VIRAGO
MODERN CLASSICS
571

Ursula Holden

sula Holden (b. 1921) grew up in Surrey and attended a
arding school on the south coast. During WWII she was with
e WRNS, and when the war ended she went to Dublin where
e worked as a model at the art school and met her husband,
th whom she was to have three children. They eventually
turned to London, and the marriage ended in 1970. Holden
worked at various jobs, and began to write in any free time she
could carve out. Alan Ross, poet and editor of the *London
Magazine*, published her first three books, *Endless Race* (1975),
String Horses (1976) and *Turnstiles* (1977), and a further nine
novels followed, including the Tin Toys trilogy in the mid-
1980s. Now living in a care home in west London, Ursula
Holden still writes daily and contributes to the *Oldie*. In 2010
she was elected a Fellow of the Royal Society of Literature.

By *Ursula Holden*

TIN TOYS TRILOGY

Ursula Holden

Introduced by Lisa Allardice

virago

VIRAGO

This edition published in 2013 by Virago Press
Reprinted 2013

Typeset in Goudy by M Rules
Printed and bound in Great Britain by
Clays Ltd, St Ives plc

Papers used by Virago are from well-managed forests
and other responsible sources.

MIX
Paper from
responsible sources
FSC® C104740

Virago Press
An imprint of
Little, Brown Book Group
100 Victoria Embankment
London EC4Y 0DY

An Hachette UK Company
www.hachette.co.uk

www.virago.co.uk

CONTENTS

INTRODUCTION

Three sisters: the eldest beautiful and mild-mannered, the middle grave and thoughtful, the youngest innocent and watchful. Bonnie, 'derived from the word "good" in Latin'; Tor, short for Hortense, 'a Roman clan name'; and Ula, which means 'owl', we are told, though it can be no coincidence that it is more commonly short for Ursula. These are the unicorn sisters, the title of the middle novel in Ursula Holden's trilogy, now collected together for the first time in this volume (the first novel in the trilogy, *Tin Toys*, was published in 1986; the third, *A Bubble Garden*, in 1989). Their mother 'Babs', an actress, is glamorous, flighty and cold-hearted. Their father is dead. It is the archetypal fairy-tale set-up – three sisters and a wicked mother – and as in all fairy tales there is much darkness, randomness and cruelty. But all three novels fall far short of straightforwardly happy endings, and the trilogy as a whole ends in tragedy.

Set just before, during and after World War II, each novel is told from the perspective of a different sister. *Tin Toys* belongs to little Ula: lonely and isolated from her older sisters, she relates the traumatic events that happen to her in Ireland, where she is sent with the family's cook following her baby brother's death. *Unicorn Sisters*, narrated by Bonnie, records the sisters' time in a comically abysmal boarding school where their prim world is expanded by the arrival of a bunch of evacuees from east London. Tor brings the series to its conclusion in *A Bubble Garden*, in which the girls and their half-brother Bo (minus Ula, who is in England recovering from polio) now live in a derelict manor house in Ireland following their mother's terrible second marriage. Each novel stands alone, but the ambiguous endings keep the reader wondering about the fate of these unlucky sisters.

Now in her nineties, Ursula Holden lives in a convent nursing home in west London, where she still writes every day on her tiny Adler Tippa portable typewriter. Although religion was 'spread on my bread as a child', she has little time for it now. One of the frustrations of the nursing home, apart from rarely being left alone, she confides shortly after we meet to discuss the reissue of her novels (about which she is thrilled), is that they don't have her 'sort of books in the library. They read Jean Plaidy – no sex at all, no violence or anything.' Sex and violence aren't in short supply in her novels, I suggest. 'Is there a lot? I suppose there is,' she replies. 'I didn't think so at the time.'

Holden was the fourth daughter of five, and grew up in a strict Church of England family just outside of Guildford in a similarly affluent world of nurses and governesses to that of the unicorn sisters. There is a striking photograph of her eldest sister, 'the beauty', on the wall; her middle sister 'was good and sweet', like Tor. 'I felt overshadowed by my three sisters, who were all clever and bright and beautiful, and I always felt like the runt,' she says. 'And then my brilliant brother came along. It was

"What shall we do with Ursula?'" Unlike her sisters, she never went to university and struggled to pass her school certificate, but 'in a funny sort of way it has worked well for me,' she says now. 'Because I could work on paper, and not be seen and not have to be clever, just use my imagination.'

As for so many women of her generation, her escape came with the war. After joining the Wrens, she 'revolted' against the stuffiness of her middle-class upbringing and went to Ireland to stay with her eccentric grandmother, who lived 'in an old house full of rats' not dissimilar to the one the unicorn sisters find themselves in. Then, she 'led a rather rickety life' as an artists' model in Dublin – much to her family's outrage. Just like a plot-line from one of her novels, she married 'rather disastrously', to an Irishman, and had three daughters of her own. Although she had started writing during her marriage, it was really only after her divorce, when she returned to London and attended creative writing classes, that she started to write seriously, going early every day, when bus tickets were cheaper, to work in the reading room at the British Library. She credits the 'huge contrast' of 'the luxury' of her childhood with the financial difficulties of her marriage 'when there was sometimes no food in the larder' and the years trying to make ends meet in her development as a writer. 'To write I do think you have to go through terrible times,' she says.

It took her many years to find a publisher, and she was fifty-four when her first novel *Endless Race* was taken on by Alan Ross, a great supporter of her early work, for his small publishing imprint of the *London Magazine*. It got 'very good reviews but no sales'. But the publication of her second novel, *String Horses*, brought real attention, with critics comparing her to Muriel Spark and Beryl Bainbridge. The shock of this success made her 'quite ill, and very thin'. In all, twelve novels, each very slim ('It's so difficult to write, I respect words, I hate to sprinkle them on the page,' she says), were published – though she wrote more. The *Tin Toys* trilogy was the culmination of this late creative blossoming.

At the heart of these three novels, as with so many of Holden's books, in particular *String Horses*, is the complex and contradictory nature of sibling relationships: one minute passionately devoted to each other, the next murderously resentful. Now all her sisters are dead, she concedes that her feelings towards them must have affected her writing. 'We were brought up very religiously so you were never allowed to show your real feelings. It was all "turn the other cheek". So, underneath, there was dislike and rage at these clever sisters of mine. I didn't allow myself to feel it at the time, but it must have been there. Your past influences what you write even if you try to keep away from it.' And poor baby Bruno, stripped naked by his elder sisters so he catches cold, and dead in the opening pages of the first book? He must have been her brother, she says. Like Ula, she confesses that she 'must have loathed him and wanted to kill him when he was born. He wasn't lovely, he was nasty. Children don't like their younger siblings coming along, at least I didn't.'

And it isn't just siblings: childhood friendships are also depicted in all their intensity, rivalry and casual cruelties. *String Horses* and *Unicorn Sisters* both examine the inevitable hierarchies of girls' schools. 'There are always glamorous girls in all schools. Everybody looks at them, longs to be like them, envies them and also criticises them,' Holden reflects now. 'I've never been the glamorous one, rather the one who watches and listens.'

This observation can be seen in her astute chronicling of the betrayals, big and small, suffered by children – at the hands of each other, but most damagingly of all by the adults who are supposed to protect them. If characteristics of her sisters can be found in Bonnie and Tor, then the vain, neglectful mother portrayed in the trilogy is quite the opposite of Holden's own mother, who was 'bossy and very religious'. But there was the same sense of a domineeringly matriarchal family, as her father – 'a very good, lovely man' – spent most of the year working for the civil service in Egypt, where their mother would join him for long periods. Her parents' extended absences account, she believes, for the darkness throughout her work. As Ula says: 'How I wished we could be ordinary, like the children at the dancing class with ordinary parents who lived with us, instead of a beautiful mother who was never there.'

Although working-class family life, especially the relationship between 'mums' and their daughters, is romanticised – 'being together, eating cramped up from the draining board near the sink. No more Nurse and I on the top floor, with my sisters down below and Maggie [the cook] in the basement' – as Ula discovers on her ill-fated trip to Ireland, shameful secrets and misery are indiscriminate of class. Ireland is similarly sentimentalised: 'God's green island', where all children are loved. And it is true that the girls enjoy rare periods of happiness there, unregulated by adults, carefree in the woods and gardens. But, as with their riotous time at the boarding school, this freedom teeters too close to chaos and real danger is never far away. For Holden, Ireland is 'a magical land' – but also one of contradictions: both the country of her liberation, and of great unhappiness.

It is no surprise that she is an admirer of her near-contemporary, the Irish novelist Edna O'Brien, identifying strongly with her early work. But the writer who made the most lasting impression on her was Jean Rhys, 'a goddess', and there are clear influences to be found in the style, as well as in the rather bleak outlook. Sparely and fluidly told, with shifting tenses and much free indirect speech, and veering between moments of unexpected tenderness or violence, the novels have a strange dream-like or nightmarish quality. And a dark sense of the absurd prevails. 'Awful things happen,' she says. 'But you have to retain your individuality and your sense of humour. And above all understand why people do terrible things. That to me is essential. Then you don't hate them.'

Despite the disquieting naivety of tone, these are emphatically not novels for children: 'Goodness, no', Holden says, 'there's too much sex and violence and dreadful behaviour.' However, as stories about the interior lives of girls on the brink of adulthood, though set half a century ago, they will have a timeless appeal to readers around the same ages as the older sisters. But these are by no means comforting novels. Witnessed each time by one of the girls, sex is seen as brutish and disturbing, the adult world as unpredictable and frightening. 'I wanted to stay being a child. Though childhood was miserable and terrible, being grown-up might be worse,' Ula thinks at the end of *Tin Toys*. And there are an awful lot of sudden deaths – often taking unexpectedly bizarre or banal forms. 'Oh, I'm so sorry,' Holden says dryly. 'But it does happen in life, unfortunately. It will happen to me too, but hopefully not for a bit now because I've got these books coming out again.' She looks down at the little pile of hardbacks, which she'd stored away modestly in a bottom drawer, now on the bed beside her. 'It really is wonderful.'

Lisa Allardice
2013

TIN TOYS

Now that my ladder's gone,
I must lie down where all the ladders start,
In the foul rag-and-bone shop of the heart.

W. B. Yeats

1

I could be certain of happiness on Saturday mornings because of
my dancing class. Each week I went there with my nurse to join
the rest, all escorted by nurses or maids. Servants were usual
then, in the days before the War, though I felt different even
then. The other little girls seemed fond of their nurses and I
hated mine. She wasn't a proper nurse but an elderly aunt, who
years ago had looked after my father when he was young. Papa
was dead now. She had come to look after me and my baby
brother and she had to be called Nurse, not Aunt. Mamma said
she could consider herself lucky, under the circumstances, to
work for the family again. Nurse seemed a suitably cold and
unfriendly name for a cold unfriendly person, whose only interest was in Bruno, the newborn boy in the shawl. She didn't like
me. Little girls were a nuisance, they fussed insistently, they
asked too many questions, they stared, worst of all they were
sneaky in their ways. She ignored me as far as possible but on
Saturdays she left Bruno and took me to Miss Dance's class. I
wore my cream Viyella frock to skip and curtsey to Miss Dance's
simple tunes and I forgot about Bruno. I would rather have gone

with Maggie our housekeeper, but Mamma preferred Nurse to take me.

The year that Bruno was born was when I first saw Lucy, just before Christmas, at Miss Dance's Saturday class. There was a Christmas tree like a silver spire by the doorway. Each pupil was allowed to place her doll or teddy bear under the lower branches before the dancing began. Our skipping and curtseying was observed by the button-eyed dolls peering from their silvery bower. My toy was different, it was a giraffe made of tin, old and dented. I was the youngest there. I hopped to Miss Dance's playing and forgot that I had two elder sisters and an awful brother wrapped in a shawl.

'Dance your feelings, my little dears. Make it a dance of love,' called Miss Dance.

I was nearly seven. Already I knew that feelings were better kept to yourself. I stamped and jumped and grinned. I liked the grand march past best, finishing with a curtsey to Miss Dance which she called 'la grande reverence'. She received our homage by the side of her silvery tree, wearing a long skirt and a silvery lace blouse. After curtseying we retrieved our toys and went home. We liked her and I'm sure she liked us. For that hour we belonged to her, twelve little girls and their dolls. To us she seemed a bright being revealing another world from her upright piano or standing beside her tree.

Children's nurses, governesses and nurserymaids were a part of life in those days. Compared with the rest of the children at the dancing class our house was understaffed. Nurse, in reality an aunt, ruled the nursery for Bruno and me. My two sisters, Bonnie and Tor, took lessons from an old governess who lived outside our town, coming to the house every day. The cooking and cleaning was done by Maggie from Ireland. Apart from

Bruno it was a house of women. My mother was rarely at home and when she was we hardly saw her. Apart from Saturdays I didn't mix with other children. Bonnie and Tor were due to start school after Christmas when Gov would retire for good. My sisters loved Gov. The schoolroom was their private world.

The nurses waited outside while we danced. They talked and held copies of *The Lady* and *The Nursery World*. Miss Dance liked to have us alone, so that our loyalties wouldn't stray. The nurses didn't read the magazines, preferring to rival each other as to the affluence and social status of the families they ruled. If a mother turned up she was made to feel inferior, having trespassed outside her domain.

Miss Dance singled me out with special smiles, because I had no father now. I was a pale child, and particularly quiet since my brother was born. I didn't know that I was pretty, having been made to feel self-conscious about a patch of white in my hair. My sisters had normal hair but all three of us had rather dingy teeth. Nurse said that this came from early neglect, but our teeth were strong in spite of their colour. Bruno, who was all she cared about, was still toothless, hairless and red.

'Very good, Ula. Keep trying. Wave your arms. Smile.'

Sometimes I practised at home when Nurse wasn't looking, pointing my toes and waving. I loved being praised by Miss Dance. I loved putting my giraffe under the tree with the dolls. I disliked dolls. That day there was a black stuffed monkey there.

'Lovely, Ula. Now for the grand march past. Take your partners, now then.'

I didn't look round. I preferred to march alone.

'Ula, you take Lucy.'

'I don't know her.'

5

'Don't be unfriendly, dear. The march is done in pairs and Lucy is our guest.'

She wanted to make Lucy feel wanted. Lucy's aunt was a friend of Miss Dance and Lucy was on holiday here. Lucy had dark curls and brilliant eyes, the colour of Wedgwood china. She was the tallest child in the class that Saturday and she had a haughty air, moving swiftly on arched feet that turned outwards. Her ankles looked delicate under her skirt of bright pink pleats. Her dark hair smelled of lavender water, her hand was cool in mine.

'Good, Ula and Lucy, point those toes. Good.'

Lucy made me feel clumsy and sticky-handed. I was afraid I'd leave a mark on her dress. It was a lovely bright shade of pink, with piped seams and short enough to show her knickers when she moved. My own cream Viyella seemed dowdy, I felt ashamed again of my hair. I clutched her hand, I kept my lips closed over my dull teeth. You had to pause when you came to the tree where Miss Dance stood, you held your skirt out, bending low over your extended right foot. I looked up. My giraffe, which I called Tin, had fallen, his legs stuck stiffly up. The black monkey, dressed stylishly in a ballet skirt, belonged to Lucy. The class was over. Time to pick up our toys and leave. Lucy elbowed me aside rudely, she pulled a tremendous face at me. We hadn't spoken to each other but I thought she was spellbinding. I had never seen anyone touch their nose with their tongue. I kept my lips closed in a line as we went down the passage to where the nurses were.

I knew Nurse wouldn't like Lucy. She didn't like me to make friends. Anyone other than Bruno was an intrusion on her time. I could think of no greater joy than holding Lucy's hand. Nurse hurried me into my coat. 'Oh hurry, Ula.' She was worried about Bruno's lunchtime bottle. I had something of Lucy's in my palm. If you kept something belonging to a person you might see them again, you might have luck as well. I clenched the wisp of pink silk from her dress and thought about her. Her dancing shoes were red instead of black or bronze, her hair was ringleted, her lavender scent and her eyes were wonderful. Nurse was rough-handed, pulling my hair from my coat collar, jamming my beret on, begrudging me her time. She had seen Lucy pulling a face. Ill-bred child, she had no place here. What a shocking shade of pink. And such curls, were they permanently waved? The girl had showed her knickers, as well as having no nurse, or even a mother. Her father had brought her, there he was waiting outside. A blessing they didn't live here and wouldn't be staying long. Not our kind, oh no. They were Irish as far as she knew.

I watched Lucy take her father's hand. She wore a dark green coat and nothing to cover her curls, more dashing than the berets I and my sisters wore in the winter. Her father wore brown tweed. Nurse pushed me ahead of her. The other nurses didn't know she was really an aunt; that knowledge would have set her apart, they would have ostracized and distrusted her. The rest met at the parties given for the children to which I and my sisters were never asked. To be asked you had to give parties back; our family kept to themselves. I didn't miss the parties, not knowing what they were like. Dressing in my cream Viyella frock was my weekly treat in spite of Nurse's resentment. She hated leaving Bruno with Maggie, who though good-hearted was untrained to English ways. I loved Maggie. 'Oh hurry, do, Ula. Why don't you smile?'

I tried to put my giraffe under my coat as I ran to keep up with Nurse along the main street of our town. She told me to have respect for my clothing and to keep my toes pointed straight, I wasn't at the class now. Nurse didn't care what I thought or how I passed my time as long as I was quiet and kept clean. I looked back at Miss Dance's window and the glittering boughs of her tree. Nurse thought that silver trees were cheap-looking, on a level with Maggie's taste.

'Will Mamma be coming home soon? Will we have a Christmas tree?' She said that my mother didn't confide in her, that Gov was her confidante. Nurse had a hoarse voice, unlike Maggie's, and angry-looking eyes.

Mamma had not been home for six weeks. Bruno was over two months old. Mamma preferred London and her theatrical friends to being with us in the country. Nurse thought her flighty and bad. I think she even blamed her for Papa's death from a heart attack. A reason for her loving Bruno was that he looked like Papa had as a baby. Nurse was an aunt by marriage, with dark skin round her eyes and hair like crinkled white wire. She had very black eyes that looked darker when she was vexed. Her yellow fingers had mauve-nailed tips. She never mentioned her own family, but only my father as a child. I had no pity for her. I had heard Mamma talking with contempt about homeless people or those of mixed blood who never fitted in. She had done Nurse a favour, employing her; other people's children were Nurse's concern, she was expected to love Bruno as once she had loved my Papa.

'Mamma wants to act, doesn't she?'

'She doesn't confide in me, I've told you. Who am I to know what she wants? Gov knows it all, I dare say.'

Both she and Maggie resented Gov who had Mamma's entire trust. Years ago Gov had taught Mamma her lessons, but Gov was differently placed from Nurse. She paid the bills for

Mamma, running our house smoothly, but going home to her own cottage at night, in Shottermill. It was Gov who had employed Maggie, Gov who ordered the groceries and bought our clothes. She would do no household chores, she returned each night to her cottage and her privacy, arriving each morning at nine. She lived apart in the schoolroom with my sisters. At night Maggie saw them to bed, and looked after them at weekends, and Bruno too while Nurse took me to Miss Dance. Bonnie and Tor were secretive, they didn't require Maggie's care. They stayed downstairs in the schoolroom with the door shut, they never let me inside. I longed to find out what they did in there, and what they learned with Gov.

Resentment over Gov gave Nurse and Maggie a bond of a sort. Gov gave herself too many airs.

As we reached our gateway I could hear my sisters talking. The schoolroom window was wide, though it was a cold day. They sounded excited, it was rare to hear them laugh or make any sound. I ran over.

'Look, Nurse. They've put up a tree.'

Nurse didn't look into the window. I went inside ahead.

Gov practised thrift and frugality, she made all my sisters' clothes: serviceable grey or navy skirts, hand-knitted jerseys to match. In winter we wore hand-sewn cotton pants under our bloomers and liberty bodices over our vests. I wore Tor's cast-offs. Nothing was bought if it could be made at home. No money had been spent on the tree in the schoolroom which was a stunted little larch, lopsided and half bare, dug from the garden. My sisters were on the floor making decorations from used exercise books, cutting the paper with careless speed. The carpet was covered with clumsily shaped dolls. Tor was trying to cut out a star. They had pushed bunches of grass and dead leaves into the tree's bare spaces. A lump of mud clung to the bark. My sisters took daily nature walks with Gov, to find specimens in ditches and fields. There was no holly or ivy in the room. One of them had tried to fashion a bell from a wire coat hanger. I gazed.

'Oh, Bonnie, it is beautiful. What is Bruno doing down there?'

Our baby brother was on the floor under the lowest branches with his head lying on a birds' nest. He wasn't wearing his clothes.

Nurse let out a scream from behind me. What had happened? Where was Maggie? Mercy. Maggie came up from the basement as Nurse called her.

'You filthy ... What are you up to? The window open, he's not got a stitch on.'

'I'm only after fetching the cocoa for the two girls, Nurse. I left baby on the chair. It's those girls.'

'His death. He'll catch his death.'

Nurse snatched him. Bonnie and Tor watched from the floor. I had brought Nurse into their schoolroom, I had interrupted, I was trespassing. Then they shook their hair over their faces again, resuming their Christmas task.

Nurse rolled Bruno into his shawl.

'Come along, Ula. Straight upstairs.'

She'd never be able to trust Maggie again with him, poor lamb in the dirty leaves. Look, grass on his head even. I cradled Tin in my arms. I never had liked Bruno. I wished that my sisters had made that tree just for me.

There were rock cakes for tea in the nursery that evening. Maggie knew I liked them, made with jam. I ate my meals with Nurse on the top floor, my sisters ate in the schoolroom below.

I ate my cake slowly; a little nest with blood in it. Maggie understood me. I wanted her.

'Nurse, I want another cake.'

'Well, you can't, Miss. Greedy. Sugar is bad.'

When she put her face close to Bruno's the world seemed to shrink, just Nurse and him, with me outside. And Bruno had a fever now, she said angrily, his forehead was all hot. If he caught a cold she'd see that Maggie was sacked.

He refused his bottle. While she was getting his nightdress from the bathroom I climbed onto the table to the cakes. I wanted another, I must have one. Even more, I wanted to disobey. Maggie mustn't leave us ever. I stretched my hand out to the biggest, so red, so pretty, so sweet.

'Greedy. Disobedient. Sneak thief.'

Nurse always punished me the same way. Straight to bed and no toys. She took away Tin. I sucked my fingers. I'd lost the scrap of silk from Lucy's dress. She'd been wonderful, she'd stuck her tongue out so comically. I must be like her, I must see her again. While Nurse muttered in the nursery about her lamb all cold and neglected under that dirty tree, I fell asleep thinking about Lucy.

2

'Talk to me, Maggie. Say something.'

I liked being with her so much, she understood everything. She knew what Nurse was like upstairs, and what Bruno had done to my life, though Maggie loved Bruno herself quite a lot.

On Sunday afternoons I stayed with her in the kitchen while my sisters played in the schoolroom upstairs. Nurse was almost happy on Sundays, she had Bruno to herself. Maggie never stopped working. There were trays to be carried up and down and all the cleaning. Mamma, if she was at home, ate alone too. Maggie's own home was in Ireland, a perfect paradise she said. The Irish loved children, I was her dotey love. She never went out at night-time, the weekends were her favourite times. She liked minding Bruno with my sisters on Saturday mornings, though my sisters weren't as nice as me. Gov was too lardy-dardy with them, Gov had made my sisters too superior to breathe. I liked pretending that Maggie was my mother while I listened to her talk of her home. England was godless in her opinion, and the way we were reared a disgrace. We lived miles from a proper church, we'd no religion. But for her we'd be truly lost. She let me play with her rosary beads, and sung hymns to me. She worried about missing mass. Her immortal soul was at risk in this country. I loved listening to her talk.

'Is it my brogue or my clever thoughts you want to listen to? Did you enjoy the dancing class yesterday?'

'I met Lucy. She's my friend.'

'Lucy what? She'll be English, I suppose?'

'I had a dream about her, it was awful.'

'Awful? Was it a bogey-man? Just you press on that rolling pin.'

She baked crusts in the oven to flatten into breadcrumbs. I grated salt for her too. Another treat was to make mustard from powder, to put into blue glass mustard pots. I liked the smell of it and I liked watching Maggie working. She had a plain round face and straight hair. Her pink hair slide pinned her hair above her right ear. Her parting showed her greasy pink scalp. Short stubble grew on her neck. I longed to wear a pink hair slide but Nurse wouldn't let me. Everything I had was plain and dull. Lucy had worn a pink hair ribbon. Maggie had small sparkling eyes.

'I wonder where Papa went when he died, Maggie?'

'To the angels it is to be hoped.' She added that I shouldn't be worrying over such things, it was morbid. She would make a batch of scones for the tea.

I sifted flour for her and wondered if we'd get presents in a stocking at Christmas. In Ireland Maggie said no child was left out. Bonnie and Tor had worked hard with their Christmas tree. I thought Bruno looked better without clothes. Nurse disapproved of Maggie's cooking; too many eggs, too much sugar and jam. Maggie thought Nurse was old-fashioned, children needed a bit of sweet. I was alone too much. Nurse gave me nothing to play with. Was it a wonder I dreamed in the night? It was Maggie who had given Tin to me but I didn't need toys if I had her. As well as being in the kitchen I liked listening outside the schoolroom door. My sisters' nature walks with Gov sounded exciting. They wore Wellingtons and kicked up the leaves. They scrambled up banks looking for lichen. Gov knew about fossils and stones. Nurse said they were wasting their time. When she wheeled Bruno outside I had to cling onto the handle of the pram. It shocked Maggie that none of us knew any prayers. She was extra worried about Bruno with his cold on his chest. Not that she blamed herself, she'd not neglected him, it was my two sisters who were to blame. They were bold and superior those two girls were, them and that funny-looking tree. In Ireland now all the trees were lovely, the one in their house was the best in the street. A good Christmas tree was like a good Christmas cake, a sign that all was well in the home. She'd miss the home-baking this year, thanks to Nursie. Imagine fussing over a bit of red jam. She sighed.

'Oh, Maggie, you'll never leave us will you? Can I empty the bucket outside?'

A cobbled pathway outside the back door led to the dustbins at the end of the kitchen garden, where nothing was growing now. I walked across the stones carefully, holding the heavy bucket in both hands. The night frost hadn't thawed yet, the cobbles were slippery, the tree branches looked whitey grey. I was never afraid if Maggie was near me. There was frost on the lid of the bin. She was methodical about waste. Newspaper bundles of refuse were tightly wrapped, there was a separate bin for ash. I liked looking inside them. Nurse wouldn't allow it, she was prudish, I wasn't allowed to look at dogs' messes on the roadside, or even at myself without clothes. I would have enjoyed poking now into the packages in the dustbin, the old bones, the peelings and tea. Maggie called me. I emptied the bucket and replaced the frost-covered lid. The bare tree branches against the sky were like animal faces, birds with opened beaks and even a baby with close-set eyes. I envied Bruno, wrapped up and protected, but I had Maggie with her pink slide shining in the light. My hands were numb when I got in again.

'Feel them. Frozen cold. Put them in water now.'

She got a new piece of soap for me with a stiff outer wrapping and transparent paper inside. I liked the smell and the taste when you touched your tongue to it. I rubbed the lather until my hands were dry, rinsing them again to soapiness. I made bubbles between my forefinger and thumb, I rubbed soap onto Tin's hooves. The brown of his spots was the same as Lucy's father's coat.

'I wonder if we'll have presents under the schoolroom tree.'

'How can I tell you? I wasn't here last year.'

It seemed to Maggie that the English did nothing properly. Back at home Christmas was a fairyland time with presents, tree, lights and feasting. Nothing had been said about Christmas fare, she'd not liked to ask that lardy-dardy Gov. The housekeeping was a long way from being generous. That dirty old tree was a show. 'Course Ma'am, my mamma, was out enjoying herself in London. Things might change here if she'd return. But what Maggie found hardest to bear was the want of any faith, for which she blamed my mother and Gov.

'Can we look at your pictures now, Maggie?'

She kept magazines under a cushion for me to cut pictures from. She liked cutting them herself as well, particularly film stars like Boris Karloff with their slick hair and signet rings. I liked the ladies best. We gazed together at Mae West's curves and filmy clothing, we were in awe of the size of her behind. She said she had lollopers the size of twin balloons. Maggie's own lollopers were floppy and soft. I liked leaning against them as I cut out the pictures. I had never seen a film or a play. She said she'd bet Mae West had a lovely tree this Christmas and knew how to celebrate the holy birth.

'What birth? What do you mean, Maggie?'

She was horrified again. Did I not even know the meaning of Christmas, when our blessed Lord was born? She spoke about the stable in Bethlehem, the wise men, the shepherds and star, while I cut out Boris Karloff's nose. I asked her what presents she'd had at her house. I pulled at the medal she wore round her neck, half listening. She said I should start learning to read.

Mamma had once seen me listening outside the schoolroom. She'd been angry. She paid Nurse to look after me, my place was upstairs with her, not listening at doors like a kitchen maid. Eavesdropping was an abhorrent practice, I would learn nothing to my advantage that way. She disliked children creeping about. Bonnie overheard Mamma and taunted me. 'Creeper, listening at doors.' I longed to be friends with my sisters, to share their sisterly world, but they neither needed nor wanted me. I wanted to learn lessons from Gov who wore tweed suits and sensible shoes, carrying a walking stick on the nature walks. Maggie got no thanks or appreciation for looking after the nursery as well as the schoolroom, carrying up trays and buckets of coal. She cleaned the nursery but not the schoolroom, Gov wanted no interference there. It stayed rather dusty and untidy, another source of Maggie's contempt. Nurse and she disliked Gov because she was not obliged to work, but came to us out of love for Mamma. She wasn't subservient. Gov had no religious faith and in Maggie's view was one of the world's worst. Maggie prayed daily to her guardian angel as well as her special saints, St Margaret and Our Lady.

'Have I got a special saint, Maggie?'

'St Ursula is a good saint. Were you named for her?'

'Ula. Not Ursula. Bonnie said Ula means owl.'

'Owl? Sweet Saviour, are you sure?'

Bonnie has been gleeful. 'Creeper. Kitchen maid. Owl.'

'Is it a fact? Are you a little birdy bones?'

I looked it, Maggie said: too solemn, too bony, a little bag of bones. She'd love to fatten me, to convert me, she'd love me to be her child.

'And you'll always stay, won't you, Maggie?'

She said she would unless Madam took a notion to leave. She might sell up and leave one fine day, you never knew. I would stay with her always. I leaned closer, her lollopers were warm. I liked listening. She complained about England, the unfriendliness, the gloom. They didn't laugh here, they hated babies, they didn't have any beliefs. She loved her old birdy bones though.

'Can we make jam rock cakes after the scones? Why has the man on your medal got a dripping bloody heart? Will you take me to Miss Dance next Saturday? I want you to see Lucy.'

She said that the other nurses wouldn't like her there, being too lardy-dardy themselves. Did that Miss Dance know the jig?

'What's a jig?'

Everyone should know the jig, she said. Watch now, she'd show me how.

She put me down, she took off her apron. Her cotton dress cracked with starch. She took her shoes off, pointing her right foot forwards, then both feet started to move. As they flew faster and faster they gave off a friendly smell. Damp patches showed under her armpits, widening as she moved. I sat on the floor by the table, she told me to hum the tune. The jig was called 'The Blackbird', her lollopers jerked in time. Soon the imprints of her black stockings showed over the tiles. Her pink hair slide flew into a corner, her belt buttons snapped and fell. This was better than curtseying and marching, 'The Blackbird' was fast and free.

'What do you think you're doing, Maggie? I can hear you from right upstairs.'

'Nurse. I never heard you come in.'

'That's plain to see. You woke the baby. You know he isn't well, he must have quiet.'

'I was only showing Ula a bit of a step. She wanted to see the jig.'

'Jig? Jig? Look at you. Button your belt. Mercy.'

'Aye, look at me, Nurse, and look at you. Is it any wonder Ula likes it downstairs with me. She gets a laugh and a cuddle down here.'

'You ought to call her Miss Ula, you're only the cook after all.'

'Miss? Very lardy-dardy all of a sudden are we not? No one is in a hurry to call you Aunt.'

Nurse's complexion went darker, she narrowed her dark-lidded eyes. She felt her lowly position and Maggie knew it. Nurse should be running the home and not Gov, who wasn't a relation and was very old. Nurse despised Maggie for being Irish, a below-stairs servant and lowly born. For her part Maggie pitied Nurse, an aunt by marriage without status or love. No relative would get such treatment in her country; no wonder Nurse was so sulky.

'Come upstairs at once, Ula. And don't make any more

rubbishy cakes for her, Maggie. They're too sweet for so young a child.'

Maggie put her shoes on, she winked at me. If she only cooked what Nursie wanted it would be prunes and steamed fish for ever more. A kiddy needed a treat an odd time, her birdy bones needed love.

'Can I see Bonnie and Tor? I think they want me.'

They never wanted me but I kept hoping. I wanted to see their tree again. They were doing their homework for Gov, until Maggie brought up their tea. I hoped she wouldn't dance the jig for them, I couldn't bear to think that. I pressed against the schoolroom door. Bonnie opened it.

'Got you. Creeper. At your nasty tricks again?'

'Let me in, Bonnie, for a minute.'

She pushed her face into mine. Her brown hair smelled of leaves.

'You heard what Mamma said, you belong upstairs. Get away from our door.'

I looked past her shoulder. Tor was at the table, using a black crayon, pressing the page hard. The tree still stood there, sad and curious, dabbed with mud and bits of straw. They had drawn their curtains early to be dark and cosy, they didn't need anyone or anything else.

3

Up in the nursery Bruno was asleep again. Bonnie had called me nasty, but I wasn't. I leaned over his cot, near to the fire. It was colder on the top floor, Nurse was getting more shawls from the landing. I listened to Bruno breathe. He was making a panting sound, almost grunting, then from time to time a little cough. His mouth looked square when he opened it, his gums were ridges of bone. His tongue was as big as mine but whitish coloured. His breath had a dry burnt smell. Nurse didn't like me touching him, especially by the tops of his legs. It showed I was rude-minded, she said, let baby have his privacy. Was his nappy fastened properly? He wet a lot. His barking cough sounded again. He didn't cry tears, nor did I usually. I tried never to cry at all. He couldn't help being ugly and unlovable, couldn't help being born at all. Nurse's black eyes went juicy with love when she looked at him, his own eyes were pale slits under invisible brows. The pulse in his pate had the faintest growth of down on it, the delicate part you must shield, the part where the brain throbbed.

'Drat my blood. Mercy. Take your hand from his head at once.'

She often made me jump with her shouting. I tried to stare and ask questions rather than show I was afraid of her. I said that Bruno was burning, he was coughing and sweating.

'It's not "sweat", it's perspiration.'

I was too much in Maggie's company she said, picking up her coarse turn of phrase. Bruno didn't even perspire, he shone. He was her shining innocent lamb. She looked closely, she listened, his cough sounded croupy. She knew all about a baby's ills. She'd send for the doctor to be on the safe side, though she was quite confident. Steam kettles were the safest for croup. She'd get a kettle now, when she went to telephone the doctor.

'I want Maggie. Can I go down?'

'You can not. Certainly not. Now don't touch him. I'll be back in a minute.'

'I want Maggie.'

'Then you must want. She's to blame for the lamb getting ill.'

'It was my sisters. They undressed him.'

'She left him with them, didn't she?'

Nurse pinched in the corners of her mouth darkly. I watched Bruno's face again. His nightdress smelled of warm milk and very faintly of flowers. If Nurse let me help her I might like him more. She went on muttering about Maggie being the culprit. And of course if Gov pulled her weight it might help. Those two girls were out of control, she herself was overworked what with me to supervise as well as the lamb. She patted his face with a towel. Steam from a kettle would ease him and plenty of warmth from the fire. She put more coal on, rattling the poker and tongs.

'And you can be putting yourself to bed, Ula. You can go without a bath.'

'Can't Maggie bath me? Could I bath with Bonnie and Tor?'

They often played at being mermaids, I could hear them, splashing and singing below. The nursery bathroom was cold with very bright lighting.

'Get along at once. You can't have Maggie. Just clean your teeth and wash your hands.'

I was seldom in the bathroom alone. Nurse liked you to do what you needed quickly without loitering. I liked whispering and playing with the taps and hated her hard fingers when she dried me with the towels. While she went for the kettle and telephoned I could stay in the bathroom and play. I leaned against the basin. Nurse didn't like dancing or Christmas trees, she was as miserable as a witch. I squeezed a long string of tooth-paste, watching it catch in the light. I squeezed it along the edge of the bath, making nests in the corners, watching it glitter, peppermint bright. Where was Bethlehem anyway? What was the thing called myrrh? More peppermint white over the sponge next. I had toothpaste in my hair and in my nose. I wiped the flannel over my face.

'Hurry up in there, Ula. You've been quite long enough.'

'I am hurrying. What's the time?'

'The time? Time you were out. Don't forget to sit on the throne.'

'I did. I did.'

The seat was cold. I jumped off before I'd been. Nurse was particular about what you called things. 'Perspiration', 'throne', 'down there'. Maggie said sweat, lavvie hole and bottom. I loved her saying 'birdy bones'.

'Are you sure?'

'Of course I'm sure.'

It was best to nod, to pretend. She didn't see the toothpaste in her concern for Bruno. I lay in the little bedroom listening to his dog's breathing and barks. My hot water bottle hadn't been filled. Nurse only cared for his warmth. Where was Maggie? Then I heard her talking. She had brought up a tray of tea for herself and Nurse. Maggie didn't bear malice for long. She pitied Nurse as well as needing her. I heard the cups rattle, the tea pouring, they had drawn up their chairs to the fire. Maggie said Nursie was wrong to stifle Bruno, she shouldn't keep the babby so warm. Maggie knew a lot about sickness in young children, too much swaddling could give them a fit. Too much heat was worse than too little, the poor babby might take a stroke. Just as well to call the doctor she agreed, but she'd not harmed Bruno yesterday. The two girls were only having a bit of fun, she'd been below getting the cocoa. Fresh air never harmed a babby, letting the air to the skin. Of course those girls were unmanageable, that Gov was a lot to blame, had a lot to answer for. They were allies again, united once more against Gov. No one remembered my hot water bottle; I listened to the click of their spoons and the poker rattling against the fire bars. I wished that I'd sat on the throne. Nurse's rule was that once you got into bed you must stay there. She didn't allow fidgeting or calling, you stayed quiet until morning time. Maggie went down again. She didn't say goodnight or look towards my door. I heard Bruno's cot being moved. He had stopped coughing. I wriggled downwards. I wasn't comfortable or warm. I had a pain down there. Wanting to go made you shiver, making a smell could help. It cured the pain for a moment. Another one, Nurse would be cross. And another, you can't help it now, you must. Now I have done something awful, something I'm not allowed to do. Bruno does it, he's a boy and a baby, I've done something Nurse won't forgive. I will lie still and pretend to forget it, I didn't, I'm not dirty or rude. I will put my hand down, I've got it, a little sticky stick. A warm stick with porridge on it, now I've got it over my hand. Push it down onto the hot water bottle, smelling awful, push it all onto the floor. Rub my hand on my pillow. There now. Someone is crying in the nursery, a man is there. Nurse is crying, I don't know why.

'Now, Nurse, please, brace yourself. For the sake of the baby, please.'

'I can't. I won't. No.'

'Where is the children's governess? Are you in sole charge here now?'

Nurse's voice sounded different, she sounded crazy. Gov didn't sleep in at night-time, oh no, a being apart. Gov had the power and the pleasure, none of the work here. Madam Mamma wasn't here either. Oh no. She and the cook general had all the worry here and the responsibility too. She knew about sick infants, she'd had the care of babies all her life. She'd cared for Bruno's father once, she ought to know. Steam kettles and heat cured the croup. Mercy, he as a doctor should know that. She'd give any medicine he suggested, but don't, just don't take Bruno away.

'There isn't any choice, Nurse. The case demands hospital care. The boy must be hospitalized tonight, if he's to be helped.'

In a grave voice he spoke of the membrane of the larynx becoming inflamed, the high fever, the child's toxic state. He spoke of a possible tracheotomy and as he spoke Nurse started to scream.

'Nurse, I am going to the hospital now myself. I won't wait to call an ambulance, I'll take the child now in the car.'

I got out of bed, I went to the nursery. I saw Nurse's terrible face.

'I want Maggie now, Nurse. I must have her.'

'Go back. How dare you. Naughty.'

'Nurse, I must intervene. The child is frightened, she doesn't know what's happening. Here, come here, let me explain.'

'I must have Maggie.'

'Fetch the cook at once, Nurse. Stop making that noise. I will take the baby now.'

'She's not cook, she's my Maggie. I want her. I want Maggie now.'

He knelt down to me, he talked quietly into my eyes. He was a doctor, he knew about illness, he was used to fear and alarm. He was used to comforting children, explaining what was going on. I must understand that there was nothing to be frightened about. He was taking my baby off to be made better. Bruno was going to be cured. I looked at his kind face. I believed him. I wasn't worried about Bruno going, but of what I had done in my bed. I wanted to tell him, I think he would have understood, but Nurse was there making that noise.

'Is Bruno going to die, then?'

'He's very ill. He won't die.'

'He liked the Christmas tree in the schoolroom. Bonnie and Tor put him there. They made the tree. It's downstairs.'

'There'll be all sorts of fun in the children's ward. Don't worry, he'll get loving care.'

I was afraid that he'd think ill of my sisters. I wanted him to understand that it was Nurse's fault, she was no good with children or babies.

Maggie came up again, her hair was on end. She stood rubbing it with her hands. She'd been washing it below, had guessed at once that Bruno was bad. Her hands rubbed slower as she stood there, gradually they stopped. She didn't want to believe her ears. The little babby would be with trained nurses, white-coated doctors would stand at his bed. He'd be fed sups of caudle, thermometers would be inserted, oxygen, with him maybe inside a tent. No Nursie to give him steam from a kettle, or to swaddle him in wool. Who would love him in the hospital? Who would pray for him? Sweet Saviour, where would it end? I pulled at her. Maggie. Maggie?

'I'm here, pet. I'm here, Ulie. There.'

'The man ... the doctor ... he's taking Bruno.'

'I know. I know. All right, I'm here.'

Maggie talked quietly to the doctor. She was experienced, couldn't she take over? She knew about quinsy and diarrhoea. Did he have to take babby away with him? He answered quickly in a low voice. Maggie shrugged and nodded her head. She'd be in charge, yes surely, she'd manage everything here. Nurse was too excitable, she was beside herself. Leave everything to Maggie May. She straightened her shoulders, Doctor could rely on her, she'd see the family through this trial. She listened closely while he spoke to her. Nurse was making too much noise to hear. Maggie took the pills that he handed her, she would see Nursie had one later on. He needn't fear, she would stay up here with Nurse and Ula while he took babby down.

Nurse sat at the nursery table, Bruno's nightdress held to her eyes. Her steam kettle, her loving attention and shawls hadn't saved him, her baby, her lamb, her love.

'Now then, Ulie, into your bed with you before I give Nursie her pill. Sweet Sav— Ula? What did you do? Your bed ... Holy ...'

'I didn't, Maggie. I didn't ... it wasn't me ...'

'Of course you didn't. It wasn't you at all. Ah God, Ula, the smell.'

She pulled the bedclothes off my bed, rolling them up, she got a clean nightdress for me, murmuring in a soothing way. 'Course it wasn't me that done it, 'twas that bogeyman all the time, and something to lay at Nursie's door. She was too strict with me, she bullied me. Imagine not letting a child to the lavvie hole. Maggie might be a coarse old peasant girl but she wasn't cruel like Nurse. A child should be let go any time, day or night. Poor little Ulie, with her baby brother gone.

'I want ... I want ...'

'I know what you want. You shall have it, so you shall.'

'Where did Bruno go?'

'With the doctor to the hospital is where. To the bathroom with you. Look at your hair.'

More Pears soap, more hot water, lapping under my chin. Maggie's soft rubbing hands were kind on me. There there, scrub my little bumbum, and a jug of water over my hair. I was her birdy bones and don't forget it. Lean back now. There. I wanted to stay cradled for ever. Warm water, sweet soap and sweet sound. She wrapped me in the big bath towel, her own clean hair close to mine. I was her dotey love, her darling, lean on her lollopers, don't be fretting. She'd need to see to Nursie next. The poor creature still in tears out there, she'd need to give Nurse her pill. After that she would take me downstairs with her, so don't go to sleep yet birdy bones in the big towel. Because I could tuck down inside her bed with her. I was nice and respectable again, clean as clean. There.

Tucked tightly into the far side of her bed by the kitchen I slept without feeling alone. The picture on the table by me was the same as the medal she wore round her neck, the man with a beard and thorns round his hair and his heart bleeding drops of red, the face Maggie seemed to love.

In the morning she wasn't there beside me. Maggie was upstairs in the hall talking into the telephone. This time it was she who was in tears.

4

Hatred and suspicion of Gov had been Nurse's and Maggie's main contact. After Bruno left Nurse wasn't the same, she barely spoke. Maggie took over my care. It was she who told Bonnie and Tor what had happened. When I left Maggie's bed that morning they were standing in their nightdresses at the bottom of the stairs, their hair hanging in tangles over their disbelieving eyes. They wore the stern look of judges, weighing up what Maggie had said. Nurse was above on the upper landing, muttering. Steam kettles would have saved him, the doctor should have left him alone. Maggie spoke through her tears.

'Be quiet, Nurse, nothing would have saved him, he was too far gone.'

'Be quiet yourself,' Nurse shouted back, 'be quiet the lot of you, it's all your fault.' Her voice trailed, she mumbled . . . must have her lamb. Bring him, must have Bruno.

Bonnie and Tor stood still. They didn't trust the world outside the schoolroom, with its uncertainty and change. I sucked at Tin's right hoof. I had hated Bruno because Nurse loved him. I'd been glad when his coughing face had been removed. No more square mouth and gaping gums opening at me. Now I wouldn't see him again. The change in Nurse frightened me. Had she gone demented, shrieking at Maggie like that? Bonnie spoke in a cold high voice. Where exactly had Bruno gone?

'Yes, where, Maggie? I'd like to know.'

I allied myself with my sisters in disbelief, dislike and unease. Perhaps they would let me into the schoolroom now. How resolute they were. Maggie said Bruno had likely gone to Limbo, yes, Limbo would be his whereabouts now.

'Where is that? I never heard of it.'

Maggie said she wasn't surprised, seeing the lack of religion here. It was a wonder we'd heard of God even. Oh why had he not been baptized? She should have thought to do it herself. A splash of water, sign the cross. Now he'd be rubbing shoulders with heathen babies, for the want of being named.

'Yes, but where is Limbo?'

Near to heaven, she said, not actually heaven, but somewhere like. Unbaptized children went there, though they might escape it if the parents had the intention, if they'd practised the faith themselves. Bruno's parents had no faith.

'All right, Maggie, we don't want to hear all that. Where is it exactly?'

Maggie explained in a pious voice about Limbo being a place of waiting, while sharing the goodness of God, not equal, not the same as heaven. Bonnie and Tor were not impressed, nor did they care to hear. By asking questions they were delaying acceptance of the fact that Bruno was dead. Death was alarming, it happened to old people and strangers. Nurse was behaving dreadfully. Tor asked if Bruno would be able to talk now. He'd have company Maggie said, but not company of the best, only those who didn't know right from wrong. Her eyes were concerned and dry now. She thought it possible that lunatics might go there, as well as the newly born.

'What about animals?'

'And toys?' I asked.

Nurse shouted again. Stop filling our heads with lies. Such talk was poison. This made Maggie annoyed. Holy church couldn't lie. She had tried to make allowances for this family, but don't accuse her of lies. Tor said reasonably that Limbo didn't sound very pleasant, and no one could prove he'd gone there. When was breakfast? Nurse was still muttering. Maggie said she'd get one of the pills. When Nursie was quieter she'd fetch everyone a snack. No sense in the whole family arguing and shouting.

She came back with the sherry bottle, a drop for herself and Nurse and suitable at such a time. Bonnie looked stern again. Gov might not like it, Gov would be here quite soon. Well, all right, but she and Tor would have some too.

'I want some. Can I?'

Out of the question, Maggie said. Little children must not drink. Bonnie and Tor could have a taste, but nothing for birdy bones. It wasn't everyday you lost an infant. I could nibble some cornflakes instead. There now, in by that Christmas tree in the schoolroom, we could all go there and sit down.

The crunch of the cornflakes comforted me. Maggie gave me some water in a glass. I waited to hear Gov's key in the lock. I wanted to hear her walking stick being placed in the umbrella stand, the flop of her galoshes being removed. Gov would make life more stable again, she would take Bonnie and Tor for their lessons. After lunch they would go for their walk. She might let me join them for a little, while Maggie and Nurse settled Bruno's affairs. Maggie was sitting in Gov's chair, leaning back in it. Nurse sat by the empty grate. My sisters were on the floor at the far side of the tree. Nurse drank from a brandy glass. My sisters only had a little drop, they'd become giggling and boisterous just the same.

'Don't start now, don't be bold,' Maggie warned. Just remember the occasion. I asked Bonnie for a taste, a sip. Please. She seized the cornflakes box, shaking it over my hair. Look at poor Creeper, out in the cold. Look.

Nurse sat in a private world, a world without Bruno now. Her face was dark and wild. Maggie wriggled her toes. She'd miss Bruno as much as anyone, dear little babby. But his passing had proved that she was important here, she felt more important than Gov. She could understand how Nurse felt, she could understand us girls. She would look after us, she would manage, was well able to run this house alone.

'Does dying hurt? Is it sudden? Or is it like going to sleep?'

Maggie knew all the answers, she was in her element, death was a pet subject of hers. In her own country they gave death attention. This life only lead up to it. What happened after death depended on what you did in life. If you were good you'd reach heaven eventually, after a spell in purgatory. If you were bad you paid. They had grand funerals in Ireland, with wakes in the departed ones' homes, with friends and relatives dropping in to pray and commiserate and a bite to eat and a drink for one and all. Food and drink helped a death in her country.

'Yes, but what is being dead like?'

Nurse made a noise like a growl. Tor asked if snowmen had souls, and what about ghosts. Maggie drew her chin in reprovingly. That was enough now. This family was beyond the light. Did we know nothing? It was up to her to enlighten us, or we'd be in danger of hell's flames. It was so different where she came from, her country could teach us a lot.

'Why did you leave then, if it was so perfect?'

Maggie went red, she was angry. Bonnie was rude, she spoke out of turn, she was impudent. She'd a good mind to pay her back. Maggie leaned forward with her hand raised.

'Have you all taken leave of your senses? Nurse, what is going on?'

No one heard Mamma coming through the front door. She wasn't expected. We'd forgotten about her. I'd almost forgotten what she looked like until I saw her. Of course, Mamma was beautiful, standing in the doorway against the light. We'd have to tell her about Bruno. What a good thing we had Maggie, well versed in deaths, wakes and sad news. None of us were dressed yet, the schoolroom curtains were still drawn. Cornflakes were everywhere as well as dried mud and grass from the tree. How I wished then that we could be ordinary, like the children at the dancing class with ordinary parents who lived with us, instead of a beautiful mother who was never there.

'We didn't hear you, Mamma.' If Bonnie was afraid she didn't show it.

'Evidently. Please explain.'

'Madam. Oh Ma'am,' wailed Maggie.

Mamma appeared to shrink into her fur coat as if she'd like to shrug off the lot of us. She'd been good enough to employ her old governess and her husband's old nurse, why couldn't they perform their duties quietly? She had neither interest nor sympathy for domestic scenes. How negligent Nurse was. She'd evidently lost her tongue.

'Ma'am. Ma'am.'

She told Maggie to stop being repetitious. And why had she been hitting Bonnie? Why was she in the schoolroom at all? What were any of us doing? The room was like a bear-garden. Nurse made a low sound. Bonnie and Tor drew closer together for comfort. At the same time they wanted to laugh. Sorrow was burdensome. Were they too glad that he'd died?

'You see, Ma'am ...'

'No, I don't see. I can see that you've all gone mad. Nurse, stop making that noise. Explain yourself. Bonnie ... don't ...'

Bonnie tittered. Her teeth showed sharp and grey. I knew she was frightened, I wanted to help her.

'You see, Mamma. Something has happened, it's rather a pity really ...'

I wanted to put it well, like a grown-up.

'Pity? What is? You're a pitiful-looking sight, all of you. Sherry? At this hour? Where is the infant?'

'He's ... he's ...'

'Fetch him. You shouldn't leave him, Nurse. What? ...'

'Sweet Saviour ... Oh Ma'am ...'

'Cook, stop being melodramatic. Ula, go on.'

'You see, Mamma, Bruno has gone. He's not coming back any more. He's gone to ...'

'Get up, Ula. Stop crawling about like a ...'

'He's at Limbo.'

'Nonsense.'

Maggie spoke her words in a rush. She had woken early, hearing the telephone ring. She'd got up to take the message, the wee babby was with the angels. Only yesterday he'd been under that tree.

Mamma interrupted. Angels, Christmas trees, Limbo. Cook's imagination was beyond control. Put that sherry bottle down at once. Where was Gov?

'She doesn't get here till nine, Mamma. You see, when Maggie answered the telephone it was the hospital, saying that Bruno was dead.'

I guessed that Mamma was playing for time as Bonnie and Tor had, refusing to consent to the truth. In clear words I told about the doctor, about Bruno's cough and croup. Then Bonnie and Tor started giggling, leaning against each other, mingling their hair. They were as uncomfortable and confused as I was, they had each other. I wished we were properly dressed. I started feeling that pain again. I licked my fingers, pressing them onto the spilled cornflakes. It was important to collect every one. Perhaps if I went upstairs now I might find Bruno there all the time, coughing and gnashing his gums at me, having given the household a fright.

'Stop spitting and licking your hands, Ula. Nurse, you had better leave the room.'

Nurse stared, not moving, hating her. Mamma was to blame for everything. She had gone away, leaving her family, leaving the wrong person in charge. It should have been her, Nurse. She was a relative, she'd been treated with ignominy, she was these children's great-aunt. Gov was a no one. Then, hardly opening her lips, Nurse hissed, 'She-devil. Mother monster, mother whore.'

Mamma's red mouth shook a little, her pointed face went pale. She turned from Nurse, she ignored her.

'Cook, will you clean up this room. Get up from the floor, children. Go up and put on your clothes.'

Nurse left without speaking again. My two sisters went to dress. Maggie picked up the glasses and bottle. I stayed, picking up cornflakes and twigs.

'It is true. He is dead, Mamma.'

'Yes, yes. I quite understand. Why don't you go with your sisters? Why are you staring? Just go.'

I said that the nursery would be quiet now, with no Bruno. Did Nurse have to stay?

'What do you want to do about her? Stop staring.'

'I've got a pain. I had one in the night.'

'Children get pains. Tell Gov or Nurse.'

'Gov only looks after Bonnie and Tor. Nurse has ... she's gone funny now.'

What would happen to his milk powder tins? Who would use his shawls and his pot? He'd been so ugly. I'd not even tried to like him.

Mamma had eyelashes like a doll. They didn't blink as she said sharply that I could hardly expect her to produce another baby to suit Nurse. My father was dead, remember? One corner of her mouth had smudged, like a tiny red scratch in the flesh. Her eyes were challenging me. I knew that we were alike inside. Mamma does what she wants.

She fights for it. I want to love you, Mamma. Why can't you stay? Why can't you look after us?

'I'd like to drink from Bruno's bottles. Can I?'

'I pay a Nurse to see to you. Ask her. Why do you stare?'

'Don't you like it at home?'

She was blunt. She had come back to collect some papers, some more clothes and to check on our well-being. She knew her duty, she would do what was necessary. Was I trying to take her to task? Did no one ever consider her point of view? Her life was far from idyllic.

'Bruno is dead,' I repeated.

'What a very obstinate child. And your hair. What is wrong with it? Does Nurse ... has she done anything about it? Are you eating properly?'

'It's nothing. I expect it will grow out. Maggie says the English don't love children. Or God.'

She said that Cook was not only illiterate and whimsical,

her ideas were subversive too. She paid Nurse to keep me upstairs.

'Bruno is dead. It's all women and girls here now.'

'I can't stay. Why can't you understand?'

I said that Nurse had loved him. Why had not she? She looked out of the window at where the schoolroom tree had once grown. She spoke half to herself. I was an uncompromising child, voicing what other people only thought. Why did no one realize that she'd wanted a son only because *he* had? Every man wanted an heir. Human nature, a son to bear the name. She had loved her husband with devotion, abasing herself to please. Each pregnancy they had hoped. First a girl, then another, the third seemed like an insult. Once more, this will be the boy. And he'd died without knowing his son. She had been left with all that burden, that responsibility which she'd created purely for him. Nothing mattered after that, no point in a life without him. There was nothing left to share without his presence. She disliked children, she'd had them for him. The boy was born, she'd not cared. Nurse wanted to come, she had done her a favour. Now was her chance to leave. Two retainers, both elderly, and that idiot peasant girl. They could manage without her, she could lead the life she'd once planned. Unwanted people longed to be wanted, they needed responsibility which she'd provided. Her own deepest need was independence, not to live through another's needs. She achieved independence of thought and action having made provision for the home. She had accommodated three lost souls who cared for her children. She had time now for herself. She turned. 'And do you know, Ula, if I hadn't married your father and had children, I might be famous now? I have always wanted to act.'

'Why did you?'

She said she'd adored, worshipped him, put him on a pedestal. A woman must have love. He'd longed for his son, that poor little boy. Too late, all too late.

'You realize Bruno is dead?'

'Dead? I can't accept ...'

'Stay. Won't you, Mamma?'

She had come for some clothes, she repeated. She had enrolled at a school of acting. Three children in Sussex wouldn't prevent her. How strange to have white in my hair. Children grew, they would cease to cling. She disliked and discouraged clinging, we must learn to stand alone as soon as possible. What she had done, and would continue to do, was for our good. Nothing would stop her career.

'Are you glad about Bruno? Do you wish we had died too?'

The look she turned on me was worse than an actual or threatened smack. She whispered my name. Ula. I was insensitive, I was crude-minded, I was ugly. I would grow into a loveless young girl. How could anyone be drawn to me, or admire me. She had just lost her son. Get away.

She went to the telephone to contact the hospital. Later on she left again but this time she took Bonnie and Tor with her. Moral support for the various signatures and formalities. My sisters looked proud and pleased.

Maggie explained the night's happenings to Gov when she arrived. Together they went up to Nurse. I stayed in the hall. I lifted the telephone receiver. 'Hello. All hail. Hello nonsense, hail lies.'

5

'And so, Ula, I'm sending you off with Cookie. Don't you think that's a good idea?'

'When? Will Bonnie and Tor go?'

'Just you and Cook. To Ireland.'

Mamma said that my sisters were to go with Gov to her cottage. Poor Cook deserved a rest too; she'd been a tower of strength since ... all this had happened. So, Ula, you can be happy, with your beloved Cook to yourself. Nurse was leaving, Nurse was ill, it was best that she left quite soon.

'Where to? Where will she go?'

Because Nurse hadn't spoken for days, not since she'd been rude to Mamma. She'd stayed on the nursery floor swallowing her pills in silence. Maggie waited on her. She was sorry for Nursie all right; because of Nursie we'd have to change our lives. Mamma couldn't bring herself to mention the funeral.

The night after Bruno died Nurse had howled in her sleep. She ground her teeth as well. Maggie had to shake her awake before taking me down to her bed again to be her dotey child, her own birdy bones, her hope. Mamma had quite changed her opinion of Maggie: the girl was rough, but a jewel. She relied on Maggie now as much as she relied on Gov. She'd be happy to trust me to her care entirely.

Mamma hadn't lost her temper with me again since the morning that Bruno had died, nor had I seen much of her. I wanted to know if she would be famous like Mae West, if she would put kisses on Boris Karloff's mouth. I went to her bedroom secretly to poke and pry in her things. She loved clothes. I smelled her flowers and her soaps, I looked in her cheval looking glass on the stand. Here she scanned her hair and her eyelashes, here she dreamed her golden dreams. She had no grey hairs; I checked her hairbrush entwined with dark auburn hairs. I looked at her rows of coats and dresses, linen, satin, silk. She had quantities of shoes with glossy heels, I tried them, my feet weren't much smaller. The gold kid sandals with thin-as-string strapping fitted me. I tapped up and down before the looking glass. 'If I hadn't married I might be famous. I have always wanted to act.' I rubbed some red onto my lips, stretching them. I too would have bosoms one day. She'd be angry again if she knew I'd been here. Spying. Creeping.

'How long shall I stay away? Does Maggie know?'

'Of course. I don't know yet how long. I'll discuss all that later with Gov.'

Mamma depended on Gov but she was bored by her. Gov was old, staid and dull. Mamma liked her bedroom best, trying clothes on, altering her hair and thinking about acting.

Nurse was given her notice to leave on the morning of Bruno's funeral. Mamma went up to her alone. I stayed in the hall listening. There was silence after Mamma had spoken. Then Nurse made a nasty sound. Bonnie and Tor left the schoolroom to join me. Nurse's wails upstairs increased. My sisters held hands, their free hands held the banisters. I took hold of Bonnie's skirt. We waited, our raised faces staring up. I noticed that Tor's clothes smelled a little like Maggie's clothes. Tor sweated when she was scared and I knew that they were like me inside. Then Maggie came up from the kitchen. She said she hoped Nursie wouldn't become dangerous, some people went strange after a death. But not to worry, she'd look after us. Nursie had mixed blood in her don't forget, poor old person, she'd brought a lot of this on herself.

Mamma's face was paper-white when she came down. Her pointed mouth stood out darkly red, she didn't look at us but went to her room. Acting was probably easier than motherhood, you only had to think of yourself and get the words right. The noise upstairs continued. Maggie said again not to fret, she'd take the sherry bottle with the pills. Nursie mustn't go to the funeral, no telling what she might do.

We were dressed in our darkest clothes. Maggie's little eyes were calm. We would remember this funeral for the rest of our lives, the day our baby brother was laid to rest. The death of a baby was special, what a shame there would be no wake. It grieved her too that the service wouldn't be Catholic but she'd seen there was no lack of flowers. The little coffin was covered with blooms, with Maggie's red roses like a crown on his head. The bouquet from me and my sisters was star-shaped, Mamma's was a pillow of tiny white flowers. Miss Dance sent pink and white carnations wired cunningly, but nothing from Nurse who had loved him best.

Mamma's black veil covered her eyes, her cheeks showed theatrically pale as we all got into the car behind the hearse. Bonnie and Tor kept close together, I would have liked to have held Mamma's hand. As we moved from the house the nursery window was thrown up and a chamber pot flew out hitting the roof of the hearse. 'Drat my blood, take that. It's all you're worth, the lot of you.'

'Sweet Saviour,' Maggie moaned.

Mamma stared through her veil at the flowers in front of us. Bonnie and Tor squeezed closer. Later they would talk and laugh about the happening. Mamma said quietly that the woman must be out of the house tonight.

I never heard anyone say 'drat my blood' again, I never saw Nurse again. 'Poor old soul' Maggie said afterwards, packed out of the house like a dog, it was worse than morbid. She kept me with her downstairs, after the funeral, and nobody saw Nurse leave. I asked Maggie if she would miss her, why she didn't say goodbye to her. It would just make a bad job worse, she said. Nurse might put a curse on her, she was capable of it. Together we listened to her feet clumping down the staircase, the bump of her black leather bag. Never again would I feel those bony fingers washing me, never again feel her pulling my hair. No one waved or hugged or smiled at her. The door banged; she was gone. We could get on with celebrating Christmas now, Maggie said. And just as well we were all going away. Back home in Ireland there would be proper decorations, proper food as well as religion.

'Where will you go for Christmas, Mamma? Do you mind being left alone?'

She said my questioning and staring was ill-mannered. She was doing what was best for us all.

'I only asked what you will do.'

'Questions, questions.' Life continued, I would understand it better one day. And I was to remember that she had loved my father and for his sake had borne him a son. She was not deserting us, she was providing for us, let me never forget that. I knew she wanted me to be loyal to her, to admire and love her if I could. I smiled. She said that it was sad that my smile was rare. Had my life been so very grim? She had never heard me laugh.

'I laughed more before you came. I don't like you seeing my teeth.'

She murmured that they were a poor colour but I had good bone structure. Good carriage was as important as looks. I told her I would like to look like her, which pleased her. Learn to walk well she advised, with confidence, grace and pride. She hoped that Miss Dance had taught me something, she'd paid enough. She never wanted to see me or my sisters as we were in the schoolroom, undressed, unwashed, uncombed.

'But *how long* shall I be staying in Ireland?'

'I keep telling you, it's not arranged. Gov is too old to work for much longer. Your sisters will be going to boarding school.'

Would Gov be fired too when she wasn't wanted? Had Mamma a truly cold heart? She said I was lucky to have this chance of travelling. She'd heard tales about Ireland. A romantic island somewhat given to rain. It was to be hoped that Cookie wouldn't let me run barefoot, or get nits in that grey hair of mine. Remember Ula to smile with confidence and grace.

'Shall I be learning dancing there?'

She doubted if I'd find the equal of Miss Dance where I was going. No doubt some rustic antics went on. They were a picturesque people, particularly the peasantry, fond of leprechauns and beer. She wanted me to enjoy the holiday with Cookie. I must learn to stop looking so sad.

'She isn't Cook, I told you. Her name is Maggie.'

'Yes, I quite understand you. I'm simply doing what is best.'

43

'How do you know what is best? How *long*?'

She supposed I would eventually go to the same school as my sisters. Did I want to go to school?

I wanted to knit dusters and make a scrapbook with pressed flowers in it. I didn't want to learn to read. Mamma had no experience of school. Her childhood with Gov had been charmed. A shame that Gov was so old now. She'd do her best to find a nice school. I must learn to be less critical of my elders. It was her own business what she called her staff. Those in lowly positions, porters, waiters, cooks, were most frequently addressed by the work they did. People simply forgot their names. It was the custom and moreover gave the workers a little dignity, especially as their work often had none. They were subservient, they were expendable but useful.

'Is that why we never called Nurse "Aunt"?'

She was in another category, Mamma said quickly. No blood relative, her employment had been ill-advised. That behaviour from the upstairs window had been iniquitous. Mamma went silent. We wouldn't mention it again. My sisters would be leaving shortly. I would go after Maggie had cleaned up the house.

When I had waited in the hall with Bonnie and Tor I had hoped we might become closer, united by apprehension, but they hadn't changed. I didn't expect them to think of me when they had gone. I didn't mind so much now, I would be having a proper Christmas with Maggie in Ireland, I'd be wanted and needed, I'd be the only child there.

I watched them leave for the cottage in Shottermill. They went without saying goodbye. I watched them go out of the gate and down the road on either side of Gov, talking excitedly. Later they would sit round her fire, having gathered the logs and twigs to make it burn well. They would listen while she read them stories. Would they sing? Would they play Happy Families and Snap? They had no fears or worries about boarding school, they had each other, they could read and do sums. They had never been lonely or treated unkindly. They would expect to be treated at school as Gov did at home. What you expected you often got.

I went into the schoolroom for another look before Maggie got there. Soon the tree would be taken down. There was a faint spicey smell of the cloves that Tor had stuck into oranges to make pomander balls, mixed with a thick smell of old dust. Under a chair was a wooden knitting needle with a length of unravelled floorcloth. Gov liked all handiwork to have a use. Without my sisters the tree looked even more beggarly. Most of the foliage was shed on the floor. Maggie had asked me not to hang about being idle, she had the whole house to make clean. People who left muddles were selfish, someone else had to pick up the mess. The tree for instance was the height of rubbish, I'd see a difference in her house at home. They made a special fuss of kiddies at Christmas, as well as the old and the sick. Poor old Nursie, it was disgraceful, like a dog with nowhere to go. Not that she wasn't pleased Nursie had left us. But whoever would bury her when she died?

I went upstairs again. No nurse now to call me greedy or a sneak thief. All was bare and silent and clean. No coughing or wheezing or breathing, just cold wind outside rattling the window. There was a faint smell of floor polish and soap. I climbed onto a chair to reach into the top drawer of the tallboy. It was empty, my fingers felt cold. I felt something soft and woolly, a white woollen bobbled sock, last relic of Bruno, caught in the back of the drawer. I put it back and got down again. Bruno's cot had been taken away, and the mattress from Nurse's bed. The bedsprings looked sharp and ugly. My own bed in the little room had no bedclothes, and a chair was on it. The grate was empty, all the curtains were taken away. The cold and the emptiness wasn't the worst. This must be what they called the feeling of death. Maggie thought that though my Mamma had a right to do anything she chose, as she was the one paying the bills, still it was a wicked thing to run from your own children, worse than murder, and they needing love and care. Without Gov and herself we'd be right little lost souls. Gov, though lardy-dardy and lazy about dusting, loved the two elder girls. Maggie had no great opinion of actresses. She liked to cut out pictures of them but they were best left in books on the whole. A poor class of person doing a poor class of work. She didn't think you'd find many actresses in Ireland. Her people knew right from wrong. I heard her calling me.

'No sense in brooding up in the cold. Come now and give a hand with this tree.'

I went round with a little brush, sweeping up mud and leaves. I found more knitting under the sideboard, tangled with swirls of dust. A trail of cloves lay along the skirting board, their cracked heads split from the stems. I sneezed. I had free access now to the room I had longed for. I was dismantling it bit by bit, removing the magic. Soon it would be clean and soulless as the nursery. Never again would I listen at the door, begging Bonnie to let me in. I would never hear them whispering, wondering if they whispered about me. Maggie threw open the window. You would think someone of Gov's education would be more par-ticular. Now then, Ula, that tree.

We placed it on its side on a dustsheet, rolling it into a long tube. I walked behind as she dragged it downstairs and out to the dustbin, where it stood propped up alone.

Time now to be thinking of our own packing, she said. I wished I had something new to wear.

'Mamma,' I asked her, 'could I have a pink dress for Christmas, a silk one with rows of pleats?'

I knew she would say no, though she had so many lovely things herself. She said pink pleats sounded frightful, I already had my cream Viyella. Maggie could buy me what I really needed, no pink pleats mind, nothing frilled. Some heavy shoes perhaps, Ireland might be muddy. And a sou'wester for the Irish rain.

Maggie got me two jerseys as well as new shoes. She wasn't buying a sou'wester just to please Ma'am. We were going to the city, not the bogs out in the wilds.

'Say goodbye to your Mammy now. Look up there, she's waving, see?'

I looked up as we drove off in the taxi. I saw her pointed face and her thin bright mouth. Was she sorry now that I was leaving her? Did she have no misgivings or fears? She hadn't kissed me goodbye or even touched me. She was at the window where Nurse had thrown the pot. 'Take that, it's all you're fit for.' I wanted to love you, Mamma. I wanted you. Now you are truly on your own.

6

Maggie wasn't used to travelling. Her only previous trip had been leaving Ireland to come here. She looked forward to showing me the sights on our journey, she knew what children liked. My Mammy had no need to keep telling her to keep me close to her, she knew all about youngsters' ways. The two of us were off to have the time of our lives; anyone would think she wasn't fit. In Ireland each and every child was cherished. Cruelty and neglect were unknown. I'd be safer with her than in Buckingham Palace, I'd be her family's ewe lamb. She'd make certain that I put a bit of weight on, I was too skinny for my size. She had only tossed her head when Mamma had questioned her about the troubles, about the dark stirrings in the north of her land. The only trouble she expected for me to run into was that I'd be spoiled from too much fussing. Her parents were expecting us, she had written. They were lonely since she'd gone away. A child in the house would bring Christmas alive for them.

As well as keeping close to me Mamma insisted that Maggie should not influence me with any religious talk. She wanted us to be free thinkers, she didn't agree with church. Mamma agreed with Gov; countries that made too much of religion often ended with civil strife. Nurse, if she'd had a faith, had kept it to herself, and Nurse didn't matter now. So Cookie, Mamma had repeated, no praying or church-going for her child, who must grow up with uncluttered ideas. Cookie's beliefs were quite hysterical, stalwart though she was in adversity. Troubles brought out the good in some people, so mind now, no preaching, no idols, no hymns. The death of the baby, followed by Nurse going off her head, had put the household under enormous strain.

'You'll miss your mammy all the same, I dare say.'

I would like to miss her, I ought to miss her. Can you miss someone you don't properly know? I ought to want to stay and comfort her. I couldn't wait to leave. My sisters were happy with Gov in her cottage; soon I would be happy too. I waved up at Mamma's pretty face at the window. I took hold of Maggie's hand. She loved me, she loved having me, now we both had each other to ourselves. We were heading for God's green island to enjoy a real Christmas.

She had made a picnic for the journey. Maggie distrusted buffet-car fare. There were sandwiches of soda bread and oranges to suck, in case our throats became parched, as well as a few jam rock cakes for the boat. Maggie loved all children, my mammy ought to know that, she'd no need to tell her what to do. You got a right rough crowd journeying to Ireland now, she told me not to speak to anyone, some folk were apt to make free, especially ones that had a drink on them. We would keep ourselves to ourselves. She'd packed some magazines in her basket, and I had my old tin toy.

We were taking the mail boat across the Channel. We left home early to catch the train from London. At the entrance to the station I saw another tree. A charity tree, Maggie told me, in aid of a sick kiddy fund. It was undecorated apart from the presents dangling from it, tied up with glittering threads. More parcels were piled at the roots of it and a placard that she read out. 'We always care this time of year; help us to care more.' She said not to stand gawping at it either, I'd be getting presents too if I was good. A man was playing a saxophone. Maggie said it was a Christmas hymn, hurry now or we'd miss getting seats.

I had never been in a train. It was so long I couldn't see the end. The platform was thronging with people with cases, the train windows were filled with faces. Most of them were men, of all ages, shouting and pushing their way. More cases and bags were in the aisles between the seating; there were rucksacks and coats in the racks. Most of the men were smoking pipes or cigarettes. Mamma had told Maggie to get into a Ladies Only compartment.

'The smell gets into my nose, Maggie.'

She said not to start annoying her, the train was packed but we had got a window seat. I'd get used to the smoke if I ignored it. She smiled at the man who had given his seat up. Very obliging of him. She didn't look at me as she spoke.

I hated the smell. I had seen Mamma smoking thin Russian cigarettes but no one else smoked at home. Maggie had always said what a dirty thing it was; she didn't seem to care now. There was too a greasy smell of empty crisp packets and a smell like old shoes, newly cleaned.

'Can I have an orange, Maggie?'

'The train hasn't started. Greedy.'

She had spoken to me just like Nurse. She peeled the orange carelessly, squirting juice over me, keeping her eyes on the man. She put a segment into her own mouth, chewing with mincing movements. The orange was a sour one, a pip got between my teeth.

'When shall we have to go to sleep, Maggie?'

She said we'd be having a lay-down on the boat, but I was not to keep fussing now. Her voice sounded different, telling me to look out of the window at my last sight of England before it got dark. Tomorrow I would see Ireland's green. She had spoken often of the colour of Ireland, the grass and the snow were brilliant. People said it was the wet weather and the quality of light. Maggie said it was a symbol of Tightness, the Irish didn't neglect their souls. The Pope himself thought the world of Ireland, the land that had never lost faith. My first glimpse would show me, after England's soot and grime. Any churches you might find in England were nearly all of the wrong kind. You'd have to come to Ireland to see what she meant, the country that did things right.

I sucked my tooth with the pip in it. Would I ever see Lucy again, or listen to Miss Dance's voice? It was a pity I'd not kissed Mamma nor waved to her.

'Look, look, Maggie, another tree. A Christmas tree in that window.' We were passing sooty tenements, most of the windows were dark. Maggie ignored my pointing finger. She said I had Christmas trees on the brain. She was still looking at the man opposite who had given up his seat. He was holding a bottle. After having instructed me so firmly not to look at anyone, let alone stare or smile, she was looking and smiling at him. Her voice sounded silly.

'That's a ferocious-looking pet your wee girl has there. Is it a goat or a lamb?'

The man leaned and offered his bottle to Tin who I was holding on my knee. I thought him stupid; anyone should know a giraffe. Maggie giggled and shifted her legs. I had never heard her laugh like that, nor seen her cheeks look so red. He stretched to touch my cheek with his podgy forefinger. I saw that he had bitten nails. I wouldn't answer him. He was trying to interest Maggie by showing an interest in me. Because of him she was using that silly voice, as if she had swallowed something too hot. She said she would take a drink from him if he insisted, she didn't normally indulge. But Christmas was Christmas, the smoke in the air had a parching effect, didn't he agree? Plus a drink helped make friends and pass the time. Was he partial himself? She hadn't taken the magazines from her basket. She only had eyes for him.

He proffered the bottle. And would her wee girl fancy a drop? Maggie leaned over and whispered. Not her own child, no, she was minding me. My father and my brother had died, she was taking me home to her family for the Christmas. She sniggered when she spoke my name. Imagine it, Ula, named after some sort of bird. Had he heard the likes of it ever? I felt betrayed, she was poking fun at me, she was laughing with one of the right rough crowd.

'Yes, please. I would like some.'

Maggie didn't stop him from pushing the bottle into my mouth, she did nothing to stop him when I choked. The drink had a dirty taste, my tongue burned, he pushed the bottle further. I gagged, my eyes watered, I struggled and Maggie laughed. Her giggles got louder, poor little birdy girl, getting a drink to herself at last. He saw what was happening, he got up, he pushed himself between us. He patted my back with his thick hand. His handkerchief smelled vile as he put his face near and wiped me. It was Maggie he wanted, not me. His eyebrows had greasy roots and were thick as lichen, growing outwards over his eyes. One of the hairs pricked my forehead. I smelled his ears and the smell of his breath. A drop more of the hard stuff would put hairs on my chest, he whispered. Named for a bird, was I? He could think of worse things than that. He liked birds himself, birds of all kinds, he liked them big and soft. He looked from the corners of his eyes at Maggie's lollopers. Maggie had the bottle now.

At the other side of the aisle were his friends, dealing a pack of cards. The cards made little flapping sounds on the table in front of them. Their cigarette cartons and crisp packets were pushed aside. Would they deal Mick into the game, they called over. Would his lady friend like a hand? Maggie answered in her new mincing voice. She never played cards, thank you, never played games at all. The eyebrow man laughed coarsely, digging his elbow into her. No games at all? Was she sure of that? He rolled a cigarette, offering her one. She was welcome to join his friends if she'd a mind to. He'd be happy here talking to the wee girl. Oh what is wrong, Maggie, what happened to you? You are smiling and talking to a stranger, you are holding a cigarette in your hand.

The men smoked their butts down to the length of finger-nails, cupping them into their palms. They forgot us when they started their game, they put money in a small pile to win. Good luck to Mick getting off his mark with the lady. They had their own bottle to drink.

Mick sat against Maggie now, pushing his big thighs close. His greasy brows, his coarse trousers and his voice offended me. How dare he take Maggie away? It was getting dark. I held Tin to the window. Mick laughed again. Was my animal looking for food now? Was he looking to munch the stars?

The journey seemed very long. The card game was fin-ished; Mick's friends started to sing. Then Mick joined in and gradually the rest of them went quiet. He sang the hymn that we had heard earlier on the station platform, 'Oh come let us adore Him'. I thought I had never heard such beautiful sounds. The carriage stopped what they were doing, they stared, they listened, sitting very still. I forgot everything but the sound of him, forgot Bruno's death and Nurse getting mad in her head. I forgot that Mamma didn't want us. Nothing mattered except the song. The rattling train, the smell of drink and smoke faded, I was happy. I believed he was singing to me. I was going to a magic green land, where the people sang like angels and where every child was loved.

When I woke up next I was in a hard bed under a scratchy sheet. I was sweating, there was a bad taste in my mouth, there was a throbbing sound. I was in a small room in a bed fixed to the wall. What shocked me most was that I was still wearing my shoes. My feet felt bruised. I sat up. My bed was high, with another one underneath. There was a washbasin with small taps and a tooth glass and a rack to put your clothes on.

'Mag-gie. Mag-gie . . .'

Her voice answered sounding muffled. Stop annoying her, she was only outside the door. She still sounded as if she'd swallowed something. I got down. I put my head to the door jamb and wailed. I banged my head, I made noises of sobbing though not real tears. I very rarely cried. I put my heart into pretended weeping, I rubbed my eyes to make them red. Please, Maggie, please come.

'Sweet Saviour, stop that racket, you'll have us put off the boat.' She pushed me into the top bunk again, tucking the narrow sheet. She looked even redder, her face looked itchy, her mouth was swollen now. She forgot to hug me or call me birdy bones. Her eyes were silly and strange.

'You must stay with me, Maggie, you promised not to leave me.'

'In a couple of minutes I will. Stop pulling at me.'

'I'll tell Mamma you left me alone. You didn't stay with me on the boat.'

'Ah God, Ula. What has got into you? You spoil my sport, you spoil everything.'

She half stumbled, then sat on the lower bunk, her grumbling voice sank to a whisper, she lay on one elbow, then lay back with her knees sprawled.

She kept her coat and her shoes on but she didn't leave me. She was quiet except for her loud rude smells. Then she started to snore. I knew now why Mamma had worried; it was because of the right rough crowd. You couldn't trust them, they had tried to take Maggie away.

A grey edge of light showed round the curtain covering the porthole. Someone was banging our door. The engine had stopped, there was no more throbbing. We must have got to Ireland now. I leaned over to look at Maggie. She was covered by her sheet now.

'Everyone off the boat now. Now please, passengers, everyone off the boat.'

Maggie's head wasn't visible except for a lock of hair hanging free. I pulled her sheet, her face was puffier, with crumbs in the corners of her eyes. She opened them, she looked blank. She remembered then. Going home. The boat. Mick.

'There's someone calling, Maggie. They want us to get off the boat.'

She jerked to a sitting position, then she got off the bed. Was Mick waiting for her? Was he looking for her? Wait now, Mick, she'd be out in a minute now.

'It's not Mick, Maggie, they want us to get off the boat.'

Her hair was in spikes, she looked older, her body seemed huge and sad, nothing like the Maggie who had danced in our kitchen, more like a huge clown. Why oh why hadn't Mick waited? Was I sure it was one of the crew? Where was he? She must get him, it was my fault for making that fuss. She should have stayed with him. Hurry, Ula.

'I must wash my hands, Maggie, you know I must. You know I have to look clean.'

I ran water into the small handbasin, I unwrapped the piece of soap. It was like a doll's washing place for toys and children. I was delaying purposely while Maggie complained. I repeated in a virtuous voice that surely she wouldn't want me to arrive in her country looking neglected? And look, she'd lost her pink hair slide. She clutched her hair, making it wilder. Not her lovely pink hair slide? We looked under the bunks for it, we crawled round the floor space. It was her lucky charm, she mourned. Her Da had bought it for her. I wanted to find it. With her hair proper again she might be the Maggie I knew, proud of me, wanting me, happy to be taking me to her home. She must forget Mick with the eyebrows, he was awful. Where was the pink hair slide?

We didn't find it. We pulled her sheets off. Maggie had a headache now. She peered up and down the passageway. No Mick. He'd such a grand singing voice. All my fault for nagging and interrupting. The two of them had got on grand.

'Your eyes have got yellow in them. Why don't you wash them?'

She told me not to be bold. I said he'd got horrid eyebrows and nasty trousers and I was glad he'd disappeared. She started to raise her hand to me when we heard more banging. 'Hurry please now, passengers, last call.'

She asked the steward if he had seen her friend at all, a curly-haired man on the stout side, with a grand singing voice, travelling with friends. He said that everyone was with friends this time of the year and a good many sang as well. In the bar had her friend been?

Maggie took my hand again. Ah God, life was unkind to her. It was also very unfair.

'I'm here, Maggie. I help you, don't I?'

She had no man, she said, to support her, no kiddy or home of her own. She hadn't much money, nor the world's prettiest face. She'd not complained, tried to look on the sunny side. Meeting Mick had been a gift in her hand. Where was he? What happened? Where was the man with the darling voice?

I told her how much she had changed when he'd come. She didn't even sound the same. Didn't she want me any more, now she'd found him?

'I do, Ula. Oh I do. It's just ...'

'What is it? Tell me.'

She said that she'd like me *and* Mick. She never seemed to get what she'd really like, very little went right in her life, she seemed to have lost her luck.

She searched again in her basket for the hair slide. We couldn't see Mick anywhere.

7

The streets looked drab in the dawn light, with the shops still shuttered and dark. There were few people on the wet pavements, moving quietly in their shabby coats. Most of the women wore headscarves knotted under their chins. The men had newspapers rolled to keep dry; the sports pages were precious. They paused under lamp-posts to confer with each other, their breath forming steam round their heads. I could see little colour anywhere. I looked for grass or a tree, even an empty flowerbed. There were no spaces even for weeds, only low buildings with broken doorways under the fanlights in empty narrow streets. Small shops on corners had lit windows. Some of the women pushed babies in prams. 'It must be cold out for a baby. Where are the gardens?'

'Don't mind these parts here. This is the outskirts.'

'You said it would be green. I just wanted to know where. I can see a green letterbox.'

She pointed to a church with people, mostly women, going in and out. There you are now, just as she'd said, people living right, observing the faith. See the statue of Our Lady, see the people blessing themselves. The men with the newspapers lifted their caps as they passed. A holy country all right, there was proof. Holy God lived in the churches, they were proper churches here.

'I know, Maggie, you told me. Where is the green?'

'Stop annoying me. It's early yet. You'll see plenty of green soon.'

She wished I'd drop my habit of pestering, it was a torment so early in the day. Ireland was as green as a parable, she could promise me that. Meanwhile she was hungry, she hoped her Ma was making a fry. She didn't mention Mick again.

Our taxi stopped at the end of her street outside another church, her church, she wanted me to see. Behind the railings and iron gate was a crib under a thatched roof with figures standing round a manger. There now, she pointed to it. See the beasts standing waiting, the camel, an ass and the lamb. See Mary and Joseph's pleased faces. I saw that they were looking down but no baby was inside the manger, only artificial hay.

'Has the baby died already then?'

She said I was morbid and heartless and no wonder, that was what ignorance did. The holy child would be there by the morning, He'd get born at midnight mass. The priest would come out of the church and lay Him down there in the hay. We could start Christmas then. See Our Lady's happy expression, see poor St Joseph's faithful eyes. She'd a particular devotion to St Joseph, Maggie had.

'Why?'

'Never mind the why. See the goat hiding in the corner?'

'Can I come to midnight mass?'

She said I might if I stopped pestering and tormenting, and I wasn't to annoy her Ma. Her Ma wasn't at all strong in her head these days. Understand, Ula? Look now, there was the green. Green grass growing all round the holy family. Satisfied? I didn't tell her that the grass was just green raffia like the mock hay in the crib. St Joseph had raffia hair, their faces were lumps of clay, but I wanted to see the baby getting born, let Maggie think it was grass. She pointed out the star on the crib roof, the star of Bethlehem pointing down. Mind, she added, Christmas wasn't just presents and excitement, it was praising the holy child. She looked sincere and tender, her face was less puffy now, as if she could see into the future. Perhaps she could see me being accepted into her church, with herself as godmother standing near. That mamma of mine had much to answer for, neglecting her children for her own pleasures, leaving them to others' care.

We walked down the street of terraced houses, which seemed even shabbier than the ones we had passed. Slates were missing from the rooftops, windows were boarded up with tin. The front doors opened onto the pavement; each one had a single stone step. Few of the windows had curtains. Maggie's door was battleship grey. The Christmas tree in her window shone out like a beam of light. The panes were sprayed with frost to which cotton wool blobs adhered. I looked in. Red and green paper chains twined from lanterns, tinsel whorls were tacked to the walls. The tree was immense, with spun glass birds on the branches. The top branches pressed the ceiling. A bird with blue and yellow wings was arranged as if swooping, its opened beak stretched to the door. The tree almost filled the room and the foliage was barely visible under the thick tinsel twisted round it. Coloured streamers hung from the small lights which kept flashing on and off all over it. I kept very still as I gazed at it. This was a real tree. I stood on tiptoe to see more of it. The bottom branches thinned into dwindling roots which stood in a bucket weighted with stones. There was no carpet in the room or any furniture except for a card table spread with newspaper. It was worth coming to Ireland just for Maggie's Christmas tree. I wanted to stay and look at it for hours. The grey door opened.

'Don't stand there gawping outside, Maggie May. You'll have the neighbours wondering again ...'

'I've brought her. This is Ula, Ma.'

'I see her. I have eyes in my head, haven't I? Don't be standing gawping out there.'

The Ma had been watching out for us since first light, she told us. Whatever had kept us so long?

'Don't fret yourself, Ma, aren't we here now, safe and sound?'

'That child's hair, what is wrong with it? Come inside before you're seen.'

Maggie explained to her mother that my hair had been like that since birth. She couldn't help it, it wasn't her fault, whitey patches from a baby.

'Well, come on in then, child.'

The mother pulled me from the window. This street was nosey and the family were proud here, they liked to keep themselves to themselves. I was already frightened of her, I hated the feel of her, there was something strange about her hands. She caught me by the point of my chin, peering closely at me with eyes that didn't look straight. How old was I? Was I a good child? Her hands felt like cloth on my skin. She had a short body on stumpy legs and her hair jutted out in a fringe over her unfocusing eyes.

'Leave her now, can't you, Ma?'

'Giving out the orders again, are you? And you scarcely over the step.'

'Ah, Ma. Stop.'

'Was life not what you hoped the other side? Did you not get yourself a man?'

'Ma.'

'Decided to honour us again, did you? It's a wonder they spared you the child. I've been on my own waiting.'

'I like your Christmas tree very much. Why isn't there any star on the top?'

I hated them quarrelling as soon as they saw each other. I must make the Ma want me.

'Well you may ask. I couldn't reach is why. I've not had any help.'

'I'll put the star on, Ma. The boat was late. The crowds were fierce, we were delayed getting away off the boat.'

I wondered why she didn't mention Mick. I was glad that she hadn't. Maggie explained about the lost pink hair slide, the one which had brought her luck. She'd need to buy another later. She pushed her hair behind one ear. We had searched for it, looked everywhere, we were worn out from lack of sleep. Was the back bedroom ready?

The Ma stared, her little cross eyes looked worse. England had given Maggie notions all right. 'Is the back bedroom prepared' indeed. Would milady like breakfast in bed? Would the whitey-haired child like its bum wiped? Was it able to tie its own shoes?

'Hush, Ma. Don't.'

Maggie said something in a low voice, about my brother and having no Da. And we'd neither of us eaten since last evening.

'You wrote about the wain dying, Maggie May. I heard it before.'

'Maggie, where is your father? Isn't he here today?'

The Ma answered before her, drawing her chin back so that it made one line with her neck. Nosey too, was I? One of the curious kind? English wains were good at being nosey, she'd heard.

'I just wanted to know where he was.'

She told Maggie to take me upstairs, and then come on down for a wash. The house felt colder inside than it had been in the street. Their staircase rose steeply from just inside the grey door. The back bedroom was opposite, at the top. It was barely bigger than the bed inside it and had a stuffy smell. It smelled worse than a zoo, Maggie said, opening the window. She forgot the broken sashcord; to keep it open it had to be propped up. She put the alarm clock under it and the cold air blew in on our hair. There now, did I think I could sleep in this room? With Mick forgotten and out of her mind she looked at me in her old way. I didn't mind the cold or the bare floorboards and the smell. This was Maggie's Irish home.

The room faced the back, overlooking the cracked chimney cowls and grey roofs that made a jagged line against the sky. The back yards were crammed with dustbins, old broomsticks and bicycles. A tin tub was hanging in Maggie's yard from a hook in the broken fence. A cat ran along the fence, jumping across the gap. A woman's voice called sadly, 'Tibby, Tib-bee.' Apart from the nail on the back of the door there was nowhere to hang our clothes. We would leave them in the cases and push them under the bed. Her curtains were pieces of sheeting tacked over the window-frames, trailing now onto the floor. The nails in the boards had their heads beaten sideways, the small heads scratched your soles. Draughts blew through the spaces where the floorboards ended and the skirting boards began. A dream of Maggie's had been to buy a red carpet to send home in time

for the Christmas. A bare bulb hung in the hall. I saw no other
lights except the Christmas tree ones. Maggie said I needn't start
pestering to use a bathroom because I'd just have to use a po.
The lavvy hole was out in their yard, that was all there was. So,
po or brave the cold again? All I wanted was to go downstairs to
where the tree glowed rich and rare. I could hear music playing.
She said it was Ma's wireless set, she listened to it all day long.

The kitchen was under the back bedroom and was where the
family spent most of the time. On the end of the draining board
was a huge wireless in a heavy wooden frame. The control knobs
were set in a design of silk pleating with wooden spokes like a
fan. Maggie's Ma stood watching the wireless with a fixed look,
her lips moved to the words of the song. She turned.

'Stop staring with the big eyes of you. Get washed, English
wain.'

'Where?'

At the sink, of course, she told me. This wasn't Buckingham
Palace here. They were plain folk, plain living and plain behaving. What water they had came from the sink. Nor would I get
waited on while I was here. Maggie had told her all about that
nursery of mine, with the trays up and down, the bathing and
fuss. I'd have to come to earth here in this place, I'd get no special treatment here. There was the towel, get washed English
child.

'I like your wireless a lot. I like your house as well.'

She looked pacified. Did I like Henry Hall? I said I thought
I did, though I'd never heard of him. We had not had a wireless
at home. Mamma being rarely at home hadn't needed one. Gov
thought it an unnecessary modern invention. Maggie's Ma loved
sweet swing music, her wireless set was the love of her heart. Her
little cross eyes stayed wistfully watching it. Next to Henry she

loved Joe Loss. She broke an egg into a cup before tipping it into a frying pan. The gas jet burned high under it. She added some lard.

'Mind Ula's clothes, Ma. That jersey she has on is new.'

It was a fawn jersey with pink stitching round the neck and the sleeves. Maggie had chosen it when she bought the shoes. I didn't think Mamma would approve. The Ma put down the frying pan angrily. Let Maggie cook the breakfast if she was so particular, she'd sit down and eat her own. She forked the egg onto her plate and sat at the draining board to eat it, leaving Maggie to cook for me. She ate slowly with quivering movements of her jaw and neck, keeping her eyes on her set. Eating increased the pleasure of listening. She hardly blinked as she ate.

The scullery was barely wider than a passage, with the sink, the gas stove and the draining board down one wall. To get to the lavvy hole in the yard you had to squeeze past anyone in the scullery. Meals were eaten at the draining board, where bread, eggs, meat-paste jars and a tea tin were kept. There was one shelf for cups and plates.

Maggie fried my egg, not burning it, spooning the fat onto it so that the yolk set with a milky-looking sheen. I'd never eaten a fried egg, only boiled ones. She cut it into a cup with squares of buttered bread sprinkled with pepper. I sat beside Maggie, all of us waiting for Henry Hall. Their spoons tasted like hot pennies, but I still loved the taste of the egg. I would be quiet, grateful and appreciative, I would make them want me there. The lavvy hole had a seat like a plank over a hole. The toilet paper was squares of newspaper pushed onto a nail in the wall. Come back in quick, the Ma shouted, or the whole street would be talking. Maggie should have put something over that hair of mine. That queer patch of white was like nit eggs.

'I don't like wearing hats, actually.'

'"Actually". This isn't "actually" England. The family is well thought of here.'

The Ma turned back to her wireless set and the signature tune of Henry Hall. Maggie told her that she would take on the cooking now, and the housekeeping. We'd buy anything we needed now.

'I wonder if there'll be presents tomorrow, underneath your tree?'

'Wondering and wanting, a true Englisher you are, on the lookout for your gain. You didn't bring anything yourself, I'm thinking. You'll be quick enough to take what you can.'

I wished I had something for her. I wasn't used to giving presents, I had never been given pocket money. Even a duster knitted by Bonnie would have been something, or one of Gov's pomander balls. Presents were something you dreamed of and hoped for, but didn't often get. The best present I'd ever had was Tin, from Maggie. I didn't know why the Ma hated England so.

The father was in the fuel trade, delivering logs from door to door. He handled Christmas trees too at this time of year, but not turf. The men in the turf trade were apart. He'd be late in tonight, he'd be kept working, it was the same every year. Their tree in the front room had been the biggest he could carry, it had taken two men to get it in place. The trees came from the country, where the Ma had lived when she'd been a girl. She had met the Da twenty-odd years ago when he'd been loading wood for the city. Her part was the greenest county of Ireland, full of lakes and wooded hills.

'How is his lordship anyway?' Maggie's voice sounded sharp. The Ma said he was middling; some people never changed.

66

And was there something wrong with my teeth as well as my hair? You'd not believe I was an English nob's child. Her woolly-feeling hands grabbed hold of my chin again. Her breath smelled of oily fried egg.

'There's nothing wrong with them. I have strong teeth. Grey teeth are made to last. Maggie told me.'

I wished she would let me alone and stop criticizing. I tried to cover my teeth with my lips, but I knew I ought to smile. If you smiled people treated you well.

Maggie said we'd get ready now and go out for the messages. There was nothing in the place fit to eat. She asked the Ma if she should get a bird or a joint of spiced beef?

'Please yourself, Milady. It's you that will be doing the cooking.'

The Ma added that it was all the same to her, she wasn't rightly fond of meat, and to make sure and cover my hair if I was going out.

When we were in the street again Maggie told me not to heed her Ma. She couldn't help her nerves being bad, it was her time of life. Nerves made a woman snappish, but as long as Ma had her wireless she wasn't any trouble. I was too busy looking at the trees in the windows to listen. They were all sizes, from doll-sized trees in saucers trimmed with silver thread to trees filling the windows. Some of them were made of tarnished tinsel, brought out and used year after year; others were real and splendid, but Maggie's was the best. I ran from window to window along the length of her street. Look, Maggie, look at that one, but she didn't seem to care.

We paused outside her church again to look at the crib. There would be singing here tonight, with candles and praying. All the families in the street would be there. But hurry now, Ula,

we had work to do first. There was the Christmas dinner to buy
and prepare, not to mention the tea afterwards when we got in.

We chose a capon. Stuffed and cooked rightly, Maggie said,
a capon made as good a dinner as any else. She liked stuffing and
basting a nice little bird, with a few sausages round it for luck.
We chose chunks of white pudding to have for this evening's
tea. A fry was lovely this cold weather, though strictly speaking
the day was one of abstinence. She'd make jam rock cakes if
she'd a minute to spare for afterwards. Did the butcher have
black pudding by any chance, black pudding went down well
with white. He looked at Maggie and winked at her. He'd plenty
of the other out at the back. Would she come in and take a look
at it?

Maggie started tittering and getting her silly look. It was happening again. She had met a man; soon her voice would change.

'Oh come on, Maggie. Let's go.'

'That's a dangerous-looking animal you have. Will I cut him
up too for your tea?'

The butcher stretched his hand out to take Tin from me. This
had happened before too. Men used Tin as an excuse to talk to
Maggie, whose eyes had gone runny again. A man was there,
and she didn't need me. When he leaned over and whispered to
her, I smelled whisky again and Maggie guffawed. Ah well,
Christmas was Christmas she said to him.

'What did he say, Maggie?'

'I'm telling your Ma that I've a pudden hidden inside, as big
as ...'

He made a gesture. I saw that his trousers had a bump in the
front.

'She's not my mother, she's ... Maggie. Maggie, we'd better
go.'

She looked angry again. Was I interfering again? Killjoy.

'You said you'd make rock cakes.'

The butcher made another attempt. A slice of cake and a cup of tea would go well with him as well. Could he get an invite?

'Maggie, I need to go to the bathroom. I need to go now.'

She looked really ugly then but we hurried off down the street. At first she wouldn't speak to me, but we had the capon safely wrapped in newspaper. She did love making nice meals. We stopped to buy tangerines bundled into red netting bags, tied with red ribbon. We looked at a pile of apples, their red skins shining from tissue paper nests. An apple after a dinner cleaned the teeth, she couldn't resist telling me, and her eyes started to look natural again. She asked if I liked ginger nut biscuits, a favourite of Ma's with tea. She liked dipping and sucking them, poor Ma did. Still, she'd made a good job of their tree, her suffering with nerves and change. Ah, Christmas in Ireland was grand, wasn't it, Ula? God's own dear land of green. What she'd missed most away from it was colour. England was such a drab land. Our house had been drab, all those grey and brown shades and Ma'am never at home. Ma'am looked after her own wardrobe all right, oh yes, Maggie had never seen the likes. Ball gowns fit for royalty, to make no mention of those shoes. But she'd never seen kiddies dressed like we did, those nasty liberty bodices over our vests, and two pairs of knickerses, those drab old jerseys and skirts. Being away made her appreciate home more. Green grass and bright blue skies.

'The sky isn't blue, Maggie, it's grey. I've not seen any proper grass.'

She said the reason for that was the snow. She'd heard snow forecast on Ma's wireless set. I'd understand what she meant when I saw the snow. The weather was dull just now, the snow would change everything. Irish snow was pure as chastity, a sparkling sinless white, and then the sky would be blue.

She made my home and country sound drab and spiritless, on an equal with our lives. She was generous with her money, she'd paid a lot for groceries today. At home with us she had sent money back to Ireland regularly. I felt ashamed again that I'd no present to give.

Maggie was staring at some flowers that a woman on the kerb was holding out. Weren't they beautiful? Roses for love. Red paper flowers cunningly twisted by gypsies and perfect in their way. She said the gypsies were bad people to cross, especially at Christmas, but she'd spent all her money now. I wished I had some to buy a rose for her. The woman spat after us. Maggie crossed herself. She'd already lost her lucky hair slide.

Now what about the lavvy, she asked me, did I still want to go? She might have guessed I only wanted attention, I could wait now till we were home. Here, take one of the apples to munch on. When I bit into the red skin the flesh was soft. Maggie bit into hers and it was brown. No matter, she said, she could make apple cake from the good parts; her Ma was partial to that as well as ginger nuts. And don't start on about rock cakes again, she would do what she could in the time. I didn't mind anything as long as I could keep her away from men. Men made her go silly and talk uncomfortably. She was still my Maggie with the greasy hands and hair who cooked nice things just for me. I said earnestly that I'd help her. I would be her right-hand man.

We heard the sounds of the Ma's wireless from the street outside. Maggie stooped, she called through the letter box. Hey Ma, we're here, let us in. The newspaper bundles in her basket slipped, the capon flopped out onto the pavement, tangerine oranges rolled into the street. Blood had dried on the beak and neck of the bird, it gazed up with half-closed eyes, its yellow claws curled inwards. I tried to get the newspaper over it again, the curled claws kept slipping free. The bird had a slimy feel. Maggie picked up the oranges. Hurry, she told me, there was a lot of work ahead. You got a bird cheap if it wasn't cleaned, and cleaning it took time.

'Ah, Ma, there you are. We're back. Is his lordship not returned?'

The Ma looked frightened when she saw blood on the newspaper. Blood at Christmas was bad luck. Maggie told her to go back to her wireless again. We'd bought white pudden for tea.

The air was soon filling with the lovely smell of it. There were thick slices of fried bread as well. Tomorrow we would be spreading a cloth over the card table and eating our dinner beside the tree. My special job would be cleaning the cutlery. I licked my fork, tasting the last of the hot penny taste. Ma suddenly leaned over and grabbed my chin again. What sort of a Christmas was I used to? What did that nurse and that governess do? Did they not take a holiday even at Christmas? Did we not eat together even then? Maggie said it was England, Ma oughtn't to forget that. It was a sad country that looked on everything differently. I said nothing, I couldn't explain that we lived separate lives always, that what I liked best about here was being together, eating cramped up from the draining board near the sink. No more Nurse and I on the top floor with my sisters down below and Maggie in the basement. This was real family life here. I looked forward so much to tomorrow's capon beside the flashing tree. The white pudding tasted as nice as it smelled, eaten with HP sauce spread into the fried bread. I poured another brown blob from the bottle, smoothing it with my knife.

'Here's himself at long last,' Maggie said, opening the oven to get out a plate of fry for her father.

'Maggie, me darling, it's my own Maggie May.'

He smelled as Mick and the butcher had smelled, a sour drink smell mixed with smoke. He had the same friendly watery eyes with crumbs in his eyelashes and his large ears stuck out each side. In spite of the look of him I trusted him, I knew that he would be kind.

'So, this is the stranger. You're welcome to the house, stranger child.'

I liked the straight hair covering the tops of his ears and growing low on his neck at the back. He bent over me to kiss me. The Ma sniffed loudly; nobody bothered about kissing her. I didn't mind the Da's smell or his eyes; he looked me in the face when he spoke to me. I knew he was glad I was there. I liked the kind way he touched my arm, I had a place in his home, more than welcome. Had I had an easy trip?

'Get you to the sink now, Da. Your tea is overcooked.' Maggie poured the sauce over the pudding slices, reclosing the oven door. Ma turned her eyes back to the wireless set. 'Oh come let us adore Him, Christ the Lord.' The Da whistled as he squeezed past us by the draining board to get to the yard. When he came back he was ready to wash. I had never seen a man wash himself. He rolled up his grey cotton sleeves, bending his long back over the sink, turning the tap on full. Cold water flew from his hair. He washed with kitchen soap, huffing, splashing, spitting. When he stood up again he was changed, his skin shone clean and pink, his scalp glowed through his white hair. When he had dried his face his eyes were clear. He had thick white even teeth, smiling at me, asking if I'd seen the tree. Maggie said he'd be of more use helping to decorate it than staying out to this time of night. Poor Ma had done it alone and couldn't fix the star.

We sat in a row at the draining board, eating and listening to the music. When the news came on the Ma turned the sound knob down. No one wanted to listen to the world's troubles on this particular day. It was teatime on Christmas eve with white pudding and HP sauce. Maggie said I'd been such a help to her, carrying the messages home, helping to get the tea, she'd let me come to midnight mass. I wasn't one of them, the Ma said sharply, I had no place in a Catholic church. Let her, the Da said, there was room for all at this time, no matter how misled or wrong thinking.

Later on we all left the house together, but Maggie walked in front linking arms with her Da, leaving me to walk with Ma. Had it happened again already? Had Maggie forgotten me for another man? The street was thronged with neighbours all heading towards the church. Most of the women carried missals and beads, some held tightly onto their men who were not walking very straight. Everyone had but one thought in mind, to get there in time for the birth, to see the holy child placed in the crib. It was more serious than play-acting, the doll-baby would be blessed, a moment to love and look forward to. As we all walked along the neighbours noticed me too, the stranger child over from England, under Maggie Mullen's care. Ma whispered to me not to mind them, they were nosey, let them stare. She had made me pull my beret down low to cover my hair, the way she wore hers. Her unfocused eyes glared at me from under the navy edge and short tufts of her fringe.

A thick crowd waited at the railings watching Mary and Joseph who waited for their child. I heard someone ask if Maggie was home for good now, and who was that English child? I pulled at my beret self-consciously; I wasn't Catholic and I was named after some sort of bird. Then we heard singing inside the church. The procession was coming. The big doors opened at last. I had never seen choir boys wearing white surplices over scarlet gowns; they marched in pairs, slow and stately, their mouths opening and closing in song. 'Oh come let us adore Him, Oh come let us adore Him . . .'

'Watch this now, Ula. Look.' Maggie pushed me forward. Here came the priest at last. Maggie crossed herself, the Da bent his head. The Ma nudged me. Could I see?

'Which one is the priest, Maggie?'

The Ma rolled her little eyes. Disgraceful. Imagine not knowing a priest from a prayerbook, what a miserable heathen child. The incense bearer swung the censer. Thick white clouds scented the air. There was the priest, gold robes glittering, more singing, more incense, bright lights. Acolytes were bearing tall candles, the priest was nearing us now. I pushed my face through the railings. The new baby was on its way.

I had expected something exquisite, a pretty-faced porcelain doll in linen and lacy frills. The priest was carrying a lump of wood in a blanket, with a roughly hewn blob of a face. It had two dabs for eyes and a smudged mouth. There wasn't any nose. It was even less complete-looking than Mary and Joseph; they deserved better than that in their hay. I looked round; no one else seemed to think it was curious, all the people's faces looked proud. Faces were smiling, they were singing. Now we could all go inside.

'You've seen it now, Ula. What did you think of it?' Maggie's face shone with delight. Christmas day had started now, we could hear mass next. I sat between her and Ma. She seemed to have completely forgotten her promise to Mamma about religion. You must hear mass at Christmas or risk your immortal soul. I didn't understand the Latin praying, I didn't understand what the priest did. Soon everyone left their seats to go to the altar to have something put in their mouths. They came back swallowing a little, with ecstasy in their eyes.

The street was even more full of people afterwards. We were joined by men who had been on the spree. It was much colder now but no one noticed it, there was a special friendliness in the air. The four of us walked in a line. Maggie had a new hair slide on that her Da had given her, with six diamonds in a row that sparkled. We looked forward now to a cup of strong tea.

As Maggie and I got into bed in the back bedroom I heard the woman calling her cat again. I saw the hair slide with the diamonds on the pillow by me, I heard Maggie breathe and sigh. It was all so wonderful and exciting, I felt that nothing would be sad again.

I woke early and lay watching the line of chimneys beginning to show against the dark sky outside. My fingers felt stiff with cold outside the blankets but I could wait no longer, I must be first downstairs to look at the tree. Last night when we had come back from the church service it had shone out like a beacon of love. There might be presents there now, or sweets perhaps. What a pity I had nothing to give. Maggie didn't stir as I slipped from the bedclothes, she was snoring again on her back. The boards were icy, I could feel the nail heads, My dressing gown and slippers weren't unpacked. I found my coat on the nail on the door and my lace-up shoes and went slowly and carefully down.

The coloured lights showed intermittently in a line under the closed door. I opened it. Yes, there was the tree. It seemed to flash even more brightly in the light of dawn than it had last night. The paper chains were more colourful, the blue and yellow bird more alive. The cotton wool blobs bobbed in the windowframe. There was something long and bulky on the floorboards, something bigger than a sack. The lights flashed again, the sack moved by the bucket of stones. It sat up. It was a man in a blanket, not a sack or a present at all, just an ordinary man, watching me with horrid eyes.

'Hullo there. Are you looking for Santa Claus?'

'There is no Santa Claus. Only babies think there is. Who are you?'

'Who am I? Who am I? That's excellent, that is. Who are *you* I'd like to know?'

'I'm Ula.'

'Ula is it? And I'm Joe.'

'What are you doing? What do you want here?'

'I'm asked what I'm doing in my own home. That's excellent, that is. If it's any business of yours, which it is not, I've come back home for the Christmas. With a gift for my sister Margaret, I've a present for Maggie May.'

'You're not her brother, you can't be. Maggie is an only child.'

'Is that a fact now? Let me tell you then, I'm her brother, I live here. I've a present for her.'

'I don't believe you.'

'Turned out of my room, I was, by you and my sister, turned out like a dog in the road. You none of you gave a thought for me, did you? Pushed out like a dog I was.'

'I thought ...'

'You thought? You'd best be thinking again. I slept here on the floor, but I'm back now, I'll have my bed back again.'

By the zinc bucket with the tree roots and stones was a newspaper packet. He picked it up.

'Here. Catch. Maggie's gift.'

It was bloody, red, dripping. Red dripped from his fingers and hand. Dark spots fell on the floor.

8

I don't remember leaving the house again that morning, or running down Maggie's street. I must have run a long time but I don't remember crossing the road. I don't remember seeing any windows with Christmas trees, or passing the church with the crib. I found myself under a streetlamp in a wide and empty street. My knees ached, my feet hurt, I was cold.

I had gone downstairs so eagerly to the waiting Christmas tree, longing to start the day. There was the capon to roast, the front room to make ready, the card table to deck with lace. Maggie had shown me the cloth they kept for special occasions with drawn threadwork round the edges, bleached as white as the choirboys' robes. I looked forward to arranging the red apples left over from Maggie's apple cake in a cracked white china bowl. The card table was to be my responsibility, I would place the cleaned cutlery just so.

Maggie had been up late last night, plucking the bird. She had let me stay up too. The Ma watched the wireless while Da smoked and had more to drink. The scullery floor had soon become white with the bird's feathers. The Da picked one up and started tickling me with it. He whispered something and I'd squirmed. I hadn't minded although his eyes had gone silly, but Maggie got angry with him. She had told him not to be crude and the look in her eyes made me uncomfortable. She told me to gather up the feathers on the scullery floor into a newspaper. They were soft and fluffy and I loved them. The capon looked smaller now, its flesh was pink and sticky-looking, with pimples where the feathers had been. What did 'crude' mean? I took a feather to taste, lovely, a soft wet squashy feel. Maggie told me not to be dirty. It was nice that Nurse had gone from my life. Helping was lovely here, I'd never been up so late. The onions were chopped, the bread crumbled for the stuffing, the apple cake had been baked. I carried out all the rubbish to the yard for her. I listened again for the sad voice calling Tibby. The last job before going upstairs was to help clean the draining board to get rid of the onion smell. Maggie poured boiling water from the kettle while I scrubbed with washing soda and a brush. All the water had to be heated on the cooker; the scullery had filled with steam. In the morning we planned to put up the star, a big one made from silver paper. We'd discussed it as we'd undressed. We had closed the window after taking the clock away in case the snow came and blew on our bed. I watched her diamonds wink in the dark as she had prayed on her beads under the blanket. She had touched my forehead, saying she was blessing me and bother her promise to my mamma. My soul was more important than any promise. I'd been to mass, holy God, and the saints would be pleased.

As I had left the back bedroom in my coat and nightdress I'd heard snores from the Ma and Da. I don't know what presents I had hoped for. I knew that the family was poor. I wasn't used to getting presents. Perhaps I expected jewels, perfumes and flowers. I didn't imagine playthings. Tin was my only toy.

The sight of Maggie's brother had been a shock to me. He wore old plimsoles and dirty dungarees. He reminded me of a snake in a blanket, he had unblinking horrid eyes. The tips of his teeth showed when he spoke to me. His voice hissed and he wriggled his shoulders very slightly. He had the same flap of hair as the Da, the same protuberant ears. Maggie had woken then; she missed me in the bed with her. She came down with her face lumpy from sleep. Before she could say anything I accused her.

'Maggie, you never said anything about this brother person. He's been sleeping under the tree.'

'Under the tree is right,' he echoed. And he was her brother, right? Why had she not seen fit to mention him? He wasn't invisible or dead.

'Yes, why, Maggie? If he's your brother you should have told me. I thought you only had parents. Why?'

'It wouldn't be shame by any chance, Maggie. Could that be it? Eh?'

His hissing voice sank lower. It hadn't always been shame, had it? A different story once, eh, Maggie? His snake's eyes watched her closely. Thick as you like, one time, oh yes, just he and Maggie May. Now, when it suited her, she ignored him. Pushed into the cold like a dog. He'd been stretched on the floor all alone, on this cold Christmas night, on account of an English brat.

'I'm not a brat. I hope you aren't talking about me. I was invited. I didn't know you were alive.'

He went on looking at Maggie, he didn't look at me. He'd more right in this house than she had. *He'd* not run off to the other side, nor had he brought shame and scandal to the home.

Nobody pointed the finger at him. Yet she had the audacity to come dancing back here for the Christmas, no apologies, no by your leave. Like a dog he'd been treated, and he wasn't having it; a dog without any home.

'Stop. Listen to me. Stop,' I shouted.

He turned. 'And listen, *you. You* stop, you're not needed here. Why don't you pack up and leave?'

Maggie begged us to be quiet. We'd wake the Ma and the Da, quietly now, for the love of the Sacred Heart. He hissed back again at her. She was a phoney and a sham. She'd done as she pleased from the very start, she'd no other concern than herself. Maggie started to cry loudly, her voice raising to a wail. Joe was a liar, and on Christmas morning. Joe was an evil star.

'You give me back my room, now, d'ye hear me? You and that brat. Out.'

Maggie clutched at her lollopers, she'd never done harm to Joe. She'd looked after the parents, she loved them, she'd always sent money home. Ma and Da needed her.

'It's true, Joe. I know it is.'

'Shut your gob, you. I didn't ask for your interference. As for you, Maggie, they need you back like they need poison. Did they ask you back? No.'

She'd always been a good daughter, she said. She'd not caused any heartache like him. Always out on the drink, stopping away at nights. Backing horses, losing at cards. He'd been better never to have been born.

'You didn't think so little of me one time, did you? Eh, Maggie?'

'Evil speaker. Muckpot. Vile.'

'Muck is cheap, Maggie. Anyone can call names. Who made Ma strange in her ways? Who made her nerveses bad?'

'You done nothing for this family, Joe Mullen. What did you bring home today?'

He drew his chin in line with his neck, like a snake getting ready to strike. What had he brung? He'd brung this then. A Christmas gift. Here then, catch it and happy days.

Maggie screamed again as the liver parcel hit her and went slithering down her front. She was bloodied, her lollopers were stained with it. He was a Judas. A Christmas curse.

There were footsteps overhead. The Da came downstairs first, his spikey hair showing patches of scalp. He wore his long underwear and stood looking at us. He seemed surprised to see Joe.

'So you decided to honour us after all, did you? What happened this time, Joe?'

He saw the blood staining Maggie's nightdress, he saw the mess on the floor. What was it? Liver? Jesus God, Joe, what is that?

Then Ma came in, smiling vaguely, looking like a bolster in her tight nightdress. She was confused, not really upset, her wireless was her soother of pain and her Joe was ever wild. The tree lights flashed again and she saw the blood. Holy saints. Holy saints . . .

'The English brat is after having a nosebleed,' Joe said in a jeering tone. She saw the newspaper in another flash. She fumbled her short fat hands. There was no music at this time of the morning, she couldn't manage without Henry Hall. What was the shouting about? What was that newspaper? Holy saints . . . Nosebleed? Why should Maggie call Joe such names?

He was still kneeling, half in the blanket. He fiddled for his cigarettes, the carton was empty, he found a butt behind his ear. He struck a match on his thumb nail, blowing smoke out like poisonous gas. I hoped we might soon all be friends again. The Da went to get his pipe from the scullery.

'Here you are, Ma, don't say I didn't think of you.' Joe threw a small packet over to the Ma. It was a small white clay pipe. Her eyes looked less anxious. She put the pipe unlit in her mouth. I was glad that someone else was claiming her attention. I hadn't liked her commenting on my looks and grasping my chin.

'Shall I get some newspaper, Maggie, and put all this outside?'

'Leave it,' Joe shouted at me. He had a few things first to make clear. Ma and Da had better listen to him, and I had better listen too. He was still the son and heir of the household, Maggie or no Maggie, he wanted to make it quite plain. He'd come in late, he'd been busy lately, he'd not seen much of them, he'd allow. But now he was back, he was home for the Christmas, alive and kicking, no harm done. He had not expected to find his bed full of people, nor the place full of English trash. He wasn't having a strange English brat usurping him, pushing him out of his home like a dog.

'Wait now, son, you've been gone a long time. Maggie ...'

'Maggie? That one, there's a few things you should know about her. She's nothing but a fraud and a—'

'Liar. Muckpot. Lies.'

The Da let out a roar. What was happening? What exactly did Joe mean? He shook his hair back from his ears. Go on then, Joe, explain. His daughter Maggie hadn't an impure or dishonest thought in her.

'That's good, that's excellent, so it is. Sister Maggie wasn't pure, since a child. You ask her about those games.'

'Lies, Liar. Lies.'

'Go on. Ask her.'

And who had started it then, yelled Maggie. Who had thought of the idea? The feathers, the tickling, the buttons. Judas. Muckpot and lies.

'Holy saints, Maggie, what's this you're saying? Aaagh.'

The little pipe dropped out of the Ma's mouth onto the floor, the tree lights wavered with a fizzing sound. Maggie's voice dropped, she sounded hoarse now. 'Twas Joe done the buttons, she'd never wanted to. She'd never liked the feathers touching, it was Joe.

'What's this about feathers?' the Ma asked vaguely.

'In her knickerses, of course. Maggie couldn't get enough.'

Ma said nothing, she went to the scullery. We heard the click of her wireless, but no sound. The tree lights crackled again, went black and stayed black.

'Jesus. 'Tis a fuse.'

From the scullery came the sound of Ma singing in a breathy voice. 'Oh come let us adore him, Christ the Lord.'

'That's excellent, that is. See what the sight of you done to her, Maggie. You made her nerveses go.'

'Now, Joe, don't talk so to your sister. Maggie never ...'

'Shut your mouth, you old gobshite. Go back and deliver logs.'

'Mag-gie. Mag-gie. I want to go to the ...'

Something wet hit my cheek, something slippery slid down my neck. Joe was throwing his liver about now. He must have gone out of his mind. It must have been then that I ran outside, away from the house with the tree.

I stood under the streetlamp with my breath wheezing and my hair sticking to my wet face. I would never go back there, I couldn't. It was a house of cruelty and fear. They threw raw meat at each other and called each other names. They didn't want me. What did gobshite mean? There was blood round my collar, my tears tasted dirty. I had no hanky for my streaming nose.

This street wasn't like Maggie's street, no church here, no crib or star. These houses had windows with curtains and front doors at the end of flagged paths. There were railings or low brick walls on either side of latched gates that protected flowerbeds or small patches of lawn. The door nearest the streetlamp had a holly wreath with red bows and 'Welcome' written inside it in careful silvery script. There must be children inside. Were they sleeping upstairs, dreaming of glittering gifts and trees? Would they dance round later in silk pleating and bows, pulling crackers and inventing games. Would they eat jelly and ice cream, showing bright teeth when they laughed? I had my nightdress on, I was aching and bloody, I wanted to go to the ... I gripped the iron gate and cried.

I heard the door with the welcome sign open. Someone was coming down the path.

'Don't touch me. Leave me. *Leave* me.'

A large hand was on my shoulder. 'It's Ula, isn't it? From the dancing class? You won't remember me. I'm Lucy's father. Come on. Lucy is inside.'

9

My life changed when I saw her again. She wasn't in bed dreaming about presents but sitting at her own kitchen table and watching me. She looked just the same. Of course, Lucy was Irish and this nice house must be her home. I had only seen her once at Miss Dance's class, wearing her bright silk pleated dress. Here she was at home in Ireland looking at me. She didn't have her monkey now.

'Oh there you are, Lucy. Is this your house?'

Her father had brought me inside without questioning me. Lucy wore her dressing gown now, of the same pink as her dancing dress, trimmed with shamrocks round the sleeves. She didn't look surprised.

'You do look awful. You've got marks all over your neck and face. You've been crying.'

Her kitchen was light and warm with two sinks and draining boards behind her at the far end. I had stopped crying but my breath caught as I breathed. The father took me to the hot tap and wiped me with a warm damp cloth. Then he dried me with large firm hands without speaking.

'You look awful,' Lucy said again.

The house was used as a guesthouse for students which he and Lucy ran alone. The kitchen floorboards were a smooth salmon pink shade to tone with the curtains and walls. Their range had a grate in it where coal was burning. A lovely smell came from the oven. They'd put a turkey in early to cook slowly; the smell was the stuffing she'd made.

She didn't question me, nor did her father; they accepted me just as I was, without clothes, filthy and tear-stained, not knowing from where I had run. She said that it was a good thing I'd got here early; their students had all gone to their own homes for the holiday. Their bird was too big for the two of them, I could help them eat it. They were setting off themselves after dinner for the country where her grandmother lived. They often went in the holidays and always at Christmas time.

Their refrigerator and store cupboards seemed to be packed with foods that I'd never seen. Crystallized fruits in wooden boxes, caviar in interesting jars, ginger in blue-painted vases, dates packed in rows with a tiny serving fork. Mock beams across the ceiling had hooks where vegetables were strung. I had never seen onions plaited, nor known about garlic roots. But apart from the turkey in the oven Lucy said it was all ordinary food. She and her father believed in keeping a good table. Did I feel like a malted milk? I said I'd never tried it. I watched the neat way she poured and heated the milk in a copper-bottomed saucepan before stirring the powder in. We drank it from pink and gold cups and saucers that had pictures of the little English princesses wearing coral beads and frilled frocks. Lucy's aunt in England had sent them she told me with distaste, she was antiroyalist herself. I looked at their curls and their faces while I sipped the sweet-tasting drink. Lucy said that her grandmother had taught her to cook. It was something she took very seriously, she had to learn all she could early because she wanted to become a chef. She'd never had any other ambition since she'd heard the Three Bears story as a baby. She'd have been ashamed to serve porridge that wasn't right. Her stuffing was a secret recipe that she'd invented herself and that she'd take with her to the grave. I remembered Maggie's humble stuffing. Lucy was a being apart. I pleated the edge of the pink linen tablecloth. I wanted to talk to her about what had happened, but not now. She showed no curiosity, repeating that I looked awful. Now that I was hearing her speak I thought she had a pretty voice with a chuckle in it. She had the faintest trace of an accent, nothing broad like Maggie had. She said that she and her father didn't keep Christmas in the usual way, they just had a festive dinner. The rest of it was too much bother and fuss. They disliked trees and decorations, they didn't exchange any gifts. She spoke with condescension about the frenzy and waste of time. She'd outgrown it all long ago. Presents and balloons were all right for babies; if she wanted something her father got it for her.

'Don't you go to church then, Lucy? I thought Irish people did.'

She stared, she smiled with scorn. She pleased herself, so did her father, she wasn't made to go when she was at home. She believed in making up her own mind when she wasn't at her convent school. St Lucy was patron of the blind, her name saint, there was more than one way of being blind. Religion was for easily lead people who preferred to avoid the truth. She turned her back on that rigmarole. Most people were like sheep. Her grandmother was a believer, but she was elderly. Lucy aimed to become a cordon bleu chef. One day people would come to her to learn gourmet dishes. And besides, her grandmother had a financial interest in Christmas: the forestry commission farmed a part of her land. Christmas trees grew in abundance behind Grandma's manor. Lucy disliked them herself. Grandma had given Lucy a set of chef's knives recently, in a polished box all graded to size. Over there on the dresser, would I like to see them? I didn't like any sort of knife. She had a chef's cap and apron, she put on the cap to show me. Her Wedgwood-blue eyes were bright.

'It does suit you, Lucy,' I said admiringly.

It would be her uniform one day, when she was free of her convent school. She'd lead her cordon bleu institution before becoming a master chef. She'd work in the best kitchens of the biggest hotels.

'I don't go to school yet. Only Miss Dance's class. My sisters are going to boarding school soon. I'm not very fond of knives. Can I see your school uniform?'

She pulled a face at the memory of Miss Dance. She remembered me there all right. Had I still got that giraffe?

'Yes. Have you got your black monkey?'

She had no time now for stuffed animals, she'd left him behind with Miss Dance. I thought she was very grown-up. I agreed earnestly when she said dolls were boring and that vocations mattered most. She only ever read recipe books. What books did I like best? I was ashamed to tell her that I couldn't properly read. I said I liked books about films.

Lucy had a lot of stuffed animals left over from her younger days, all named after hotels. There was Gresham, Hibernia, Shelbourne; her monkey had been called Wicklow. We'd go up and look at them soon. I had forgotten that I was still in my nightdress. My feet felt warm again now. Her father had left us alone with our Horlicks. He was kind. I was all right here. When he asked me where I'd been staying I was confused again. It couldn't be far away if I was there this morning, Lucy said sharply. Surely I knew where. Fancy coming all the way from England and not finding that out. What a baby, worse than a newborn lamb.

'She's three years younger than you, Lucy. She's had an upsetting time.'

Her father would telephone my mother in England. Meanwhile I was not to fret. He was delighted to have me here, I could stay. His Lucy needed a friend. We heard him speaking in the breakfast room through the hatchway, where the telephone was. What would Mamma say to him? I tried to imagine her, alone now, with her face perhaps petulant from sleep. Had her peace been disturbed again? Had she no escape from a child even from across the sea? Was she happy? Was she in her dressing gown? It was Christmas. Would she marry someone else?

'Ula,' he called to me. My mother wanted to speak to me.

'I don't want to. I can't . . . '

'Just say hello. To let her know you're . . . just hello.'

'Hello? Mamma? Hello?'

So far away, such a tinny sound. Could that voice be Mamma? I wasn't used to the telephone. At home I whispered into it without asking for a number. I was expected to talk now and listen.

'Darling child, what has happened? You're not unhappy, are you? You don't want to come back? Why?'

'Mamma? Mamma?'

'After all my instructions to Cookie, what was she thinking about? Imagine letting you out alone so early. I hope she's not making you pray.'

'Mamma?

He took the receiver from my hand, dampened from where I'd clenched. What a good thing she couldn't see me, all tear-stained, with liver blood down my coat. Lucy was grinning again.

'You do look awful.'

We listened while he spoke again. 'Unhappy' ... 'troubled house' ... 'lost her way'. He slid the hatch across but we could still hear him. He was talking about the visit to his own mother later in the day. I held my breath. When he came back to us in the kitchen he said that my mother had agreed. I could stay on here, I could go with them to the country. I'd be most welcome at Lucy's grandmother's home. She had a big house further north.

A country estate sounded grand. Perhaps the grandmother had a title. It was to be a manor in the country for me instead of Cookie in the slums. Finding Lucy was a turning point; I knew I'd have peace of mind, though my head still felt thick and giddy and my eyes hurt. It was natural and peaceful here with wonderful Lucy, an anti-Catholic, an anti-royalist, a cordon bleu chef-to-be. The father said he'd let his mother know at once to expect me. She'd be charmed. He had found out Maggie's address from my mother, no question of my going back there. He'd go round now and pick up my things. My mother had given her authority. We would eat our dinner and leave for the country. We must leave in good time because snow was forecast.

I sighed and waved my toes. Lucy and I were alone.

We went upstairs to her bedroom to look in her fitted cupboards all along one wall. There was her pink frock with the silk pleating that I'd remembered. There were her red dancing shoes. Her convent uniform was maroon with a Latin motto on the blazer pocket which meant 'God is love'. She hated her nuns and their teachings. They made you have a bath under a sheet. The food was awful and they slapped you. She occupied her time in the chapel services by inventing recipes and making secret plans. She wouldn't remain long in a hotel kitchen, she would work in a palace one day.

'Which palace, Lucy?'

A large one, she said, but not in England, of that I could be very sure. She hummed and looked at her hair in the mirror, beautiful, calm, sure. She said there was her cot of stuffed animals, each with the hotel name. If I wanted I could put my giraffe in with them later. I knew he'd be better alone with me; his sucked hooves and flaking tin spots would be sorry and out of place amongst all that furred opulence. Lucy believed that childhood was far from pleasurable, it was a time to be lived quickly until you were free. She had already invented a celebration cocktail for when she started periods. I didn't ask what she meant. I wanted to agree with her over everything. Only yesterday I had longed for Bruno's bottle and to be wrapped in woolen shawls. Meeting Lucy had changed my course. She inspired me. I too would stamp in high heels before drinking whisky and blinking at men. She said that I had a lot to learn about life; those servants in England had me spoiled.

'Has your grandmother got servants?'

I imagined a manor house would be staffed with butlers. Only cleaning women, Lucy said. Not that her grandmother wasn't prosperous; more importantly she was quite a good cook. The manor was a remote place in large grounds. Only Lucy was allowed in the kitchen besides grandmother.

'Oh, Lucy, I love your bedroom.'

More salmon-coloured curtains were at her windows, but with a tiny blue sprigged pattern matching her bedspread and

frilled dressing table. Her ceiling was a silvery blue, her bathroom opening from the bedroom was blue, as blue as her lovely
blue eyes. It seemed that she already did live in a palace. She
and her father had taken me in knowing nothing about my worries. Did she know that my brother had died? Had she noticed
my white hair? Soon I would be in a country estate. They had
a lake with swans on it. Foxes and deer lived in their woods,
coming up near the house in bad weather. I hoped to see the
deer stepping daintily over the lawn or a fox sniffing round the
bins at the back. Long ago there had been peacocks on the
lawns to parade amongst the flowerbeds, and gardeners were
employed. The family fell on hard times and the estate declined,
the peacocks disappeared. They were stupid and small-minded
birds, Lucy said; where one went the others followed. Legend
had it that they were broken-hearted, they were beautiful but
without brain. God punished their vanity by giving them an
ugly shriek but no song. There was said to be a ghost peacock at
the manor but Lucy hadn't seen it, nor did she believe in ghosts.
She disliked legend and lore as much as she disliked religion and
royalty.

'Are the lawns there green as a parable?'

She told me not to talk rubbish. We would go down now and
get on with preparing the meal. Her clothes were already packed
for the country. When her father got back again I didn't ask
what he had thought of Maggie's family or if she had asked
about me. I was ashamed of her. I wanted to forget all of them
as well as the tree, the church with the crib in that street. They
hated each other, they weren't loving and affectionate. I didn't
understand them; I didn't want to.

Lucy said that we'd eat in the kitchen, we'd be informal and
save time. She moved lightly from the stove to the table. She let

me put out the mats. Although it was the kitchen it seemed formal and festive. The refrigerator lit up when you opened it, showing all the beautiful coloured foods. I was glad not to eat near the telephone in case Mamma wanted to speak to me again, Lucy and her father sat at opposite ends of the table, I with my back to the range. I was dressed properly again in my skirt and jersey. Lucy wore pastel blue. We ate mashed potatoes whipped with sour cream and herbs. The small green sprouts were lightly steamed. I had never tasted such rich gravy. Lucy's cooking was best of all.

'Oh, Lucy, your cooking is wonderful.'

I wanted her to be glad that I'd come there. I said I could understand why cooking was her life's work. Her father dismembered the turkey carefully, laying portions onto an oval plate for their student guests when they returned. The cuisine was the pride of the guest house. The refrigerator was never bare. We ate cheeses and fruit after the turkey, before our coffee and turkish delight. Lucy was contemptuous of mince pies and puddings, the popular fare for mindless sheep people. I had never eaten a slice of melon served with ginger or seen turkish delight in an icing-sugar cloud. My piece tasted like Mamma's rose water with nuts in it. I listened to Lucy's pretty voice. Her dream world would become mine. I too would become polished and sophisticated. I too would choose a career. Her father asked what plans I had, what I would do when I grew up. I faltered. A mother, I supposed ... to become married.

'Is that all?' Lucy said loftily. Her father was talking about a vocational future. I hadn't decided, I might be a vet I said. For rare animals naturally, nothing ordinary. My name meant 'bird' actually, I added in an offhand way. Lucy said I should study ornithology, if I wasn't too bird-brained to work. Outside their kitchen was a paved yard with urns for plants to grow in. There was a bird table and a stone birdbath. Go out now and put scraps for them, Lucy ordered. I was proud to feed their birds. There was a bag of nuts for the blue tits. I looked at a sparrow pecking at a bread crust and thought of the ghost peacock bewailing its pea-sized brain. Mamma had a gauze dress in peacock colours, multicoloured, iridescent, divine.

I sat in the back of the car with Lucy for the long drive to the manor house. Her father tucked a rug lined with fur over us; coney fur Lucy told me, a posh name for rabbit skin. I stroked it slowly. That little scrap of fluff from her dress at the dancing class had brought her to me after all. I asked her what the tune she kept humming was called. She smiled and didn't reply. Did she know a tune about Come adore Him? She pulled a face. Don't ask her to think of hymns, she wasn't at the convent now. She told her father to drive faster, she had a lot to tell Grandma tonight. She was like a princess in fur, giving orders. I'd see the green countryside soon, the delight of Maggie's heart. The county we were visiting was agricultural, with many lakes to make everything lush.

'Maggie's mother came from there, I think it was there.' I felt bolder about mentioning them now. I wondered if they were still shouting. Was the Ma watching her wireless still?

It felt nice to have Tin with me again. Because of my tired feet I wore my bedroom slippers for travelling, their brown pompoms soft as two old friends. I would need Wellingtons for the country, they told me. The walking was wet and rough. My eyes felt heavy but I didn't want to miss the scenery and the sight of the yellowish sky. It would snow tonight, the father said. It was weather to keep folk at home. Not that he minded. It meant that we'd have a clear run.

We drove through the small towns of Ireland. Some were just a single street. They all had pubs and churches. The houses opened onto the pavements like the houses in Maggie's street. The doorsteps were cleanly whitened in honour of the day, though there were few Christmas trees in the windows. I saw no decorations or coloured lights. A few general stores selling everything had greetings cards on display. A bearded Santa Claus made of cardboard had a sack of net Christmas stockings containing holly sprigs and cheap tin toys. Nothing looked exotic, precious or rare here. The Irish country seemed bleaker somehow. A live kitten was curled on a white baby shawl, the sign said 'For Babies' needs'. A window was devoted to first communion clothing with little plaster models wearing white. They held rosaries in their stiff plaster fingers, their mouths simpered under cheap cotton veils anchored with wax orange blossom wreaths. Lucy made a 'yuk' sound in her throat. On a bare stretch of road I saw a wayside shrine with a lone statue holding shrivelled flowers. I turned back to see the face, watching travellers, pale and cold, wondering which saint it was. Lucy showed no interest; such effigies were for sheep. There were no other cars for miles.

They always stopped at Cootehill; it had become a ritual. They went to the hotel to let the grandmother know they were almost there. Grandmother was particular about punctuality. She must not be upset, being elderly. Lucy's father was her only son and Lucy her only grandchild. How lucky she was not to have to compete for attention and to have a country and a town home.

While her father went to the telephone she and I went to the lounge. Her voice was loud and assured as she ordered malted milks before sitting on a red plush chair. I sat opposite her, hoping my bedroom slippers weren't absurd. I pulled my coat over my legs. I'd never been in a hotel. Lucy drummed her long fingers on the table top. She'd asked for a whisky for her father as well. What confidence you have, Lucy, how I admire your verve. The milk drink, when it came, tasted different from her brew, more like honey and much too sweet. I gazed at her while she sipped disdainfully. She was twice as nice as my sisters and her father was wonderful too. He drank his whisky quickly like Maggie's men had, but without their runny eyes and watery smiles. I watched the way his fingers held the glass, loosely, with splayed tips and very short nails. He leaned forward over his knees a little, but keeping his back straight. I liked his brogues and his ribbed socks. Lucy, how lucky you are. Outside the street was deserted, inside the hotel seemed full. The lights shone white and glaring in the bar next to us. I watched a woman there, speaking with a loud voice. She leaned across to kiss the bartender, showing full breasts under her blouse. She whispered, fluttering her eyelids yearningly, her blouse neck slipped some more. Was this the world my mother wanted, lipstick, admiration and men? It's dangerous to have too much feeling. Don't feel guilty, don't involve yourself, self comes first.

Lucy showed me the cloakroom. She had to go often like me. It made a bond between us, I thought happily, as we walked along the passageway. Her shadow towered above mine as she waved her arms, pulling a face. 'Look out, here comes a ghostie.' I kicked my slippers. 'You are funny, Lucy. I do like you.' She could still touch her nose with her tongue.

We washed under the same jet of hot water after soaping lavishly with pink hotel soap. We licked the lather from our hands, we smeared it, we rubbed until our lips were sore. I asked if she liked Jeyes fluid, or the smell of syrup of figs. She liked soap flakes and scouring powder she told me, and that pink powder for cleaning knives. Don't forget her heart lay in the kitchen. That was enough of playing baby games, dry my mouth and follow her.

Before we left the cloakroom we polished the surrounds with folded towels. We breathed on the brass taps before buffing them. We folded the towels corner to corner. We arranged the toilet rolls to hang exactly. We rubbed the door handles and locks on the lavatories, breathing with concentration and care. We peered into a cleaning cupboard and found a vast vacuum cleaner surrounded with snakelike coils. Lucy patted her hair complacently. Could I really not even boil an egg? The steam from our labours had turned to little diamonds in the fuzz round her temples. She wondered if the white parts in my hair made me an albino. You got freaks in animals too. She'd seen an albino blackbird once. Still, I'd made a good job of the taps.

'The last lap of the journey,' the father said, tucking the rabbit rug round us again. I loved the feel of it on my knees as much as I loved him caring for me. Lucy pointed at my hair again, had he noticed? He said it was distinguished and that I'd be glad of it one day. I shouldn't allow anyone to scoff. I was a pretty child and I'd be prettier when I was older. I knew he meant that Lucy was the best.

He told me to look out on the left side of the car; I mustn't miss the first glimpse of their lake. It was said to bring luck when you saw it, provided you didn't speak first. Many Irish lakes had legends attached to them; they were especially proud of theirs. It wasn't large but was interestingly shaped, with a dense growth of woodland around.

It was almost dark when we turned into the big gates and along a twisting lane. Humped shapes of rhododendrons grew on

either side of us, their stiff leaves tapped at the car. In summertime the blooms made a fine sight, mauvey reds, orange and
pink. Now you couldn't see any colour in the failed light. The
tall conifers stretched upwards behind the bushes darkly filling
the sky.

'There now, Ula, that's the lake, see?'

'Where? That? Where are the swans?'

A break in the trees and rhododendrons showed a stretch of
what looked like mud. As the moon came from behind a cloud
it glistened weakly. It was hard to tell what was mud and what
was water. The land round the tip of the lake was marshy, the
father said, and the only point where the water could be
reached, the woods elsewhere being thick and impenetrable.
The lake was actually heart-shaped, a heart with a twisted tip.
We stopped and watched. Then the moon hid itself and we
drove away, turning another bend. I asked again about the
swans. They nested in the reeds and sedges, being shy and retir-
ing birds. The old wood was a reserve for wild life now, since his
mother had been in charge. It was the birds' and animals' sanctuary, and had become their sole domain.

'I can go in,' Lucy said boastfully.

'No. You know the rule.'

The new wood behind the manor was cultivated for
Christmas trees. It was a source of income for the grandmother
and gave work for local men. I would see everything in the
morning. Lucy started humming her tune again. We were nearing her second home.

We drew up before a big house with a pointed gable and its
windows blazing with light. In the pillared porch stood the
grandmother waiting with stretched arms to us. She was taller
than Lucy's father, with white hair and a clinging shawl.

10

'So, Lucy, my childie, you and Ula shall go early to gather green for the party.'

'Not a Christmas tree, Grandma, you surely don't mean a tree?'

The grandmother laughed. Indeed no, we'd all had enough of trees. Weren't there enough outside the house to fill the universe? Her voice had the same chuckle as Lucy's had. I was awed by her stately height. She was relying on our help for tomorrow's party, the one she held every year. She always asked the same guests to it, quiet people without many human ties. They relied on the grandmother's St Stephen's Day tea party as a part of their yearly feast. The big hall was decked with greenery, the long refectory table was loaded with food. Games followed later, with hot punch round the fire at the end.

Lucy and I must gather as much greenery as we could carry. There was plenty growing on the edge of the old wood. Bring in all the holly and ivy we could find. Grandmother was delighted that I'd joined them, she could well use another pair of hands. Just take from the edge of the wood, not inside it.

'I hope I see that ghost peacock. Who is that man in the picture?'

'There isn't a peacock, I told you,' said Lucy. No one had seen it, it was rot. The man in the picture was her grandfather, his face peered from a heavy frame. Because he was dead a lamp burned there. It was the first thing you saw when you got inside. The great hall had big fireplaces each end of it where wood and turf burned high. The mantelpieces were marble under carved gold mirrors. The grandfather's picture was like a shrine. When he'd been alive much of the country round had belonged to the manor but all was sold now except for the two woods. Grandmother stared at me piercingly. Had Lucy explained about her animal sanctuary, the woods where no one must go? I could run as much as I wished in the new woods and admire the plantation, but not into the old woods at all. Come now to the fire and talk a little. I had had a tiring day. She wanted to explain about the tasks ahead of us, the most important being the greenery. There was last-minute baking, scones and jam sponges, and setting out the table with the best china. Had I a suitable frock for her party? She didn't mention my hair. She questioned us about church-going, her voice and eyes quite severe.

'Daddy and I went to midnight mass, Grandma.' Lucy said quickly. And I knew she was afraid of her. You did what the grandmother wished or lied about it. You kept busy, you practised the faith. She expected you to rise early, not to be idle and to keep a cheerful face. She said that if we were warmed through we should go up now to our bedrooms.

'Can we share, Grandma?'

'Share, Lucy? I beg your pardon, what do you mean?'

'Ula might be lonely. She's not used to sleeping alone, she might get frightened.'

I felt my cheeks go warm with pleasure. It must mean that Lucy wanted me. Or was she just belittling me? The grandmother's reply was terse. No question of sharing at the manor, Lucy ought to know that. The rooms must be silent upstairs, bedrooms were for sleeping and praying, not chattering, especially at night.

She walked up the wide stairway with the polished treads and banisters that lead upwards to the gallery. Her strap shoes made little taps. Lucy was behind her, I came next, the father followed with our bags. I looked back over the banisters at the grandfather's picture, following us with his eyes. I felt the heat rising from the two burning turf fires. The grandfather's eyes seemed to burn as well. The stairs curved round to join the gallery. The grandmother moved like Lucy, her back straight, her small feet pointing slightly out. She turned. She would put me in the room next to Lucy's. Lucy always slept in the room on her own. It was quite unnecessary for me to feel strange here, Lucy and she would be near. The father would sleep at the end. The rooms facing the back of the house overlooking the new wood were kept closed in winter, the cost of heating was high.

My room was beautiful. It was large, sparsely furnished and warm. Instead of curtains shutters were in the windows, another fire burned in the grate. The grandmother crossed to bolt the shutters, they were the best thing for keeping out draughts. Before I slept, she warned me, I must open them; fresh air was important at night. The age and size of the house made heating difficult, they only used turf and logs. I was responsible for the fire in my bedroom, I must take care to use fuel with care. She bent to put another sod on it. The ash was an orangey shade. The bed near the fireplace was ready for me, the sheets and blankets turned down over the eiderdown. Tidiness was a virtue, the grandmother said quietly; the care and condition of my room depended on me. I looked at the dark grey eiderdown that matched the carpeting. I looked at the white satin striped walls. There was an antique dressing table and wardrobe and a small grey armchair by the bed. Looking after this room would be a pleasure; I already felt proud and calm. Over the bed hung a crucifix inlaid with mother of pearl. Everything was tended and appreciated; there was nothing cheap, flashy or worn.

'I went to church last night with Maggie. I saw the holy child get born.'

The grandmother smiled indulgently. She was glad that I had a little faith in spite of my English ways. Faith was an anchor, it sustained you, faith kept you from straying from right. Lucy interrupted her. I wasn't Catholic, I didn't know anything about faith, didn't even go to school. I had no father, I didn't know a single prayer at all.

'I do. I do. I know "Hail".'

'"Hail"? Go on. Hail who?' sneered Lucy.

'That's enough, Lucy.' We were not to bicker, said grandmother, it was time now to go to bed. She would call me herself in the morning. And remember, I must make my bed. I could use the bathroom at the end of the gallery, but separately, not together with Lucy. Bath in the morning, not at night-time. The boiler didn't run to extra water at night. And no more talking now, children.

I had never seen or smelled turf burning, a delicate and romantic smell, like a bonfire only heavier. I lay in bed sniffing it, feeling rested. I watched the stuked sods sending sparks upwards; they glowed redly before sinking to ash. I was frightened of the grandmother, I'd make her like me. I would gather piles of holly and ivy and earn her praise. Before she left to go down again she had bent over me. Her cold closed lips just touched my head. Remember, child, fresh air, let the fire die out and, if I could manage it, say some kind of prayer. Any prayer was better than no prayer, the intention would be pleasing to God. If I wished I might call her Grandma. And now, Ula child, goodnight.

I put my hands over my face, I knelt by the bedside. 'Hail. All hail. Hello nonsense.' What were the prayers that Maggie had said? Was that tapping from where the crucifix hung? Perhaps Lucy was trying to signal. I tried to knock back but my knuckles felt useless. More sparks flew up the chimney making patterns on the fireback. I was safe and comfortable here. Sleeping alone wasn't alarming, my bed was lovely, though my feet were still a little sore from the shoes. Tomorrow I might see deer on the lawns outside my window or the track of foxes' pads. Did the deer sleep standing up or lying? It had been a long Christmas day.

'It's six o' clock now, Ula. There's been a heavy fall of snow.'

'Does that mean we can't get the greenery?'

Grandma said the snow had stopped now, plans remained the same. As soon as Lucy and I had finished breakfast we must start on our first task outside. They could lend me a Burberry and Wellingtons, my tweed coat and shoes wouldn't do.

Downstairs Lucy's father had already refilled the turf and log baskets, having raked and relaid various fires. Smoke was rising from the two fireplaces in the main hall; soon the flames would start to flare. The cleaning women who helped Grandma wouldn't be coming today, but Lucy was here and Lucy would be famous one day. Lucy made delicious fruit cakes, Grandma told me. And she'd find me some little jobs in the scullery. I would feel useful, I had no need to feel left out.

We sat at the refectory table for breakfast. Grandma said that monks had sat there once. They had used the same polished chairs that we were using, so mind now how we behaved. She didn't sit down herself but strode up and down with her porridge bowl in her hand. Each time she passed grandfather's picture she paused and looked at it. She never sat for breakfast, preferring to organize the day while she ate. She watched Lucy and me critically. Ula, don't hold your knife like a pen. Kitchen manners were difficult to break later; the result of giving servants too much power. My mamma would see the change in me when I returned to her, I would benefit greatly from my stay. As for herself she was delighted to have me, I'd be such a help with the chores.

Drifts of snow had pushed between the opened windows and the shutters during the night, little white walls of it. Lucy and I knocked them down with our hands. A larger wall of snow was inside the porch, up against the heavy front door. Grandma gave us two brooms. We must sweep the snow onto the path. There were shovels and a huge brush and pan. Outside I blinked, the glare was blinding. Maggie had been right after all, Irish snow was different, as different as Irish grass. It did look whiter, brighter, a blinding spiritual white.

'The sun makes the snow look like diamonds, Lucy.'

She banged the head of her broom down, giving me a pitying look. Next Grandma gave me a pail of peelings and tea leaves to carry out to the bins. The kitchen and back scullery overlooked the new wood with the plantation. There were the Christmas trees growing in rows, bordering aisles of untrodden bright snow. The trees looked paler, a delicate yellowish green, not tall yet but enough of them to stock the windows of the world. The air was still. I could hear nothing. I stood by the bins listening and watching. I didn't want to go in.

At breakfast Lucy had asked for brown sugar; Grandma had frowned and refused. Porridge was eaten with salt at the manor, Lucy ought to know that. She didn't encourage the development of a sweet tooth, particularly in a child. She herself used little sugar even in making cakes. I told her that I liked salt myself, and vinegar and mustard too. At home I used to help Maggie grate salt blocks. I crushed breadcrumbs and took rubbish to the bins. I had tidied too and cleaned saucepan lids, I liked being with Maggie best. Grandma had smiled coldly and approvingly. Quite the little maid of all work, wasn't I? I'd be most useful here. She repeated that she liked well-brushed teeth at the breakfast table as well as well-brushed hair. What was the red ribbon I was wearing? It didn't look very neat. I hadn't had time to tie it, I explained. It was from the tangerines that Maggie had bought. 'But you are not with Maggie now, child, are you? Do remember, sparkling teeth.'

'Hurry up out there, scullery maid,' Lucy called me. Time to gather greenery now. The father was stacking more logs. The snow on them hissed when he put them to burn, the turf smelled even stronger now. He asked Grandma if the usual assembly was coming. She nodded; her lonely ones who were dear to her. Would he organize the hot punch as usual? Her guests liked to warm up before they left. There was the vet who appreciated his toddy, and with whom she was on most friendly terms. They had common interests concerning animals, she in providing a sanctuary, he in curing their ills. The man with the travelling van came each year with his daughter; he supplied sundry items to the locality. Biscuits, shampoo sachets, boots and corn plasters were brought to remote cottage and farm dwellers. The van man's daughter helped take the change. The two spinster sisters from Cootehill did dressmaking for local people. They loved wild life too, especially birds. They stood in the porch each year with their backs to the big doorway, hoping to see a whooper swan or a long-eared owl while they waited for Grandma. The ban on entering the old wood was a disappointment. They would have enjoyed a walk there with notebooks and field glasses. The five guests knew and accepted each other's foibles. The sisters were brought by the van man, the vet came each year on his bike. Lucy's Wellingtons had been bought from the van man; she showed me them in the cloakroom.

'These will fit. Put them on. Here.'

'They're too big for me, Lucy. Much too big.'

'Don't fuss. It's your feet are too small.'

She hoped that I wasn't going to complain all the while and spoil everything. Here, take this mac, put it on. Her eyes had the hard blue colour of happiness as we started over the upper lawn on the snow. There were few red berries about this year, but she loved gathering holly branches best. I closed my lips over my teeth to stop the cold hurting them. Lucy went much too fast. My feet slipped in the boots, I couldn't keep up with her. The mac was too long as well. I squeezed my eyes up. I only needed to see Lucy, making a dark shape ahead in the snow. The holly trees were on the edge of the old wood, the ivy trailed over nearby shrubs. She had brought her biggest chef's knife for the branches, spurning Grandma's secateurs blunted from age. Inside Scots pine grew, larches, oak and silver birch. Seasonal evergreen only, Grandma said, just holly and ivy. There was plenty of this outside the wood. Lucy flashed her big knife importantly, she shook the branches, snow slithered down in little showers. She'd made me take her smallest knife before we came out, though I hated it. To please Grandma I'd gather a lot of green, both ivy and dark prickled holly leaves. She'd see then how clever and useful I was.

'Wait, Lucy, don't go so fast.'

'You're afraid, aren't you? You're a milksop.'

'I'm not afraid. I'm not a milksop. It's the boots, they're far too big.'

Her own boots fitted her trimly; she made accurate prints in the snow. As well as pointing them outwards like Grandma they had the same coloured eyes as well. She paused, staring upwards as the snow showered, she whistled that strange little tune. It looked like more snow falling when she shook the branches. In the dark shadows below were frosted drifts. Were there fox and rabbit holes under us? Did the squirrels nest over our heads? Snow fine as powder clouded the air again.

'My collar's wet, Lucy, don't do that.'

She made a face. Scullery maid. I ought to be grateful instead of complaining. If I couldn't keep up I shouldn't have come. She slashed at a higher branch. There was no room for milksops here.

'I'm not. I'm not.'

'You are. Inside, you know you are.'

We were just inside the old wood now. The trees grew closer. She was working systematically, flashing her knife back and forth. The holly branches were soon piling on the snow. Scullery maid. Milksop. Complainer. Why hadn't I stayed at home? She seized a hard chunk of snow.

'Don't, Lucy. It's cold. I'm your guest. Don't throw it.'

She hurled it, missing me. Guest? Don't imagine I was needed or wanted here. No one wanted a complainer. 'Scull-ery maid. Milk-sop. Complain-er.' More chunks flew through the air, then some twigs, then a stone. The stone grazed my cheek, it hurt, it could have blinded me. Had the old wood turned Lucy's brain?

Where was the friend I'd longed for? Who was this stranger with snow and knives? She came closer, she waved her knife again. Poor milksop, did I want more?

'Stop. Stop, Lucy.'

'Why? I don't want you. Nor does Grandma.'

I felt the knife-tip touch my neck.

'I'll tell Grandma and your father if you don't stop.'

'No one will believe *you*.'

I felt the knife pressing.

'I'll do anything. I'll give you anything.'

'You haven't a thing that I want. Pauper. Milksop. All right then. I'll take that old tin giraffe.'

'But you can't. You don't like toys, you don't play with them.'

The knife pressed. 'I'll take the giraffe.'

I'd unpacked Tin and forgotten him since I'd been here. I was being paid now for neglect. She didn't want or need him, she'd no interest, she only wanted to wield her power. Her bears in the cot with hotel names meant nothing to her.

I couldn't bear to think of Tin thrown aside.

'Lucy, just because you have a father and two houses and a grandma ...'

The knife pressed harder. It hurt. 'All right, you can have him ... You can have him.'

She lowered the knife, smiling again. Right then, we still had a lot more to do. She wouldn't forget my promise. I watched her in silence as she cut down swatches of ivy. I had betrayed my toy. In a sharp tone she told me to gather it. I was a hindrance more than a help. Soon she had cut quite a pile. We took our raincoat belts off to bind the branch ends, ready to drag them back over the snow. I had cut no greenery. We didn't speak again until we'd reached the porch, pulling the branches behind.

'Remember, you promised. I'm having that toy of yours. Don't think I'll forget, I won't.'

I went back to my room quickly. There was poor Tin with my red ribbon round him, balanced in front of the fire. The room felt lovely again after the bitter air outside. I put more turf on the fire, doing it carefully. I watched more sparks fly. I didn't want to go to the party. It was safe here and smelled lovely in my room.

Grandma called and I had to go down. I hid Tin under my knickers in the big wardrobe. I brushed my hair to make it lie behind my shoulders. Should I try and walk like Lucy, with my toes out? I wished my eyes were a bit more blue.

Grandma was in the kitchen by the big range. Her apron was whiter than her hair. Lucy was measuring butter at the table. There was a smell of nutmeg, milk and dried fruit. Rows of fresh scones lay cooling on wire cake racks. There was a lump of dough waiting to be rolled and cut into circles.

'Will you make jam rock cakes too, Grandma?'

'Jam? In a rock cake? Fruit, Ula. A rock cake is made with fruit.'

She instructed me to flour the dough and then roll it. Great heaven, not like that. Lucy must show me, knead it evenly, then take the round scone cutter and press.

Inside the house Lucy was quiet again, her eyes lost their malicious gleam. She was afraid of Grandma. Away from her she was different. I resolved to keep near Grandma's side. Lucy showed me how to push your palms forward, curling the fingers from the dough like a cat. My hands weren't as agile as hers were. I could feel she despised me when we touched. I wanted to be back at Cootehill with her, washing together, being friends.

I set scraps of sugared cherry into the fairy cakes. I cut green angelica to look like wings. I breathed the lovely smell of baking. Lucy, why can't you be my friend? Tin is part of me, can't you understand that? He's all I have with me from home. Even when I forget about him I need him. He could never be yours because he's mine.

The refectory table was transformed now, looking like a church altar with white linen and gold. The best white tea set had gold edgings, the crested spoons were prettily wrought. In the centre of the table was a candelabrum to be lit when the guests arrived. The log baskets were filled to bursting. Most impressive of all was the green. All down the stairway holly and ivy had been tied to the banisters and threaded with red ribbon bows. I thought of Maggie's church again. It was exciting. Cold green leaves, candlelight and sweet smells. I must change my dress next, Grandma told me, it was almost time for her guests.

I stared at myself in the long mirror. I wished I had something pink to wear. The people had different ways and ideas in Ireland. They worried more about what religion you had than what you thought about. Only Maggie had really worried about me. Are you worrying now, Maggie?

The big porch bell rang, the guests were arriving, the yearly treat had begun. The van man was first, and his daughter. She clung to him because she couldn't speak. She had the young old face of a dwarf or a lady giant, you couldn't guess her age. Her mouth trembled, she hated strangers; she ignored my out-stretched hand. Her father was proud of her, proud of her dependency, she was his speechless only child. He boasted that she was afraid of her own shadow, wouldn't let him out of her sight, she relied on him. But he relied on her help on his work rounds, putting the change into his customers' hands.

Sometimes she carried shampoos and potatoes to back doors for him. She was a great girl, so she was; he was proud enough to beat the band.

The vet was next, wearing a great coat that smelled of ether. His breath smelled of drink and smoke. Grandma didn't allow smokers to smoke inside the manor house, there were no ashtrays or lighters or spills. But now she smiled gaily, he was an exception, for didn't he heal sick animals and birds? She had the place looking gorgeous as usual, he said loudly, without taking his pipe from his teeth. Gorgeous, Marm, gorgeous, and greetings to one and all here. He inspected the holly and red ribbons. Not many berries, a sign of more snow. Gorgeous, though, no other word for it. He looked at Lucy's father. All set for the punch-making? It seemed that they made it together, it was the custom. He handed a parcel to Grandma and I guessed rightly that it was drink. Mick on the mail train, Maggie's Da and that butcher, all smokey-smelling, all fond of strong drink. It made them silly and watery-eyed but made them friendly. The vet patted me on the head. This drink was special, he'd made it, a treat for Grandma to enjoy every year. The van man fingered his pioneer badge. He mustn't criticize, the vet did good work, a grand man.

The big hall was ready, the baking completed, the games were planned, when would we eat? The Cootehill sisters were a long time taking their coats off and settling their wispy hair. They wore dresses that they'd made themselves from stockinet oddments with lace modesty vests at the neck. They both wore brooches in the shape of swans, flying. They twittered with joy over the leaves tied with red ribbon, they yearned over the white and gold plates. 'Beautiful. Beau-ootiful as always,' they chorused, slight envy behind their eyes. When it came to style they could spot it, it was their livelihood. Everything here was the height of style. Their gift was a tin painted with shamrocks, designed to hold packets of tea. 'The cup that cheers but does not inebriate,' the vet uttered portentously. At last the teapot was brought in. I had helped to polish it with pink powder and a chamois leather earlier, after arranging the scones and cakes. Lucy sat at one end with her father. I helped Grandma to pour the tea, pouring milk into the white and gold teacups. I offered the scones that I'd helped to knead.

'Gorgeous, gorgeous,' the vet murmured, topping his cup with a small flask, refusing the food.

'Beau-ootiful,' the sisters whispered, moving their mouths, peckingly like birds. The van man and his daughter both ate heartily, making a lot of crumbs on the floor and round their plates.

The first game was always Hunt the Thimble, the same games were played every year. There was Spin the Trencher, then Blind Man's Buff, all of them strange to me; I'd never played any games. Maggie had tried 'I Spy' with me, but not knowing spelling made it dull and we both liked talking the best, or looking at her film star books. Maggie had been a true friend, except when those men were about. I wouldn't think about what would happen next to me. Not knowing, not even wondering was best. The van man's daughter behaved rudely with her fairy cake. The handicapped or young babies could behave as they wished.

'Let Ula have first turn hiding the thimble. She's never played before.' Lucy's voice sounded sugar-sweet. For the sake of the van man's daughter, to humour her, the thimble was hidden in the same place always. Everyone pretended to close their eyes. 'On the frame of Grandfather's portrait,' Grandma whispered. The van man's daughter grunted with fun. It was she that found it each time. No one behaved as you'd expect in this country, especially inside their homes. 'Great girl, great girl,' her father applauded. It was Spin the Trencher next. The one who spun the board called the name of the one who must catch it. If it dropped before they got it they paid a forfeit.

'Let Ula have first turn.'

Are you trying to discomfort me, Lucy? I don't know the people's names. Grandma said she was too tired to play now, she would save her energy for the other games. Her cheeks had two flushed spots of red in them; she sat by the fire alone.

'Lucy,' I shouted, turning the trencher, dropping it. It rolled under the refectory table, falling flat before she could get it.

'I'll pay you out for that, you'll see,' she whispered.

Charades came next. 'What is Charades, Grandma, I've forgotten?'

'Poor Ula, she doesn't know.'

I was to pick one side, Lucy the other. I'd learn the rules as we played. 'I'll pick my own father,' Lucy said proudly. I called Grandma's name. Lucy had everything, she was cherished, encircled with love and care. She knew the games, knew the people, knew the mansion. And where had Grandma got to now?

'I'm here, I haven't deserted you. Just putting the bottle away.'

She and the vet emerged from the back scullery, her cheeks looked a little more red. He said, swaying slightly, that Charades was a gorgeous game, gorgeous, nothing like a game of pretend.

Like Hunt the Thimble they never changed it, they chose the same word to act every year. The interest and charm of playing was in the acting, the word they chose was 'legend'. The first scene must include the word 'leg', the second, 'end', the whole word must be said in the last one. All the games were made easy

for the van man's daughter. Perhaps one day she would understand. I picked the two sisters as well as Grandma who explained
what we had to act. Someone must fall and break a leg first. As
we were planning the scene the van man's daughter made a terrible gobbling sound, she left her seat, rushing at us, whirling
and waving her arms.

'God love her, she's excited,' apologized her father, leading
her away with him. Didn't that prove now that she had a heart?
She couldn't endure to watch people hurting themselves.

'I have it,' the vet said in a throaty voice. 'The word is
"legend", no need to act out the play.'

Everyone clapped and applauded; the van man's daughter
clapped loudest of all. Grandma said we'd go straight on now to
Hide and Seek, no more Charades tonight. She didn't want any
of the guests overtaxed or fatigued; she would hide first as usual,
in a nice little easy place. She'd just pop out with the vet to the
scullery and see that the punch-making was under way. Hot
punch was a grand drink to end the evening. Lucy remarked
cheekily that some people liked it at the start. Her father was to
stay at the base to help the vet with the drink-making, the rest
of us were to hunt in pairs.

The Cootehill sisters had each other, the daughter clung to
the van man. Lucy's father and the vet would join in later, so
Lucy and I were left.

'Can't I ever get away from you?' she said. 'We've been
together all day.'

Each of the hunters was provided with a flashlight; the game
was to be played in the dark.

'Close your eyes now, everyone,' Grandma said in a thick
voice, emerging from the scullery again.

The lights were switched off, we waited round the fireside.

The Cootehill sisters settled their skirts. Was that the tap of strap shoes going up the stairway? Was that the grey shawl catching at the leaves?

'Grandma is going upstairs, Lucy. I'm sure I heard her.'

'She'll hide outside, she always does.'

'Outside? But the snow. And the woods, they're dangerous.'

'Not to me they aren't. I know them.'

'But they're out of bounds. Grandma said.'

'You know nothing about it. Milksop. You know nothing about the rules.'

She laughed excitedly, this was their tradition. We must put our macs on again now. Come along, follow her. More snow had fallen since this morning when we'd dragged the leaves across the lawns; there was no trace of that now, only pure snow and some footprints. Lucy was the first out, moving quickly, picking her booted way in the light of the moon. We had no need of our torches yet, it was brilliant. I looked back at the manor house gable, shaped like a giant Christmas tree, with the moon and stars for lights. Our boots made slushing sounds. Lucy moved so quickly. I would have liked to hold her hand. She wanted to be the first to find Grandma, she didn't want me along too. She called over her shoulder to pick up my Wellingtons. I was slow as well as afraid. She and Grandma knew every inch of the estate, just follow and hurry, do.

'She wouldn't be inside the old wood surely, Lucy? Not after what she said.'

We were by the holly trees where we'd cut branches. Lucy gasped. Look. Tracks. Over there. I lit the torch. Grandma must have crossed the lawns and gone straight inside the old wood.

'The snow is deeper now, Lucy. You're going too fast again.'

'Complaining again, scullery maid. I've *got* to find her first.'

Her voice was as cruel and impatient as it had been this morning. Being outside made her worse. Whatever happened, I must keep Tin, she wasn't fit for him. I wanted to get the game over and go inside. I looked back at the other seekers; their torches made dots of light.

'Lucy, the Cootehill sisters are old. The van man's daughter can't move fast. Lucy, wait for the rest.'

'Feck the lot of them,' I thought she answered, but I couldn't be sure in this snow. I could see her torch far in front of me, darting beneath the dark trees. The Wellingtons were still uncomfortable, my feet slipped. The mac was too big. It seemed that the hunters lacked spirit, all nervous, all lost, all cold. Lucy should wait for us, she was selfish. Lucy, your heart is cold.

I tried to hurry, my torchlight was dimmer. Worst of all was the soft deep snow. Lucy surely wouldn't want Tin after this evening. My worst punishment was happening now. The wood felt evil and dangerous, only safe for animals and birds. Perhaps the trees will put a curse on us, or the owls peck and the swans lunge. A stag can attack and kill you, a savage fox can bite. Grandma can't have intended disturbance in her sanctuary. How much of that drink had she drunk? The snowdrifts are deep and icy, the trees are thick, where are the stars?

'Lucy, wave your torch again. Please, Lucy.'

There was a sound. Was that her chuckly voice? Was she whispering? 'This way, milksop. Over here.'

There were no lights. I pushed forward. Was that a thicket?

'Call again, Lucy. Don't leave me, please. You must stay close, it's the rule.'

Stick to your partner, whistle if you get separated, wave and flash your torch. Last one to find the quarry paid a forfeit. Was that a whistle? Was it Lucy? Was she whistling that strange little tune? She wanted Tin because I did. Being cruel gave you power.

I felt something like a hole. Was it a footprint? Was she trailing a wild beast? Grandma can't be in the old wood, she loves animals. I want Lucy to be my friend. Please, Lucy, I need a soul sister. Wave your torch. Be my companion. I hate you, Lucy, whistle your tune.

I heard twigs snapping, snow shifting and falling. I sensed that someone was near. I went forward, I must not be frightened. I can see something shining ahead. A glittering patch all bright and frightening, cold-looking, the shape of a twisted heart. Lucy, I can't see you. Have you found Grandma? Make a whistle. I'm by the lake.

The ground is muddy, marshy, squelchy. The marshy part at the tip of the lake. I feel something spikey. Rushes. These cold spikes are rushes in my hand. Something else, something is pulling me, someone is pulling my hand.

Lucy's hands are cool, thin-boned, delicate. Don't pull me, Lucy, I'm falling. Someone is breathing. Quick breathing, then a watery sort of gasp. There you are, Lucy, all the time.

They said afterwards that the little knife that she'd lent me that morning had been pointing downwards as I fell. Still in my pocket, the point went straight into her. She pulled, I slipped, I fell onto her, the knife pierced her white childish throat. Lucy, I can't find you. Why did you leave me? Your face is wet, why did you run? Speak, Lucy, can't you say something? Lucy, why did you run away?

Everywhere was confusion and shouting. There was moaning in my ears. The Cootehill sisters made noises of dementia. The van man told them to whisht. He would go back for the two other men, they'd bring bandages, they'd know what to do. His daughter started her noises again, sounding terrible in the dark by the lake. She clung to turn, she pulled and impeded him and Lucy made no sound on the ground.

By the time help came the sisters were praying. The combined flashlights of the hunters made a weak light in the mud. Lucy's father and the vet brought lanterns, shining them on Grandma and Lucy. Lucy hadn't spoken, nor had Grandma, who was paralysed, stiff from shock. The three of us were muddied and wet-looking, we were stained with splashes of dark. Blood looks black in the darkness. The father picked up Lucy, her hair trailed over his arm. Her hands dangled. Lucy, speak to me, I know you're teasing. Why did you run away?

The party left the old wood and walked over the lawns again. The vet led the way with the lantern, then came Lucy in her father's arms. I kept saying her name aloud over and over. If I called loudly enough she'd be all right. Lucy? I know you're teasing. Lucy? Inside the porch he turned.

'Why are you calling her? What have you done to her? Don't you realize Lucy is dead?'

11

Grandma didn't speak until she got inside. She had been the last in the cortege through the wood. The Cootehill sisters had pulled at her hands. She was an abject sight compared with her earlier self. Inside the manor she revived a little. She told me to go upstairs and wait there until the doctor and the priest had been and gone.

'I don't want to go up. I want to stay here.'

They had put Lucy on the refectory table. They were all round her. I couldn't see.

The elder sister pushed me to the bottom of the staircase. Lucy's soul had gone to God. The doctor would come to put the seal of officialdom on her leaving. The priest would pray for her safe arrival, though of that there was not a doubt. Lucy's soul had been pure and stainless from her Christmas confession and communion, her soul would go straight to God. More lies and rubbish, I thought darkly, as I went again up the stairs. They could sign documents and pray as much as they liked. I could go into Lucy's room now if I wanted. You pulled me down, Lucy, it's your fault. Tin is mine now, for ever and ever. You shouldn't have run away.

I can hear the bell ringing for the praying and signing. Blood looks nearly black in the dark. The grandfather in the picture will look down on them with painted eyes. All the rest will have eyes full of tears. They will bow their heads, they will cross themselves, their mouths will murmur in prayer. I never learned prayers, none of us did. Would Lucy meet Bruno now? I imagined she would despise and bully him if she could manage it. Poor Bruno, I rarely thought of him now.

When Grandma came upstairs I didn't want to look at her, I didn't want to see her candle-white face. The whites of her eyes were pink and terrible. She still managed to look severe. She leaned from her height to kiss me, just brushing her lips on my head. Maggie's kisses had been loud and smeary, often having an onion smell. Grandma's were a breath of lavender. Lucy was ready now. I could come down. I was not to indulge in self-blame for the accident. I must come and honour her remains. Thanks to the good Cootehill sisters Lucy looked radiant as a picture. God wanted her back, his holy child.

'Yes. Where though? Is she near Limbo now?'

'What are you talking about? Limbo? Lucy made a happy death.' Lucy was with the saints and the angels. Come down and see. I'd soon understand. The good sisters had been so wonderful. I would understand when I saw.

'I don't want to see her.'

'Ula.' Her voice was sharp. I must learn to do as she bid me. She would never believe that Lucy had deceived her, that she'd been a fraud, had given up praying, had not been to mass. She didn't believe in God any more. If there was a God he'd probably not want her, he would be disgusted to have her near. I didn't want to look at her, she'd been my enemy. But I must do as I was bid.

I was still wearing my cream Viyella. There was a line of mud now, along the hem. I had changed into my bedroom slippers with the brown pompoms. Grandma took my hand on the stairs.

The red bows in the greenery were gone now. There was a hushed and churchy smell. You knew I didn't like knives, Lucy. I never meant to hurt you. I hate that old wood with the lake. It's sad, it's frightening, it's dark. It's bad luck too, shaped like a twisted heart. It's your fault for going in there. The vet must have made Grandma drunk.

'There. Doesn't she look seraphic?'

I didn't think she did. She looked awful, lying there. The refectory table had been pulled well back from the fireplace. She was at the far end, in a white lace robe that reached below her feet. She looked taller now and her face was stiff as the frills on the pillow she lay on. There were lit candles at each end. Was it Grandma's nightdress she was wearing? Why couldn't they have left her in her pink? Was it muddied and bloodied after the accident? White didn't suit her, nor did frills. She looked like a tall ugly doll now, lying just where she'd sat at tea. She'd been buttering scones with those fingers; now they held rosary beads. Her face looked so stiff.

'Isn't she beau-ootiful,' they whispered. They had done this to her.

'A seraphic picture,' Grandma said.

'I don't think so at all. Why didn't you leave her pink frock on?'

Grandma's hard fingers pinched me. Bold and truculent child. The sisters both hissed with disapproval, and they after working so hard. They'd made a beautiful corpse out of Lucy. Trust the

English child to complain. I had neither respect nor understanding of life here, they didn't wish to be told what to do. In
any case, her pink dress had been ruined, the ... occurrence had
rendered it fit only for scraps. Lucy was so pure and holy the
pink might even end as relics in the future. The white was perfect; they as dressmakers should know. They'd a deal of
experience with deceased persons, they were in demand in the
country around. They were sent for when loved ones passed
over, their piety and taste were famed. They'd been sad not to
have had more flowers for her laying out, it was the wrong
season of the year. There was enough holly about to fill a cathe-
dral, but holly wasn't right for a corpse. The collar of her
nightdress was turned upwards, her little red wound didn't show.
I wanted to wrench her eyes open, explain, make her listen. All
of this had served her right. She shouldn't have taken her knives
here. I hated knives. Now I'd keep Tin.

I looked at her father standing behind us, his face set. He
looked older, grey. He wasn't looking at Lucy but at the floor in
front of him. He wasn't holding any beads. The candles made
guttering noises, the beads in the sisters' hands clicked. Your
father knows about you, Lucy, and I know. You're a fraud, you're
not holy at all.

'Kneel, Ula. Try and say a prayer.'

'Why is the fire out, Grandma?'

You had to have cool air near a corpse, it seemed. I put my
hands over my face again. 'Hail nonsense. Hello rubbish. You
may look like a seraph to some people. I think you look like a
dead doll. It's all your fault, you know it is. Oh Lucy, I wish you
were here.'

Her hair was arranged glossily under the candlelight. She
liked her hair pulled back from her face. A chef mustn't have

hair falling about. 'I've seen you, Lucy, put your tongue to your nose.' 'Pray for us sinners now and at the hour of our death,' intoned the sisters. Their worried breathing smelled of tea.

'I think Lucy ought to have her chef's hat on, and perhaps a recipe book in her hand.'

'That's enough, Ula. Upstairs again.'

'I want to stay down here with you, Grandma. I don't like it up there alone.'

She looked sharp again. Her eyes were still pink-tinged and terrible. I was too young to stay down, too ignorant of their ways. The grown-ups would keep a watch here until the morning. 'What age is she?' one of the sisters whispered. What an impossible child. No wonder the English grew up bad.

'But I don't like it, Grandma. Please, let me stay.'

The father raised his head and looked at me but said nothing. I felt he thought I should stay. My world too had been shattered; a child's grief was potent too.

I went up to the long gallery, my brown slippers making no sound. I opened Lucy's door and went in. It was a larger room than mine with a darker carpet. The fire was out, the shutters closed. I shivered; the coldest part of me was in my head. I opened the big wardrobe; no pink dancing dress. Lucy, where are you now? You were wearing the dress when I first saw you. You left your monkey, you didn't want it. Now you have left and I'm behind.

There was nothing lying about except her knife box, with the smallest knife not in its place. A few cookery books were on the bookshelf. She'd been old ahead of her time. Her blue nightdress edged with shamrocks was under her pillow. I could sleep in her bed if I wanted; no one would know downstairs. She had a big washbasin in a recess with a light in the mirror over it. The washbasin had a crack and the pedestal was unsteady. It was the first worn object I'd seen here. Grandma had said no bathing at night-time. I would wash here in Lucy's room. I tried the hot tap; the water ran brown at first, then clean and hot. I went to my room to fetch Tin. When I got back there was a dark stain on the carpet spreading wider and wider. I turned the tap off. What would Grandma say? Would it seep through the ceiling and splash on top of Lucy? Would it hiss on the candle flames? I tried mopping with her face flannel. Then I washed and got into her bed.

I gave a jump when the bedroom door opened, expecting Grandma's disapproving face.

'Who is in here?' the father's voice asked. Who was in his beloved daughter's bed? He'd come up to say goodnight to me. Why was I not in my own bed? I tried to sound adult and casual.

'I'm in Lucy's room tonight. I thought it would make a change.'

I pulled the sheet up, I didn't want him seeing me in her nightdress, but his own grief was his main concern. His face looked like the oldest in the world, grooved with sadness round the eyes and mouth. I would have liked to comfort him, but didn't know how to. I didn't think he'd like me on his knee or holding on to him. He stood awkwardly, hanging his hands. I looked at his broad fingertips again; the fingers themselves were quite thin. His nails, though short, had conspicuous half-moons.

'I thought ... I thought that ... ' I expect that he'd thought I was Lucy, in her bed up here, not dead downstairs. He was bound to miss her, I told him in a wise voice. One day it would seem like a bad dream.

'You're too young to have all this to bear.'

'Yes. I didn't mean to have that knife. I hate knives.'

I didn't tell him that I liked wearing her nightdress and lying in her bed. Being there made me miss her less. I wondered if he knew about her knife-brandishing and cruelty and how much I'd envied her.

He picked up Tin from the eiderdown, his palm covering the painted spots. Lucy had never owned toys like other children, she'd stopped playing with bears and dolls. He'd encouraged her to be practical and resourceful. He would be thrown onto his own resources now, he'd be put to the test. When all this was over he must go back to the city and his livelihood. Life would never be the same. I thought of his students returning from the holiday to a house without Lucy. The salmon-pink kitchen would feel melancholy without Lucy whistling and humming while she concocted her stuffing and stews. Who would put scraps out for the birds and order her father about? The animals with the hotel names would be given away. What would happen to her school uniform and her chef's aprons? Surely no one would want to use her knives?

'My father died you know. And my baby brother. He was quite young really, just a few weeks old.'

I wanted him to know that he wasn't alone with his sorrow, that I'd some deaths to bear as well. I hadn't missed my father, I didn't mind not having one until I saw Lucy with hers. He said quietly that he'd been self-indulgent, he'd tried to burden me with his own loss. I'd already suffered too much. I was so young. His excuse was that I had a listening heart. Forgive him. Could he put my clothes on the bed? He removed them from the small stuffed armless chair and pulled it near to me. This was where he used to sit with Lucy; they liked quiet talks before she slept. The Christmas party last year had been perfect, everything had gone with a swing.

'Did you play Hide and Seek outside last year?'

'Of course. The same games every year.' It was their ritual: the same decorations, hiding the thimble in the same place, acting the same word for Charades. His mother always hid first in the old wood, on the edge by the holly trees. Only ... this time she'd gone inside. Her eyes were weak, she'd not been well recently. Their guests loved the tradition of the party, they felt bonded and needed. What would happen now?

'Don't think about it. I'll tell you about my family.'

About Bonnie and Tor, my two sisters who had no time for anyone but each other and never any time for me. How Bonnie was derived from the word 'good' in Latin, though Bonnie had never been good to me. Tor was short for Hortense, a Roman clan name. They had their governess in Shottermill, they were happy there. I had never had a true friend, that's why I wanted Lucy. Then I told him about Maggie, how I'd helped her in the kitchen on Sundays while Nurse stayed with Bruno upstairs. I'd grated salt, made crumbs from bread crusts, I'd emptied rubbish into the bins. I told him about her film star books and cutting out pictures of stars. How Maggie had danced the jig for me. Did no one dance any jigs here? I used to love being with Maggie. It all changed when Bruno died. I wanted to explain it to him. How Nurse, who wasn't a proper nurse but a great-aunt with black blood in her, had loved Bruno truly. When he died she'd gone off her head. I didn't tell about the pot flying out of the window. I wanted him to understand about my old world, about the kitchen and Maggie's comfortable smell.

'And your mother? Where does she fit in? How is she? How does she feel?'

'"Feel?" Mamma?'

I never thought about Mamma having feelings. What was

Mamma really like? I told him about her wanting to become an actress. I couldn't imagine her being like the ones in Maggie's pictures, with big lollopers, big teeth and behinds. My sisters were going away to school soon. Mamma hadn't said what I would do yet. I wanted to stay being a child. Though childhood was miserable and terrible, being grown-up might be worse. Maggie had said that Mamma might sell our house and leave.

He said I shouldn't pay too much attention to what Maggie said.

'Who? Maggie? Why?'

I wanted him to be interested in me, to question me instead of thinking of Lucy. He must know she'd been a bully, she'd been far from sweet and angelic to me. I liked his neat hair with grey streaks in it. I liked him not smelling of drink. His coat and his brogues matched each other, like turf sods just frosted with snow. I wanted him to tell me where Lucy would be taken. If I knew that I might not worry about where I'd go next. I asked when I would see Maggie.

He said it was unlikely that I'd see her for a long time, if ever. I ought to forget Maggie now.

"What happened? What did she do?"

It would be ill-advised, he said, to contact her or her family again.

'She had a brother, you know. Under the Christmas tree, lying there. I wanted to tell Lucy, I didn't get a chance.'

Someone must listen now, I had to explain. The Ma's tears had sounded so desolate. All that horror, the liver and blood. Some grown-ups seemed so sad. Maggie loved me. Her Da was kind. Irish families knew how to love, she had said so. Was her family different, was it religion? She'd told me too about

Ireland having no snakes or toads, as well as no king or queen.

He said mutual respect and tolerance were universal. In some families, no matter which country, things went wrong. It all started from within the family, success or failure later in life. Maggie's mother was weak in her mind. Maggie herself had been a mother, did I know that?

'Poor thing. What is it called? Where is the baby?'

Her child had been born prematurely, more than that he didn't know. He'd nothing against Maggie, she'd gone to England to get away. He'd been horrified by the poverty, the overcrowding; slum dwellers paid a price the world over. Her family were deprived.

'Yes, but did you see their Christmas tree? Did you see Joe too?'

He said Joe, in his view, was jail fodder. It was the mother he felt pity for. So many mothers had it hard. I thought of my own mother again, Maggie's mother, Grandma. I wondered where Lucy's own mother was.

He sighed groaningly again, his thoughts returning to his own loss. When he leaned to hug me his eyes weren't thinking of me but of Lucy, his pride and delight. He tried to make his mouth smile as he left me. Don't go, Lucy's father, think of me, I'm here.

I put my face into her pillow again. I had her nightdress, I had her room. I had Tin.

The elder sister came in the morning, her face bleached dry from her tears. Crying and exhaustion made her more kindly to me, or perhaps it was the effect of the death. Her cheeks felt rough as her lace frilling. Her voice was even more whispery now. She fumbled her hands. Look at your clothes, childey; who tossed them like that over the bed? You couldn't learn tidiness too early, an orderly room pleased the saints. I asked her where Grandma was.

It seemed she was unwell. The night had been too much for her, her heart was never strong. She was in her bed now, while Lucy's father was seeing to things. I guessed that soon the men with the dark car would come for Lucy. She'd be leaving the manor soon for good. The sister told me to go through to the back kitchen for my breakfast. So I wouldn't have to look at the refectory table again.

The younger sister was stirring porridge. She wore Grandma's apron which reached to the floor. I asked if I could have brown sugar with it and she said why not? Extra sweetness would be no harm on this day. Grandma had strode up and down yesterday, with her porridge bowl in her hand, pausing to peer at Grandfather's picture. Today she lay in her bed sorrowing, with a weakly beating heart. I took a spoonful of porridge, having stirred the sugar to runniness. I swallowed, it wouldn't go down. I stirred again with the crested spoon. I couldn't eat it, it tasted vile. The sister said not to worry, porridge could be difficult. Would I take some toast fingers instead? And some milk in this pretty cup now. There, wasn't that quite the thing? It was cold outside, but not too cold for a walk. A little walk would do me no harm. Then, after I got back, later, things would be ... normal again.

'I suppose you mean that Lucy's body will be gone then? Will the fires be lit again?'

She answered with a fresh gush of tears. She wiped her face on the apron string. Respect for the dead was something I'd not learned. Go out now through the back door quickly. Ah, what it was to be a child.

The Wellingtons that I'd worn yesterday were by the back

door waiting. She joined her sister for a last round of tears and prayers. The boots didn't feel as big and alien. The raincoat felt damp and cold. There was no blood on it. Had the sisters cleaned it? I put my hand into the pocket; there was no knife. I hadn't wanted the knife, I hated knives. All of this was Lucy's fault. I didn't want to walk in the new wood either, or anywhere outside at all. How awful she'd looked in that lace.

The back of the manor was in shadow. I breathed in the icy air. I walked through the yard past the bins and outhouses. The early sun came out, a faint warmth shone on my face. In the bottom of the right-hand pocket was a small rent; I poked my finger through. What would happen to me? Soon Lucy's father would be going back. I had killed Lucy yesterday in holy Ireland. I was the first one to walk on this snow, all brilliant and silvery white. Ahead of me stretched the new wood with the Christmas trees, little pointed green shapes, hundreds of them, all similarly sized. This was Maggie's green as a parable Ireland, under white as chastity snow. I'd expected to be loved and needed here, the country of legend and lore. I had envied Lucy, I had hated her, loved her. I was alive, she was dead. I walked between the lines of trees, making tracks where no one had trodden. Up one avenue of trees and down the next, my feet pointing outwards, crushing the silvery snow.

I heard a sound, I looked upwards. A bird was flying over the manor, a long-tailed brilliant shape. I saw the tail feathers trailing, I could see the small head and small cold eyes. It came to rest in front of me, I could see the turquoise blue neck feathers shining, the gold and brown eyes on the tail. It looked at me impassively, then rose slowly and flew back over the gabled roof. It had left a feather in the snow, small and fluffy with a hint of iridescent blue sheen.

'Hail. All hail. Hail,' I whispered. I ran back into the house.

'I've seen the peacock. I've seen the peacock,' I told the sisters. Where was Grandma, I must tell her.

'Aye, go you up to her. Don't make a noise mind.'

She was in her bed looking older and smaller, her face between the hanging white plaits looked thin. Her eyes looked as if she'd cried the colour from them. She put out her hand.

'I saw the peacock, the ghost peacock. It's not a ghost, it's real.'

'That's grand. For your luck, child. Grand.'

'What's wrong? Are you ill, Grandma?'

'Just resting. That's grand about the bird. They say that those it looks on will be in for a bit of a change.'

'He looked at me. He had little hard eyes, round like beads.'

I showed her the curled fluff of feather, the proof that he'd been there. From under the wing, she thought.

'Has Lucy left the manor now?'

'She has gone, yes. But you must stay. Stay as long as you'd like to.'

'You mean you'd like me to? You want me? Me?'

She whispered that Lucy had needed a friend, that she'd loved me. I must stay here, treat the manor as my home. She'd already spoken to Lucy's father. He'd make the arrangements. And my two sisters could come too. I could have anyone I wished to stay here. Anyone I wanted. Did I like the idea?

12

Bonnie and Tor came to the manor. That spring and summer I was happy, I blotted what had happened earlier from my mind. I remember the games we played, I can still hear the sounds our voices made.

We kept to the gallery at first, hardly whispering. Then we crept down the wide stairs, running round the refectory table, then gradually out on the porch. Bonnie and Tor were afraid of Grandma, but their fear turned to respect and then need. Grandma didn't vary, she was there constantly, though apart from cooking and eating meals with us she stayed in her room. Her health worsened after Lucy died.

The summer that year was long and dry. We stayed alone apart from meals. We played late into the evenings, staying on the upper lawn close to the manor's grey walls. We knew that Grandma was upstairs, we were protected. My sisters never asked about Lucy, or what had happened down by the lake. They didn't look towards the old wood or want to go there, nor did the new wood at the back interest us. We were involved in our games and ourselves on the upper lawn, nothing else mattered. I was included at last. Once in the night I thought I heard the peacock crying, but it could have been an owl. We loved the bats that flew over our heads in the twilight, we chased them and tried to copy their sound. We ran barefoot races, we played statues. They taught me Grandmother's Steps. I loved the feel and smell of the dewy grass under my thighs as I rolled head over heels, I loved to hear Bonnie and Tor call. I loved running round the upper lawn till I was giddy, dazed, touched with glory. I loved holding their hands, touched with joy. I put the past behind me that summer. I never saw Maggie again.

That September the war came and another life started. I went with my sisters to school. During the holidays we stayed there. Mamma joined a company, touring to entertain the forces, but I was never as lonely again because I had Bonnie and Tor. They were mine and I was theirs.

I never went back to Ireland. It all happened a long time ago. I came across Tin in a box of old trinkets; there was a brown scrap of feather too. Tin is smaller than I remember, and shabbier, his painted spots have gone. But for finding him I might believe that I'd imagined the events of that strange sad Christmas. I don't think I have exaggerated, but I wonder.

UNICORN SISTERS

1

'You'll miss me, darlings, I know you will. I know I'll miss you, too.'

Once Mamma had decided to leave us again she kept repeating this, like the refrain of a song or a prayer. She said we must be brave soldiers, she knew what was best for us. The three of us were to go to a boarding school, a place of safety, out of reach of Hitler's bombs. She hugged me and my two sisters, leaving wafts of perfume in our hair. She touched our hands which embarrassed us, we were not used to the touch of adults. We were used to her being away.

I loved the soft feel of her fur jacket, the feeling of fur against my face. She wore her collar turned up to frame her cheeks and hair. When she was at home I used to listen for the tap of her coloured heels, the swish of petticoats. She was perfect.

She had red hair that September when war was declared but sometimes it was just mouse brown. Mamma was relieved to be getting rid of us so conveniently. War was declared. We must go at once.

She was stage struck; we were used to her going away to her

acting. This time we were leaving her because of the present emergency.

'And, Bonnie darling, I leave you in charge. Promise me you will take care of your sisters. They will feel strange at first, at school.'

Her hair clung beguilingly to her fur collar. While we were safely in the West Country she planned to sing and act for the troops. She would join a company, tour the country to make the army smile.

So then, it was settled, she would miss and think of us constantly. She had discovered the perfect school where we could stay in the holidays as well as the term, a school which catered for girls with absent parents. We only had Mamma, our father was already dead. Entertaining the forces would be Mamma's war effort, more valuable than fighting with guns. There was no question of us staying with her. She needed to be free.

'It's a charming place, run by two sisters. I've seen the prospectus. They cater for girls from six to sixteen. So, Bonnie, you'll be substitute mother, won't you?'

She widened her lashes, her beautiful eyes appealed. 'Bonnie, darling, I shall miss you. You're my right hand, my aide-de-camp.'

I looked away. I didn't want to co-operate. I wanted her to stay. In wartime children needed parents more than ever, not just because of bombs but because everything had changed. We didn't want to go to strange teachers in a strange school in a strange county. Why should I act as a mother when I was their sister? I needed her, so did Ula and Tor.

The three of us had been in Ireland earlier, for a holiday. Home had seemed far away. When we got back there were soldiers everywhere, on motor bikes, in lorries, peering from the tops of tanks. The atmosphere felt hectic, with housewives won-dering and worrying about soap and biscuits and other household articles that might become in short supply. There were first aid courses at the town hall, there were gas masks to be collected. You needed air-raid shelters to keep you safe from raids. But the soldiers looked carefree, shouting at girls to make them giggle, revving motor cycles and whistling. The girls nudged each other, the wailing notes of the whistles made them blush and comb their hair after the soldiers had passed. I couldn't imagine anyone wanting to whistle at me.

Mamma had letters and telephone calls that made her anx-ious. The War Office wanted to requisition our home. When we left it soldiers would move in and live here. A regiment was sta-tioned in our town. The War Office would pay Mamma for the use of our house; a help, she said, towards the fees of our school. While we studied in the West Country Mamma would be singing for soldiers, uplifting their morale. She would stay with the others in her company, we must not worry about her safety. She knew that we would love our school. Our uniform was only to be obtained at Liberty's. Imagine, darlings. And we must be fitted with gas masks too.

A man with ARP on his shoulder put rubber masks on our faces and made us breathe while he checked for a correct fit. The rubber had a choking smell like cooking stoves which I hated, but Ula was thrilled. They were kept in cardboard boxes with string handles, they must be carried at all times. Notices read: 'Have you got your gas mask?' Mamma thought they were deplorable; they messed your hair and spoiled your skin. When she was singing for the army she might get a better one with long breathing tubes like the soldiers. Ula patted and examined hers, swinging it with pride. Tor didn't say what she thought, she never did. I could usually guess what she was thinking, she and I were so close.

The day after we got our gas masks we went to London for the uniform. We were quite vague about why the country was at war, we only knew it made a lot of changes.

We walked through the revolving doors of Liberty's. Ula showing off with her gas mask. I already felt responsible for my sisters because I'd been put in charge. Soon we were in our vests and knickers, trying on uniforms. I had made Tor and Ula leave off their bodices, in case they were laughed at in the shop but the assistant was motherly. Until now no one had bothered about our clothes; we wore ugly skirts and grey jerseys. Now the fitting room became piled with tunics and blouses that gave off that special wool smell. Mamma, smelling of attar of roses, sat smiling and watching us change; the perfect fond mother kitting out her daughters.

The uniform was a light rust colour with contrasting tomato red or coral pink. Our blouses were tussore silk, our underwear Chilprufe, our velour hats had rust-coloured turned-back brims. I never dreamed that I would own so many lovely clothes. Our feet danced as we left the school outfitting floor. We were like three princesses dressed extravagantly for an unknown future ball.

On the ground floor Mamma paused at the perfume counter to replenish her essences and her beautiful rose-smelling soaps. When she sang the soldiers would be able to smell as well as see and hear her. She sprayed the air round my face. 'Lovely isn't it, my sweet Bonnie? How I'll miss you.' The assistants watched and whispered. What lucky children. What a lovely mamma.

We went to a restaurant where a three-piece band was playing. Romantic tunes accompanied our tinkling spoons.

Mamma hummed in a throaty way; she never tired of that song, she said.

'Sing the words, Mamma.'

'When I grow too old to dream, I'll have you to remember. When I grow too old to dream, your love will live in my heart.'

She sang too loudly, but I liked it. I watched her biting into a sandwich, looking lively and exotic. Her real world awaited her, her world of cocktail parties where people discussed love affairs and gossiped about stars of film and stage.

'I love cream cakes,' Ula said, reaching for another.

'Sweet child, don't make yourself sick, will you? You're not in Ireland now.'

Ula choked. She asked why we had to go so far away.

'The bombs, darling. Hitler is the culprit. You must be educated. It's unfortunate, I know. You have your sisters. Bonnie has promised to look after you.'

'Do I have a choice?' I muttered. But the school uniform was worth the bother and upheaval of war.

The London streets were crowded with soldiers in their best uniforms, off duty now, their guns and packs put away. With boots and buttons glistening, they had their loved ones, and money to spend. Those without a girl looked lost and lonely, standing at corners and waiting, or bunched in groups looking at maps. Freedom was sweet.

At the next table an officer had sat with his fiancée. With chairs touching, they had eyes for nothing but themselves and their diamond ring. They hadn't noticed when Mamma had sung.

Sandbags were piled in front of windows to protect them from shattering. Underground exits had boardings to protect travellers from blast. There were crash barriers where crowds might gather. Above our heads the barrage balloons floated in the clouds, like huge, unlikely-looking whales. There were posters everywhere urging and encouraging: 'Dig for Victory', 'Careless Talk Costs Lives'. Ula wanted to know what 'Save for the Brave and Lend to Defend the Right to be Free' meant. She couldn't read yet. Tor read the slogans aloud. Mamma said that it was a good thing to stock up on perfumes, anything might become rationed in wartime. Now that I had my uniform I had no interest in the war or rationing. I would miss Mamma but I still had Tor. We had never been apart. We had shared our schoolroom and had been taught by an old governess. Mamma was like a remote perfumed butterfly; when she alit you longed to keep her. I could only guess at her real world that she liked best.

'I'd like to wear a tin helmet,' Ula said. 'I'd like to be an ARP man.'

'We must all make sacrifices for our country,' Mamma said, looking dreamily at her rings. The couple at the next table had kissed their ring before kissing each other. Mamma's rings were glittery and precious, put on her fingers long ago by Papa. Soon she would be telling us that she would miss us for the last time. We would smell roses, feel her hands on our hands. She'd be gone. I decided to wear the velvet collar of my tweed coat turned up like hers. I would experiment with the brim of my hat. The school was called Magnolia House. The headmistress was called Miss Gee.

'I love school,' Ula said.

'How do you know? You haven't tried it. Don't be so sure.'

'Not long now. Hurry, my darlings, or we'll miss the six o'clock train home.'

And then it was the first day of term and we were driving to the West Country. It was a low building behind a white wall, the autumn evening was damp with fog in patches. On the school gatepost was a small unicorn.

'And look, Bonnie, they've got a magnolia tree.' Mamma sounded nervous now. We looked at the knobbly branches growing in a tangle in front of the conservatory to the right of the front door. There were no plants on the front lawn, no autumn daisies or chrysanthemums, just grass and the wet grey branches of the tree.

'I like the unicorn,' Ula said in a small voice.

'It's so quiet. Where are all the girls, Mamma?'

'Children, darlings. This is where I leave you. We'll part here, I won't come in. Look, your headmistress is at the window.'

We saw a thin person behind the magnolia branches standing in the conservatory.

'Stay, Mamma. Don't go yet.'

'Don't linger, darlings. Go in. Kiss me. Quick.'

'Mamma . . .'

Remember the feel of her hair on your cheek, her perfume, her wide open eyes. Remember the rings on her white fingers, put there by Papa long ago. You mustn't go yet, Mamma, you must meet Miss Gee, you must talk to her. I have never met or spoken to a teacher. I don't know what to say.

'Bona? What a tall girl. You must be the eldest. But why did your mother not wait? How strange.'

'She's very busy. It's her war work, you know,' Ula explained.

Miss Gee moved stiffly back through the white doorway. She hadn't smiled, her face was thin and stern. Her clothes, her skin and hair were a pale greyish shade. She spoke through half-closed lips. She closed the door. We were cut off from Mamma. We heard the taxi drive off. We are alone now with Miss Gee.

Her study was severe, with just a desk and a cupboard for her files. Mamma had left without seeing our bedrooms or the rooms where we would work and eat. Did she even know what we would be learning?

Tor and I could read anything. We had learned from the same books that Mamma had used, because Gov had once taught her too. They were mildewed and had broken spines mended with brown paper. When you turned the page you got a smell of church. We had learned no maths or geography or languages. Ula had done no lessons at all apart from Tor teaching her letters. We used to keep her out of the schoolroom, it was our private domain. No wonder she looked forward to being with us. Ula wasn't afraid of anyone, not even Miss Gee now. She reminded me of a knight on a tombstone, stony-faced and grim.

She wrote our names in her register. She asked about our health. Had we had measles, chicken-pox, mumps?

'I don't think we ever had any illnesses.'

Not having mixed with other children we hadn't caught their germs. When we were little we had gone to a dancing class. Our health was good because we had stayed at home with our governess. A lump came into my throat when I thought of her. She had been deaf and she'd slept a lot but was good-humoured and fond of us.

'Except for our brother, Bonnie. Don't forget about him. He died of croup.'

'Ula.'

I hated her for mentioning our brother. Having no father and a mother who ran off without waiting was bad enough. Whatever would Miss Gee think of us?

She didn't answer but went on writing. When she looked up her eyes were cold and sad. Was there any food that didn't agree with us? Nothing? Very well. We were to sleep together in the larger dormitory. The smaller one was not at present in use. The school, she explained, was not operating at full capacity. Owing to the war the pupil quota had been reduced. The term did not start until tomorrow. Why our mother had seen fit to leave us a day early was a mystery. The other pupils would arrive tomorrow, the official start of term. What a pity that our mother had not stayed a moment, had not troubled to make herself known.

'We thought we had to come today. Mamma must have made a mistake.'

'A pity. I like to interview new parents.'

'Our mamma is going to sing for the army. The war is going to move into our home. I like your school, Miss Gee. I see you have that message "Save for the Brave". We saw it in London.'

The slogan was printed on the lid of a cash box on the windowsill. I explained that Ula was excited, that she wasn't used to school. She was naturally talkative. Miss Gee mustn't know that she couldn't read or that Tor and I knew no algebra or French. Ula could remember the shapes of words once she'd been told what they said. If only Mamma had talked to Miss Gee. If only we hadn't come a day too soon. She continued writing without answering. She wrote with a steel nib dipped into an inkwell. She blotted her copperplate writing with clean blotting paper. Now, new girls. Come with her. I wished she would smile.

I wished that Mamma had seen the drab dormitory with the faded curtains that separated the beds. The ceiling was cracked like a piece of china. Upstairs was much shabbier than below. Perhaps parents were not encouraged up here. Mamma never had concerned herself about our education or our activities. We had never been taught religion. At this school it seemed to be important, there was a chapel room downstairs.

'If a bomb fell that ceiling might fall on us, Miss Gee.'

Miss Gee didn't answer Ula. She went downstairs.

'Don't talk so much, Ula. It's best to keep quiet until we know the ropes.'

Tomorrow eleven girls would arrive. Fourteen pupils was not a large school, more a group than an establishment. I looked down the dormitory with the double row of waiting beds. I stroked the tussore silk sleeve of my blouse. I had fawn silk stockings for Sundays, I had brown strap shoes with little heels. When we had looked into the chapel room Miss Gee's face had gone gentle. The school assembled there every morning, it was the focus of the school day. She had said that the girls were encouraged to be self-governing, school was but a training for life. An old gardener had carried our suitcases up, they were waiting beside our beds. The grey curtains hung from metal poles by rings. They clattered when you gave a pull.

'Don't break them, Ula. Take care.'

The window curtains were lined with black cotton to comply with black-out rules. Enemy aircraft could attack at night, not a chink of light must show. Every street light, every traffic light and car light must be dimmed now because of war. We would feel better when we had unpacked our clothes. I would put Mamma and the war out of my mind as I unfolded new sweaters and vests. I would gloat again over my tussore silks and tweeds. Even our hankies were pastel coloured; we were like three pink and rust butterfly brides. We moved from our suitcases to our beds, sorting and piling. I helped Ula to refold her skirts. She worried and annoyed me constantly with her high spirits and thoughtless remarks. She had stayed in Ireland for longer than

Tor and me. Before we got there a dreadful thing had happened to Ula which cast a black shadow over our lives. She had accidentally caused the death of her friend Lucy and we never spoke about it. Ula hadn't shown any grief but it would probably affect her always. It had happened soon after the death of our brother Bruno and we rarely spoke about him either. Probably this war would affect us all deeply, though Mamma was too old to change.

The responsibility fell on me, I would keep my promise. Ula was wriggling over the bedrails like a snake, crumpling her clothes again.

'I'll sleep in the middle, shall I, Bonnie?'

'No you won't, thanks very much. Tor and I stay together.'

Ula stared with her silly smile. She had a freak streak of white hair over her forehead which stuck up sometimes like a little horn. If only she were not so noticeable and talkative. We all had rather poor-coloured teeth but I was the prettiest and the one most fond of clothes. Ula started wrapping a pink hankie round her gas mask, rocking and kissing it like a child. She never took offence, was always cheerful. Tor hardly spoke at all. I knew and understood her, she liked to read and keep a diary. Both were even-tempered and never spiteful, I knew their good qualities too.

At the end of the dormitory was a row of wash-basins that you tipped into a drain behind. They were thick and clumsy, too heavy for Ula. I watched her struggling. Tor went to her help. The water swished. We heard it gurgle; the plumbing seemed to be old. We sat on our beds and looked at our clothes again. There were no carpets anywhere.

When we had put everything into the chests of drawers we went downstairs again. We felt hungry.

There were long tables in the dining room. Miss Gee had made the tea herself because we had come early. After today there would be just a light supper at night.

'What's in this sandwich, Miss Gee? I like it.'

She told Ula that it was called Patum Peperium, made from anchovies, which some called Gentlemen's Relish. She hadn't smiled yet. Did she pity us or despise us for having dead or neglectful parents? She didn't speak any more but kept her eyes on a list of names. As well as fewer pupils she seemed to have a servant problem, another result of this war. The dining room smelled of old frying pans. Ula was greedy about the sandwiches. I was deeply ashamed to see her wiping her mouth on a lock of her hair.

'It isn't dark yet, Miss Gee. Can I go and look at that unicorn again?'

Miss Gee said that the front of the school was out of bounds without an adult, no girl was to go near the gate. There were few rules, that was one of them; do not go near the gate. We might put on our Wellington boots if we wished and walk round the croquet lawn but stick to the paths, please.

Our Wellingtons were brown. The label said 'Made in France'. So far the nicest part of coming here was the clothing. Mamma had spent a lot, she must care about us. The boots squeaked as our ankles brushed together. They made slushing sounds in the wet leaves. The twilight air was bitter against our faces, we felt too awed and nervous to jump or run. At home we used to love kicking autumn leaves or catching them as they fell. The croquet hoops made crooked loops against the cold no-coloured grass. Ula pushed her boot into one of them. 'Look, Bonnie. I'm an animal in a trap.'

'Get off the grass. The lawn is only for teachers. You heard what Miss Gee said.'

'What teachers? I haven't seen any except her. Look, a mole has been here, look at that mound over there.'

'Do get off. It's not allowed.'

'I want to see the unicorn. I must.'

'You heard. No.'

But I wanted to see it too. Even more, I wanted to hear cars passing. We were cut off and silent here, with only the slush of leaves and the squeaking of our boots. By now Mamma would be home again. Was she thinking of us while she sipped her evening cocktail? A lot seemed to be expected of me. Miss Gee had said that she liked those with long hair to wear it plaited. Ula's wasn't long enough, Tor wore hers quite short and straight. I hated plaits. There would be no supper tonight. Come back, Ula, you are not to go in the front.

I ran round the side of the building after her. She was standing by the magnolia tree looking at the unicorn. It was difficult to see now in the dying light, just a small lump on the gatepost with a horn sticking out. The magnolia tree was a blur.

'You must do what I say, Ula. You've got to learn.'

I put my hand out and pinched her, that would teach her. She clutched her neck. 'That hurt, Bonnie. Don't.'

I had never hurt her physically before and I felt ashamed and sorry. She was only young after all, she couldn't help having accidentally killed someone, she couldn't help her irritating ways. I resolved never to hit or hurt either of them while I was their guardian, I would love them and keep them from harm. 'I'm sorry, Ula, honestly.'

'Oh, all right. Is that a rat or a rabbit over there?'

'It's just leaves, you fool. Come on.'

We had to use a torch in the bathroom that separated the large and the small dormitories, there were no blackout curtains there yet. The three baths were divided by wooden partitions that you could see over if you climbed them. We could listen to each other splashing peacefully. Miss Gee had told us to use separate baths. Modesty remained a virtue despite war. She gave me a torch. I must keep this pointed low; remember no light must be visible from the sky. As important as modesty and the concealment of light was the saving of hot water. The level must not rise above the mark painted round the bathtub. Fuel was needed for the war effort. 'Save for the Brave and Lend to Defend the Right to be Free'. And please draw the cubicle curtains when dressing and undressing.

I aimed the torch under the partition. I could see Tor's bony little feet. Each cubicle had a slatted mat to step on to. There was a wooden rack for your sponge. Ula whispered that there might be spiders. Tor said that cockroaches were more likely. She had hardly spoken since we got here. At home we used to collect spiders, not having other pets. They always died. If I hadn't felt so responsible and homesick I might have enjoyed the bath. Faint starlight shone through the window. Was it dark enough for a raid? I heard my sisters' watery sounds, I heard Tor drop her shoe. Ula liked practising whistling in the bath; she hadn't learned it yet. Water was supposed to improve sound. Tor was finished first. I loved and understood Tor better than anyone, we never quarrelled or got bored. There was no need for anyone else when we were together, but I wished we'd bought something to read in bed. I stared into the starry blackness and imagined a castle made of roses, snow and moonlight for us to live in. I supposed we'd have to let Ula in too.

'Hurry then, Ula. We're getting into bed now.' Mamma had given each of us a tube of face cream. The water at school might be hard. The West Country wasn't mild like the south, the winds might roughen our skins. Nightly creaming ensured good looks later, use it, darling, don't forget. We sat up in bed spreading the cream diligently, not forgetting our necks. We patted it round our eyes. The cream was made in France like our Wellingtons, it shone pure and shiny white. Ula gasped; she'd been using her toothpaste. 'It's all pepperminty. It stings, Bonnie, what shall I do?'

'You might get a disease. Wash it off quickly, Ula.' She made a lot of noise heaving and banging the washbasin. Tor went to her help again.

In the night Ula made more noises, groaning and grinding her teeth together. She often did this at home since the accident in Ireland. I shook her shoulder. She had her gas mask under the sheet with her. She looked so innocent and startled. I must never hurt her again.

'You must try and sleep quietly. You must learn to fit in. The girls won't like you to be different. You must try and get your own friends and do what I say.'

2

I woke early. Today was the real start of the Christmas term. Soon we would see the other girls. They would know each other, they would know the staff and the timetable. I worried for my sisters' sake the most. I put my hand to the heating pipes above my head. I guessed they'd be almost cold. The black curtains fitted the windows without any light showing. At home Mamma would be snuggling into her pillows, pulling up her eiderdown. Her life would soon change too. When your country needed your services, you were told what to do, you obeyed. Some people liked being instructed, liked being fitted with gas masks and planning shelters for raids, liked growing vegetables and saving fuel. Mamma would like singing to soldiers while she left her family to me. I hoped we wouldn't be laughed at for being backward, for having no father and rather poor teeth. The uniform was my mainstay and comfort, even my pyjamas were new; soft pink and rose coloured stripes. My face cream was like a talisman, smelling a little like Mamma's rosy scent. There was no sound, no swish of passing traffic, no flushing cisterns or clattering plates. Soon we would see the mistresses as well as the girls. Would Miss Patrice, Miss Gee's sister, be as strict and stern as her? Tor's bedsprings creaked.

'Are you awake, Tor?'

'I've been awake for ages.'

'Do you think I should plait my hair?'

The neat-fingered one of the family, Tor was good at drawing and making raffia flowers. Her animal drawings were so real you could almost feel them, her writing was tiny but neat. She moved quickly, she learned quickly, she never got in a panic. Though two years younger she was more clever than me. She got out of her bed and huddled under my blankets. Her feet felt cold and small. I rubbed my calves against them while she started combing me. You must remove the tangles before you could make plaits. The hair must be pulled straight and even. It was lovely being close again, almost like our room at home.

'What are you doing, Bonnie? I can hear you. Tor's with you. Can I come too?'

'No, you can't. She's plaiting my hair.'

'Let her,' said Tor.

It was to please Miss Gee that I was suffering this combing and pulling. Tor was patient, she tried not to tweak. She had a kinder nature than I had. In Ireland when the three of us had played grandmother's steps it was Tor who showed Ula what to do. It was Tor who read the names of streets aloud and helped Ula with anything too heavy or tall. Ula was an embarrassment, she walked with her toes turned out, her skirts always looked too long. She was inquisitive and cocksure. At nearly eight she should know how to behave. Tor and I looked like perfect schoolgirls in our uniforms; no one would think we had a run-away mother and a sadly disorganized home.

'You're hurting, Tor. It's pulling me.' My eyes were watering.

The hair grew in a fluff on my nape. Tor said you must pull as hard as possible to plait properly. My neck felt stretched and raw.

'Your skin looks all red, it's nearly bleeding. Oh stop, Tor, leave her alone.'

Blood and knives terrified Ula, the only things that made her afraid. She had her gas mask in my bed with her, her feet were warm against mine. Tor said she would make one plait like a pony's tail, which wouldn't pull as much. We lay squashed together with our knees tangled. My neck still hurt but my sisters were there. It was easy to make Ula happy, you just had to include her. I wished that Tor spoke more than she did.

Ula said in a kind voice that I was probably nervous this morning because of the other girls.

'I'm not nervous, you fool. But just don't tell anyone about our home.'

'You mean about Mamma leaving us because of Hitler. Don't worry, I won't tell.'

'Not Hitler, stupid. I mean about our home being occupied. Don't talk about Bruno, or Papa . . . or anything.'

I meant her friend dying in Ireland. She understood me. She started whispering to her gas mask. Then she tried her whistling.

'Help Tor with my hair, will you? The plait hurts. It's no good.'

Their fingers tickled as they eased the hair out. At last my neck felt normal again. I looked at my face, white and serious, in the mirror over the chest of drawers. Perhaps Mamma would send coloured ribbons to tie in bunches over my ears.

No one had said when we should get up. We pulled the curtains back and got our dressing gowns. I reminded them to say 'dormitory' instead of 'bedroom'. It was 'form' here, not class or schoolroom. We must make the best of it and forget Gov and our old schoolroom. There would be no making raffia flowers here. Tor and I used to play a private game about animals. I was nearly twelve and too old for imaginary games.

Outside a bell rang, the kind of bell pulled by a rope. Did it mean breakfast or should we go to the chapel room? We hurried into our clothes. Ula started being stupid again, wanting to wash her gas mask. Did Miss Gee know what Mamma thought about religion?

'Let's go to the dining room. Food is what I need.' Ula skipped downstairs ahead. The chapel-room door was closed, we could hear voices that seemed to be arguing. One voice sounded tearful. A notice on the door said 'Biblical Tableau Practice 3 pm'.

The dining room was empty. Through the door to the kitchen the old gardener was making breakfast. He wore a sacking apron and thickly soled boots. The boots made him seem taller but he was bent and wizened. He was heating baked beans. There were tinned tomatoes as well.

'Hullo, what's your name? I'm Ula.'

'Oh, ah. Gumm.'

He was helping indoors to oblige. He was the gardener by rights. His lock of hair hung over the beans. His moustache made him like a miniature Hitler, he had knotted hands. He smelled like Tor, sweaty, but very strong. Tor had sweated since I could remember. I hoped she wouldn't do it here.

'I like fried bread better than toast, it's what we had in Ireland,' Ula said, squashing her tomatoes till the juice ran pinky brown. She was eating our school colours, red tomatoes and brown fried bread. She offered some to the gas mask. Grease ran down her chin.

Tor wasn't enjoying this food. I moved closer. We had never

had baked beans. Her sweating was a worry. She washed a lot. There was no one we could ask. Gov had been too old to know about bodies, Mamma was too busy or away. I asked Gumm for some butter.

'It's margarine, Bonnie, remember it's the war. Where is Miss Gee, please? Is she in the chapel room?'

He sniffed. 'She never told me about all this. No staff. No cook. What am I supposed to do? Too much.'

His job was maintaining the property and the grounds. Some people expected too much.

'Do you mean there is no one to run the school now?' Ula leaned forward, licking her fingers.

'Ah, new girls. I trust that you will assist Gumm in any way you can. After today we shall meet in the chapel room and settle our routine.'

She looked as grey and serious as she had yesterday. Had it been her we'd heard crying? She looked critically at my hair. We would adjust to curriculum.

'Who will teach us, Miss Gee? Where is your sister?'

Miss Gee looked at Ula. Miss Patrice would be along presently, she would be our form mistress. Meanwhile we would find text books in our desks. We would use the same form room. There were changes this term, not only on the domestic side, she glanced at Gumm, but academically too. She would announce the changes when the other girls arrived. Meanwhile we should copy the timetable written on the blackboard and pin it inside the lids of our desks. She closed her eyes when she'd finished speaking. Gumm crashed the plates outside.

The form rooms were at the back of the building, with the dormitories above them. They overlooked the croquet lawn and kitchen gardens. More leaves had fallen in the night from the beech tree, scattering the grass in pale brown piles. The form room was a little warmer than the other rooms. The desks, the walls and floor covering were brown. Miss Gee's copperplate handwriting covered the blackboard. Tor read it aloud. There was Biblical Tableau Practice every day. I chose the double desk at the back for Tor and me. We would prop the lid on our heads and talk in private. Ula banged her desk lid in front.

'Tor, shall we be all right here?'

'We'll have to be. There's no choice.'

The text books were newer than Gov's ancient ones. We had never owned exercise books before. Tor had her precious diary. Gov had given me a pen and pencil set and Ula some coloured crayons. Gov was as far off as if she were dead. She had taught Tor and me to read and write, we had never been bored with her. I still missed her. Miss Gee had left sheets of brown paper to cover our text books, we must label them with the title and our names.

Tor's thin hands moved precisely. She had finished *Men and Women of History* before my brown paper was creased into shape. There was *Mathematics Made Magic*, the *Geography Lover's Guide* and *Easy French*. The look and feel of the books made me anxious. Tor's writing would be the best in the school. My own was large and childish. We'd never learned tables. Life was best if you did things well. Tor liked learning, Ula tackled anything with gusto but we'd never had to compete. Ula crumpled brown paper in front of us, getting Gripfix in her hair. She was pleased to be doing real work in a real school, with her elder sisters near. She put her rubber in her mouth crossways and started humming.

'You're not a dog with a bone, Ula. Don't hold your pencil like that.'

She went on making dots and scribbles, pressing dents into the paper. How the girls would jeer.

'What, Ula, are you doing, pray?'

'Hullo, Miss Gee, I'm just busy with something. I am looking forward to sums.'

'Bona, you as the eldest should have shown your little sister what to do. Look at this book. I am disappointed.'

'I'm sorry, Miss Gee. You see Ula can't quite read yet. She could never manage *Tiny Tales of Yore*. I'll cover it for her when I've finished mine.'

'Not read? What a disgrace.'

'Mamma didn't agree with a lot of lessons. I'm Bonnie, you know, not Bona.'

'I prefer the full nomenclature. No lessons at all, you say? What a tragedy. What negligence.'

'What's negligence?' Ula was jaunty. Tor read her anything that she needed to know. As long as she had us nothing upset her. Miss Gee said it was assumed that her girls could read and write prior to arrival here.

'But we aren't really your girls, are we, Miss Gee? We belong to our Mamma.'

'Shut up, Ula.'

Miss Gee said that I should allow Ula to express herself. Self-expression, self-governance, self-determination were admirable. Magnolia House aimed at democracy. She added that Ula was entrusted to her care, in one sense she did belong to Miss Gee.

I hated to think that this might be true. It was war, there was no one else, we must obey her. The lessons, especially that biblical one, sounded ridiculous. I dreaded the arrival of the girls. I smiled.

'It's quite absurd I know. But Ula *is* backward. What *shall* we do with her?'

'We are not equipped for retarded pupils. Learning should start early and end late. I emphasize the need for prolonged application for all three of you. Hortense, that handwriting is far too cramped. As well as lessons we aim at elegance, that inner grace, some call it *"je ne sais quoi"*.'

We looked blank. She wrote our names on separate sheets of paper. When the book binding was completed we should practise writing copperplate, repeating our names until we reached the foot of the page. Ula must hold her pencil correctly, in the right hand please, and do not press. I liked my writing, Tor's print was beautiful. It was insulting to be told to change.

'Slowly, Ula, do not touch the line above or the line beneath.'

'I like it large,' Ula said, pressing and breathing aloud. With her rubber back in her mouth she was happy. Miss Gee walked between the desks. She paused at the blackboard. She erased 'gymnastics', substituting another lesson of Biblical Tableau practice.

'What is that, Miss Gee, please?'

She said it was the important subject this term in particular. The school enacted a pageant every Christmas which parents came to watch; it was the yearly tradition. She took Ula's gas mask, she showed us the hooks on the wall. All masks must be hung there during lessons. As government property they must be treated with respect.

'And perhaps, Bona, you will be good enough to refill the ink-wells. Ink replenishment is a monitor's task.'

'Does it mean I'll be a monitor?'

Prefects and monitors were elected yearly by the two head girls, at present Phoebe Pillcock and Margaret Pierce.

The heavy stone bottle slipped in my hand. Miss Gee had left the room. Ula said the ink smelled like Gumm's apron, cross and bitter. Don't sniff at it, it could be poisonous. She was longing to write in ink. With her steady hand she was as diligent as Tor. By the time she reached the bottom of her page her name was neat. I filled each ink-well with care. If I was made a monitor I would see that my sisters were well treated.

Ula hoped that Miss Gee's sister would be as nice as she was. I despaired of Ula. Couldn't she understand that Miss Gee was an enemy? We should distrust her until we knew her better. We should tread warily and try to please.

We waited in the conservatory behind the magnolia. No one could see us; we could watch the girls arrive. There were no plants there except for one dying cheeseplant. We could see the unicorn again, wise and aloof in the daylight.

One by one the taxis and cars drove through the gate, pulling up in front of our tree. Seen from this side its branches were like a face, the criss-cross boughs making wrinkles.

Except for one girl they came with their parents, who came into the school with their daughters in the proper expected manner. Some of the fathers were in uniform. Though serving they had found time to come and talk to Miss Gee, to leave instructions regarding their girls. Voices murmured from behind the study door about extra French, piano practice and games. Miss Gee's door opened and closed.

The parents looked sad-eyed when they left. Mothers and daughters cried and clung, fathers cleared their throats. We had a good view of these partings shielded by our magnolia. We watched the final waving, the wiping of forlorn tears. It started to rain. The unicorn looked on with blank eyes.

'Now it's a proper school full of proper girls.' Ula hopped

round the cheeseplant. We could hear the girls in the hall. Minutes earlier their faces had been wet with tears. They recovered quickly. They shouted catch phrases. 'Don't be so *feeble*', 'Same to you with double knobs on', 'I admire you more than somewhat', 'Oh catch me someone, ere I swoon'. The laughter sounded false, so soon after the farewells. Timidly we left the conservatory.

With faces pink and dry again the girls shook the rain from their hair. The aura of parents' fur coats, morocco leather and cigars was replaced by costly shampoo, well-scrubbed skin and laundered clothes. No one noticed us, they were engrossed in their reunion.

So we went back to the form room again to practise more writing. At our desk at the back of the room was the tall girl I had seen earlier who had come without parents or friends. I had noticed her pale hair, the way it hung round her cheeks and neck. She was looking at my pen and pencil set.

'Three sisters. My oh my.'

3

Phoebe was my first meeting with a real live schoolgirl. I would never forget her name or her face. She spoke slowly, drawlingly, her movements seeming slower because of her height. Her skin reminded me of moonstones, a kind of transparency. She had long-fingered hands. Her faintly greasy hair was pushed behind her ears. Her eyes seemed colourless, staring unblinkingly.

'I can tell you've been here for ages. Your uniform is so old.'

'Don't be so cheeky, Ula.'

'Your infant sister is right. It's more than ages. It feels as if I came before the flood.'

Her skirt was skimpy, with worn seams, her jersey sleeves were too short. The jersey was back to front, the vee neck backwards; her sleeves were pushed up to give a short-sleeved effect.

I had felt so proud of my uniform. I felt fussy now, over-dressed. I wanted my own hair in a low parting with a pushed-back fringe, to wear my own clothes back to front. She crossed her arms, gripping the elbows, she spoke with her long chin raised. She preferred rags to a new uniform. She was just

162

living for the day when she left this prison; she'd be sixteen soon, praise be.

'I like this school, Phoebe. This is my writing. Miss Gee told us that you were the head girl.'

I said quickly that Ula was slow at writing, but she didn't glance at Ula's page. She asked if we had any brothers.

'No, we haven't.' I spoke quickly before Ula could start talking about Bruno. I said my age and that I wasn't sure yet about school.

'I have one brother. A godsend, *je vous assure*.'

'Why "godsend", Phoebe? What is "*je vous* ..."? We did have ...'

'Ula talks too much, she's impossible.'

Phoebe smiled without interest. She said that we were only allowed outside the school with a relative. The Gee sisters had a complex about safety. Her brother collected her whenever possible. There was a hotel in the town, the Black Lion, did we know it? They served decent cocktails there.

'We saw you arrive in a taxi. Are your parents away as well?'

They were dead, she said, but not unhappily; she didn't feel the loss. Her uncle in America was her guardian. Sometimes she spent her holidays there. Once or twice she had stayed here, at school. Her closest friend and relative was her brother. She and Midge organized the school.

'Midge? Is that Margaret?'

'No one says "Margaret". Take no notice of what Miss Gee says. She's too old to be running a school. Her ideas are antique.'

Perhaps Phoebe would be here in the coming holidays. I would learn to move and smile like her. And she was clever, speaking French and travelling by taxi alone.

'Where is the younger Miss Gee? We haven't met her.'

'Probably still trying to locate some staff. Not that it makes a difference. The teaching here barely exists.'

She went to the blackboard, rubbed out Biblical Tableau practice and substituted Gym. She yawned. Her teeth were square and big. She had a large pointed tongue.

'Come on, everyone, let's go and unpack our things.'

Her red leather luggage had been taken up, her suitcase had labels of hotels in foreign countries. She loved and was used to travel. She piled quantities of clothes on her bed. Not much longer for her in this feeble and antique place, praise be.

'That isn't uniform, Phoebe. What are those clothes?'

Ula picked up a green frock with smocking across the yoke. Phoebe took it back and held it to her chest. A frock like green woollen cobweb, a frock for a grown-up.

'Mufti, of course. I'm not staying in these rags all day.'

'Mufti? What's that?'

I guessed it would be something to discourage us. It seemed that everyone wore their own home clothes at night except for the little ones. We were the new girls; we would look different, every night.

Phoebe went on throwing clothes about, she had no idea of my dismay. Tor wasn't the same, clothes didn't affect her or Ula so much. Another dress of holly-berry red, more sweaters in beautiful shades, a velvet bolero to match a skirt. I looked at Tor; she ought to realize, our uniforms were not enough. Each night we would stand out like fun figures. Would all their clothes be like Phoebe's, luxurious and distinct? She went on casually handling the soft shantungs and linens. She had a jewellery box with seed pearls in it and a string of coral beads. Why hadn't Mamma read the prospectus properly? Phoebe was putting on high-heeled velvet shoes.

'Oh Phoebe, wear the green dress to match the shoes, they're lovely.'

Ula was like a jester, jumping about, waiting on Phoebe the queen. She didn't envy Phoebe, she just liked serving her. Phoebe changed casually without drawing her curtains, standing white and tall in her vest.

'You've got lollopers, Phoebe, I can see them. Bonnie's aren't as big.'

'Be quiet, Ula. Shut up, can't you?'

'Don't be severe on the infant, she's harmless. The girls here call them "*pommes*".'

There was a lot of school jargon to learn it seemed, mostly words to do with bodily growth. I felt hot and uneasy, I didn't want to know about it. Often I just wished to stay a child. I wanted a figure like Phoebe's without the pain of growing, the pain of change. The higher you were in the school, the more jargon, to be kept a secret from the rest. Phoebe puffed herself proudly under the green smocking. She had brassieres if she wanted, too. She settled the soft pleats over her thighs. She didn't want to know about us or what we were feeling, she was interested in herself.

'Can I brush your hair, Phoebe?' Ula waved her tortoiseshell-backed brush. Phoebe had her hair cut expensively in London, and singed to get rid of split ends. She showed us, she smoothed her parting. She wanted no infants banging her head with a brush. At Christmas her brother would take her to nightclubs, she'd wear a backless gown and spindly golden heels. That was providing her brother was still in the country. He'd joined the army. Lucky beast.

'Why lucky? Will the war last long, do you think?'

She hoped it would last long enough for her to join up. She

admired her reflection, she clicked her heels and gave a salute. How much pocket money had we brought with us?

'What pocket money, Phoebe?'

The horror was starting again. Couldn't our family get anything right about coming to school?

'You mean you didn't realize? *Zut alors!* No money at all to buy anything? You'll need some. The food here is muck.'

Each girl brought money, Miss Gee encouraged it. Miss Patrice kept a Saturday shop. You could buy stamps, soap and stationery. There was jam, fruit, biscuits, even eggs. Phoebe said I should write home and ask for money. Was our father serving in the forces?

'Oh, he died. Ages ago, like your father.' I spoke quickly before Ula started again about death and disaster. But Phoebe was only interested in her own family. Her parents had died in an Indian earthquake. She had her rich uncle and her brother. No complaints. Brothers had friends, especially in the army, brothers could be useful. Was she thinking of boyfriends?

'Our mother is in the army, in a way she is.'

'The ATS? Why didn't you say?'

'She's going to entertain troops, as a singer. She was going to go into films.'

'A film star? You've succeeded in impressing me. I'm all ears. Tell me more.'

It wasn't true. There was nothing to tell her unless I invented it. Mamma had spoken about film work before the war. I knew nothing about films, I'd never seen one. I'd never been to a play. Ula used to cut pictures from film magazines with our cook in the kitchen. I didn't know a single film star's name. Phoebe's interest waned, I might have known it would. She went on admiring her hair, smiling to herself. If I'd answered she wouldn't have heard.

There were noises outside. 'Here they are, here comes everyone. Midge, I've been longing for you more than somewhat. You're here at last.'

Footsteps, voices, laughter, our future schoolmates crowded in. Cases banged, curtains rattled, hats and coats hurled through the air. Gasping, grimacing, shrieking, shoving. 'Same to you with double knobs on', 'Catch me someone ere I swoon'.

'Midge. At last.'

She was another tall girl with little dark eyes and bright cheeks. When she laughed her eyes creased into their sockets. She had very curly hair. All the faces looked pretty and confident, all smiling, all with friends. These were our future companions, squabbling over beds and cases, swapping holiday experiences, not asking us our names. 'My dear it was *him*, he actually *smiled* at me.' 'We were going on this cruise but Daddy wouldn't, he cancelled it. The *political* situation, my dear.' 'Has Gubgub lost weight? Hold me ere I swoon again.'

Gubgub was the plump one with red hair and a bangle above one elbow that looked too tight to be pulled down. Did all schoolgirls look and talk like this? Were they all affected and boastful, waving their brassieres around?

A tiny girl with a face like a monkey said that the waiter had stared at her pommes. 'Every time. Can you imagine?'

'My dear Barbie, have you any *pommes*? I hadn't noticed.'

'You're cruel, Phoebe. How is your brother? And how is you-know-who?'

'Hush, mice have ears.'

Phoebe was the most exciting, Gubgub was the fattest and

the most giggling, fingering her gold bangle. Barbie was the one they teased. I liked Midge's face, she seemed the friendliest. Phoebe said tonight she would sleep near the film star's daughters. Tomorrow she might move away. Midge and she were a team, friends of long standing, they sat close on her bed, whispering. Midge had delicate thin ankles, the rubber soles of her shoes were newly heeled. I had spilled ink on my blouse sleeve, I rubbed at it. I would wear my jersey turned back to front and push the sleeves up. I would stick out my chest and pull my cheeks in to look alluring. I parted my hair differently, combing it flat. Midge smiled at me.

'You haven't said your name yet. I'm Midge.'

'I know. A midge is a mosquito.'

She didn't mind me saying it, she smiled with her eyes. I felt I could trust her. I said our names and that I was worried about pocket money, stamps and mufti clothes. Her eyes seemed like gleaming slits of kindness. She had lots of stamps and clothes didn't matter. She had no interest in clothes or high heels. Which did I prefer, gym or games?

'We never did either. This is our first school. I'm dreading French and maths.'

She understood about liking to kick dead leaves or run on damp grass. She said I shouldn't worry about Biblical Tableau practice, it was just one of Miss Gee's fads. She treated me as an equal, not a newcomer. She had a large family of brothers and sisters. She was the eldest. She loved and missed her home. When she'd first come here she'd suffered from homesickness; she liked to welcome new girls now. I told her about our house being empty and how the army would be moving in. About my sisters and me being backward about lessons, about Ula letting us down. I knew that when there was privacy I would tell her about Ula's dark secret, how a child had died at her hand. And also how Bruno had died of croup after Tor and I had undressed him and left him naked under the Christmas tree. She was trustworthy and understanding.

'Sit by me at supper,' she said. I was chosen. I raised my chin to show my smooth neck rising from my jersey.

On the first night the girls ate alone without any staff present. No staff had been seen this term. We heard the crashing of plates in the kitchen, the squeaking of trolley wheels. The little girls treated Gumm with cheekiness, unafraid of his Hitler frown. 'Gumm, Gumm, eat your chewing gum.' Ula joined in excitedly.

It was cold corned beef and the potatoes were hard. Some of the girls had supplies of dried fruit and biscuits. Their voices shrieked above the plates and cutlery noises. 'Golly gumdrops, this meat is antique.' 'Catch me ere I swoon.'

Midge was by me, Tor on my other side, Ula was opposite, gobbling everything she could. Tor ate a little meat. The smell of the dining room took away my appetite. Midge, Phoebe and Gubgub were an accepted threesome. There were three little girls as young as Ula. The tiny girl with the face of a monkey was like a midget with Shirley Temple hair. She was thirteen.

Phoebe languished over her plate; she yawned hugely. 'I can't eat this. Give it to the hungry new girl.'

They all laughed and looked at Ula. I hated them but Ula didn't care, eating the food with enjoyment.

'Take no notice,' Tor whispered. 'Don't let them see you mind.'

Phoebe ate a banana that she'd brought with her. She licked it, her long jaw moving slowly, her long fingers barely touching the fruit. Except for Midge and the little ones they'd all changed for supper. Dresses vied with pinafore-topped skirts and thin blouses. Each girl had a cherished look. They picked at Gumm's supper and chattered.

'Enough, enough,' Phoebe called, flapping the banana skin on the table edge. 'I can't hear myself think. Remember the film star's daughters are here.'

I went red. Ula piped, 'She's not a film star. Mamma is singing for soldiers.'

'*Mamma?*' There was a chorus of mirth. '*Mamma?* You did say Mamma? Oh catch me Mamma ere I swoon.'

'Where did you spring from, Mamma's daughters? Did you come from Mars? How too antique for words.'

Ula laughed with them, she didn't understand malice. Tor and I looked at our plates.

'She's their mother whatever they call her or whatever she does. Leave them alone, they're new.'

I might have known Midge would stick up for us. Phoebe got up and left the dining room. Come on everyone, time for the game. The rest followed her in a flock.

'What is this game, Midge, please?'

It was played on the first night of each term. It was called 'Raiding', the whole school played. You picked sides. You took turns travelling from one end of the dormitory to the other by swinging on the curtain rails. If you touched the ground you were out. The trick was to lift yourself high, using your shoulders, swinging your hips and knees. You undressed and got into pyjamas first.

The basins thumped back and forth, plugs gurgled, lights flashed on and off. No one cared to remember blackout curtains or saving hot water, 'Raiding' mattered more than war. Ula brushed her teeth excitedly. She would play a real game at last.

Tor was sweating, she was nervous. She hated being despised or mocked.

'The little ones can stay with me, Phoebe. You and Gubgub head the teams.'

Midge guessed that Tor was frightened; no one need play if they didn't want to. 'Raiding' needed courage and strong arms. Tor kept her company on the bed with the little ones. I wouldn't show fear, I would try. I must make Midge and Phoebe admire me, my sisters would be proud of me.

'I'll have the film star's daughter. You, Bonnie, come with me.' Phoebe had picked me, I'd been elected. I would be gossamer light, quick as a bird. I would reach the basins without a falter, they would see I wasn't antique or quaint. Tor was on the bed with Ula, wringing her fingers. Ula had wanted to play but hadn't complained. Her white lock of hair was my mascot, their sympathy gave me strength.

The beds were pushed apart, the curtains drawn back tightly. My turn now, the railings are cold. My clean hands slip on the iron, I'm moving. One hand over the other, watch me swing. I'm flying like an angel, watch me, Ula. Look, Midge, I can do it. Lift your hips, swing your knees, work your shoulders, don't look down. Watch the curtain rail, watch your fingers, my sisters are cheering, they believe in me. 'Come on, Bonnie. Bonn-ee.' Little Barbie is weightless. Gubgub has fallen. Watch your hands, don't look down. My arms ache, my chest hurts, I'll show them. We're Mamma's children, you owe her respect. She's better than a film star, she's perfect. 'Bonn-ee. Bonn-ee.' She left us without pocket money or mufti, she's perfect, she's our mamma. Barbie, the midget, is wearing a nightdress, her toes are like sparrow's claws. Phoebe's pyjamas are piped creamy satin, whatever she does or has she's the best. Watch me, I'm a flying angel. Look Ula, look Midge, look Tor.

'Ah. Aaah. What a shame.'

I heard the groan before I realized I'd fallen. I had banged my foot, lost my grip. The curtains broke the fall, I slithered and flopped, my heels hit the floor, Barbie fell after me. There's only Phoebe. Phoebe won, she always does.

'Not bad, Bonnie, considering you're a novice. For a first attempt not bad.'

Someone laughed. I sat by Tor. She knew I felt vanquished. I was panting, I wasn't beaten. I would teach them to laugh.

'I say, can anyone here do the splits? Watch, this is how you do it.'

I had never tried any acrobatics, another voice had come from my mouth. You stretched one foot forward firmly, the other one behind, you went down. You could do anything if you made up your mind to it. It is will-power and determination. Push down, never mind the pain.

Phoebe watched and smiled. She put a foot before her, she sank like a bird on wings. Her thin legs settled at right angles to her body, she put her hands above her head, she watched me, she smiled at me.

'Phoebe, you're wonderful, you're the tops. I admire you more than somewhat.'

They cheer her, they congratulate her because they love her. Darling Phoebe is sublime.

I have pain in my thighs and humiliation. I have been punished for showing off. No one can outdo Phoebe the wonderful; I feel so ashamed I could die. I cannot die, my sisters need me. I must keep the promise to Mamma. It's Tor I worry most about, she's so thin and silent, she's not spoken to anyone here. This school is too grand, these girls are different, they are rich, we'll never fit in. They are cruel, they're contemptuous and shallow. Trying the splits has given me a pain.

In the night I woke up with the pain again. I walked barefooted between the beds, each containing a sleeping girl curled into various shaped lumps. The lavatory light was on. I must not pity myself, mustn't cry. It's just a pain, I'm not frightened. If a bomb came down I wouldn't care now, if my sisters died with me. Blood in my pyjamas, it can't be. Don't scream, it might be a dream. I will wake up in bed having dreamed of an air raid. A rusty splotch of red in my dream. I have injured myself inside from showing off, I tried the splits, now I'm paid. It's a dream of an air raid, a dream of a game, don't be frightened.

I leaned over my knees, I heard myself cry. Midge came to my help again. She pushed the lavatory door. Come, Bonnie, you're not dying, stop that crying. You're just menstruating, someone should have told you. About that blood coming, running and red. Blood that would come every month, nothing to do with splits, just menstruation. You would have it for most of your life.

'Don't men have it? It's disgusting.'

'Men don't have anything. It's to do with having a child. It hurts sometimes, it's nothing serious, even if you do have pains.'

She hadn't started yet, but she was ready for it. She had sanitary pads in her drawer. The older girls brought them in preparation. Sometimes they called it 'the flag'. The little ones didn't know about it. The older ones had their own lavatory. I might as well get used to the idea and be practical. It was how women were made.

I began to feel less afraid and more curious. I had learned an important secret of the school. I was a woman now, Midge told me, not like Tor and Ula. I'd never be quite the same, never be young again.

When I was in bed I thought Phoebe whispered something. 'Well, well, put out the flags.'

I got up early to look again. The pad had smudgy marks like the writing of a thick nibbed pen.

4

Having no pocket money or mufti was bad. Not knowing what to say was worse. We had never mixed with anyone, let alone children. There was the worry of the school slang. I must make Phoebe like me, I hoped that Midge already did. Showing off was frowned on. I heard Gubgub say that I was a swank. The thought that I would be a woman once a month was comforting. I mustn't mess my new pyjamas. Being a woman could be a messy nuisance in spite of the importance you gained. Midge didn't mind being a late starter, you might go on having that blood for at least thirty years. If you had a baby it would stop for a while. Midge was shocked over my ignorance. Babies, bodies, growing and blood were both lovely and awful, it was best to realize and understand as soon as you could. Being frightened was a hindrance. Knowing things early was best.

Gov must have considered these things too secret to be mentioned. We had never asked questions about our bodies, we stuck to knitting and raffia flowers. Midge gave me another towel rather reluctantly. Don't use it unless absolutely necessary, she said. She had a secret use for her towels that no one knew about. She might show me when the right moment came. I wanted to please her, but I didn't know how to stop the blood coming. I would try and let it drip into the lavatory if I could. At her home, she said, her family were open about everything; it made a difference to life.

'What is this secret, Midge?'

She would show me on Sunday if she could. I was to write to my mother and ask for the biggest pads. 'Remember, Bonnie, the largest, that's all I'm saying now.'

There were three sizes. The outsize ones were called Maternity Wear. The one I was wearing felt like a rabbit's tail. I needn't have worried, though, the blood stopped coming the next day. As I grew older my cycle would settle, Midge told me. Don't forget the letter to my mother.

School assembled in the chapel room. I looked forward to seeing Miss Patrice. The sisters didn't always agree, it seemed. Miss Patrice believed in more practical and physical pastimes. There were other ways of achieving inner elegance and grace besides Bible studies and handwriting. She would have been happy to teach tree felling or dairy farming; as it was she taught us games.

Miss Gee stood on the dais in the chapel room, still wearing grey with a white blouse. Miss Patrice was by her. She was quite different, with a big face and mottled, sallow skin. Her long lashes looked out of place, her eyes were brown and large as a cow's. She watched but she didn't join in the hymns and prayers required by her sister. Ula liked singing, she liked showing that she knew the tune though she couldn't read the words. 'There's no discouragement, Shall make him once relent, His first avowed intent to be a pilgrim.' I could see that Miss Patrice didn't agree with religion. Midge said that Miss Gee was high church. I imagined a tall steeple and a choir that sang very high notes. Miss Gee gave thanks for the school comradeship and good food. We prayed to win the war and our soul's guidance, we prayed to retain pure hearts. I moved my lips, I wanted to fit in, I thought of Mamma again. I didn't think it was true that she'd miss us. I missed and thought about her still. She ought to know that I was beginning to become a woman. This praying was the final straw.

Midge had showed me the prefects' lavatory near the boiler room. In the corner was an enamel bin for used pads. The stained lumps wrapped in paper gave a sweetish rotten smell when you lifted the lid. It was called the 'flag bin' by the prefects.

'But I'm not a prefect, Midge. Are you sure?'

'I'm sure I'm sure. You'll be a prefect. Phoebe and I choose.'

I felt too new to be a prefect. I was wrongly dressed, without pocket money or knowledge of French. Under the cover of singing, Phoebe hissed, 'How is Mamma's girl this morning? Put out the flag yet?' She turned her blind-looking eyes to the window before I could tell her I was a prefect. She had combed her hair so flat you could see her scalp through it; she was still beautiful, though she had as much colour as a piece of string.

The praying and singing ended. Miss Patrice took her place on the dais. She had an announcement to make which was more in the nature of a request. The present emergency was testing; we must memorize the national slogans. 'Dig for Victory', 'Save for the Brave', 'Careless Talk Costs Lives'. My sisters and I knew no one in the forces, whose whereabouts we might let slip to the enemy, though we'd liked to see them passing in lorries. Soon soldiers would sleep in our home. Phoebe's brother was going to be an officer, Gubgub had a cousin at sea. Various girls' fathers had positions in the Admiralty or the War Office, where they would probably stay until peace was declared. Miss Patrice spoke of saving soap, and the economical use of stationery. We could save on laundry by taking extra care with our clothes. Meanwhile her Saturday shop opened each week, the proceeds of which went towards the war. Now for her special announcement regarding digging for victory. Each of us was to own a garden plot and grow vegetables. We would plant and eat our own potatoes with pride.

Midge put her hand up. 'Does it mean we should take orders from Gumm?'

'Midge, you have anticipated me.' She spoke about the reduction in numbers of pupils and of staff. At the present time there was just Miss Gee and herself. The girls looked glad. It seemed that the two sisters were to teach all lessons this term. For the sake of convenience we would work in one form. She relied on her prefects and monitors to help the younger girls in need of coaching. Her eyes were a warm fudgy brown, she spoke with missionary zeal. How could I coach anyone when I knew nothing? I was used to Tor helping me. Gumm was to take over all the cooking.

'What about games?' Midge asked.

Miss Patrice looked strained. It was a question of the croquet lawn and the front lawn; which was to be used for games and which for the allotments? Miss Gee tapped her ruler on the edge of her hymn book. The front lawn must remain untouched. No ball games, running feet or digging spades must sully the grass in front. The green peace of the school entrance must remain undisturbed. No digging or ball games in front.

So the croquet lawn must be sacrificed for the growing of

home produce. The chapel room must be sacrificed for the use of indoor games. Was this why the sisters had been arguing yesterday morning? Miss Gee's chapel room was also the strongest room in the building. Until a shelter could be built, it would be used during air raids as a place of safety.

'So, girls,' Miss Patrice called decisively. 'Indoor games indoors. The croquet lawn to be dug into plots.'

'And girls,' reminded Miss Gee, 'remember your gas masks, carry them at all times, make use of the gas mask hooks.'

Midge explained the Off Games book. Those who had the flag could sign their names there. The sisters didn't agree over this either. Miss Gee allowed you to lie on your bed and feel delicate. Miss Patrice was brisk; it was self-indulgent to give in, a run with a skipping rope round the lawn was her remedy. Differences over religion, menstruation and the use of the grounds were causes of friction. Barbie, the tiny girl, liked to eavesdrop, she had heard them argue in their private quarters beyond the conservatory. The sisters vied for power. Gubgub had once woken to find Miss Gee bending over her with a hot-water bottle. They referred to the flag as 'the time of the month' or 'being off colour'.

The chapel room had no equipment for use as a gymnasium, no parallel bars, no springboards, mats or ropes.

I signed my name in the book with the pencil attached by a rubber band; I wrote in copperplate. I was pleased not to have to leap with a skipping rope and run the risk of spoiling Midge's clean pad.

'Don't look so glum,' Miss Patrice said. She had a bouncing walk, moving on the balls of her feet. The creases of her pleated tunic scarcely moved, remaining sharp. You couldn't imagine her in anything but a dark blouse and navy serge but she must have once been young. Had those fudge-coloured eyes ever loved? The younger girls became giggly when she came near. 'Catch me, hold me someone, it's *her*.' But they didn't mean it, they were showing off. Midge said that both sisters were too old for their job, that the present poor staffing was their own fault, nothing to do with the war. They mismanaged, staff didn't want to stay here. The school was badly planned, badly managed without enough space for games. The rush of new entries that they'd hoped for turned out to be just me and my sisters. The girls left this school with few educational attainments. Some went on to finishing schools. Phoebe's uncle had planned to send her to Switzerland. Because of the war she hoped it would be the ATS instead.

Miss Patrice told me to walk round the croquet lawn while the others did indoor games. While they jumped their ropes or passed clubs from hand to hand I would kick leaves outside again in my boots. I heard them shouting. Was that Ula laughing? There was the hoop she had pushed her foot into, there was the mound of dead leaves and the molehill. I was alone and it was autumn. I was still happy with the Wellingtons.

The school pageant was planned for 21 December. There was Biblical Tableau practice every day. Miss Gee tapped a rhythm on the radiator with her ruler while the girls walked round the dais. The little ones sang in the corner. Bedspreads were wrapped round the older ones to make them appear biblical; they were portraying ancient times. Midge was Moses, holding the stone tablets up. I didn't know the difference between the Old and New Testament. I knew about the birth of Jesus but not much else. I dreaded being asked to sing. 'I'm off games, Miss Gee.' Perhaps she would let me lie down.

'Join the little ones in the corner and sing.' It was the same hymn.

'Sing up, Bona, I cannot hear.'

'Though fancies flee away, I'll fear not what men say, I'll labour ...'

'Enough, Bona. Stop singing. You are tone deaf. I suspected it from your speaking voice. Just move your lips to the words.'

I blushed deeply. Everyone had heard. The film star's daughter couldn't sing a note, she had an ugly speaking voice. How more than somewhat bad.

Miss Gee leaned closer towards Ula's singing face. Ula knew she sang well. Miss Gee smiled with radiance.

'A natural soprano, pure and high. Sing, Ula, as loud as you can. Bona, you had better go and help with the bedspreads. Then sit down and keep quiet.'

'Well, well, wardrobe maid,' Phoebe said, in contempt of the whole affair. Religion, gym and pageants were nonsense to be endured until she joined the army. I pictured her relaxing in officers' bars with a peaked cap on her head. Long cigarettes would dangle from her pale fingers while the officers declared their love.

I couldn't help feeling proud and delighted with Ula, though I was jealous too. As the leading choir girl she would wear angel's wings and sing a solo. I supposed I would have to settle bedspreads to fall round her toes and comb her hair fluffily. Our Irish cook must have taught her to sing. We would have no one to come and watch the pageant. I would beg Mamma to come. I hadn't written yet, because of the embarrassment of asking for sanitary towels.

'Dear Mamma. Please will you try and come to our play at Christmas? Also could you send some stamps? The other girls change each night into other clothes but we can't. Love from Bonnie.'

On Sunday I saw Midge's secret. In a way it altered my life. She led the way past the croquet lawn, down the path to the potting sheds. At the end of the garden was Gumm's hut with a corrugated tin roof and a large metal incinerator on legs with an odd chimney-like lid.

'Where's the surprise? What is that awful smell?'

'It's for burning rubbish. It smells worse when it's just been lit.'

It was Gumm's job to see to the incinerator. The surprise was in his hut. We were out of bounds, but there was no one to see us. We pushed open the door of his hut. Midge said that in summertime he sat with his pipe and a flask of tea. The war had changed his life too; now he was indoors cooking meals. There were bundles of newspapers and sticks there. Under some sacking in the corner was the surprise.

'Midge. I had no idea. Can I hold it?'

'Not yet. She must get to know you.'

She had trusted me with her secret pet. I felt suddenly different. My face felt as if it had broken. I hadn't smiled for so long, not since Ireland. I knew Midge's secret and the whole world had improved.

We watched her run to the bars expectantly, sniffing and tame. When she smelled Midge's fingers her whiskers trembled, her nose and forepaws raised. She ran to the exercise wheel, paddling her paws on it; the wheel squeaked as it turned. Then she came back to Midge's fingers. Was she hungry?

'How do you know it's a she mouse?'

'It's obvious, can't you see? That's why we need sanitary pads, her babies should be born soon.'

Midge had a pad in her raincoat pocket. I helped to undo the gauze. We tore the wool into fluff, we relined the nesting box at the other end of the cage. Cleanliness was important, she told me, the nest must be warm and fresh. Mice were nervous, they took fright easily, if threatened they might kill their young. We fed her with toast fragments, we fetched fresh water from the tap outside. An apple core or a carrot was good for them but their basic diet was oats. Milk was good for nursing mothers but too much made their urine smell. The cage had an enchanting frowstiness. I pressed my face closer. Midge had trusted me, I trusted her, I didn't feel anxious or alone. I asked timidly about the babies. How did they get out, how did they start? I added that I did know about it of course, but I'd forgotten. The details had slipped my mind. Would she remind me? I knew she would not hold me in scorn.

She explained patiently about the mouse's life cycle, from birth and copulation to death. She showed me the enlarged stomach, the little entrance under the tail. It happened there, the male mouse put in the seeds, eighteen to twenty days later the babies came out. She kissed the sweet nose lovingly. Nature was magic, wasn't it? Those dots were nipples for breast feeding. She ate a lot, especially now. Getting to the hut was a difficulty sometimes, that was why Midge had made herself a garden prefect. I would be her garden assistant now. I would have the authority to keep the others away. She spoke of pets in general while the mouse's nose went on quivering.

At Midge's home each child owned something, a rat, rabbit, guinea pig or bird. That was how she knew about animals. The pets were allowed in the house at Christmas to run freely beneath the tree. The family sang carols and opened presents while the animals looked on. We'd never had presents or a tree like other people. The one that Tor and I had when we'd undressed Bruno had been a stunted little lopsided larch, not a proper tree. It was the night following that he'd caught his croup and died. No one had said it was our fault, but they thought it. Like Ula's knifing episode in Ireland, it wasn't mentioned. Midge's Christmas sounded lovely, with other children, presents and singing, candles and exciting food. This year I would be here with just my sisters.

'I'll give you one of the babies if you like, Bonnie.'

'Midge. Are you sure?'

'I'm sure I'm sure. But absolutely no one must know. No one at all.'

'I swear it. You can trust me.'

'Not even Phoebe knows about the mouse. Don't ever let me down.'

'She's your best friend, isn't she? She's not like you.'

'We've known each other for years. I understand Phoebe. She's not as confident as you might think. She needs to impress everyone, sometimes it makes her cruel.'

Then I told Midge about our family secrets. About Ula killing her friend. About our brother dying after being left naked to catch cold. How we never mentioned these sad awful happenings. She swore that she'd never tell. But said that some secrets were less frightening if other people knew them, someone who understood and didn't lay blame. I felt relieved to have told her. I would have trusted her with my life.

'When can I have the mouse?'

I must be patient, she said, they weren't even born yet. And mind, Bonnie, not a soul must know. No pets were allowed in this school, the Gees didn't approve. They believed that their girls should show kindness to each other rather than to pets.

Their policy of self-governance was muddled when it came to animals and religion.

At supper Phoebe waved a letter from her brother. He'd started his officers' course. Then he might take off for anywhere. How she envied him. Join the army and see life.

5

I waited for an answer from Mamma. She didn't write but a parcel arrived.

'Look, Tor. Oh, Tor. Look.'

Mamma had gone to Liberty's again. Now we too could wear angora wool at supper time, we too had patent leather shoes. The dresses had wide collars and belts that laced in front with a thong instead of buckling. Oh look. We're as good as Phoebe now. And I knew something about Midge that Phoebe didn't know. Midge and I trusted each other. I had felt the mouse tail curving my wrist, felt the cool prick of its claws. Mamma had no time to write, she had too much on her mind. She had found time to go to London for our sakes, she had remembered our sizes in clothes. She had remembered that I liked blue. Blue stood for hope and remembrance, blue for the colour of our eyes. Had she paused at the perfume counter on her return? I sniffed the dress, was that her scent? Had she sipped tea and nibbled a sandwich at the same restaurant, while the band played that dreaming tune? Lovely colour, lovely material, lovely unpressed pleats. Who cared about stamps, pocket money or sanitary pads.

Before long I would own a mouse. The mother mustn't be disturbed for three weeks after the birth, when the babies would grow fur and open their eyes. You must separate the males from the females before they started interbreeding. I felt clever and knowing now about mice. I put my blue frock on, I felt like dancing. Something rustled, something in the pocket, something more, another surprise.

'Look Tor, another present.'

Mamma had bought me a precious keepsake because I was the oldest, I was the one in charge. The hands were shaped like little arrows on the gold face. It had a rapid tick. It was valuable, it was nicer than Phoebe's. I would put it under my pillow at night. Midge had a cheap one, her parents were not well off. Her brothers and sisters went to grammar schools and lived at home. She and Phoebe had come here at the same time, which must be why they were friends. We all slept in one dormitory now and worked in one class. When the Gee sisters left us alone we did as we liked. Midge, Gubgub and Phoebe helped with the younger ones. No one mentioned French or maths. The form room was warm when we were all in it. Only the gas mask hooks on the wall were a reminder of war.

The croquet lawn was disappearing to be replaced by plots. First the croquet hoops were taken up, the grass dug over. The rabbits and moles must find new homes. Tor and I shared a plot, Ula was next to us. Our fingernails broke, our backs ached but we were close. I longed to confide my plans for mouse ownership. I couldn't betray Midge's trust. The cold wind blew our hair in our eyes. I waited for the signal from Midge. She told me to take the stones and weeds in the wheelbarrow to the rubbish dump. 'Be ready to come to the hut.'

Each girl piled her rubbish on the path ready for collecting.

'Can I come with the wheelbarrow, Bonnie? Why can't I?'

'Midge chose me. Get on with the raking.'

Ula wanted to grow mustard and cress in shapes to come up next year. 'Hail Unicorn, Welcome Spring'. We had to explain that it wasn't possible. Phoebe refused to join in work outside. As head girl she chose to remain apart. Gubgub was kind, comforting the little ones if they scratched themselves on brambles, her red hair bright in the cold air. The school relied on the prefects and monitors, the Gee sisters looked so tired. I longed to tell Ula my secret, it would make her happy. Midge was coming, I could hear the barrow wheels. She paused by each girl. The frost-stiffened sods of earth and grass were piled into the barrow with the leaves and beech-nut casings. Midge was breathing hard. I took one handle of the barrow and we moved off down the path. We tipped it on to the rubbish dump. Now was the time for the hut.

'Don't make a sound, Bonnie, I'm warning you.'

I felt the warmth of her breath. Her cheek had a mud smear, her slitty eyes gleamed. Remember, Bonnie, not a sound.

I smell the beloved and unmistakable smell of mouse again. The cage is empty, no mouse to welcome us. We push our faces closer, listening, we hold our breath, it's too wonderful to believe. Tiny rustlings, silence and our breathing, tiny squeakings, silence again. Listen to the rustling and squeaking of motherhood.

'They're born. Born at last.'

We felt proud as if we'd worked a miracle; no midwife could have felt more joy. The mother had no time to run out and greet us, she had her family, her destiny for which she'd been born. We didn't speak again, we left food and crept away. What we felt must be holy rapture.

'Why were you so long, Bonnie? Your face is red. Are you cold?'

'It's the wind, stupid. Will it be lunchtime soon?'

My sisters were still squatting by their allotments. A fresh gust of wind blew grit over us. Tor had always longed for a pet. Midge was my benefactress, she knew our secrets. Why couldn't my sisters find their own friends? Tor was too dependent, too clinging, too silent. Did proper mothers feel as I did, bored with their children, stuck with them, wanting to get away from them? How irritating they were, looking and questioning. I'd never have real children. I wouldn't marry until I was old.

Tor had been quick to learn the school jargon but she never used it. She only spoke to Ula and me. She had her precious diary to scribble in, that was all she wanted. I couldn't remember her laughing for months. Ula was perky, she could tell the time now, they both deserved normal fun. I didn't want them bothering when I was thinking of the mouse family. I could have smacked their faces for two pins.

It was Saturday, we did no lessons, just gardening or hanging about. There was no recreation room, just the form room. We sat at our desks at night. Midge lent me *The Study and Care of Rodents*. It became my Bible. I sat learning it while the rest gossiped or combed their hair. The Gee sisters were spending more and more time in their rooms beyond the conservatory. We did as we pleased, even eating supper at our desks. Gumm did less cooking now, often just sandwiches and perhaps some plain biscuits which we washed down with tea. My period was an important landmark in life for me. Finding the mice had brought me joy.

Miss Gee continued to pray for the war effort. Miss Patrice exhorted us to dig for victory and to save for the brave. The war was quite important and interesting for grown-up people to worry about. What mattered most was my sisters and me.

'Midge, I'll write to Mamma again. This time I will ask her. The babies must have everything they need.'

The form room door opened. Phoebe stood there.

'Hullo everyone. He's here, he's come to fetch me. My brother came. We're off for the weekend.'

I only glimpsed his face and hair the colour of pale string, like Phoebe's. 'A bientôt,' Phoebe murmured.

The girls giggled with jealousy and excitement. So handsome, so debonair. Lucky Phoebe, she was the prettiest and most favoured, off now for celebrations at the Black Lion Hotel. We all envied her more than somewhat, it was swoon-making. We were stuck here with just old Gumm.

6

We ate our supper sandwiches and speculated. Was Phoebe drinking champagne or cocktails, eating roast duck with orange segments by the light of candles? Was she discussing the war? Would her brother tell of his regiment's destination? We had seen his photograph, now we had seen the man. He was real and wonderful, he had her languid expression, her long-fingered hands. What would we not have given to be in her place? Gubgub spoke with yearning of smoked salmon and tiny peas. Midge liked lamb hash with carrots. Everyone had a favourite dish except Tor who didn't join in. Ula liked rock cakes made with jam in the centre. I liked hearing about food as we ate our frugal meal. I had never drunk alcohol except for some sherry once, when Bruno had died. I had only eaten in a restaurant once, that time with Mamma in London. I had never been close to anyone in love except the couple at the next table who had the diamond ring. I would always think of Mamma when I heard the dream song or smelled roses. I even thought of her when a spoon clinked.

'Midge, do you know a song called "When I grow too old to dream"?'

She said she did, it was rather sad. We discussed songs then. There was one called the Umbrella Song on a record. Barbie had a gramophone though it was broken. You had to start winding the handle as soon as the tune started, otherwise it wavered and wailed and became unrecognizable. If you wound without stopping you risked breaking the spring inside. Barbie didn't mind lending the gramophone but she stayed near it, her tiny arm working the handle like a piston. You got the idea of the tune in spite of the distortion; it was something to do besides talk. No one wanted to think about war news, though seeing Phoebe's brother made it all more real. He was the only soldier I knew by name, though I had barely got a glimpse of him. Mamma probably knew a lot of soldiers now. Miss Gee didn't mind Phoebe going out. Her brother was one of the fighting forces for whom she daily prayed. I thought of Phoebe lying under a black silk eiderdown printed with peonies in a room in the Black Lion Hotel while we slept in two rows here. Barbie was given to snoring, Ula moaned and ground her grey teeth. How would I manage my mouse at Christmas time when my sisters and I were alone? It would be grown and active by then. I longed to feel its whiskers, its slender tail curving my wrist. The claws of a mouse felt ecstatic. Grown-ups missed a lot by regarding them as pests.

'I've never had champagne,' Ula said boastfully. 'I know about whisky, of course. There's poteen too, that's illegal.'

Carried away, she added that she wouldn't mind a night in a hotel, it would make a pleasant change. Gubgub said sharply that she was just a bumptious little child too much given to showing off. Midge, the peacemaker, said they didn't have alcohol in their home, that it made you sleepy and rude. Each child in her family had certain tasks, they had no servants like the other girls here. Sending Midge to this school was a sacrifice for her parents and they were not satisfied. Midge wasn't learning enough. Unless the situation improved they had written to say she must leave. I had never seen Mamma holding a duster or boiling water. We had had our governess and nurse and our cook. The more I heard about Midge's home the lovelier it sounded, especially at Christmas time. I supposed that our house would be full of soldiers now. Would they respect Mamma's chintz furnishings? Would generals sleep in our beds?

'Let's put the Umbrella Song on again, may we, Barbie? I'll wind it, let me.'

'Can I see your book, Bonnie? What's it about? Mice? How sweet.'

'Anyone want to play noughts and crosses? This French waiter said noughts and kisses, my dear.'

'Let me wind, Barbie, you're too little.'

'Same to you with double knobs on.'

We missed Phoebe. We expected to see her pale, half-blind stare again in the doorway, to hear her sarcastic drawl. I had a dream that night of furless rats and mice gnawing each other; the rats had long red teeth and sightless eyes.

'You blame Ula for making a noise, Bonnie. You were moaning in your sleep just like her.'

All three of us had awful dreams sometimes. We couldn't climb into each other's beds for comfort, you couldn't do that at school. I thought of Phoebe again to help the dream to fade. Was she sleeping under the peony eiderdown or swaying to a jazz band in her high heels and her bra? She didn't mind having no real home or parents. Joining the army was her sole goal.

I would choose a white mouse if there was one, with peaceful, pale pink eyes.

On Monday morning Miss Gee spoke through grim lips from her dais. We sang no hymn, prayed no prayer for the war effort, she had important news that would affect us all. She paused, holding her ruler as if for strength. Had something happened to Phoebe? She hadn't returned last night. Miss Gee had had a visit from the local billeting officer. It seemed there was a problem with some children evacuated from London who had failed to settle in foster homes. Local householders in the town were hurt and uneasy; the children wouldn't respond to care, their manners were rude and disruptive. As our school was not carrying the full number of pupils, Miss Gee had no alternative but to offer a sanctuary. No patriot could refuse this call. The country needed us, she and Miss Patrice had agreed. The children would arrive shortly. There was silence. Miss Gee stood like a sentry on duty. Any questions, girls?

'Will they do lessons with us, Miss Gee?' Midge asked.

The strange children would continue their studies in the town. Their own teacher had come with them from Clerkenwell, a person used to their ways. 'We are short of staff here, don't forget, Margaret.'

'I'd like them to learn with us. Our lessons are sometimes—'

'Ula, put your hand up before you speak, please. The children will sleep here only.'

Their weekends would be spent at school. It would be fresh opportunity for patriotism. Our land called, we would give up our strength and our beds. This was a new meaning of lending to defend. She had not anticipated Magnolia House becoming a refuge for less privileged children. Midge asked where they would sleep. Would they obey the prefects and monitors?

Miss Gee made it clear that the strangers must submit to our school regulations while under its roof. We must realize that they would be unfamiliar with etiquette and *savoir-faire*. Elegance and inner grace would be unknown qualities. We must be patient. Any questions?

Ula put up her hand. 'Will they have fleas?'

The girls tittered. I hated Ula again for making herself so conspicuous. I admired her too. I didn't want any strange children invading us just when school was getting better. They might smell or steal my watch. I put my own hand up.

'How many children, Miss Gee? How long will they be here?'

'That is not for you to question, Bona. This is war.'

War was silly. Loving your country was silly. No one asked us if we wanted to fight or take in strangers. Old Gumm was upset this morning, the toast was uneatable.

Miss Patrice was in a state of exhilaration. London children held no threat for her, she welcomed the challenge. This was her opportunity to assume leadership from her sister. Miss Gee was feeling her age. Miss Patrice wore her thin locks flattened into a dark-coloured bandeau like a little soft crown. These strange children were our war bonus, she said earnestly, a chance for each one of us to shine. She would like to offer a prize to the most helpful Magnolia girl. The strangers would be homesick, we must welcome them with arms opened wide. They might not be used to English properly expressed; we must talk clearly and slowly. Their manners might seem quaint, their hygiene less than adequate.

'Do you mean they don't wash?'

Miss Patrice didn't rebuke Ula for her practical questions. Remember that we were asked to save fuel. Share with those less fortunate. Poor Gumm would be even busier. She counted on her Magnolias to help both indoors and out.

I thought that the two old ladies and the elderly gardener already had enough to do. Miss Gee had been silly to accept.

'Cockneys are renowned for their courage and their humour, girls. Instead of doubting, worrying and wondering, let us pull with a will and smile.'

She hoped that we would share our good fortune with enthusiasm. She would like us to go to our allotments now and start sectioning them into halves. We would welcome the strangers with a gift of land.

There was no sign of Phoebe. The two sisters were too perturbed to notice she was still gone. We grumbled as we put on our raincoats. Why should we share our gardens? I liked having my sisters near, without strangers listening to us. Miss Patrice gave us wooden stakes and lengths of string. Measure and mark out portions for the strangers. Generosity was better than gold. Drive the stakes, wind the string, make ready the precious soil. Land was heritage, give it freely. Share and care, girls, care and share.

Ula had broken a plate at supper. She had collected the china pieces to make an edge for our plots. I missed the croquet lawn, the molehills, croquet hoops and leaves. The cold brown earth looked unfriendly, with the stakes, string and broken china. I cut Ula's string with a pruning knife, remembering her fear of knives. Miss Patrice patrolled the path as we laboured, her rubber soles quick with joy. I felt under my sleeve for Mamma's gift. I would always wear it to be on the safe side. The Clerkenwells might be light-fingered, they might hate us and do us harm. I didn't know what heritage meant. I guessed that Tor was feeling as I did, excited, curious and annoyed.

'They won't be sharing lessons with us, Tor. At least we can be thankful for that.'

Miss Patrice heard me. She stood still, her fudge-coloured

eyes looked sad under her little cloth crown. Sharing was caring, Bonnie, remember that, the strangers were far from their homes. We had so much here, practise *noblesse oblige*, consider others. 'Yes, girls, I am speaking of love. This is your chance to practise charity.'

We tittered and felt uneasy, she embarrassed us with her lectures. Generosity, patriotism, sharing and caring. Same to you with double knobs on, go away, leave us alone. Her face had a melted look in the cold weather, her eyes were liquid with zeal, her nostrils gleamed. She said that with Christmas approaching some of us might like to ask a stranger home with us.

'Does that mean they won't go back to Clerkenwell for the holiday?' I asked sharply. Would our holiday plans be upset? There was my mouse to consider now, as well as my sisters. How Miss Patrice's face irritated me. How silly all the girls looked kneeling by their plots. Where was Midge with the barrow?

Then she appeared wheeling it carefully past the potting sheds, but she wasn't looking at me but behind me.

I turned. A group of girls appeared round the school. These must be the Clerkenwells arriving before we'd had time to imagine what they'd be like. What struck me was that they looked annoyed.

They'd been turned out of their town billets without being consulted. They looked shabby but far from abject. Their coats were too short and tight under the armpits, they wore plimsolls or sad-looking shoes. They stared back at us with knowing eyes. A bus had brought them from their school in the town with their luggage. The girl in front had a red beret. Her coat didn't button. I saw a row of little warty spots round her neck like a necklace. She took her hands from her pockets. Her dirt-rimmed nails had flaking red polish on them. Her wrists were bony and she wore lipstick. My sisters and I were still kneeling with stakes and string in our hands.

'What you lot doing? This a prayer meeting?'

'Did you see our unicorn? You should have come in by the front door, not the side.'

'Be quiet, Ula. That's one of our headmistresses, Miss Patrice, over there.'

Miss Patrice rushed forward, her lashes damp with welcome.

'Cordial greetings, we extend our welcome. I speak on behalf of us all.'

'Yeh? Ta. Where's the other head lady? The old one.'

Miss Patrice explained that Miss Gee was feeling tired. That we were preparing and dividing our plots to give our guests as a welcome. Working in pairs we would till and cull, dig for victory, lend to defend. We offered them land.

'What, grubbing in this cold? No ta.'

Miss Patrice blinked. We were preparing the soil for spring vegetables, though the little ones might be allowed flowers. A few button daisies or pansies perhaps, but culinary produce was our aim.

'Don't fancy vedges. Other than tin peas.'

The rest closed behind her in a sleazy-coated scowling band.

'Well, well, put out the flags,' drawled Phoebe's familiar voice. She was back with her coat round her shoulders like a cloak, her hat brim making a halo round the back of her head. Our queen had returned from her weekend at the Black Lion. The visitors sniffed, unimpressed by Phoebe's soft silk stockings, her shoes with little heels. Their own socks or laddered cotton stockings creasing into their lamentable shoes didn't shame them. Phoebe was too big for her boots.

'Phoebe, child. You are back in time to welcome our London guests.'

'London guests? *Zut alors.*'

Phoebe didn't ask why they were here; she assumed that the Gee sisters were mad as usual. She should have stayed at the Black Lion with her soldier brother. She must be missing him. It was war and he had gone. I would have been happy for her to turn to me for consolation. I would heal her broken heart. The strangers were not impressed. She was just another toffee-nosed cow with more swank than sense. The Magnolia girls rose from their cramped positions. The hems of our raincoats were damp, our Wellingtons were smeared with soil. I wiped my hands on my hanky. Miss Patrice said, adjusting her bandeau, that Phoebe should have been here a moment sooner, in time for the welcome. Phoebe shrugged; the party of cockneys were of no interest.

'What's that animal in front on the gatepost?' The girl in the red beret seemed to be their spokesman.

'Our unicorn, dear, our mascot. The unicorn is a symbol of protection.'

'You mean bombs and that?'

Miss Patrice explained the legend about the unicorn protecting the other animals, thus it was held in high esteem. By dipping its horn into poisoned waters they were made safe. The girl in the beret sniffed.

'Figuratively speaking, my dear. The beast is heterogeneous. Did you notice the lion's tail? It is an aggregate of other animals. It has elephant's feet.'

'Can't say I did. Where are our beds? We got to get our things straight.'

Miss Patrice hoped that their stay here would be companionable. Would each of them like to choose a Magnolia girl to be her guide and mentor?

'Guide? Eh?'

'We want you to look on our girls as godmothers or aunties. Come girlies, choose a chum.'

'You joking? We got to find our beds. We got to get back to school. Oh all right, I'll have you.'

The beret girl walked over to Phoebe who yawned in her face. They walked ahead back inside the school. The rest of us followed. Miss Patrice ought to have warned us; we didn't feel godmotherly or even friendly towards these children. I supposed we would have to give in. But Midge had other views.

'I don't want to be anyone's godmother, thank you, Miss Patrice. Being head girl is quite enough.'

And she was in charge of the grounds now that Gumm was indoors all day. She wanted to make it clear that Bonnie was her second-in-command outside. Just Bonnie, no one else.

I would do anything for Midge. I would heave rocks to the rubbish dump single-handed, I would clean the potting sheds, render the incinerator odourless as long as our mice were safe.

By the time we were back in the dormitory Phoebe and the girl in the beret whose name was Red had arranged to sleep next to each other. The other five could choose to sleep in either dormitory. Red and Phoebe drew the curtains round their beds at the far end, away from the clank of the basins and the gurgle of the bath plugs. Red thumped her case down. 'Tell me all,' I heard Phoebe say. They whispered, occasionally they laughed. Red's laughter was snickering; Phoebe laughed almost soundlessly, on an indrawn breath with her lips pulled into a square. In no time they had become an exclusive society with a membership of two.

The school felt different, already the smell had changed. Keatings powder, greasy hair and plimsolls took over from talcum powder, toothpaste and new clothes. Midge was sitting on her bed reading, with her hair hanging over her face. Had Phoebe forgotten her now that she'd found Red? Midge was too proud to show that she cared.

The other strangers were slow to speak. We all strained to hear what Phoebe and Red were saying. A smell of vanilla essence seemed to creep through their curtains. It was Red's perfume. Her boyfriend liked it. It lingered on your clothes. The Magnolia girls were alerted; none of them spoke openly of boys. They had crushes on waiters they'd seen on their holidays, they giggled over 'you-know-who', they swooned at the names of each other's brothers. Their 'you-know-whos' didn't exist. Red made the word boyfriend sound thrilling and wicked. Midge thought all that sort of thing absurd. Red was a novelty; we were agog.

Miss Patrice had spoken to the billeting officer about the strangers' health records. She needed their London addresses. Had she noted Red's warty looking spots? I tried to peer through the gap in the curtains. Red was using a disgusting puff on her neck. She had an almost lipless mouth. Phoebe was holding

Red's tin compact as if it were platinum. Red, with her boyfriend and vanilla perfume, engrossed her. She saw me watching and closed the curtains. The other visitors tipped their cases on to their beds as we had done when we arrived. Their cases were cardboard, split and broken, they had threaded the strings of their gas mask cases through the handles. The clothes in the cases looked like rags washed to no colour. A girl kept sneezing and coughing. She wiped her eyes on a piece of torn vest. Another girl gave her a piece of cough candy with paper sticking to it. They found a comic and started to read, their mouths making sucking sounds between the coughs and sneezes.

'Can I look?' Ula asked.

The comic looked exciting and colourful, you could understand without needing to read. Ula was used to film magazines but we'd never had comics. Tor had gone out, probably to the form room. The visitors showed no interest in our school. They didn't require godmothers or friendship, they needed to get back to their own school. They looked at our bath cubicles with dislike and suspicion. Too much hot water made you soft in the head.

'Now, girlies, settling comfortably?'

Miss Patrice was busy and happy. Had everyone chosen a fairy godmother? Where was Phoebe, her trusted head girl? She cleared her throat. Sharing cubicles was not encouraged here. The visitors would soon learn our ways. We aimed at grace and inner elegance. Magnolia House was democratic, we worked toward the common good. Now, did everyone understand the itinerary. Each weekday the bus would take them to their school in the town. On their return to Magnolia supper would be waiting. Their weekends would be spent here. The Clerkenwells and the Magnolias would be expected to share the chores, putting shoulders to the wheel. The everyday running of the school would fall largely on the girls. Both teaching and domestic staff were reduced owing to the war.

'No more servants to do your work, diddums?' Red didn't bother to lower her voice.

Miss Patrice suggested that we might like to work in teams. What about Maggies and Clerkies? Red made a face of nausea. She snatched her gas mask and went downstairs. No one was interested in team spirits, democracy or elegance. Miss Patrice stood at the top of the stairs and called down. 'Pride, girlies. I'm talking about pride. In yourselves, in the school, in England.'

Red looked back. 'Look, Miss, we need more pillows, we none of us can sleep flat. We ain't dirty, we don't need baths. Pillows.'

Miss Patrice had observed their bad posture, their congested breathing and coughs. One pillow aided deportment. Bad posture and poor hygiene took toll.

Phoebe yawned again. She liked lounging on pillows in preference to fresh air and gardening. Also she liked deep scented baths. If she paired off with Red I could spend more time with Midge. Midge would turn to me. She had spoken again of her parents' dissatisfaction with the school. She was learning nothing. She wanted to study animal ailments, she wanted to be a vet. She was different from Phoebe who just wanted a good time in the army. Midge must have a career, she mustn't waste her time. A veterinary training took years; all her books were about animals. She had sympathy for people. She was quite concerned about the Gee sisters. The war was a burden for the elderly.

That evening the visitors glared at the undercooked rice pudding. The sausages had been raw. They noted the way we held our cutlery, the way we sipped water without gulping. Nothing impressed them. They pushed their plates aside.

'Do you always eat this type of food? I wouldn't give it to my dog.'

'Where is your dog, Red?'

'With Mum and Dad, of course. Clerkenwell.'

Red was used to proper teas in the kitchen; good strong tea, not this dishlap. Thick bread with chips. Sundays in Clerkenwell they ate jellied eels and mash. This rice pudden was raw. Phoebe agreed. Red was *absolument* correct, it was uneatable. She had another banana, she gave half of it to Red. Old Gumm should be put out to grass. We had heard about her dinners with her uncle at his Mayfair club. She had had steak with her brother at the Black Lion.

'What do you do after this lot, then?'

'We read or we play Barbie's gramophone in the form room. The babies go to bed.'

'You got a grammie? Where?'

We explained about the broken spring and only owning one record. Red thought it was bad having no sitting room.

'Do you know the Umbrella Song, Red?'

'Course.'

'What about "Run Rabbit Run"?'

'And "South of the Border".'

'"Begin the Beguine", "Deep Purple", "Roll Out the Barrel".'

We wanted Red to know that we knew the right tunes, were up to the minute with songs. She fiddled with her spoon, pinching her thin lips inwards. Her permed hair was like a bush beside Phoebe's flat locks. Both were stylish in different ways. Red called to Gumm. 'Hey, Hitler, you trying to poison us? This the best you can do?'

He turned away.

'Come on you lot. Leave Hitler to his slops.'

I hated Gumm being humiliated. He had done his best here for forty years. He must long to fight for his country with younger men rather than cook for impudent girls.

The form room seemed smaller now, filled with so many girls. The babies stayed up tonight. Barbie's gramophone was by the gas mask hooks. Phoebe had brought back a surprise from her weekend, a record of 'There's a Small Hotel'.

'And look, Tor. On the other side it's our song.'

She looked at me strangely, then turned away. Didn't she want to remember that happy tea in London, the cream cakes, Mamma's throaty voice, the couple with the diamond ring? She made me feel disloyal. I was spending too much time with Midge. I still loved her, she must realize that.

Red was impatient with slow tunes. Play something with a bit of life, not that waltzing slop. 'Come on, you twerps. Let's dance.' She and her lot were used to real dancing. Push up the speed, Barb, faster than that. Come on, Phoeeb, bugger the rest, let's do some dancing.

Phoebe's myopic eyes started to shine. Her brother danced formally, guiding his partners over the floors of nightclubs with practised hands. Red danced wildly. She needed a fast beat and room to move. She and Phoebe had already formed their private way of talking barely moving their lips, a secret language. Now they danced. They moved so fast their bodies seemed to whirl. Red pushed and pulled her, showing her. Don't be so stiff, move from the neck down, move the whole body, loosen your shoulders and knees. They touched, they broke away, rejoined and parted, every inch must be alive. You got it, Phoeeb, I'm learning you, it's easy if you let go. The record finished. They were panting. Red had learned from her boyfriend at home.

Ula wanted to know about the boyfriend. Wasn't Red a bit young?

'Never too old or too young, kiddo. Watch out, keep out of our way.'

They were off again. Ula looked serious. She felt uneasy about boyfriends because of the way our cook had gone off with men. We had met few men ourselves, few boys and were not used to having friends. Red's perfume and dancing gave an entry into a private and forbidden world of which we knew nothing. Scrawny, mean-lipped, spotty-necked Red knew about life. Ula stamped her shoes, sideways and forwards, sticking out her bottom. 'I'm dancing. Look at me.'

'Who you supposed to be? Charlie Chaplin?'

'Ula, don't try to show off.'

I snubbed her but I wanted to dance too. I wanted to dance better than Red and Phoebe, I wanted to outshine everyone here. They must watch me, not Red and Phoebe. Why should they get all the praise? I had tried the splits and got menstruation. Did you always pay for showing off? Ula went on jumping busily, showing her awful teeth. Phoebe and Red were leaping dervishes. The gramophone sounded like animal squeals. Phoebe our goddess and dirty Red were magical. 'Good old Phoeeb, not half bad. Come on, you lot, have a try.'

We joined in, trying to copy, moving the best way we could. The Clerkenwells were used to letting go in their playground and jumping in the London streets. They weren't self-conscious, they could dance without effort. The Magnolias were stiff and ill at ease. It was our turn now to be awkward, lacking grace, elegance and style. We had never seen or heard of this sort of dancing, it was very different from the waltz. Gubgub could dance the Gay Gordons, and there was the Lambeth Walk. Midge took hold of Ula.

'Come on, Tor. Let's you and I try.'

She moved away from me like a stranger. I caught a whiff of her sweat. Why was she angry? Didn't she know I'd never forget her?

'Come on, Tor, let's try.'

'So kiss me my sweet, and so let us part, When I grow too old to dream, your love will live in my heart.'

'Wind the grammie, faster, faster, wind it quick, you blood-clot.'

I went stiff. What a disgusting word for Red to use in front of children. Then the light was turned off. It was easier in the dark-ness, you didn't feel so self-conscious. Horrible word. I felt Tor breathing, smelled her, felt her cold fingers in my hand. We heard leather shoes scuffling, plimsolls slithering, mufti dresses brushed the visitors' rags. It was pitch-black, then gradually you could see shapes of dancers. I need you, Tor; nothing has changed, believe that. I promised Mamma that I'd look after you but I have to learn new things. The cockneys know things we've never heard of, swearing and dancing and boys. I want to be wise and kind like Midge. I want to stay a child but I've men-struated. I can't stay the same, I am older. Don't leave me, Tor, be the same.

Phoebe and Red shared the same bath. Midge didn't show that she cared. Sharing baths was worse than sharing beds or lavatories. Midge helped Ula fold her clothes. 'And we'll pull our beds close,' Phoebe said. With pillows touching they mur-mured their closed-lipped language, having splashed and tittered in the bath. Had they compared toe-nails, bust measurement and body hair, having left wet marks on the slatted mat? Red had a photograph of her boyfriend wearing battledress. We all wanted to see his gap-toothed smile and sleek hair combed straight back. Phoebe's brother was framed in silver. His bony jaw impressed us and his neat pale hair. Red looked at him, then kissed her own picture smackingly.

'Let me see, Red. Please?'

Ula wanted to know what ITALY in the corner meant. Was he Italian? Ula was beginning to read now.

'Blimey. Ed an Eyetye?' Red kissed her picture again. I Trust And Love You was what it meant. Phoebe jerked the curtains close round their beds, the bed springs creaked, they were alone. Red was filthy, the bathroom stank of her, she had spots and said disgusting words. She was only thirteen but we all wanted to listen to her, would like to be a little like her. Her life in Clerkenwell sounded better than our lives. She went to Saturday night pictures and the market with her mum. She could roller-skate, her dog was called Bony. Her dad came home shouting from the pub. They ate in the kitchen, the table had newspapers, they had winkles and meat pies from a stall. Their parlour was kept for Christmas and birthdays. She missed that parlour and Sunday teas. Boys liked you to have tits in front and lipstick for kissing, they liked frizzy hair and hot perfume. Best of all they liked you alone. Imagining her home must be like watching a film, though we'd never been to one, except for one about bees making honey in our town hall. Red's home sounded so friendly, she'd never wanted to come away. When she married she wanted one kiddy and to live in Clerkenwell near her mum. They'd eat winkles and drink sodas while they gave eye to the kiddy. She didn't want to join in the war. Her dad was a fire fighter in the city, it was dangerous. Her mum and her and the kiddy would be sunny as larks. She wasn't like Phoebe, wanting to join up for travel and glamour. Red believed in family ties.

I didn't feel tired or sleepy. The war was horrid, the way it changed everyone's lives. We might never see Mamma again, but at least we'd met the Clerkenwells. My nipples hurt, I hated having pubic hair. Tor made me feel trapped and guilty. I envied Ula, still just a little child. She was sitting in bed rubbing on face cream. We didn't want to catch Red's spots.

Red was rude again in the morning. 'Look, chum, whatever they call you. We can't eat this slop. Worse than sick.'

Gumm looked at the porridge, then looked at her spots. 'Cook it yourself. I'm off.'

8

'Not like that, Phoebe, you clot. You're burning it.'

'It should be well browned, Red. I had it once with my uncle.'

'Bugger your uncle, he ain't here. They can put jam on it.'

'Not *jam*, Red, this is a savoury.'

Ula pushed in. 'I love jam, Red. Jam on fried bread is nice.'

'No one asked you, kiddo. Phoeeb and I are the cooks.'

Phoebe ran her hand through her fringe. She let Red take her place at the stove.

'Red, what does "copulation" mean?'

'You'll cop it if you get in my way. Phoeeb, you're burning it.'

School supper was called tea now. Phoebe and Red ruled the kitchen, smoky now with burning fat. Midge was cleaning potatoes in the corner. Gumm had kept his word and left.

Red said his food was dangerous, he'd better not show his face. Miss Patrice's sallow face had lengthened. A faithful retainer had been insulted. We were now without paid help. She had pleaded in vain. Gumm was unused to rudeness, he would not change his mind. She didn't wish to lay blame on one person, the school must bear the shame collectively. A servant had been treated inelegantly. Her sister had been made ill. Now Miss Patrice took morning assembly alone.

'What is wrong with Miss Gee, please?'

She was prone to stomach upsets, any friction could set it off.

'Told you. Poison,' Red muttered.

Miss Patrice still wore her bandeau. It looked careless, her hair pushed it to one side. She looked worn out. She was now asking the school for further endeavours. Would we cook as well as keeping the premises tidy? She looked at Red, a hint of cold-ness in her fudge-coloured eyes, their lids pink now as if from crying. Because of Red we must all pay the price. Red looked back at her and gave her snickering laugh. She had no time for old people, not a lot of time for these toffee-nosed girls, except, of course, old Phoeeb. But this school was better than staying in those billets; she could be with her mates each night as well as at school, plus she'd met and chummed with Phoeeb.

'And so, girls, prefects and monitors will be our leaders in the absence of domestic and academic staff, all of whom have gone to serve. Any questions?'

'What's the pay?' Red called.

Phoebe said that she and Red would take over the cooking. Midge and I were assigned all garden duties and outside control. Red complained about the Gees' meanness. They were saving wages, we should get paid for the work.

Each morning she and Phoebe rose before the rest, to make toast. Tea was made in a large enamel pot with milk and sugar added. They enjoyed themselves in the kitchen, muttering their rapid talk. Midge and I helped prepare vegetables. Red said she felt like shopping the Gees to the government. They were profi-teering from this war, two old spivs.

Supper was always late. They argued over menus. Red

yearned for whelks and jellied eels, Phoebe for pheasant or jugged hare, all impossible. They didn't know how to cook in any case. They agreed that time spent in cooking should be as short as possible, they liked dancing together best.

The larder had been a shock. Gumm had either stolen the rations or not ordered any. The shelves were bare and dirty. Rice and sugar jars were empty, a few eggs in a bowl were bad. There was nothing under the china cheese cover. There was a paper sack of porridge, some old bread in a bin. In the refrigerator was a parcel of sausages; their shiny red skins smelled. A spider ran round the tea packet. The baker said that he'd been instructed to leave old bread. A few minutes in a hot oven under a damp cloth freshened it. Red said her mum did that but you'd expect fresh bread in this place. Two spivs, nothing less nor more. Red liked bread cut into a bowl with milk and some sugar, so we had that often now. With Phoeeb's money and brains Red thought she should know more about cooking.

'Not like that, you clot. Too many servants has made you helpless.'

'I can't help it, Red. I've had no opportunity.'

'Diddums, you're getting it now.'

The Clerkenwells hadn't met Miss Gee yet, still in her room with her stomach complaint, waited on by Miss Patrice. Her walk had lost its bounce, her hair grew droopier. She spoke with less vigour about patriotism and inner elegance, the country's needs, the danger of careless talk. 'Thrift, girls, I urge you to practise thrift.'

The Clerkenwells were unimpressed by her, nor did they feel curiosity about Miss Gee. They still missed Clerkenwell.

The evenings were our happiest times. With tea eaten we went back to the form room. Without our uniforms our behaviour seemed to change. The differences in speech and manners became less obvious. We became less separate, our backgrounds didn't count. Without grown-ups to bother us, the war and its silly rules didn't count either. What mattered was dancing to the gramophone.

'Not that way, Phoeeb. Gas is too high.'

Slices of bread and hot fat hissed as Red dumped the contents of the frying pan into the rubbish bucket. A lump of lard melted into a cabbage leaf.

'I'll empty it. Can I?'

'You again, Ula?'

'Let her, Phoebe. She likes helping.'

Ula liked emptying and tidying. Red didn't want kids under her feet. She let Ula take the bucket to the back door. She wanted to go on gossiping with Phoeeb.

I spent more time in Midge's company. The winter had set in, there was still a little work to do. The paths must be kept tidy, the potting sheds kept neat. There was the incinerator and rubbish dump to see to. We spent hours with the mouse family, they led such happy lives. The babies were out of their nest now but couldn't be handled. There was the white one of my dreams, there was a black one with a slightly snouty nose. I worried about the thin pitiful one that trembled. I could have two if I wanted, Midge said, but they'd have to be the same sex. She was so knowledgeable and expert, lifting the young by their tails. They needed a protein and carbohydrate diet. Mice were prone to virus infections, salmonellosis, Tyzzer's disease. With proper care they could live for three years or more. I memorized her learned veterinary information. I would be nearly fifteen when they died.

We cleaned the cage, having removed the nesting box;

we discussed names for the mice. The rubbish and incinerator-burning took place on Sundays when the girls were supposed to be visiting the high church in the town. A bus called for the churchgoers but no one used it, preferring to stay in bed, eating toast and talking about their lives. We learned more about the Clerkenwells than they did about us; their opinion of posh people was low. Our toffee-nosed parents couldn't manage without servants. It was a shock to find no servants here and no staff. The school they went to in the town was better off. The town children were taught proper lessons and given a proper lunch. They could do easy algebra and knew the rivers and capital cities of the world. The Magnolias were freaks from freakish homes in their opinion, not knowing much and showing off. They remembered Clerkenwell with nostalgia. Cosy oil fires were better than cool heating pipes. To sit round a lit gas oven with plates warming or clothes airing was companionable. They liked being squashed together in one bed. They liked Joe Loss and Henry Hall on the wireless. They liked Roy Rogers and the *Beano* and chips. Where was the pub or the chip shop? This place was poverty-stricken, though we let on to be posh.

Red's dad being in the Fire Service meant he earned more than some of them. Red had a three-piece suite in their parlour with a rimless mirror over the fire. They had a shiny coal scuttle. Her mum made suet puddings called Spotted Dick. These old teacher sisters were mad in the head and mean with it. Red's dog did better. Once we had the grammie going in the evening, it was all right.

She and Phoebe slapped the bread slices on to plates, ladling the jam on.

'Hurry, you lot. Time for tea.'

We heard the click and tap of knives and spoons in the

dining room, we heard Ula boasting again. She liked setting tables, she liked folding tableclothes, she liked sounding the bell outside.

As the weeks passed our appearance changed as well as our voices. Red started a fashion for curling our hair. She used lead strips covered with stocking silk to wind round small strands of hair, using six for her fringe alone. Her wrists were less thin in spite of the diet, her spots didn't seem quite so bright. Frizzed hair might suit me, my hair was longer now. There were no more indoor games or Biblical Tableau practice. The hymn singing and praying stopped too. Miss Patrice asked if the head girls would conduct assembly; we forgot the end of term pageant. We shared our things increasingly with the Clerkenwells who had to dress in the weekdays for their school. They wore our uniforms when they fancied, there was no one to mend or launder, our clothes became grubby and frayed. We often kept our pyjamas on in the daytime, though we still liked bathing. So did Red.

The cupboards and drawers became clothes pools. You took out what you liked to put on, throwing things anywhere at night. We liked wearing the visitors' rings and bracelets that left green marks on your skin. Red let some of us use her lipstick. Sharing was interesting, it made a change. The important event each night was the dancing, always ending up in the dark.

The little ones went to bed when they wanted, our sweating bodies writhed. We went on until our legs ached, just like a real London dance palace. I trusted the Clerkenwells now. I was learning two important new subjects, how to dance and look after mice. Phoebe's brother sent more records. The dream song was left aside. I would never forget it, I would always love it.

Mamma hadn't written. Red got a tin watch from her boyfriend. It wouldn't tick, though she wound and wound. What you could do mattered more than what you had. Red was proud of herself.

' 'Course, if you got the army occupying you got no worries.'

'What do you mean, Red?'

She said they paid a lot to use your house in wartime, a wonder the Gee sisters didn't let this place. It wasn't a proper school, not what she'd expected. Her mum would be disgusted if she saw. Catch her stopping a minute longer than she had to. Her boyfriend Ed had put in for Christmas leave. Clerkenwell was all right at Christmas, they knew how to do things right.

'You shouldn't go back to London. You might get bombed. Don't.'

'You joking? Try and stop me. My mum's there besides. Not everyone runs away, scaredy cat.'

'My oh my,' Phoebe sighed.

They were best friends but I think Phoebe envied her. An officer brother wasn't like a soldier who trusted and loved you. No one was bored with Red around. It was rare now to hear anyone say 'Catch me ere I swoon' or 'More than somewhat'. There were no gasps or French catchwords now. The Magnolias didn't drop their aitches (except for Ula sometimes) but vowel sounds were less pure, consonants less ringing. Our favourite supper became boiled eggs.

I liked listening to the sounds in the dining room when eggs were eaten, the chip of shells, the shells being dropped. I liked the tapping of spoons, the smashing of shells when they were empty. The Magnolias stopped slicing the tops off, we peeled the eggs like buns, ate them in our hands greedily. Crumbs fell from our fingers, our teeth became crusted with yolk. Eat quickly, never mind table manners, we mustn't waste good dancing time.

'What about washing up?'

'Bugger the dishes, they can wait.'

The magic movement and music took over, we were united, without difference of background, money or class. There was joy in moving to music, changing partners in the dark. Barbie or Ula called when it was time to change, switching the light out; you left your partner, you found someone else. You pushed, you giggled, you stumbled, you must guess before the lights went on. The desks were outside in the passage now, we'd stopped using them. The music screeched. Lights out. Change. I liked dancing with Ula, she moved jauntily, in a funny hopping kind of way. Her bones felt light and brittle. I asked if she was happy since the Clerkenwells had come.

'I'm usually happy. It's Tor, Bonnie. She cries sometimes. She bites her nails, she never used to. And she ...'

'Lights out. Close your eyes. Change.'

'Midge. It's you.'

'Bonnie, I've got something to tell you. I had a letter. I'm leaving.'

'What?'

'I'm leaving at Christmas.'

'You can't. You mustn't, Midge.'

'It's true. They've found another school for me. They're coming for the pageant.'

'Who will be head garden prefect? The mice. Midge, don't leave me.'

'You must choose someone to help you. You'll be in charge.'

Midge must have a better education, she mustn't waste time here. The war would end one day, she wanted to be a vet. She'd need biology, Latin, maths, chemistry, she was learning nothing here.

'The others are happy here. Phoebe and Gubgub.'

'They're different, they're not serious, you and I are.'

Some people never acquired ambition. This school was useless if you aimed high. She had a goal, nothing would prevent
her, she would become a vet or die.

My only goal so far was to care for my sisters, and keep
Midge's friendship and respect. Without her the rubbish disposal
would be a misery, the incinerator a gruesome task. I needed her
advice on mousekeeping, I needed her for bodily matters. I had
no one to rely on. Midge you can't go.

'Tor is unhappy. You must ask her, Bonnie. She's your sister,
ask her to help.'

9

'Bonnie, dearest. Too sad to have been so remiss. It's tragic that I cannot attend your pageant but we'll think of each other.'

I read Mamma's letter to my sisters. The Magnolia girls would have parents or relatives for the pageant, but not the Clerkenwells whose parents couldn't afford the fare from London. Phoebe hoped for her brother, Red hoped for her boyfriend. Planning and hoping for the soldiers strengthened their bond. Midge would leave after the pageant. I had been hoping that Mamma might meet Midge, my first friend and my guide.

We had forgotten about the pageant. There was little time now for rehearsals. The tableaux depicting prophets and wise men of the Old Testament would be changed to something simpler. We decided on Bible Beasts. We were engrossed in dancing and cooking. Only Ula, who helped Barbie with food for the Gee sisters, had remembered the pageant when she'd seen Miss Gee's ill-looking, stone-coloured face. We heard about the dying cheeseplant in the conservatory and the cold uncomfortable rooms the sisters had. The sisters picked at their food and Miss Patrice had lost weight.

The blackboard had no timetable now, there were no desks in the form room. But we could all read, Ula too. Tor had helped her, as once she used to help me. Phoebe had appointed herself our headmistress, with Red her second-in-command. They strode about in their mixed-up clothing. Phoebe's jewellery looked pretty on Red, the Magnolia uniform fitted her. We put the Gee sisters out of our mind; patriotism and England's future mattered less than comics, dancing and curling our hair. *Savoir-faire*, inner elegance and grace stayed beyond the conservatory. Each night the Magnolias were impatient for the Clerkenwell school bus to return from the town, the fun could start then.

One evening when I was waiting at the gate for the bus I felt that I was being watched. I touched the stone unicorn's shoulder for confidence. I shouldn't be in front of the school in my pyjamas. I had lead curling pins in my hair. Was that Miss Gee's face behind the magnolia branches where I and my sisters had waited once? Her face looked twisted and contorted, she seemed to be wringing her hands. I blinked. She was gone.

No one minded Midge barring them from the garden; it was so cold now, our secret mice were safe. Phoebe and Red barred everyone from the kitchen. Girls tended to pair off in twos. Tor was alone a lot. I couldn't help it. I would make it up to her when I could. We had come to meet other girls as well as to be educated; I needed and loved Midge. The cage must be cleaned daily, the mice grew quickly. We let them run through our fingers, round our wrists, up into our hair, leaving their sweet mousey scent behind. Tor often looked at me strangely, though I hadn't seen her cry.

The day of the pageant was getting closer. The animal idea came from Midge. As her father was a rector she knew her Bible; there were all kinds of Bible beasts. We wanted to retain the religious theme from consideration for Miss Gee, this being a church school. There were the Gadarene swine who rushed down a cliff, killing themselves, there were sheep and other farm animals round the manger. Camels, sparrows, donkeys, lions, peacocks, every kind of animal was mentioned somewhere. They were nicer than people, more interesting to act.

'We must have dancing, Midge, after all our practice.'

Red suggested the animals in the ark. Two by two we would dance into it; we would continue to dance inside. The animals would need exercise and amusement after getting so wet in the flood. Phoebe and Red would be Mr and Mrs Noah looking after us. Everyone wanted to be the best animals, elephants, monkeys or bears. It was decided to draw lots from slips of paper. You drew your animal and found your mate. Ula looked sad, what about the singing? She'd looked forward to leading the choir.

'No choir,' Phoebe dictated. The show must be simple, without complications. If singing was needed the audience could be the choir. There was to be nothing churchy or high-minded about the evening, the show would be short and sweet. Those who liked could make masks and tails for our animal dancing. Come on, everyone, draw lots now.

Midge picked first, she drew a mouse. I was next, another mouse. We were still partners, there was no one I'd rather dance with. We'd played with the mice all that day. Gubgub and Barbie were the ark's two pigs. Tor was a goat, the coughing girl was her partner, her name was Pegeen. For the first time I can remember Tor objected. She'd like to partner Ula. Couldn't she change? Pegeen coughed angrily. She didn't want to be a goat either, not with Tor.

'Can't change. Stick to the rules, you bloodclot.'

Tor blushed. I hated Red for calling her that name.

Ula was left out, we were an odd number. She was cheerful about it, didn't mind being in the ark on her own. Was there an animal that sang?

'Let her be a unicorn.'

'Like the one outside. Yes.'

'There's no such animal. There couldn't be.'

'It's mentioned in the Bible often. What about psalm twenty-two?' Midge said the unicorn was famous, talked and written of but never seen. There were legends from many countries, China, India, Armenia, all had stories. The unicorn was beloved and venerated but never captured though hunters set traps with cunning and guile.

'Listen to the preacher's daughter. Swallowed a Bible lately?'

'Shut up, Red. Midge is going to be a vet.'

'Couldn't Ula be a goat with me and Pegeen?'

But Ula wanted to be the unicorn so it was decided. Midge told us that the unicorn was not allowed into the ark without a mate. He was told to pull the ark through the water by a rope tied to his horn. Brave and cheerful, the unicorn wasn't an animal of war.

So much was happening that Mamma didn't know about. Ula had a high soprano that had received notice. I was tone deaf and had periods, my fringe was curly. I was sick of worrying about my sisters. She'd had them, not me. While she sang to soldiers we'd be dancing in Noah's ark in darkness. We'd take the wind-up grammie into the chapel room. We'd play jolly tunes like 'Run Rabbit Run' and 'Roll Out the Barrel' and hoped the parents might like to sing. Red wanted 'In the Mood'. The animals wouldn't dance every minute, they'd need time for 'you-know-what'. As Mrs Noah, she would wear her black cotton skirt that her mum gave her, falling like petals round her calves. She would writhe and tangle with Noah in the darkness. Her skinny legs longed to be off.

There was no time to make costumes. We made botched attempts at finding ears and tails. The guests would proceed straight to the chapel room, having been welcomed by Ula at the gate. She hung paper chains round the stone unicorn's neck. I saw her kissing its ears.

The parents were used to watching interminable Bible scenes while the choir sang hymns year after year. Our show made a pleasant change. With our makeshift ears and tails you couldn't tell the difference between the Magnolias and the Clerkenwells who leapt and pranced before the dais. The sounds we made were mystifying to the parents, roaring, mooing, squeaking, barking; the caterwauling hurt the ears.

'Into the ark, you lot. In twos, please, you're bleeding soaked,' Red ordered.

In pairs we climbed up, welcomed by the Noahs. Ula was last, she stayed outside. Her cardboard horn was fixed by a rope round her head, she ran up and down pulling the ark. Noah held the other end. She was also in charge of the grammie, working the handle, making sure the tunes were jerky and fast. All we cared about was dancing, faster, faster. The parents started to smile. Nothing like a tune to relax and amuse you. What a quaint original show. Heels started tapping to the music, shoulders jiggled.

'Wind the grammie, you bloodclot.'

'I am. I'm trying to,' Ula answered. We were off again.

I looked in vain for Mamma, I knew it was hopeless. I saw Midge's parents and her father's dogcollar. The lights went off, we danced now in the dark. The parents' tapping and humming was less inhibited. One or two even took to the floor themselves, shuffling and swaying politely; it was after all just innocent fun. War entailed change, adjustment, classes mixed, standards slipped or disappeared. You did your best to pull with a will and keep cheerful. The music changed. It was 'In the Mood'. Mr and Mrs Noah circled each other. Mrs Noah advanced, lifting her skirts. She thrust her hips forward, put her arms up to Mr Noah, put her face and her thin lips to be kissed. The parents went quiet, someone coughed. I looked to the doorway. Was that Miss Gee in the passage wringing her hands? Her girls were unrecognizable, her pageant a mockery, we had desecrated her chapel room.

The finale came with my special tune that I'd asked Ula for, we would finish with a change of mood. 'When I grow too old to dream, Your love will live in my heart.'

The parents glowed with emotion. How lovely. Dreams never faded or palled. They stayed with you, you didn't outlive them, through wars and grey hairs dreams remained. I'm thinking of you, Mamma, I smell your perfume, this is your tune, why aren't you here? I'm thinking of the cakes and the couple kissing their ring, I'm thinking of your voice, your face, your smell.

'Bravo. Encore. More.'

We stepped down from the dais happily. Ula skipped round with her rope and horn. I was proud of her, proud of all of us. Bible Beasts was a great success.

Phoebe stretched her hand out, welcoming, explaining. Miss Gee was unwell. Yes, wasn't it a bore? Miss Patrice was nursing her, she and Red were in charge this evening. 'C'est la guerre,' she said, adding, 'vive la paix!' Red walked behind her, mincingly. 'That's right, poor old lady come over queer.' The girls done the show theirselves, glad you liked it. That old Bible stuff was old-fashioned, animals were more modern, made a change. Red fancied herself as good as a duchess, better than Phoebe, extending two fingers to touch each parent's hand. She invited them for a cup of tea. That's right, in the dining room. She ran the meals now, with a bit of help from old Phoeeb. She'd taught her how to cook, Phoeeb hadn't known nothing. She'd taught this school to dance as well. Pleased they liked it, come again next year. Cup of tea now, in the dining room, that's right. Red would make sure the whole evening went with a bang, they must leave with happy memories and bellies full.

I watched the fathers in uniform. If Papa hadn't died would he look like that? And would Mamma be by his shoulder smiling lovingly? Was it loneliness that kept her away? If she had him to love, would she love us better?

There was Phoebe's brother, more handsome than his photograph, the youngest and best-looking here. Phoebe touched his cheek with hers. 'At last, angel brother. I'd have been peeved if you hadn't come.'

He looked from her to me. He stared, I felt embarrassed. I had been so proud of my tail made of knotted stockings, the cardboard ears, the whiskers fashioned from string. I pulled at them. They felt silly. If only I had on my lovely blue dress.

'Bonnie, my brother wants to meet you. Come on, come on and be met.'

'How are you, Bonnie, under those whiskers?'

'I'm all right, thanks very much. Have you met Red?'

'I haven't yet. I intend meeting her. It's you I want to meet first. You make an adorable mouse, but I expect you know that?'

'No. Midge is a mouse too. Do you know her?'

'I know Midge. I'm interested in you. You looked so sweet and fervent during that last song. I'll bet you believe in dreams too. Do you?'

He spoke softly, as drawlingly as Phoebe. He took the hand that wasn't clutching my tail. Then he took that hand too, clasping them lightly, not letting them go. His fingers tingled, they felt exciting. He kept looking at me. Why did he want to meet me? Why did he want to know about dreams?

'I'm not sure. I suppose I do. I've ... I can't remember your name.'

'It's Percival. I loved the way you dance. You dance enchantingly. I longed to join you. Do you waltz? Will you waltz with me one day?'

'When? I'm not much good at the waltz. We never ...'

'Then I must teach you, mustn't I? You and I must waltz one day.'

Red's dancing was jerky and childish. I longed to be whirled across the floor with his arm round me while violins softly played. Outside would be a shining moon and roses smelling heavenly. But I was too shy to imagine being outside alone with him. It was safer to stay with the violins and candles, swirling and circling, our hair touching, our cheeks brushing, his pale eyes close to mine. When he smiled his cheeks flattened, he had Phoebe's bony jaw. Percival was a lovely name. He watched me as if I was special, something to be cherished. Sir Percival and the holy grail. It's you I want to meet. I longed to join you.

'You won't forget, Bonnie, will you? We will meet and we will waltz.'

'I'll never forget.' But when will it be? When?

I hadn't known my eyes were closed until I felt Red there, interrupting, spoiling the dream. Moonlight, roses, violins, candles, spoiled now, fading, gone. Go away, Red, you've spoiled everything. Get away, you Clerkenwell beast.

'You Perce? Thought you was. I'm Red, Phoebe's mate.'

Ed hadn't arrived, she hadn't given up hope, he still might turn up. Light Infantry. Christmas leave. She chewed her sandwich as she spoke, her short teeth biting quickly. That almost lipless mouth was used to kisses, she'd been trusted and loved by Ed. Percival watched with alert pale eyes. Light Infantry? Which detachment? Her boyfriend was a fortunate chap.

'And you, Bonnie. Have you someone special here tonight?'

'Mamma couldn't. There isn't . . .'

'Her dad is dead. Her mum didn't show up. Old Bonnie's been left in the lurch.'

'I'm not. I'm not.'

'Poor Bonnie. Never mind. You will remember your promise to me, won't you?'

'What's she promising you, eh? Is Bonnie a dark horse after all? Cor . . . look who . . . Stone the crows, look at your teacher.'

In the dining-room doorway was the terrible figure of Miss Patrice. 'Come at once, someone. My sister . . . my sister . . .'

Phoebe showed leadership and strength. No time now for languor or affectation. Emergency stations, no confusion please. Her velvet heels tapped to the door. Miss Patrice? Well, well, what is this? Let there be calm.

She helped her back to the rooms beyond the conservatory, leaving Red in charge. Midge only had authority out of doors. She didn't mind, she was leaving anyway, nor did she dislike Red whose ambitions differed from her own.

'Okay, folks,' Red shouted. 'Keep your hair on. Stay as you were.'

She looked at Percival. Don't you move either, she'd be back in a tick, she'd just find out what was up.

Midge's father, experienced in pain and bewilderment, followed Phoebe and Red outside. He hadn't approved of the pageant, mildly blasphemous, an affront to the intelligence, but the two head girls were coping well. He suggested that we carry on with the supper while he saw what he could do.

We still wore our ears and tails and mixed up clothing. We went on handing out biscuits and tea.

'Afraid it's serious, folks. The old head teacher is dead.'

Red was there, licking her lips triumphantly. It was a thrill breaking such news. Ula gave a whimper like the noise she made in her nightmares. Her face looked awful. What did Red mean, 'dead'? Who was dead, explain it please, which person was it who had died? Tor put her arms round Ula, she stroked her hair, which earlier she had tried to plait like a unicorn's mane. Her hair straggled from the rope with the horn tied to it. She was crying. Who could be dead?

'What I said, kiddo. Your head teacher snuffed it.' Serve her right, profiteering spiv.

I had to speak for Miss Gee and protect Ula. I said that the war had been too much for Miss Gee. Too many changes, she'd never wanted her school to be like this.

'You mean she didn't want us coming here from Clerkenwell. Well, we didn't want to come.'

'I think Bible Beasts upset her. I think she saw us.'

'Everyone enjoyed theirselves, nothing wrong with it. We were doing the Bible.'

'The dancing might have shocked her, she's not used to it.'

'You don't know nothing about it, Bonnie.'

But Red was upset, I could tell. I felt Percival near me, touching my hand again. Then Midge's father returned. Yes, the news was true.

She had apparently died quite suddenly. The doctor had been sent for but hadn't arrived in time. In due course we would know the reason. It was sad and upsetting, a proof, if proof were needed, that our lives were not in our hands.

Red muttered something contemptuous. Midge's mother put down her cup. This, on top of the extraordinary exhibition the school had just put on, was proof of what they already suspected. The school wasn't suitable, the sooner they reclaimed Midge the better. She must start after Christmas elsewhere.

'I can't bear it. I don't know what you're talking about.' Ula clung to Tor, rubbing her eyes.

'Hush, darling. It will soon be over. There.'

Pegeen offered Ula a cough sweet. Barbie squeezed her hand.

I had never seen Ula look so white and unhappy. She had known so many deaths. She had liked Miss Gee and all the grace and elegance talk. The two sisters symbolized something we'd not experienced: certainty of purpose, principles and pride. I remembered that sad face behind the magnolia tree. Miss Gee had been proud of us once. Miss Patrice would never carry on without her. Though they'd disagreed, they had needed each other.

Midge's father went to the telephone again. He stood by the teapot. He had a suggestion to make. Those parents who could manage it might like to take their daughters home now. Leave at once without waiting for the end of term. Miss Patrice was in agreement, he saw no problem. Midge's mother asked about the London girls, what would happen to them? Phoebe drawled that Miss Patrice had suggested once that the Magnolias should invite the Clerkenwells home with them. There was silence. Phoebe winked at Red. Had she a secret plan perhaps, with Percival? The parents rustled uncomfortably; they murmured, trying to conceal their dismay. The jolly tunes and dancing earlier were forgotten, they began to wish they hadn't come. The

London girls, though quaint and delightful, would scarcely be suitable guests in their homes. They lit cigars and cigarettes, they cleared their throats. It was war. To refuse would seem churlish and mean. Phoebe, the head girl, was unnecessarily masterful, urging and explaining as she moved from group to group. The girls had already been paired off for the pageant; stick to your animal partner, take that girl home if you could. She pushed her lank hair back, no need to fuss or delay. Just pack your things now and go. She told Ula kindly that Miss Gee had probably died without pain. Red copied Phoebe, pushing her frizzed hair back. Poor old person, snuffing it at Christmas. Rotten time to go. She'd not met her personally; she felt choked now it was too late. She was waiting for her boyfriend now. How about another cup of tea?

'Oh come on, Red. Percival wants ...'

Red wasn't budging without her boyfriend. Ed would turn up, we'd see. Midge was pleading with her parents. Bonnie was her partner, let her come back, please. How I longed to sing carols in Midge's home and open presents; to help them cook their Christmas meal; to meet their pets and help care for them. Christmas with Midge would be a dream come true.

'But my sisters, Midge, I couldn't leave them. They'd never manage.' And there was my promise to Mamma.

'They could all come home, couldn't they, Mummy? All three of them. Say yes, please.'

The mother shook her head regretfully. Space was at a premium with their large family, especially at Christmas. One extra yes, three was too much.

'It's quite all right, Midge, don't feel badly. We'll be quite all right here on our own.'

I hated her worrying about me, I hated pity. She said she

would give me all the mice if I liked. 'The whole cage? Are you sure?'

'Sure I'm sure.' And I must get in touch with my mother to tell her about Miss Gee dying. I didn't say I didn't know where to telephone. A cageful of mice would compensate for anything in life.

Her father must leave quickly because of the parish. It was better not to say goodbye. Midge had taught me everything I needed. Our friendship had been real, our times with the mice rapturous. I would miss her small eyes smiling and explaining. I would remember everything she'd told me, I would guard the cage with my life. I wished her farewell in silence. I will never forget you, Midge. Go forth, good friend and noble vet to be.

The dormitory was in an uproar. Parents had come up to help them pack. They were trying to behave hospitably, accepting their hostess role with grace. It was the giving time of year, the London children were neglected, poor little casualties. The ragged assortment of clothes was hard to believe. Where were the uniforms they'd so lovingly provided? Where were the soft underclothes, the expensive shoes? Barbie's mother held up a blouse with the sleeve torn out. A blazer had scraps of fur glued in place of the collar. Beds, floors, drawers were strewn with unwashed, unmended clothes. Beside the wash-basins was a communal pile of garments that no one wanted. Barbie's mother shook her head, she conferred with Midge's mother. Was this what they paid high fees for? Truly the cost of war was high, the sooner they left the better.

Red's vanilla smell was strong in the air, heightening the tension. Now that the Clerkenwells were leaving they were behaving as they had when they'd first come, silent, cold and hard. No one had asked them if they wanted to stay with these toffee-nosed parents. They were on their guard again. The days of sharing clothes, dancing and comics were coming to an end. There would be fresh criticism ahead. They didn't trust these Magnolia parents and their rich, unnatural ways. Grown-ups and teachers didn't change much, whether peace or war; you had to obey.

The Magnolias felt let down and embarrassed. Their friends were not presenting themselves in a good light. The world of school was already fading, the home world lay ahead. They bolstered their confidence with the old school slang, unused since the Clerkenwells came. They grinned and shoved each other. 'Same to you with brass knobs on', 'More than somewhat feeble', 'Catch me ere I swoon'. Basins were thumped back and forth for the last time. Curtains rattled, clothes were selected at random.

I bent over my pillow; I couldn't bear to lose Midge. She was leaving my life for ever, in a moment she'd be gone. I felt for my golden watch. I would give it to her as a memento; she'd admired it, her own was a cheap one. So much had happened since we'd stood in this dormitory and she'd told me her name. 'Midge is a mosquito,' I'd said. I looked up. Midge had left.

'Tough luck, kiddo. You're too late.' Red had seen.

They were all going. I sat on my bed with my sisters, listening and watching. 'Goodbye you three. Happy Christmas.' 'Bye-ze-bye.' 'Merry Chrissiewinks.' 'So long.'

There was just Red now, and us. She sat picking her nail polish, looking sulky. She'd shoot Ed when he turned up. Phoebe had left with that pale-eyed brother of hers; she never did trust a pale-eyed man. Perce was a typical la-di-da, unreliable. As for those profiteering spivs, the elder one was lucky to have kicked the bucket before the government caught her. She stood up, still in her black cotton skirt and someone's slippers. She'd go down again and wait for Ed.

'We'll sleep in the end beds, we might as well.' We'd become used to sleeping where we wanted, in the beds or sometimes on the floor.

Downstairs the dining room was heaped with empty plates. There was no tea left in the pot. The draining boards and kitchen table were covered with used cutlery and crumbs. We licked our fingers and pressed them to the crumbs as we used to at home. What was Miss Patrice doing? Had the ambulance born the body to the mortuary? Was Miss Gee praying with the angels now? If only Ula would stop using her hair for a hanky. She looked so frightened. These deaths were spoiling our lives.

We went to bed without undressing or washing. Red's vanilla and stale powder-puff smell had got in my brain. I would lie still and think about Percival, I would think of roses, moonlight, violins. I would remember his hands touching, his voice speaking, I would remember him for the rest of my life. I would keep my promise, I would waltz with him one day.

I heard the sound of the front door bell and then the sound of slippered feet.

'Halt who goes there?' Ula cried in a dramatic way.

'Shut your face, it's only me.'

Red was close to me, smelling of something different, like sherry, but sharper and thick. Her whispering was thick against my ear, her thin lips like little worms wet and tickling.

'We're stopping in the other dorm. Don't tell your sisters.'

'You mustn't, Red. You shouldn't. Don't.'

'You're just jealous, you little bloodclot. We don't want any spinsters spoiling it.'

She wouldn't have dared if Phoebe had been here. This was

a school for girls. She shouldn't bring Ed up. And I wasn't a spinster, I was a prefect. As a matter of fact, I could be head girl now. I closed my eyes and tried to forget her. Think of Percival again. Think of waltzing and feeling him touch you. Feel his hands, feel his flat cheek against yours. Pale lips, pale eyes extracting promises, waltzing, dreaming in moonlight all our lives.

Tor shook me. 'There's a noise in the other dorm. What is it? Wake up, Bonnie, there it is again.'

'Don't listen, it's imagination. I was having a dream.'

Ula woke. 'What is it? Who goes there?'

There was something, Tor repeated. A horrid noise. There it was again. We must find out, it was our duty; it might be Germans. Or burglars, Ula added, or poisoned gas. Her gas mask was ready, just in case.

I went first. Our bare feet were soundless. Past the swing basins rimmed with dirt. We passed the cupboards, empty now and the musty bath cubicles. Someone in the other dorm was in dreadful pain.

We stood in the doorway. I didn't want to look. I had to look. I felt sick and hot and cold. I must stop my sisters looking. It was a noise like animals. Go away, Red, it's not allowed.

There were four, two on the floor under a blanket, two on the bed by the door. The light shone on Percival and Red, they had no clothes on. Their bodies were spread, she was on top of him, her bottom jerked up and down. They rolled, he was above her, heaving and pushing. Panting, awful, they weren't wearing clothes. They seemed joined below the waist, they must separate, we must stop watching. I couldn't stop, I was excited. Why didn't they stop? They didn't want to stop, they liked it, it wasn't pain, the noises were noises of love.

The two under the blanket were wriggling and squirming.

'I'll teach you, like I done Red. Stuck up bitch, leave it to me, I'll teach you.'

And Phoebe, our head girl, our goddess, 'Don't hurt. Don't stop. Stop. More. Oh, put out the flags.'

We didn't speak or look at each other. We got into our beds again.

10

Everything was worse when you were tired. My brain was over-charged. My sisters and I might have been mistaken. Could they have been practising some kind of dance? Why had Percival been there? Why did Phoebe say she wanted more?

It hadn't been dancing, it had been sexual intercourse.

Phoebe was nearly sixteen, Red was thirteen. Was it legal? Could you do it if you had no bust? Red had no hair below either, she didn't have periods, but her spitty lips were used to kissing and being kissed. I knew about babies now, thanks to Midge. A man put his dangling thing between your legs and put juice there. Red called that part her naughty-naughty. Could she have the ingredients of a child in her? Midge hadn't told me about noises or heaving. I had never seen a dangling thing, except for Bruno's, under the Christmas tree, before he died. I had imagined that both people would have to keep quite still as it went in, barely breathing and keeping straight legs. Now I saw why it had to be done in bed or under covers. It was so noisy and so rude.

The whole thing was Red's fault, I'd never forgive her. But for

Red, Phoebe would be safely asleep in a room next to Percival
at the Black Lion Hotel. I never wanted to set eyes on her, rude
Clerkenwell beast. She had spat on the hospitality of our school,
had disgraced the memory of Miss Gee. The whispering behind
curtains with Red had been the start of Phoebe's downfall, her
mind had been poisoned. Clerkenwell people were different, the
children grew up quickly. It wasn't necessary to do sexual intercourse until you were married and wanted babies. Red was
tainted. If only Midge were here.

A car drove out of the drive very early. Did Phoebe know we
had seen? We heard sniggering and splashing in the bathroom.
Red came to collect her clothes.

'Don't go in there yet, spinster.'

She was disgusting, I'd never use that bath again. Could a
dangler go into you in a bath, did it work under water too?
Midge said that nature was beautiful and miraculous; she might
not think that now. They had used Magnolia House for disgusting purposes, without asking. They hadn't even paid. Ed,
who had sealed his picture with a kiss for Red, had never met
Phoebe. What could Percival have seen in Red? She'd called
him snotty-nosed, la-di-da and treacherous, why had she
changed?

Percival had held my hands and made them fluttery. I rubbed
them now on my sheet. They felt as if they'd been bitten. I
wasn't a spinster, I was my sisters' elder sister.

'What's up? Cat got your tongue?'

I wouldn't answer. Let her do anything she wanted as long as
I didn't know.

'Red, wait. What about breakfast? Who will make it?'

Trust Ula to think about food. Red called back to make it
herself. 'I ain't stopping here with you lot. Murderers.'

We were silent. What had she meant?

I will put Red out of my mind for ever. I will forget that Clerkenwell exists. The fire-fighting dad and his beer on Saturday, that mum making bangers and stew, the shiny coal scuttle, the dog warming its fur by the fire, are all contaminated. I will never again think about Ed. The four of them had lost their reason. People had mental blackouts in wartime, they got shell-shocked and did strange things. Nothing mattered if my sisters were safe. I haven't changed, I'm the same, my sisters' protectress and friend. I will look after them this Christmas, make it up to them. Happiness shouldn't have to be earned. Midge thought that all knowledge was important and useful. I wish we hadn't been there last night. Phoebe of the sophistication and elegance will join the army. Her boredom and string-coloured beauty won't fail her. I don't think she'll ever have inner grace. Pale-haired Percival, knight in armour, did you really want to waltz with me?

Tor stroked my hands. 'I'm here. Don't look like that. It's not your fault that everything is suddenly horrible.'

'Tor, I want to show you something that Midge and I did. You mustn't tell anyone, not even Ula. I'm going to need you to help.'

'It's in the garden. I know about the incinerator. And about periods.'

'I hoped you didn't. You're too young.'

Anything to do with bodily development, sexual intercourse or death was better left unknown as long as possible. Tor believed that if you learned things early they didn't frighten you. It was your own brain that made things bad.

'You'll like the surprise. It's small and wonderful.'

'Will I?'

'Oh yes.'

I would teach her to tear up nest wool and handle the babies. With time and effort we might even teach them tricks.

While Ula made the breakfast Tor and I went down the path. We were close again, it was like the old days, before school, before meeting Midge. Tor had been left out. We were reunited. I would always love her more than anyone, because I knew her so well. We might even become world famous mouse experts.

We passed the allotments, ready for the spring planting of vegetables. The school had no staff left. When we went, there would be no girls.

There had been another hard frost. We breathed like dragons to make smoke come. On the path was one of the croquet hoops, forgotten from the lawn. I kicked it, chunks of frost fell off. I thought of our first night here. We had kicked the hoops and Ula pretended to be trapped and we had expected to be here for the rest of the war. I must write to Mamma today.

'Remember the sun in Ireland, Tor. The war spoiled everything. Oh hurry up, do.'

She said things might have changed in any case, because of getting older. She wanted to say something, must I go so fast?

I couldn't wait to get there. I wanted to see her face. Past the incinerator smelling sickly, past the rubbish dump and potting sheds as tidy as little homes now, thanks to Midge and I.

'Wait, Bonnie, I want to tell you . . .'

'Shut your eyes now, Tor. Breathe in. Smell. Can you guess? Tor. Oh Tor. Look.'

I couldn't stop screaming, I couldn't stop shouting. Someone had opened our cage. The mice had escaped, they had been murdered. There were traps in a row on the floor. In each trap was a bloodied mouse. There was the black one with its eyes bulging, dried blood on its snouty nose. There was the sweet piebald with its neck broken, there was the mother stiff and cold. There was one pale tail apart from the mousetraps, its pink root tipped with blood.

'They've been killed, they've been murdered. They're gone, Tor.'

She was shaking too, her cheeks were wet, tears dripped and splashed from her face. 'Oh, the poor things, look at them, oh, the poor things.'

'I'll write to Mamma. Blow your nose.' I had never seen her crying properly before.

'I haven't . . . Oh, Bonnie, what shall we do?'

'Use mine. Who could have done it? Who could be so wickedly cruel?'

'We'll have to bury them, we can't just leave them. We mustn't let Ula find out.'

'She hates blood. We must do it now. We'd better find a spade.'

We parcelled each corpse in twists of newspaper. There was no proper prayer we could say. 'Run in peace,' we whispered, folding each packet. We would bury them outside the hut. We must leave here now, it wasn't suitable for children. I wouldn't wait to tell Mamma. We took it in turns with the spade, trying to dig, pushing and kicking it. We could barely dent the frost-covered ground.

'Listen, there's Ula calling. She mustn't see.'

I ran to the potting sheds to call to her. We're coming, don't come out in the cold, we're coming.

'We can't bury them, Bonnie, it's too hard. What shall we do?'

We flung the bundles into the incinerator. Don't think about it, think of your sisters, just throw them away and run. This is worse than Miss Gee dying or Bruno, worse than the orgy in the dormitory, it's the saddest thing of my life.

'Listen to me, both of you. We're leaving here. At once.'

'Why, Bonnie? We must have breakfast. I've made it. What were you both doing so long?'

'We were just tidying. What did you make?'

'Tea and bread. I found some raspberry jam.'

No wonder Tor was small and scrawny and Ula had spots on her chin. We hadn't eaten properly since we got here. We'd had no lessons and no clean clothes.

'There's a letter from Mamma, Bonnie.'

'Darlings, I hope your Christmas at the school will be jolly. Isn't it a shame the army commandeered our home? I'm staying at the White Harte Hotel at present. I may have news for you all soon. The company travels north after Christmas. I think of you and miss you.'

'Going north? Where in the north?' We must leave at once, we must see her.

There was no answer when I knocked at Miss Patrice's door. She was sitting at Miss Gee's desk like a statue. Her head was down, she stared at the blotting paper pad, her hands lay upwards on the desk. Her hair was dry and neglected.

'So you see, Miss Patrice, we can't stay. There's no one to look after us. We've decided to go home. If you'll just lend us our fares.'

She didn't look up or answer me. I took two pounds from her box on the windowsill. 'Save for the brave'.

Was she fit to be left? Was it safe? 'I'm sorry for the trouble,' I murmured. My sisters came first.

'We mustn't forget our gas masks.' Ula was excited, getting

her case out, trying to whistle again. There was nothing much left to pack. We found three old coats from the communal pile, with rips in them. The word 'uniform' had lost its charm. I would never wear any again if I could help it. I felt for my watch. I'd so wanted Midge to have it. I had so much to remember her by. She had nothing of me. My watch was gone. There was a note. 'Midge told Pheeb about you and your sisters how Ula killed that girl and you and Tor letting your brother catch his death. You needn't give yourself such airs I seen those dead mice too Tor done it. So long Ethelreda.'

Ethelreda? It was from Red. So Midge had told Phoebe about our family secrets, Phoebe had told Red. Did the whole school know? I could trust no one, they were all traitors. It didn't matter now. Tor would never do anything cruel, I wouldn't believe that. It had probably been Gumm who had trapped the mice, or even Red herself.

I longed for my scruffy home clothes again, my old-fashioned bodice, my jerseys. The magic of disorder and muddle was over. Everything here was a bad dream. Miss Patrice had smelled of mould, we smelled nasty ourselves.

We had learned little of importance here that would help in the outside world. We could write copperplate and dance and make tea. I had failed in the keeping of mice. I hadn't even buried them. They lay in filth in the incinerator with half-burned sanitary towels. I had rolled that single bloodied tail in my pink hankie. Run in peace.

The taxi drove us past the unicorn. We saw his face for the last time. I didn't look back. He was just something made of stone, no protection against betrayal and death. No wonder the cheeseplant was dying in the conservatory. The whole place was as good as dead.

Now we are back at our own station, the platform is empty, the waiting room is locked. No stationmaster or porter to smile and take our tickets. Have they too been called to fight? The little side gate is open, we are on the road now. We will walk up the hill to our town.

'Here's the White Harte. Perhaps Mamma is in there. I can't see anyone.'

Ula craned her neck to the windows with their old-fashioned leaded panes. She started pushing the front door. We must ring for attention at the reception desk; she'd been in Irish hotels, was used to them.

'Don't start showing off again, Ula. We'll go home. Mamma might be there.'

I didn't want them to know that I was afraid of hotels. I wanted home as much as I wanted Mamma. It might be bombed or altered, our things might have disappeared. My head felt light and dizzy as if nothing was really true. Could this be happening? Had we really run away from school? And did Mamma realize that Ula was a sort of murderer and that Tor and I were almost as bad? Bruno had seemed sweet without his clothes, we'd meant no harm, nor had Ula. Red saw us as criminals, three guilty sisters with blood on our hands. I couldn't blame Mamma for wanting to be a film star or a singer, she was probably ashamed of us. We were three killer daughters who got on her nerves.

Soon her rose-smelling kisses and orange curls would cast their spell again. We would see her and start to adore her. She should have warned me about periods and intercourse, we should have known more about death. Midge was right, worries increase if you don't discuss them. I must find out more about Ula in Ireland, I need to talk about Bruno's death. I don't think

Tor is well – all that sweating. When we find Mamma we must talk.

Lorries filled with soldiers kept overtaking us, convoys were passing through our town. Soldiers in waterproof trousers and tin helmets rode on motor bikes. An officer in a mud-coloured car swished past, the tyres making crunchings in the frost. Our gas masks and cases felt heavy now. I wanted a cup of school tea.

'Fancy a ride? Jump up, kiddo.'

'Don't smile at him, Ula. We don't know him. Do hurry, we're nearly there.' Perhaps the soldier was from London. Red said 'kiddo'. Don't smile.

And then we were home again. Changed-looking, cold, unfriendly, under frost-covered tiles. Our curtains were gone, our front door was open. Where had our hall carpet gone?

Was it to save it from soldiers' dirty boots? Why was the standard lamp missing and the coat rack? Where was the letter tray and the umbrella stand? What was the funny smell?

Through the open school-room door we could see a filing cabinet and the corner of a table. Someone was using a typewriter. The sound of plates clattering came from the basement. We were hungry and thirsty, we wanted dinner. A drawer slammed shut in the school room, boots sounded on the boards.

'Hey up. This is army premises. You're on army property here. No kiddies, no civilians, what's up then? Eh lass, no need for tears.'

He looked down at the manilla envelopes he was holding, avoiding my face until I felt better. I blinked.

'Just ... we wondered if Mamma was here. It's our home, we used to live here. Mamma is at the White Harte, but ...'

'No babies, no kiddies, no mammas. Who is she? She did live here?'

'It's our house, I told you. Mamma is an actress, well, she's a singer now really. We must find her, she's going north, you see.'

He shuffled his envelopes. Steady now, calm down, girl. Nothing was worth being that upset. He shouted down the basement stairs.

'Illingworth, come up here will you? Some kiddies are asking for their mam. She sings, she's a singer seemingly, used to live here. Happen we can help, eh? You'd better come.'

11

Illingworth's army plimsolls seemed almost as long as his shin-bones. A dishcloth hung from his khaki apron. He threw another cloth like a ball from hand to hand.

'Oh, hullo, do you live here too now?'

In spite of Ula's troubles she was never frightened of strangers. Her lock of hair stuck up questioningly, as if she'd whitened it with frost.

The men's faces both looked well lived in, with wrinkled skin round their eyes, but they weren't old. They looked at you straight when they spoke to you, they had flat accents and came from the north. I knew they were kind from the way they looked at me. They had hard, scraped-looking jaws. I'd never spoken to a soldier apart from Percival. Was it for these men that Mamma sang?

Singing was more elegant than dancing. I wouldn't like her kicking up her knickers in front of men. Would she sing special songs for Christmas? How I wished we had gone to Midge's family to sing round her tree with her pets.

Our school room was called the orderly room now. The soldier in charge was Oxenbury. Both spoke with shortened vowels and called us lass a lot.

'Our piano has gone,' Ula said, coming from our drawing room across the hallway. The men ate there, sitting at long tables with folding legs and wooden fold-up chairs. Our lesson table with the chenille cloth in our school room was replaced by Oxenbury's desk and files. He had wire baskets for his letters, labelled 'In', 'Pending', and 'Out'. He had a modern telephone that you held in one hand, instead of our old one with the separate ear-piece that you hung on a hook at the side.

His typewriter was called the 'Good Companion' and was kept under a cloth cover. He was dapper, with short scrubbed nails and hands. His trouser creases were like knife blades, the tucks in his battle dress were pressed like fans. Illingworth moved swiftly in his light soles. The kitchen work was heavy, all food must be carried upstairs. The hair over both their collars was so short that their necks looked shaved. The curls grew strongly over their crowns. With their odd speech and their thick eyebrows they might have been brothers. They were best mates and they liked us, you could tell. Oxenbury was the gentle one. Illingworth spoke less but didn't mince his words. Children were not allowed but we made a diversion. The rest of the section were out on manoeuvres on this frosty afternoon.

'Happen you fancy tea, then?'

'Yes please, Illingworth. Just what I wanted. Can I help you?'

'Ula, we don't live here now. Don't be cheeky.'

Ula was letting the family down as usual, strutting about with her toes turned out, touching their telephone, poking at the Good Companion. Now she had the cheek to want to serve tea. We didn't know these men.

We sat at Oxenbury's desk feeling better. The newly painted

hot pipes smelled like lentil soup. Our home looked more
sombre now, the army furnishings were plain. They had had
problems, Illingworth said, with the heating system; army maintenance had soon put it right.

'Do you like our house?'

'Not a lot to complain of, better than some billets I've seen.
We got rid of the dry rot. Did you know you had dry rot, back
of the pantry sink?'

'What is dry rot? I've never heard of it, Illingworth.'

Ula fiddled her fingers into the mesh of the In tray. If only she
would keep still. Illingworth said you paid dear for neglect of
property, but my family would stand to gain in the long run,
thanks to the army who let nothing go to rack. He was a regular soldier, he'd moved around a lot. Not like Oxenbury here, in
for the present emergency. Come peace, Oxenbury would be off
home again.

'Tor and I never went to the basement very much. Ula did.
We never knew about the dry rot.'

I wondered if humans could catch it. Perhaps Mamma had
dry rot of the heart. I wanted to defend our home and family
from criticism. They should realize that our father was dead, that
Mamma had done wonders, that but for this war we'd be living
here now. I asked Oxenbury what he had done before he joined
up, if he'd always lived in the north? He took a comb from his
pocket to repart his curls. He had worked in a wholesale drap-
ery business in Scarborough, had been in charge of stock
control. Army life suited him. He'd like to be a quartermaster,
that was his dream. He liked order, liked things done right. He
flicked his Good Companion with his handkerchief. Aye, army
life suited him champion. Not but what he'd be back to civvy
street when time came, choose how.

'There'll be changes. Old life won't be the same. War was bound to happen. Change for the best.'

'What do you mean, Illingworth? What kind of change?'

Illingworth spoke of class struggle, of social change that would affect one and all. Servants had gone already, good luck to them. So-called gentry must do their own chores. Stately mansions would be a thing of the past come peacetime, turned into museums or blocks of flats. Upper classes took too much for granted, working man must have his chance. Too much was owned by too few people, present capitalism was due to die. He wasn't like Oxenbury, he believed in red politics.

'They're kiddies, Illingworth, don't confuse them. You're too quick to start waving the red flag.'

'I quite understand, thanks very much. What I want to know is where are our things?'

Capitalists, dry rot, flags and changes, what we needed was our old home clothes. Once I had my skirt and jersey, my brain might begin to feel real. I was wearing Pegeen's vest under this awful overcoat. Ula had the blazer with the glued-on fur. Oxenbury told us that everything in the place was army issue. Any inquiries regarding previous effects should be addressed to War Office.

'We had a brother once. Our nursery was on the top floor. But he's dead now, he died last Christmas.'

'*Ula*. Shut up, can't you?'

She was without dignity or shame, blurting out our private affairs to strangers. I was sick of her. Before Tor and I had left Ireland we'd planted a magic stone to draw us back there. If only we could be there now.

'Eh, lass, she meant no harm. Don't get yourself upset again.'

'I'm not upset. I was just thinking about Ireland. We stayed there before the war.'

Oxenbury had a sister living there himself. He said everything ended some time, both good and bad, else how would there be change? Folk often only realized a good experience when it was over. He spoke so kindly, I longed to confide. I wanted to explain about my sisters and how I wanted a rest from them. I wished they were like other children, who hadn't had deaths to put up with, who hadn't lived so much on their own. Ula was eyeing the soldiers' gas masks as if they were diamonds. They had webbing straps and long breathing tubes hanging from large face-pieces.

'Fancy a biscuit?'

Oxenbury kept chocolate ones in his desk drawer for hungry moments during his important office work.

'Yes please. I'm quite hungry. I'll just look upstairs first, just in case, if I may?'

'Ula, Mamma isn't here. You know she isn't.'

Oxenbury said let her look to satisfy herself. But make haste before the section returned. She'd find all changed upstairs any road.

'Oh, all right then. Hurry, Ula.'

What had Illingworth meant about homes being turned into flats? Wouldn't we come back to live here? I would hate to be like the Clerkenwells eating chips and playing in the slums.

'Cheer up, lass. Look on the sunny side.'

The biscuits were digestive with chocolate on one side. They made a chocolaty burst when you bit. A luxury not often seen in shops now, he said. Tor ate slowly, Illingworth dipped his into tea, Oxenbury made polite little rattlings in his throat when he swallowed. We shared the serviceable army spoon.

'Chocolate biscuits, my favourite,' Ula said, coming down again from checking upstairs. From her face I knew she had seen something peculiar.

'What did you find, Ula?'

'Our eiderdowns and beds have gone.'

'Are there curtains?' Or did the soldiers have to dress and undress themselves in the dark? The orderly room windows were criss-crossed with brown paper to stop glass shattering in an air raid. Outside in the garden where our lavender used to grow were sandbags piled like a little wall. Ula said that their beds were miserable. Their mattresses split into three sections that they stacked in a pile during the day. Illingworth said they called them 'biscuits'. The rooms smelled of Jeyes fluid and everything was painted brown. I knew Ula had seen something that had upset her.

'Did you look in the nursery? Well, did you?'

'Captain's room is at the top now,' Oxenbury said. And he'd be in right trouble if it were known he'd let strangers in there. He glanced at Illingworth. The lass should have stayed below with us.

'Ula, what was it?'

Just an ordinary bed, she said, with a mattress and bedspread. There was a bedside table and proper curtains and ...

'What, Ula? And what?'

'Happen you saw a picture, lass? Yes?'

'What picture? Who of?'

She twisted her fingers. She'd seen Mamma's photograph. Taken long ago, with us when we were young.

'How could it be us? No one knows us here now.'

Could Mamma have given the captain a souvenir because she was going north? Film stars gave photographs to fans. I didn't want anyone looking at us here. Our house was all brown paint and change now, we didn't belong. Nothing felt real.

Oxenbury said slowly that a picture was nothing to get worked up about. Our mam was a singer, he'd seen her himself, they both had. The three of us should feel right proud. He smiled at us with his kind dog's smile. He didn't understand how much we missed her or how much she had let us down. In his part of the world mothers were probably different, more like Clerkenwell ones. They made nice dinners and put the children first. If they worked it would be for the children, not to amuse themselves. These men probably wrote home each week and got letters back. Was it possible that the picture was an advertisement for Mamma's show? The lovely singer with her children at home. I was proud of our lovely mother. Oxenbury didn't understand. I was angry with her, I hated her. She never gave a photograph to me. It was Christmas, where was she now? Did she have her arms round us? What clothes did we have on?

I explained that she had wanted to be a film star, she was a singer now instead. It was her war work. Illingworth said in a dry voice that neglecting kiddies might not seem so patriotic to some. Not just term but holidays too. Some might not understand that. Did anyone know we were here?

'It's the bombs, you see,' Ula explained.

That was why Mamma wasn't here. She wanted us to be safe. She couldn't be expected to know the headmistress would die.

Tor said nothing. She'd been wonderful about the mouse slaughtering. In an emergency she didn't fail. Nothing would ever make me believe that she'd hurt them, she was loyal. I wished she could be more like Ula and Ula more like her.

'Magnolia House is a small school with a lovely uniform. Mamma bought it herself, it cost a lot.'

I looked down at our awful clothes. No one must think ill of Mamma. Ula started rustling in the drawer for another biscuit. 'And please excuse my little sister. She's had a tiring day.'

'Aye, it would seem so. Don't you worry, girl. Captain is a good bloke.'

'As I said Mamma is a singer. Actually she's a … *chanteuse*.'

A rose-scented *chanteuse* of distinction waiting for us to join her.

'We know. We heard. We saw her. Listen up, that's Captain now.'

A car drew up, heavy feet sounded, lighter ones followed. Steps crossed the hall to the orderly room. A man is in the doorway, Mamma is behind him. She is here, Mamma has come.

'Bonnie? What's this, what are you doing? You naughty … why are you here?'

I had never seen her look so red and furious. She was trying to smile, she had little lines round her eyes. Her face was like a cracked dish. Why had we disobeyed her? She'd made arrangements for us. I was a naughty, disobedient girl.

'We couldn't stay. Miss Gee died. We had to leave, so we came.'

'Dead? She can't be dead. I saw her. When?'

Mamma had said she'd miss us and think of us. She had this captain now by her side. We were a nuisance, we had turned up unexpectedly, we were just a nasty surprise. The captain was the man we'd seen earlier in his shiny mud-coloured car. His face was like a ferret, staring now at Mamma.

She tried to settle her expression, smiling harder, twitching her shoulders. The captain mustn't see her looking upset. She spoke in a silly way, as gushingly as the Magnolias when they'd arrived at school.

'These are my three pets, aren't they sweet?'

'Mamma . . . I . . . I . . .'

'Don't mumble, darling child. Bad manners. Now then, we must make a plan.'

'What kind of plan? We're here.'

'A plan for where you should go. Oh my god, Bonnie, what *have* you got on? Look at you.'

My vest, Ula's glue-furred blazer and Tor's blouse were a show. She was ashamed of us as well as vexed. We had interrupted her life, what must the captain think? Oxenbury and Illingworth had shown more welcome.

Ula spoke. 'What Bonnie meant was that school turned out horrible so we came back to you. I can sing now, Mamma, and I can read.'

'*Marvellous*, darling.'

'At our pageant I was a unicorn. I was alone. Where shall we go now?'

'Let me think, my sweet. A plan, we must make a plan. Let me think.'

'Hurry and think, please, Mamma. Bonnie is upset. We came by train.'

Ula was speaking her mind bravely, defending us without thought for herself. I wanted to hug her.

Mamma touched her bright curls. She gazed at the captain. Such a dilemma, what should she do?

Lorries were coming to a halt outside. Soldiers were shouting, manoeuvres were over. They would stamp across our hallway and up to our bedrooms, they would wash in our basins, blow smoke out of our windows, eat supper in our drawing room, having read the letters sorted by Oxenbury. The ferret-faced captain would go to the nursery to look at Mamma's picture.

Would he sing while he shaved his face in the nursery bath-room? Would he plant a kiss on her face before he slept? His hair was short like the men's hair, he had blue stubble over his neck and chin. His nose jutted over his long shaped mouth. It wasn't that he was ugly that made him unlikeable, it was the way he looked at Mamma.

'What *shall* we do? I'm at a loss.'

'Do? I fail to see a problem. They must simply go to the hotel.'

'But . . .'

'No buts. I shall see to it. I shall take you. The four of you shall come with me now.'

He looked better when he smiled, his eyes went kinder, but not as kind as Oxenbury, not the smile of a proper friend.

'And drive in an army car?' Ula squealed with pleasure. Could she sit in front?

We were a proud party, walking past the soldiers and the lor-ries; we were the captain's guests. A weak sun was coming through the fog now and it didn't seem as cold. We would be spending Christmas with our Mamma. We would stay at the White Harte Hotel.

'Really, darlings, those *clothes*. What have you been up to? Where is your luggage?'

I explained that we'd just brought our washing things. Where were our old home clothes? She closed her eyes exhaustedly, she leaned her head back against the seat. So many decisions, so many problems. It seemed the army had requisitioned her life as well as her home. Her poor lambs were destitute and travel-stained, they had scarcely a stitch to wear.

'We couldn't bring anything. Miss Gee died, I told you. And everything went wrong.'

She said we looked pale. We seemed larger. Had we got taller?

'Ula has. I might have. But not Tor, she never grows. I . . .
Mamma, I'm older . . . I . . .'

'I know, my sweet. I can see you are. Tell me later all about
that.'

Her eyes looked at me, she didn't see me. She was thinking
about the captain in front.

Then we were at the White Harte again, with the wisteria
branches round the leaded windows. In the summer its flowers
would be mauve. We were to share a large room overlooking the
road.

'I can see the lorries passing.'

Ula would take the single bed by the window. Tor and I
would share.

'Couldn't I share with you two, Bonnie? Why is it always you
and Tor?'

'It isn't. Not always,' Tor said quietly. Ula should be allowed
to join us sometimes, it wasn't kind or fair to keep her out.

12

'Did you hear Mamma come in last night, Tor? Did she say goodnight?'

I had tried to stay awake, I had listened to the convoys of lorries passing and wondered if all those soldiers would get blown to bits. This must be the troop movements that Miss Gee spoke of. Our careless talk could cost their lives.

Our room was beautiful, we had loved it immediately. We had our own bathroom in the passage outside. Our clothes cupboard was like a separate room that you could walk in, with rails and shelves inside. We had hung up our raggy coats and explored our bathroom. We had arranged our toothbrushes and sponges on the shelves. We had brushed our hair and watched our reflections. Ula tapped her toothbrush on various surfaces to make different notes. Glass made the highest ones. Tor and I smiled tolerantly at her. We were three sisters come to rest at last in a hotel. We smeared our faces with Mamma's cold cream again. We lay in hot water to our earlobes, forgetting about saving for the brave. Freedom was the White Harte Hotel, doing what we wanted, knowing that Mamma was near. In deep water you could forget growing older and being responsible, your brain and your feelings worked as one. Magnolia House was a distant nightmare, Mamma's room was on the same floor. She would look in to say goodnight after her show. Had she brushed kisses on our sleeping foreheads? I sniffed my hair for the scent of roses. 'Ula, did you hear Mamma?'

'I was watching for lorries. I was awake ages. I heard the people leaving the bar downstairs.'

She looked pink and normal again but Tor still looked sickly. The road was quiet. It was foggy again. The fog came in swirls, the sounds outside were muffled, once or twice a plane passed overhead. Runnels of wet ran down the little windows. Ula had put 'U's in each pane. It was early still, Ula wanted to go to the bathroom again, excitement made her like that. Mamma's bedroom faced the back.

I had a bedside lamp with a switch hanging from a length of silkbound flex. I felt it and remembered the mouse tail. Tor was rooting in her attaché case on the floor.

'Are you looking for your diary? Listen, Tor, I want to tell you something.'

'What are you saying, Bonnie? You always have secrets. You're leaving me out again.'

'Nothing, Ula. Watch for lorries or something.'

'Tell me. Tell me.'

'Don't keep her out, Bonnie. Tell.'

'Oh, all right. I was asking Tor if she remembered our game.'

It was more a phantasy than a game which she and I had played for years. Once at Magnolia House I'd forgotten it, there had been neither privacy nor time. We used to make lairs in our beds and pretend to be animals. You could play it alone but it was better with Tor. We could pull our beds together to make a smooth base for a cave or nest. We made our eider-downs and sheets into passages, propping the roof with a coat hanger or even a chair. Wriggling and snuffling we became hedgehogs or badgers, moles or squirrels; we preferred bur-rowing animals rather than fierce ones, though Tor used to choose yaks or camels sometimes for a change. Then we'd drape clothes over cupboards and tables. Our game had no beginning and no end, our time was mostly spent in preparing the hide-outs. Tucking and smoothing and hoisting was a pleasure. This large hotel bed would be ideal. I didn't want Ula playing and spoiling it. I explained that it wasn't a proper game, she wouldn't enjoy it. Look for lorries and leave us alone.

'There aren't any. Please, Bonnie.'

Her cheek had a red mark from the crease of her pillow, her white lock of hair was on end.

'Let her, Bonnie, don't push her out.'

'Oh well. Think of an animal. Make a nest.'

'I'm a fly. Buzz buzz.'

'A fly isn't an animal, you fool. It's an insect.'

'I'll be a stone unicorn then.'

'If it's stone it can't make a nest, stupid. Play properly or you can't play at all.'

'I was the unicorn in the pageant.'

'Remember what Midge said about unicorns, Bonnie? They did exist once.'

The game was my invention. I didn't want Tor making the rules. Ula made me feel ashamed. She was fiddling with her pencil in her curls, trying to make another horn. She was so babyish and eager. I wanted to forget school and that unicorn on the gate and the pageant.

'Bonnie, why don't you be a mother unicorn? Then Tor and I can be your young.'

'I'm not being anyone's mother, thanks very much. And put that pencil down.'

'Let her, Bonnie, it won't hurt us.'

'They aren't real. No one ever saw one. It's stupid.'

My feeling of not existing was starting. Think of who you are and why you're here. Christmas is coming, nothing is terrible, you needn't feel afraid any more.

'Oh, all right.'

Ula thought that unicorns might sleep in grassy glades with ferns for covering. In summer they might lie on a lawn. We walked round quietly on hands and feet, shaking imaginary horns. Ula pawed the air looking solemn; she made little humming sounds. Being fond of moonlight it was probable that they sang at night. They would eat rose petals with jam, and a little fruit in the summer months. Unicorns were loving animals who didn't quarrel or fight. It was calming to roam round our room, being neither male nor female, adult nor child, just three sisters in accord. We played until we were tired of it, then we lay on the floor under our beds.

'Let's remember Ireland.'

The lovely warm summer seemed like years ago when we'd run and rolled on the grass. We had searched for four-leafed clovers and picked daisies, breathing that special summer smell. We had listened to bats squeaking and unseen dark night birds. We had run races in the twilight, never caring who won or lost. We were without past or future, only the present mattered. The war came and we'd had to come home. Why should good things have to end?

'The captain is Irish,' Ula sucked her hair.

'He isn't. Is he, Tor?'

'Ula was there the longest. He might be. Ula should know.'

'I don't trust him.'

Tor said he was kind to get us here, he'd been responsible. Mamma liked him.

'You don't think ... ?'

Mamma wouldn't do anything stupid would she? We were used to not having men by now, a stepfather would be a burden. We didn't need one so why should she? Just because she wriggled and blinked at him didn't make him special.

'Mamma likes being looked after and protected. He's kind. She's been alone for so long.'

I said I didn't see why, she'd got us, hadn't she? Tor had a way of tucking her chin in when she was being sensible. She was too wise and old-fashioned for her age. She understood grown-ups and children better than I did. I was too old now for playing games on the floor but I'd enjoyed it. After what had happened to Ula you'd think she'd never want to see an Irish person.

'Feel, Bonnie, feel my horn.'

'Shut up, don't be so stupid. I'm thinking.'

Mamma had soldiers listening and watching her every evening. If she was lonely it was her own fault. Why choose the captain? She'd be better off with Oxenbury. The sooner she moved north the better. Perhaps the captain would get gassed or shot. Our family could do without Irish ferrets joining us.

'Stop worrying, Bonnie. Remember Ireland.'

What an innocent she was. Had she forgotten what happened there and the terrible death of her friend? It had happened before Tor and I joined her. She'd grown taller since then, she'd put on weight.

On our backs in a row in the big bed it felt as if we were the same age, the same size, though Ula was taller than Tor now. Why didn't Tor grow? I'd never find anyone nicer than my sisters, though Ula could be loathsome at times. She said that perhaps the captain had put an Irish spell over Mamma; the Irish could do that.

'Spells, indeed. That's rubbish. Spells are against the law.'

Mamma was not unhappy, she had no need to marry someone. Both my sisters were wrong.

Ula said that Mamma had once confided in her. She'd been miserable when Bruno died, though she'd not shown sorrow. If she'd been happy she'd want to stay with us. She didn't want to be reminded of children.

Grown-ups should never be unhappy or unreliable. They should be there when needed. They shouldn't die.

Ula said she probably didn't know what she did feel, she was muddled. She had bought the uniform and that nice watch for me.

My watch was twinkling in Clerkenwell on Red's wrist now. I had to admit that the captain had arranged this room for us beautifully. We had mauve striped curtains and mauve carpeting and the special room for our clothes. He'd asked particularly for a large room, guessing we'd like it. Our bathroom was a joy.

'I wish we had something to read.' Ula was as fond of books as Tor was, now that she could read. She liked reading aloud to prove that she did it properly, following the print with her finger. Outside in the passage was a bookcase with a row of dictionaries, which we'd never been taught how to use. There was a thin book with a brown cover, *Creatures of Myth*. Ula read the chapter headings in a loud proud voice, checking to see if we were impressed.

'"The Basilisk", "The Cockatrice", "The Griffin", "The Sala-mander". And "The Unicorn". You see, Bonnie, they are real.'

'It's mythical, you fool. That means it's not true. It's fable, not a proved fact.'

She held up the picture of an uglier unicorn than the school one, with a longer horn and a look of contempt round the mouth.

'Read about it.'

Her singsong voice continued. '"The other animals held the unicorn in esteem, because of its noble birth."'

'Go on.'

'"They preferred to wait until it had dipped its horn into the drinking water to ensure freedom from poison. The horn was a cure for all ills."'

'What rubbish. Anything else?'

'"If the other beasts gave chase out of envy the unicorn flung himself over a cliff in a somersault. By impaling himself on his horn the fall didn't harm him."'

'What a feeble thing to do. Any more?'

'"When the Genghis Khan invaded India he was greeted by the unicorn abasing himself so courteously that the great man reconsidered his campaign and returned with his troops, thus India was saved by a unicorn."'

'Oh, really.'

'But listen to this part, Bonnie. "The unicorn loved to rest his head in the lap of a fair maiden so huntsmen used maidens as bait. Because the maidens loved the unicorn they protected him so the plan failed."'

'No one is going to rest their head in my lap thanks very—'

'Oh come on, Bonnie. Play some more.'

13

We were feeling hungry. When we heard noises downstairs I told my sisters to get washed and we stopped being equals. I couldn't avoid being the oldest for long. I looked at myself while I waited for them. Midge said that your glands would change. Adolescence might bring greasy skin or spots. I felt old before I'd started living properly. At least I didn't have warts round my neck or dandruffy shoulders like some Clerkenwells. One day I'd be as lovely as Mamma was with well-kept skin and hair. I would wear a long bob with a fringe dangling into my spiky eyelashes, I would drink red or green cocktails from long-stemmed glasses. I'd never desert my sisters; we needed each other. Phoebe's brother must have been suffering from war fatigue. Had they been drunk, perhaps? I hadn't smelled drink when he'd taken my hands and spoken of waltzing. War made people rude and muddled. Putting on uniforms made things go wrong.

I combed my hair flat again. Phoebe's sophistication was a veneer for her weak will. She craved attention and admiration, she was inwardly shallow. I and my sisters were deeply serious, one day we'd all be wise.

Tor's diary was still in her attaché case. I knew everything about her except what she wrote there. It was a fat little book with shiny covers and ruled lines. The first page was thickly written with two words, 'strictly private'. You could hardly see the paper under the ink. Inside the writing was even tinier. I held it close to the lamp. No margins, no punctuation, no spaces. I oughtn't to read it. I must.

September 1939 This is a war record not about England but the way it changes things Mamma says we must to go school we went to london for our uniform Bonnie thinks clothes matter Mamma saw us in our vests when the band played at tea she had tears in her eyes Bonnie is bossy

October 1939 The school has a unicorn Mamma was afraid to meet Miss Gee Bonnie is afraid too inside Ula and I are like Papa the other girls are silly especially Phoebe this diary is my survival I guessed Bonnie would fall in that game she got a fright when her period came

November 1939 Bonnie goes round with Midge now Im alone I know what theyve got in the garden its a cage of mice I blame them for everything Id like to kill them Xmas will be awful . . .

I held the page closer. I couldn't believe it, not my gentle Tor. She'd known all the time about our secret. Yet she'd cried so when we'd found them, her tears had dropped on to the corpses. I would never know who had murdered them, I didn't want to know. I would love and trust Tor until death. Run in peace.

'Put that down, Bonnie. How dare you.'

She was standing in the doorway with Ula behind. Both had toothpaste on their cheeks. I'd never seen Tor look like

Mamma, the same cracked dish expression, the same furious eyes.

'I was just looking, I wasn't snooping. I never knew you ...'

'It's private. It's my diary, my own private affair.'

'I'm sorry.'

'Swear not to look again. Swear ...'

'I'm your sister. We never have secrets, we've always told.'

'Liar. You never told about the mice.'

'That's different. I promised Midge.'

'It's not different. You're a creeping sneak.'

'What mice? What mice are you talking about?' Ula butted in. I couldn't bear Tor calling me names. She loathed me.

'Swear, Bonnie. Swear you won't do it again.'

'Yes, you'd better swear, Bonnie. Swear as a unicorn.'

'Don't be such a fool.'

'Do as Ula says. Swear.'

They made me swear on my honour as an animal of peace to obey rules of privacy. I would never touch Tor's book. I felt foolish saying it. Ula was satisfied. Tor must have enjoyed humiliating me. Were they babyish because they didn't want to grow up?

Mamma was wearing orange. She seemed to light her corner of the room. The other guests looked drab and serious, eating toast with downcast eyes.

'Can we have boiled eggs, Mamma?'

'Ula, my sweet, I've ordered fruit. You need vitamins. An apple a day keeps acne away.'

I felt ashamed of our clothes again. Mamma looked so lovely. The marmalade in the crystal jar was the exact colour of her blouse. What would the White Harte guests think of us? I peeled a green apple. Should Mamma or I write to Miss Patrice? We'd left so suddenly and she had looked so ill. Mamma was looking at Ula in disbelief, that filthy fur on her collar looked like an animal.

Ula started to explain. We had lost our clothes because the Clerkenwells preferred our uniform to their things. Mamma begged to be spared the details until she had drunk her coffee.

'We have nothing to wear, Mamma. There are no clothes for us anywhere.'

Then she would have to see to it, Mamma said. In the meantime did we have to talk quite so loudly at this hour of the morning? The guests were listening, though keeping their eyes on their toast. The beautiful singer had her schoolgirl daughters home for Christmas, wearing strangely tattered clothes.

'Mamma, can't I just tell you about the pageant? Bonnie and Tor were mice and goats but I pulled the Noah's ark.'

'Shut up, Ula.'

I couldn't think of the mice without a pang, without seeing their bodies lying red and torn, the worst sight I'd ever seen.

Mamma put down her table napkin. From the look of us we evidently had suffered some sort of emotional upset. She would have something to say to that headmistress, the school had not lived up to its claims. Hadn't we learned anything apart from speaking with rather common accents?

I thought of the dancing to the grammie, Barbie's thin arms winding it, I thought of the wartime songs. I thought of Midge's mouse book. A pain went through me.

I bit into my apple. I choked. Fragments of apple flew from my mouth. It was that pain again. That shooting sensation was a period. I had no one to help now, I had used up all Midge's pads.

'My sweet child, whatever is it? Is the apple sour? What a face and what a fuss.'

She wants us to look healthy, to eat fruit, to care for our looks and be a credit to her. We must speak nicely, carry ourselves well and not bother her. We are a disgrace, our clothes are disreputable. Ula has spots. Tor looks starved.

'Mamma, I have periods. I've started. I never knew.'

I bent over the green apple peel, I couldn't speak. I felt Tor's thin hand patting mine, silently comforting.

'How monstrous. How appalling. You mean you were not prepared?'

'How could I? I never heard of it. No one told me. No one said.'

'Didn't Gov instruct you? You mean you were not ... she didn't ...'

Tor spoke. 'Mamma, you should have told Bonnie about menstruation. You are the mother, after all. There's such a thing as motherly interest. I think Bonnie has a pain now ...'

'Period of what? Do you mean weather?' Ula dug the spoon into the marmalade. 'Don't cry any more, Bonnie. It's not your fault we lost all our clothes.'

My two sisters were defending me, braving Mamma for me. I could forgive them anything.

Then Mamma left her side of the table. She embraced me, ignoring the guests. She knelt on the floor by me, she put her face close, she rocked me back and forth like a child. She'd had no idea, she hadn't realized, could I forgive her? How remiss she had been. Come now to her bedroom with her. She'd look after me, come along now.

The room was coral pink with cream-coloured walls and overlooked the garden. Mamma pulled the curtains, she lit the gas fire, she pulled back her eiderdown. I must rest, I must stop whimpering, I was safe. She lit the lamps each side of her bed, her room was rosy. Come now, Bonnie, don't be self-indulgent. Crying was ageing, it swelled the eyelids, dried the complexion. No more self-pity. Just relax.

She opened a drawer in her wardrobe, felt under her secret underwear. There. Protection and comfort, large size, go to the bathroom.

'I'll go with her, shall I?'

'Shut up, Ula. No, you can't.'

Tor told Ula to look at the sundial outside. Remember the lawn in Ireland? We'd never seen a sundial before. Ula fiddled with Mamma's dressing set, touching the silver jars and bottles. Why was Bonnie so upset?

Mamma was combing her hair when I rejoined them, examining her streak of white. She said that one day Ula would be glad of it, streaking was sophisticated. Ula stood proud and still, being praised for her appearance. Tor waited her turn to be combed.

Mamma said our clothes were like something from a bonfire night, we'd have to be fitted out again. But Bonnie darling must rest now and forget her troubles. I climbed into her wide pink bed with her hot-water bottle, I stretched down my feet with joy. Put the bottle on the stomach, she said kindly, warmth helped pain. She offered me milk with honey in it and aspirin. Her face was sweet, the aspirin was vile. I wanted the pain to stay now, she was so kind to me. I was a nasty colour, she said. Sleep a little but no more self-pity. She went downstairs to the telephone.

I was where I wanted to be, in Mamma's bedroom with my sisters perched on either side of me. They watched with grave faces. I was warm, free of pain and beloved.

'Let's see if the captain's picture is here.'

Ula couldn't sit still, she rustled about again at the dressing table, lifting the silver-backed brushes.

'Of course not. Why should it be?'

I wouldn't let a picture of that ferrety man spoil my happiness. I turned away my head.

'Behind the looking glass. Mamma hid it. He hasn't put SWALK.'

Tor looked at it too, framed in silver like Percival's, an officer's peaked cap on his head.

I would never put a picture of a man in my bedroom. Soldiers were faithless and treacherous. Had Percival really wanted to waltz with me? Had I imagined it? (Yes, oh yes. *When?*)

'Now children, darlings, everything is settled. We'll go shopping later on. Bonnie, will you be fit enough?'

'I'm afraid not, Mamma. I didn't sleep last night.'

I closed my eyes. Did she really expect me to sit in the captain's car again while he made eyes at her? I would stay at the White Harte alone.

14

'Mamma, I must talk to you. Alone, please, before you go.'

'So intense, so emotional, my sweet. Learn to take life lightly. I have had to. I assure you it's best.'

She had listened while I spoke of Tor who was too thin, too small, too sweaty and quiet. Someone must worry about my sisters. People always let you down.

She smiled in a vague way saying that children differed as much as adults. It was rare to know someone totally and completely, unless . . .

'Unless what, Mamma?'

I had trusted Midge with our life secrets, she had told Phoebe, who had told Red.

Mamma raised her hands in protest. Midge? Phoebe? Red? Such a catalogue, spare her more please. I must learn not to be so fervent. I was getting positively overwrought. It was a great mistake to expect too much of people, she had found, particularly when you were young.

'Yes, yes, I quite understand, Mamma. What exactly did Ula do in Ireland?'

Her face went stiff again, her eyes changed. A painful time. Bruno's death, a time of loss. And imagine, Bonnie, I wasn't there for it. The shock, to arrive home ... my only son ...

'You were never there, Mamma.'

'How unforgiving you are. How can a child understand, presume to judge? When your father died my interest died. Each time I looked at you three ...'

'You haven't got a photograph of him. Why?'

'Have you no conception, no idea of pain?'

'You never asked us if we wanted to be pushed out. To Ireland, to that awful school.'

Her face went patchy, she started bending and pulling her fingers like Ula. I mustn't think that she didn't want us.

'We did think that. We think it now.'

Did she know that Tor and I had put Bruno naked under the Christmas tree? His dangler was like a tiny snail.

'The war ... I ...'

'What about the war? You like singing, don't you? It suits you.'

'You're so critical. Your sister Ula has more sympathy.'

'She's a baby still. She shows off. She'll probably go mad one day. I'm not critical. I'm telling the truth.'

'Darling Bonnie, I look to you. You're my second-in-command, my adjutant, remember? Why are you letting me down?'

'I don't want to be any more.'

'When your Papa died, all my happiness—'

'Your happiness? What about ours? You shouldn't have had us.'

I wanted to give her as much hurt as possible. We had been lonely too. She'd been left without an heir, we'd had no mother.

'You're too young to understand adult despair.'

273

'I'm trying to, Mamma. I'm trying.'

She said children only understood what they already knew and had experienced. How could we understand aridity of the soul?

'Aridity? Are you bored with us? What did happen to Ula? She grinds her teeth in her sleep.'

She looked shocked. Did I think Ula might have worms?

'What happened?'

'I thought you knew. She caused her friend's death in the dark. The knife in her pocket slipped, the little girl's throat was pierced. A freak accident. Imagine letting children run round with knives.'

'You never knew what we had. You weren't there.'

'Accusing me again. You are merciless!'

'I'm not. You are.'

'You liked Ireland, didn't you, Bonnie? We'll go back there, all of us, one day. You'll see.'

She couldn't help the war, she said. She had thought we were happy at school. She'd always had a singer's ambition, the army needed her.

'So did we.' I added that the uniform had been nice at first. The beautiful rust and tomato colours reminded me of mud and blood now. Clothes didn't ensure friendship or stop you feeling left out. 'And, Mamma, you should have told me about ... you know ... growing up.'

She protested that she'd bought a book on sexual development.

'I didn't read it. Tor did. Tor keeps a diary.'

'Keeping diaries can be morbid. She's an introspective child.'

Had anyone tried to frighten me with old wives' tales? Had I been frightened? Did I understand everything now?

'It's not just that ...'

'What is it, sweet child?'

I mustn't think of Red in the dormitory, mustn't think of those dreadful sounds. Those feet sticking out from the blanket, that smell like stale fish in the air. I will forget heaving bodies and dangling things. There are things I would like to know. How did the dangling thing get into you? It was too floppy. Was it pointed? Did it bleed? Probably Red knew more about bodily things than Mamma, she was more open. Mamma's face was still blotched and nervous-looking. Was she secretly afraid of intercourse?

'Are you sure there is nothing more you need to know?'

'Quite sure, thanks, Mamma.'

She looked relieved. She peered in her hand mirror, checking her mouth. I could hear my sisters in our bedroom. Ula was trying to whistle. Mamma put down her mirror. She wanted to talk about love. I must try and understand, one day I would love someone myself. Love was a blessing, you treasured it having sought it. Some women only loved once. Love, once found, stayed in the heart. It was almost holy.

'Holy? There was nothing much holy or precious when we saw it.'

'Saw? What did you see?'

My mouth felt horrid. I could nearly smell what we'd seen. My words jumbled as I tried to tell. Red and Phoebe, the look and sound. No clothes. That horrible sound. The bed. The blanket moving on the floor. The bed, the moving blanket and the sounds.

Mamma went quite white, her curls seemed to jump round her white face and staring eyes. Did I mean to say that we had actually stood and *watched*? She had put my sisters in my charge.

I had let them watch like peeping cats. Why had I not gone to my headmistress? Why had I not spoken before?

'Miss Gee had died. We never mentioned it, not even to ourselves.'

Was love and sex something to praise and extol but never watch? Miss Patrice had spoken of love in the same melting way as Mamma.

She said it was quite monstrous, her own children in their own school.

'We were upset.'

We must put it quite out of our minds now. And believe her, love was miraculous when it was right. One day I would change, one day I would fall in love.

'I won't. I promise you I won't.' Loving my sisters was bother enough. Why should adult love be better?

'Is there anything else on your mind?'

'Why have you got a photograph of the captain if Papa meant so much to you? Why has he got one of you?'

She closed her eyes. She might have known I'd be merciless. Creeping round other people's bedrooms, prying, continually interrogating, taking her to task.

'I'm not interrogating, just asking.'

She gazed at her third finger, thinking, I expect, of another diamond ring that the captain might put there. She murmured that she was a young woman, despite widowhood. Was she allowed no second chance just because of motherhood?

'He's Irish. Look what happened to Ula there.'

'Don't be absurd. You're talking wildly. You loved Ireland, you know you did. And the captain is from the north.'

'How can you love someone with a face like that?'

Because of Ireland Ula was a manslaughterer. I was just

advising, not criticizing. We were just three ordinary daughters wanting an ordinary mother, was that too much to ask? It was Christmas, better forget him and concentrate on us.

'Everything is going to be different, Bonnie, you'll see.'

'Then could you move your bedroom nearer to ours? We'd like it.'

We'd feel more like a family. We would know if she came in late. Her face lightened, she'd be delighted. Would I like to help her move her things?

I would trail back and forth with joy for her, I would carry armfuls of lovely things. I wouldn't let Ula or Tor help me. I would arrange her shoes in coloured rows. Her new room by ours had its own clothes closet, I would be queen of her castle of clothes. I would be her personal maid, her seamstress, her sec-retary; no one else must touch those dresses and hats. She would share our bathroom opposite her doorway. Her oils, creams and rose-smelling powders would oust our sponge and toothpaste smells. Our little tubes of cream must be put in a corner. Mamma must have all the space she required. We would wait our turn for the bathroom, we would keep watch, she must never get away. We would hear her coming and going like an ordinary mother. She would brush our hair and worry about our health.

'Look, Mamma, this petticoat is ripped. How did it happen?'

The rose-coloured satin with lace inserts was in two pieces. I will stitch it daintily to make Mamma immaculate again. She will rely on me, tell me her secrets. I will help her, she will help me. We will make merry this Christmas at the White Harte, we will wear more new pretty dresses, we'll teach Mamma dancing. The clothes we are wearing must be burned.

We needn't have a Christmas tree, they had brought us bad luck in the past. Our bedroom had an open fire, we would burn logs there. We would buy cards for our friends with robins, lanterns and snowmen.

'Which friends?' asked Tor quietly.

Christmas was a time of forgiving and forgetting. Should we send a card to Red? Would Midge think of me on Christmas morning, busy with presents, her pets and tree? We would make our room light and magic, with red knitted stockings to hang before the fire. We had never believed in Santa Claus. We were like three Cinderellas, our chance had come.

'Mamma, when we buy our new clothes can we go to that restaurant? We might hear Bonnie's tune.'

'What tune, sweet child?'

Ula hummed. Mamma observed that she had a sweet voice. Perhaps she would be a singer too. Acting and singing were often inherited. She smiled at her singing child. Yes, we would revisit the restaurant, and Ula must learn to eat slowly, not gollop like a little pig. How was Bonnie? Better now?

'I want to finish moving your things. I'll mend the petticoat, Mamma.' I would lie against pillows stitching, stitch her to us tight as a shadow while they went shopping. The name Mamma was old-fashioned and ridiculous. 'Mummy' was like the Magnolias, 'Mum' like the Clerkenwells.

My sisters put on those shabby overcoats. Ula was bending her knees stiff-jointedly, she was sniffing and pawing her hands. She wasn't thinking of new clothes or restaurants, she was being a unicorn.

'Goodbye, Bonnie, I wish you were coming.'

Goodbye, Tor, beloved friend. I picked up the petticoat, the busy seamstress. This time Mamma wouldn't leave us, she belonged with us. No more goodbyes. I waited until they had driven away and the road was empty. I got my coat and ran up the road again.

Our hall door was open still. I heard the clatter of the Good Companion. Oxenbury's kind dog's smile was the same.

'Hullo, Oxenbury. I've just come to ask you something.'

'Thee again, lass? What's up?'

'It's Mamma. She's too old you see, it's unsuitable. She's got us, that should be enough.'

'Too old for what?'

'She seems to have an infatuation. For ... you know ... that captain. She's too busy and she's too old.'

I was breathless. I wanted Oxenbury to agree with me. I needed support. I knew I was right.

'Too old for what?'

Illingworth was there again, with his dishcloths and tennis shoes. Kiddies on the premises again? He and Oxenbury would get cashiered.

'Cashiered? It's Mamma, Illingworth, you see. It's possible she might want to marry your captain.'

'Happen she might at that.'

Oxenbury asked how my sisters felt.

'They're too young. They don't understand. He's from Ireland, you know, the northern part.'

'We knew where he's from. He's Company Captain. Does your Mam know you feel this way?'

'She's not said anything definite. It's just that I worry.'

Oxenbury said I should tell her our feelings. Illingworth looked amused. Maybe it was a shot-gun arrangement, we'd better lump it, choose how.

'Mamma wouldn't shoot a gun at anyone, she wouldn't.'

'Don't tease her, Illingworth. Their mam could go further and fare worse.'

'She doesn't need anyone. She's got us. Don't you understand?'

Oxenbury said that life moved on, you had to let go of people. All a bit of a mystery was life.

'What do you mean?' I'd had enough of secrets and mysteries.

As Oxenbury saw it you had to let things take their chosen course. We couldn't put a rope round our mam and tie her, it would help no one.

'Well, never mind all that. The captain is quite unsuitable, apart from being from the north of Ireland.'

The captain most likely had a stately home back in the old country, Illingworth said, and able to keep the lot of us in style. He only hoped the place would be in a better state than this house had been, not a heap of rubble fit for demolition. He threw his dishtowel from hand to hand. The captain was champion. Be fair, now, wait till I knew him. I should be pleased for the sake of our mam.

I said that he never smiled or talked to us. He looked like a ferret.

'Happen he's shy of you three. Have you talked to him?'

'I've nothing to say to him, I just dislike him.' He'd never fit in with our complicated thoughts and lives.

I liked Oxenbury and Illingworth more than any men I'd met yet. They took me seriously, they were kind. They hadn't told me what I'd wanted to hear. They hadn't said that the captain was wicked, that Mamma ought to send him away. But I felt more settled and comfortable when I left them. I think they did understand.

Mamma's bed was wide and comfortable. All her things were nicely put away.

'Look, Mamma. I've finished your petticoat.'

I held it for her to see. Lovely stitching, she said, what a clever child. What a help I was going to be.

'Come into our bedroom in a minute, Bonnie. You're going to get a nice surprise.'

15

I stood in the doorway of our bedroom. These strangers couldn't be my sisters, playing with a lot of toys. Our room had changed into a sort of toyshop with toys everywhere, on the floor, on the beds and chairs.

'I thought you were supposed to have been buying clothes. Have you all gone off your heads? Where are the new clothes?'

They were still in what they'd put on this morning, that be-furred blazer, that dreadful blouse. Our room was alive with stuffed animals and clockwork playthings. There was a lion almost as big as Ula, with a hectic yellow mane, a crocodile with a jointed backbone, its open mouth sharp with teeth. There was a wild-eyed mule made of leather and a family of pigs made of raffia that fitted into a basket, there were insects that flapped tin wings when you wound their tails. On the floor surrounded by more toys was Ula; she was kissing a grey velvet lamb. I had never seen her kiss anything except her gas mask. There was a high whining sound.

Tor was playing with a spinning top that flashed red, silver and gold. As it turned more slowly the humming got lower. Tor looked at me and smiled. A child's voice was singing a carol. Mamma had actually bought a gramophone. 'The stars in the bright sky looked down where he lay, The little . . .'

'Oh stop, all of you. You do look silly.'

They took no notice. The child went on singing, the top went on spinning, Ula went on kissing her lamb. While I had been worrying about our future Mamma had been spending foolishly. We still had nothing to wear. I wanted to hit her; as if my sisters weren't babyish enough. I had organized her new bedroom, I had discussed her marriage future with the two soldiers. Was I the only one with any sense? You couldn't control grown-ups, you could only get attention by being ill or unpleasant, they did as they wished in the end. I had so longed for her, now I almost hated her. I wouldn't be like her when I was old.

'You are silly, Mamma. I suppose I can be thankful you didn't buy any dolls.'

There was a toy engine with wooden wheels and a chimney. There was a water pistol and a pop gun that shot a cork. Ula said she'd wanted to buy dolls. They had stopped her.

Tor plunged the spindle of the top again. The humming sound increased. The top skidded over the floor towards me.

'Do make it stop, Tor.'

The carol ended. Mamma wound the gramophone. 'Away in a manger, no crib for a bed.'

'Oh shut up, all of you.'

The three of them looked pretty and carefree in the light of the logs burning in our grate. Mamma looked as young as my sisters, all playing with Christmas toys. There was nothing woebegone about Tor and Ula now, in spite of the awful clothes. Mamma still had her fur jacket on, her collar framed her face. She took a little parcel from her pocket. Don't think she'd left

me out, she'd not forget her right-hand man on such an important day. She'd bought up the last toys to be found in London.
Factories had to make munitions now, she'd had a spree while
the going was good.

I started picking up wrapping paper. I was still angry. I ignored
her little packet.

'Open it, Bonnie. I didn't buy *you* a toy.'

It was a string of seed pearls in a box with a velvet lining,
nicer than anything Phoebe owned. Three turquoises were set
in the clasp, blue for my eyes, Mamma said, blue the colour of
hope.

'Thank you.'

'We had every intention of buying clothes and Christmas
cards for your friends. We saw the toyshop, we couldn't resist.
We ran out of time.'

And she had taken my sisters to the hairdresser. Ula's curls
just touched her shoulders, her white lock was part of a fringe.
Tor looked like a young and even thinner boy now, with dark
rings round her eyes. All of us needed cheering up, Mamma said,
she had done the best she could. At least she had not insulted
me with games and animals. My sisters were not interested in
the pearls, they were too engrossed in their toys.

'Do you feel better now, Bonnie? Let me fasten it.'

Was she pleading? Was she a little afraid? Her fingers touched
my neck. Were the pearls to atone?

'While you were out I went to see Oxenbury and Illingworth.'

'Who? You mean you went home after what I said? I told you
not to go there, Bonnie.'

'It's our house. Why shouldn't I? The army don't own it. We'll
be going back after the war.'

'You had no right. Besides, why should you want to?'

'They're my friends. I like them.'

'You are never to go there again.'

'You do. You go there.'

'That is different. The captain is a personal friend.'

'Oxenbury and Illingworth are my friends.'

'That is absurd, that is entirely different.'

'Why?'

'I entertain the regiment, you know that. Apart from which, he's a family friend.'

'He's not my friend. Don't include me.'

'You are a child but you could make some effort to understand.'

'One moment I'm a child, the next moment you're giving me pearl necklaces and making me responsible for my sisters. Well I'm not a child, thanks very much. If you'd like to know, I went to ask Oxenbury and Illingworth about you and that captain.'

'You *what*? You went gossiping and sneaking to the troops about my private life? Are you out of your mind?'

'No, I'm not. I was afraid you might do something silly, something we all might regret.'

'I find it difficult to understand your lack of loyalty. Pray, what was the outcome of this top-level inquiry? What pearls of wisdom did you glean?'

She had blotches round her mouth again, her eyes were hard. Tor went on making her top hum, the child went on singing, Ula crooned to her lamb. I have made Mamma furious. I have caused her pain. I'm glad.

'Well, Bonnie?'

'They told me not to interfere. If you want to marry someone it's up to you.'

Mamma, look after us. Don't go off with that ferret man.

'For which gracious permission I'm supposed to be grateful? Perhaps you'd like me to go on my knees?'

'They quite like the captain. They admire him. They probably like you too.'

She was quiet. Had I appeased her? Mamma, I just want you to stay.

'Mamma, what is to become of us? We can't go back to that school.'

'We'll have to discuss it, naturally. It's your ... hostility. The other two are so much easier.'

'They're young.' How could we become better friends until she became more real, more of a living mother. You couldn't make things right just with a lot of toys or clothes.

'You should have come with us on the shopping trip. You are overwrought again. Fancy running behind my back and tittle-tattling.'

'I told you, I was worried, I had to tell someone. Mamma, will you be marrying that captain?'

'Don't call him "that captain". His name is—'

'Don't tell me, I don't want to hear, I don't care what his name is.'

Her eyes were pleading again. She said I was her special daughter, she relied on me, she always had. Why must I keep probing and attacking? Couldn't I just wait and see?

'You mean I'm useful to you while you go on singing and falling in love?'

'Bonnie.'

'Do you tell Tor and Ula they're special? Do you know how they feel about anything? They might not want the captain around.'

'Bonnie, when I marry again – *if* I do, it *is* possible – you'll

always be my special child. You were born first, my eldest daughter . . . '

'As if I didn't already know.'

'You could be my bridesmaid, you could walk behind me.
Think of it, darling. Wouldn't you like that?'

'I was right, then. I guessed you wanted to marry him. No
good will come of it, you'll see.'

'Don't say that, darling, you mustn't. This should be a happy
time. I've thought it all over most carefully. It's an important
decision, you mustn't be cross.'

'It's not just you, though, it's all of us.'

'I know. And a wedding would be wonderful. It's what we
need, a happy occasion. Something to celebrate as a family.'

'We were never a proper family.'

'We could be. A real family with a father again.'

'Would my sisters be bridesmaids?'

'I hadn't thought. They could be. I don't think so. I'd rather
just have you.'

I am not like my sisters, to be bought by playthings. I don't
trust flattery. What use would a father be now?

'If I did decide, what would I wear?'

'A dream dress, long and floating, don't you think? We could
go to London again, just us two. We could get something made
or we could try Liberty's.'

I hate your power, Mamma. I adore you. I would die for you.
Will I never be free from your spell? You hurt me, you ignore me,
you delight me. Must I always dance to your tune? Why should
I walk behind at your wedding? I'm not your little dog to order
about. I will bite your heels, I'll mess on your wedding dress. I'll
howl at the people in church. Bridesmaid? Not me, thanks very
much, not for a bride with dry rot of the heart.

'Let's see now. Blue for you again, I think. Blue for your eyes, blue for hope.'

There would be nothing hole and corner about this wedding, a day to remember, a pageant of love. Mamma was transported, planning, deciding. We must hurry to London again, for clothes. They might become rationed, they might disappear for ever. We might be old ladies before peace was declared. Buy now, buy and enjoy ourselves, just her and me. Oh yes and that restaurant, just her and me, we might hear my tune. It will be lovely, Bonnie, won't it?

'Will the regiment be going north?'

'Hush darling, careless talk costs lives. We mustn't discuss troop movements.' One thing she did promise, she would never leave us again. Perhaps we could attend a day school. The captain would help, he was so businesslike, so fond.

'Magnolia House was miserable. I didn't ...'

'I know, darling child. Don't think of it, it's over. The important thing is I have a secret to tell. I want you to be the first to know. It's exciting.'

'What secret? What is it?' I'd had enough of secrets, I was sick of them.

'Wait and see. Wait until we go to London for our outfits. I'll tell you when we're quite alone.'

As the train left our station with Mamma and me in the first-class carriage I leaned from the window to wave to Ula and Tor. They were happy to be alone for the afternoon, they would do without me today. They pranced down the empty platform, being unicorns again. They waved their paws in the cold air, they kicked and frisked in their shabby clothes. Gas masks, deaths and separations were forgotten. Run sisters, run faster, run in peace while you can. I will never leave you, I will protect you, I will care for you. I'll teach you to waltz one day, we'll waltz by moonlight, the violins will play our tune.

'Close the window now, darling. Now, my secret.'

The train increased speed, louder, faster.

Too-old-to-dream. Too-old-to-dream. Too-old-to-dream.

A BUBBLE GARDEN

1

Everything that had happened to him before Bonnie was a foretaste, marking time, so it seemed. His childhood, his adolescence, his move from Streatham to Clerkenwell before his war service all led up to him meeting her. His real life started in Ireland when he'd seen his dear one.

He had never been there before, the thought made him sentimental. He would see that green grass, drink their Guinness, hear talk of leprechauns. The people there were amazingly kind, known for their welcome.

His invitation was timed perfectly. A civilian again after his army demob, he hadn't yet found the right job. He had bumped into his old Captain accidentally. After that meeting the letter came offering him a job in Ireland. Peace-time in London was uneasy for Eden, the kind of job he looked for was scarce. Whole areas of the city were demolished. He was at a loss to find anyone who might help. It was good to renew old times in the army with Bradwell. The letter following the meeting was a surprise.

'I don't promise you anything definite but there may be a job here for you. The Grange has been empty during the war years. Now I need an overseer for the farm, whose duties would include staff management and general duties. The hours would be flexible and the work varied. Come and see. Stay as long as you wish. Yours, Bradwell.'

The offer seemed Godsent. He had accepted with speed and high hopes. Overseer on an Irish estate, steward of a stately home, agent, administrator, bailiff, he would cheerfully be any or all of these. He would do anything he was asked to get out of London. He'd had enough of city life.

He had no qualms, he was quick on the uptake, unafraid of work, prepared to learn any skill. He wrote that he would come immediately.

He had told Bradwell that he'd worked in insurance, that he'd like something less sedentary now. He would welcome responsibility and challenge He must have impressed Brad. He also sensed that Brad missed the army. Hitler's antics had changed many lives, war rendered them topsy-turvy; it was hard to settle to peace again.

As far as Eden was concerned, he didn't fancy being ordered like a lackey any more. Having been commissioned, he'd a taste for authority; he didn't want desk work, he wanted power.

In actual fact he had never worked in an office or even owned a bank account until he joined the army. He had turned his hand to anything, been jack-of-all-trades in his time. He liked jobs to do with money, handling cash, putting it to better use. He had worked for a firm supplying penny-in-slot machines to pubs and arcades. Eden had emptied them, keeping tally of the cash. For a short time he had been a meter collector for the gas company. He had spent a long time on the Stoke Newington to Hammersmith bus route as a conductor, counting his takings with accuracy and speed. Making figures balance on paper was a joy and pride to him. Give him a column to tot and he didn't complain. He was above working on the buses now, having been an officer; he had experienced a better way of life. He could find nothing to suit him in London. Ireland was the answer. Ireland would bring him luck.

He had been curious about Bradwell's marriage to a widow with three daughters of her own. Since their marriage a son had been born. He had heard that the girls were good-looking and gifted. He looked forward to meeting them as much as he looked forward to a stately home. Landed gentry in Ireland were famed for comfortable living. Life in London was bomb damaged and depressing. A change would restore his soul.

There would be formal gardens, lawns shaded by yew trees. There would be greenhouses for rare blooms and fruit. Away from the mansion would be stables for horses and cattle, hen-houses for the poultry, walled gardens for vegetables and more humble fruit. Figs on sunny walls, tennis courts, fountains awaited him. He would learn to fit in to high life, in the land of singing. Shamrocks would wave in the breeze.

Very likely he'd be put in charge of the accounts, he would handle the staff wages and check the invoices. From his office he would settle disputes with tradesmen who relied on the local gentry for their living.

Conditions might be difficult to start with, Brad having been away for so long. He, Eden, would restore the Grange to its former glory. He didn't expect to eat with the family each day, he'd have his own quarters over a garage or in an annexe, he wasn't fussy. A butler or housekeeper would bring him trays.

Irish landowners were famed for their tables, the food would be supreme as well as the wine cellars. He was almost thirty, time to put down some roots. Where better than in the county of Armagh? He had health, quick wits, energy, he might even acquire an Irish wife.

He would wait until he had settled before stocking his wardrobe. He would see what was needed first. No doubt the list would include tweeds, jodhpurs and a hunting jacket (he disliked the idea of animal slaughter, loathed violence of any kind). Fishing tackle would be provided, very likely, as well as guns. He'd want a dinner jacket. The list seemed huge. Clothes bought locally would be cheaper and probably better cut. He had made inroads into his army gratuity, but he had a cheque book and no family ties.

He booked his ticket, via Liverpool, to Belfast on the *Ulster Monarch*. Life looked rich and wonderful. Work lay ahead in the country of colleens.

2

The taxi driver refused to drive him through the main gates, a small set-back and an indication of what lay ahead. The paint peeling from the gate posts was another sign. One gate was off its hinges, lying propped against the bank where it looked rather charming, with wild flowers pushing through the struts. Buttercups and dandelions tangled with a mauve flower that he thought was called vetch. Fuchsia flowers bloomed in the hedges. He paid the driver, who had barely spoken, he took his case and started to walk.

It was hot. The curving drive was bordered by horse-chestnut trees. He couldn't blame the driver for refusing to go further, the ground was pitted with potholes and what looked like cartwheel tracks. On his left was a disused cottage, probably a gardener's lodge once. Now a wild rose straggled round the door which opened in two halves like a stable ... The windows were without glass. Piles of rubbish lay round it.

He enjoyed the walk, in spite of the heat. The mud of the drive gave off clouds of dust, making the weeds and grass each side look grey. It was mid-summer, there had been no rain for weeks.

The taxi man had been silent about Bradwell and his family. It was obvious now that the Grange wouldn't be grand at all. But he'd been invited, he was needed. Obviously there was work here, but not the kind he'd imagined.

The fields each side of the drive were empty, except for one boney cow. Far in the distance a donkey brayed. Clouds of flies buzzed round his head. More buzzed round the cow's head and tail. The swish of the tail, the cropping cow's jaws and the far-away donkey were peaceful sounds. The cow's nostrils were pink and wet. Eden didn't mind the heat, though he sweated heavily. He was in the country, with cows, flies, dust and dandelions. He'd meet Brad's family soon.

He paused by a clump of laurel bushes behind which lay the Grange and the lawns. He heard the singing before he saw them. He stood behind the bushes where they couldn't see him, peering through the leaves. He saw Bonnie first and his heart was lost. He knew that, no matter what the cost, he must stay.

There were two lawns, an upper and a lower, sloping down from the house, with steps to connect them. Bonnie was trying to wheel her little brother down the broken steps in a doll's pram: the boy was thin with longish hair. His legs hung over the pram wheels, he trailed his sandals in the grass. He had sticking plasters on his limbs and was sucking a grass stalk. The middle sister had a bowl of soapsuds; she sat on the steps blowing bubbles through a clay pipe. The third sister wasn't there.

They seemed heedless of anything but themselves and their bubble world. Theirs seemed a magic capsule which he longed to enter. They looked invulnerable. The house behind was derelict and much smaller than he'd imagined. Tiles were missing from the roof, damp patches lay like blots on the walls, windows were boarded up. Ivy growing round the front door had loosened the pointing, the door itself looked rotten. There were no well-tended paths, no flowers or rose bushes, the two lawns were more like fields. He didn't mind; he'd seen Bonnie, lovelier than any flower. He listened.

'I'm forever blowing bubbles, pretty bubbles in the air. They fly so high, nearly reach the sky, then like my dreams they fade and die. Fortune's ever hiding, I search everywhere, I'm forever blowing bubbles, pretty bubbles in the air.' Bonnie's voice wasn't beautiful, more like a croak, but her beauty enchanted him.

The boy beat time languidly with his grass stalk. Bonnie half turned. Had she seen him? He stepped back, he mustn't interrupt their magic moment. He wanted to watch them for hours. She bumped the pram down, reaching to burst a bubble, her small breasts showing through her shirt. Her thighs were bare, all three wore shorts and old sandals. She went on reaching with her pretty hands. Was she doing it for him? Did she know her buttons were undone? He liked thin girls. In spite of her lovely smile she had an air of sorrow.

He cleared his throat. The boy spoke. 'Bonnie, someone is there.'

She started dramatically, moving a little towards the laurels, not looking at him. Then she buttoned her shirt.

She said loudly that the rubbish dump was the place for him. She pushed him onto a pile of weeds and grass cuttings.

'Sister, darling, you'll pay for that. You'll pay with your life.'

He was a handsome boy of about seven with a rather ratlike face. He lay and kicked his heels.

'A man is watching you, Bonnie. Look.'

She walked over to Eden, holding out her hand. 'Hullo, you must be Captain's friend. I'm Bonnie.'

Her speaking voice was beautiful, in contrast to when she sang. The way she referred to her stepfather by rank seemed delightful. He'd been disappointed that no one had met him in the town, but he was getting his welcome now. Her hand was petal soft. He wondered where the parents were.

'Mamma is ... busy, I'm afraid. Did you come in the town taxi?'

Tor, the younger sister, came over, the quieter one. The three of them were like figures in a play against the gloomy building behind. He didn't care if they were rich or poor, they had class, theirs was the world he wanted. Tor was thin, with cropped hair and narrower eyes than Bonnie's, less brilliant. She wasn't very much taller than the boy, still by the grass cuttings, waving his heels in the air.

He took Tor's hot hand. She smelled of fresh perspiration, like dandelion juice, not unpleasant. She didn't speak. She had a piercing gaze.

Bonnie was the hostess in her mother's absence. Had he had a pleasant trip? What time had he left London? He basked in the light of her smile. His life was changing. Birth and breeding surmounted poverty. A family tree cast a long shadow; doubtless theirs went back hundreds of years. He explained that he'd travelled on the mail boat.

The boy examined the sticking plaster on his knee. His limbs were scratched and scabbed. He gave his curiously rodent smile and asked if the sea had been rough.

'Stop asking questions. Get up, Bo.'

Bonnie said that her brother Boris was too inquisitive. The name Tor was short for Hortense. Ula, the youngest sister, was still in England, in hospital.

'Nothing serious, I hope?'

Bo told him that she had polio, the poor creature, had been flat on her back for months. He spoke with a fluctuating brogue but his sisters spoke with the kind of purity that Eden most admired, that you heard on the BBC. He told them he'd enjoyed his trip and was delighted to see Ireland at last.

In fact he'd been up in the bar all night, listening to the other travellers celebrating their return home. He wanted to save buying a berth. He had drunk almost nothing, but was exhausted now. Nothing so far had turned out as he'd expected, but he didn't regret coming. There was work here, he would be needed. There was Bonnie. He would make sure that these kids needed him. Yes, he'd enjoyed the trip.

'You served under my father, didn't you? Did you kill anyone? Did you like the war?'

Eden explained to Bo that he'd been in Tunisia with Bradwell for a short time. War was not something to enjoy, you made the best of it. War caused disruption, if not catastrophe. Death was not something to glorify.

He had a horror of bloodshed or rage of any kind, but he had enjoyed the war. It had opened his eyes to another way of life, he had met new people from new backgrounds. He liked order, the mindless drilling on parade grounds; the cleaning and polishing were good discipline. As an eventual motor transport driver for officers, he'd become ambitious. Finally, he'd become an officer himself. His acceptance into the Officers' Training Unit was a landmark. He would never return to his old way of life or mix with his old companions. The pip on his shoulder gave him a new pride and opened new doors. He had done everything to the best of his ability, but patriotism, the war effort, defeating Hitler, held no interest for him. His own self-improvement counted more. His uniform flattered him, an officer had an active social life. He'd been sorry when the war had stopped.

Meeting Bradwell again was a stroke of luck. He was here, the sky was the limit now.

Bo lay on the grass still, his hair fanned over a patch of clover. He stared up with light-coloured eyes. He'd like to be an army band master. He wouldn't mind being the Pope.

'You look like a casualty of war,' Eden said, pointing to the sticking plasters.

Bo pointed two fingers at them. 'Bang-bang. You're dead. How old are you?'

'Stop it, Bo,' Bonnie said.

'I'm only after asking because of Dadda needing someone young to help.' Bo reached for the soap bowl, blowing into it through his grass stalk, making the foam rise.

'Where is your father?'

'He'll be in soon. Mamma ... is ... lying down,' Bonnie said.

'Not ill, I hope? The heat ...'

Bo said that his Mammy lay down in her room often. The one he missed most was Ula, poor creature.

'Well, she's not here. You must make do with Tor and me.'

'Sisters three, ah me, ah me,' Bo sighed poetically.

Tor leaned over him. Ula would write to him soon.

He blew another mournful blast down his grass stalk. The women in his life were suffocating, he said. He wanted to go to the Christian Brothers' school.

They left the pram on the lawn and went in.

Lunch was eaten in the kitchen, overlooking the stable yard at the back. The long pine table, the copper pans on the wall, the heavy plate racks were evidence of past wealth, but now the table had a broken leg, the pans had holes, there were no plates in the racks. Some of the floor tiles were cracked or missing; a fern forced its way up near the sink. There was a smell of sour milk and must. Eden noticed these details with pleasure; the more neglect there was, the more work for him both inside and outside the Grange. The light bulb flickered. It was pleasantly cool and dim.

He went on observing and listening as they sat round the table. The torn napkins, the miserable utensils and cutlery confirmed the truth; Bradwell had hit on hard times, was very likely in dire straits. Why didn't he appear? Where was the mother? She'd been resting now for hours. The kids seemed very much alone. He mustn't stare so much at Bonnie. Lunch, made by Tor on an ancient range, was a sort of soup of potatoes and milk; he had to force it down. There was an open fireplace that needed cleaning. Each time Bonnie opened her mouth for her spoon he glimpsed her sweet pink tongue and his longings started.

A duck waddled across the back doorstep, its eyes were a cold, unfriendly black. At least they had some poultry as well as one thin cow. Bo jumped up and snatched his duck. It was his pet, his lucky duck. The bird flapped and squawked, freeing itself. In the yard was a gulley with a trickle of water, the duck retreated into the heat again.

Bo was responsible for the egg collection. His duck might lay anywhere.

'Only one duck?'

'We did have another. It died.'

Sometimes the eggs smelled, having lain undiscovered for weeks. Ducks made good mothers, Bo said, being more intelligent than hens. Their eggs tasted oily. He waved his spoon about as he gave this information. Would Eden like to help him look for eggs? His careless little birdeen sometimes laid indoors.

Eden was still wondering about their mother. Shouldn't they take her some lunch? It was all so quiet.

Old dung lay round the yard. The door at the end of the barn led to the back field. No kitchen gardens, no greenhouses or fountains, just one duck and one thin cow.

But when he was in charge, he told himself, it would all change; the Grange would prosper again. They found an egg in a patch of thistles. Bo wiped it clean, smelling it. Rotten, as he'd feared. Ah me.

Eden was already starting a mental list of requirements. That yard was insanitary; they'd need brooms, shovels, a proper wheelbarrow. He would need building materials. He would need to learn about crop rotation and the rudiments of poultry keeping. He would forget grandiose ideas. That barn looked reasonably weathertight. The house needed rewiring, the damp parts cut out and restored. There was enough here to keep him busy for years ahead. He'd wanted a change, wanted challenge. Here it was.

'Bo, exactly where is your father? It's getting late.'

Bo blinked, he put his hand in Eden's. The boy's hand was sticky, he felt the sticking plaster against his wrist. Was he accident prone? He mustn't upset him. Why did he speak with that brogue?

The state of the rooms upstairs was what you'd expect. The bathroom had to be seen to be believed. The vast iron bath on claw feet, the tangle of piping, the rusted geyser, were from another age. On the window sill was a huge artificial rose. Someone had spilled tooth powder.

Eden had the room next to the girls' room at the top of the stairs. There were no carpets on the unpolished boards. Bo had the tiny room by the bathroom. There was one attic room on the top floor, the domain of his host and hostess. He still hadn't seen or heard them by night time.

Eden pressed himself against the wall that separated him from the two girls. He heard one of them laugh. No one had laughed downstairs. Were they talking about him? He went over the bubble song in his mind.

3

A mosquito hummed by the window, then by his bed, annoyingly close to his head. He grabbed at it, there was silence. Then it started again. It was too hot for pyjamas, even the air was too much on his skin.

He had pulled his bed under his window to overhear what the sisters said. Outside he could make out the laurel bushes, a lumpy shape in the dark. Was Brad even in this country? Did they have a mother at all?

He'd not liked to keep asking questions, there'd been no sound from the attic overhead. These kids were too young to be left alone; though Bonnie wasn't a child she was defenceless.

He pushed his sheets onto the floor. He liked a firm mattress, not a lumpy one; this one was what you'd expect. He stared out again. A thin moon showed from behind a cloud. He was moonstruck over Bonnie, he must reach up to his goddess, make her his own.

He couldn't sleep for thinking about her. There was no sound now from next door. Were her eyes like forget-me-nots or hyacinths? Her hair was so silky, her infrequent smile so sad.

She'd made a brave effort to welcome him, she'd been a mother to her little brother; putting him to bed, putting fresh plasters on his scabs, washing him, singing in that odd, growling way, almost one note. She must be tone-deaf, that wouldn't change. Bo liked being petted, insisting on being sung to sleep.

He mused over the events of the day. The Grange was a fiasco, this country a let-down, but he'd found her, all else faded.

His bedroom had only a bed, a chair and an old-fashioned washstand. Someone had put a branch of hawthorn in a jamjar on the marble top, it had bitter-smelling blooms. Had Bonnie put them there? Beautiful Bonnie of the luminous eyes was next door to him, sleeping the sleep of innocence.

He'd found a bulb for the kitchen light but the flex was damaged. Most of the switches were corroded, he'd got a mild shock off one.

Those eyes were familiar, he'd seen them somewhere, he couldn't place her. Had she travelled on his bus years ago? He had a long memory for faces, hers was elusive. He'd made a habit of listening and watching all his life; his method of self-improvement.

If he had a weakness, it was a hatred of reading; he never read a book or even a newspaper if he could avoid it. Reading was time-consuming and tiresome, a retentive mind was as good as the printed word. He'd been forced to study at the Officers' Training Unit; since that time he'd lived by his wits, listening, practising, copying.

He was particular about cleanliness, the state of this house came as a shock. He'd be needed, that was what mattered. He'd even take to reading if Bonnie wished.

As a child he had lived with his aunt in Streatham; they had not been happy years. He had loathed his time at school. His real education didn't start until he'd left Streatham and put Aunt from his mind.

As he lay in the heat thinking of Bonnie, he remembered something that happened with his aunt. He'd been about eleven, wearing a pair of new long trousers, sitting at the table waiting for tea. Somehow the plate had been knocked from Aunt's hand as she was putting it in front of him, his new trousers had been spoiled. He had watched scrambled egg trickling down his fly buttons, along his thighs and into his shoes. Aunt's anger had been more upsetting than egg in his buttonholes. She had dabbed her cloth at him. Nasty little boy, had he no idea of decency? Dab-dab. Look at the state of him, did he think new trousers grew on trees? Couldn't he control himself? Dab-dab, dirty brat. She'd never asked to have him, didn't need or deserve him. Dab-dab. He was nothing but extra work.

He had run upstairs to get away from her, had stood by his bed holding himself until misery turned to comfort, his body eased. He glowed with warmth, he clutched harder, his jet spurted, again, again. Forget Aunt, let it go, release it. Yes. Over the blanket, over his trousers, egg and sperm in a widening stream. He mopped at it, breath panting. Aunt mustn't see, mustn't know about it. She would kill him if she knew.

They had shared nothing but the roof, he'd never confided in her. When he got bullied at school, he'd not told. The boys sniffed and sniggered, boys with parents and noisy homes. You became secretive early, you survived by cunning, you learned to imitate and to lie. He'd made a point of keeping quiet and neat, of making no mess, and keeping out of Aunt's way. Was she a real aunt or a foster parent? Mustn't be a nuisance, mustn't ask questions, so he never knew. What mattered was learning to please. His anxieties over his sexual development must be ignored. The down on his upper lip, his body hair, his voice that squeaked up and down must be ignored. Don't question, don't draw attention to yourself. Listen and watch, bide your time.

The egg episode was a small landmark, but by the time war broke out Streatham was a memory. By then he was on his way up in the world, he'd never gone back, never written, hardly thought of her. She used to fix him with her small eyes, her damp grey lips and given this advice: 'Be content with your lot. Ambition killed the rat.'

He was destined to climb, he'd known it for years. At fifteen he was on his own. Though he'd never lost his feeling of lone-liness, he'd grown used to it. He had set himself to learn what and what not to do. He'd learned how to make girls interested, using flattery and kindness, had learned how to make them say yes. Not being tall, he naturally preferred small slender girls. He'd found a room in Clerkenwell and settled to improving himself.

At first he had joined a boys' club. He'd learned wrestling, then, more importantly, he'd learned ballroom dancing. Dancing became a passion as well as an opportunity to socialize. His first real girlfriend had been thirteen, but looked older, with a foxy face, thin lips and ginger hair. He had taught her to tango; later, when jiving swept the dance halls, they'd been champions. Together they studied pornographic magazines, knew where blue movies could be seen, and had been happy. She'd needed no teaching in bed. It came naturally, whether dancing or making love. When the war started he'd joined up and moved away. She'd been young enough to be evacuated to the country. They had vowed fidelity, the war kept them apart. Neither were keen letter writers; sometimes he regretted leav-ing school early, but hating books as he did, he'd had no choice.

He became a student of life, with three interests; wrestling, ball-room dancing and making love. These interests narrowed to sex and dancing. He took up simple book-keeping instead of wrestling. He seemed to have been acquiring knowledge all his life. To please his aunt he'd learned housework in Streatham, had shopped, washed dishes and cleaned. He brought tea to her bedside each morning, he cleaned and lit her kitchen fire before leaving for school.

His fires were a source of pride to him. First you raked the ashes, setting aside any clinkers to lay each side of the grate. Newspaper must be crumpled loosely under the kindling wood, the layer of fresh, small coal pieces was the finishing touch. Aunt would come down, see the blaze but never thank or praise him.

He hated her, she resented him. The egg episode strengthened his resolve to leave when he was old enough. He'd acquired patience and a few basic skills in Streatham.

When he was called up he'd left his job on the 73 bus route, said goodbye to his red-headed girl friend and started to climb further in the world. At the end of his service his sights were set, his ambition crystallized, he would be middle class in future, Streatham and Clerkenwell didn't exist. He would look different, he would speak correctly, paying attention to each inflection, each vowel sound. He would be assured and easy in all situations, would bask in affluence and leisure. He never wanted to see a bedsitter again. He never wanted to open a rent book or put money in a slot meter or deal with a landlady. He was through with cheap dance halls and cheap girls. He would be quiet and moderate in all things. The army had taught him to hold his cutlery correctly, to move in a measured way, to open doors for ladies and the elderly, to give orders firmly when the occasion arose. He had little money and few specialized skills, he had boundless ambition, he was a power-house of energy.

He'd been working particularly hard on his vowel sounds when he'd bumped into Brad in Piccadilly. His greeting, 'Hey I know you. I remember you,' had been faultless. Brad's invitation was his reward. His appearance had altered as well as his speech and behaviour. Gone were the crooked teeth, the slicked and greasy hair of the army days. With straightened teeth, expensive barbering and small moustache he was another person. His eyebrows were thinned, his nails manicured, he sometimes smoked a cigar. A daily bath was something he took for granted now, the hint of grey at his temples was just right. He was a fitting recipient for the invitation to Ireland.

The poverty he'd found here didn't dismay him. Nothing overruled breeding and class.

He lay pondering in the stifling room. He must be consistent, reliable and calm. He repeated a little rhyme he'd invented for his vowel sounds: 'Brown frowned on his way down town. He must save to pay Jane's way.' His stomach rattled, he'd eaten almost nothing all day. At least his aunt had fed him, he could say that for her. Not like these kids. He felt clothed all over in damp. He stroked himself slowly, with finesse, to induce sleep, climaxing without intention, warm spouts over his hand; and, in coming, he remembered. He *had* seen Bonnie before, years ago. She'd been at the posh boarding school in the West Country where his redhead had been evacuated for a short time. He had visited her for an illicit night. Yes, Bonnie had been one of the girls there. Little did he think that he'd ever be visiting one of those stuck-up kids, as an equal, as a guest. They were not entire strangers, though they'd not spoken and he, of course, had changed totally. He lay still, marvelling at fate.

He must get a hanky, mustn't mark the mattress; to leave stains would be ill-bred. It would dry, he could turn it over. He rolled up his hanky and put it in his case. He was starving. What kind of parents would leave these kids without food?

He made further plans as he drifted to sleep. He would start in the kitchen; they must have proper light, though he'd had little electrical experience. He'd be their benefactor.

The morning was dull and sunless, very likely they'd have storms. He washed and shaved in the terrible bathroom, not liking to risk the geyser. He trimmed his moustache, rolled up his sleeves and went down.

Tor was eating porridge by the stove, holding her bowl in her hand. Bonnie was sitting by the window with a mirror balanced against the sill. She was combing her hair over her face, covering it. She wore a pyjama top over her shorts, she was examining the tips of her hair. Bleached gold from sun and wind, it shaded darker at the roots. It *was* the same girl he'd glimpsed briefly all those years ago, he was sure of it. You couldn't forget those eyes. She looked at him through the darker and light-coloured hair, so piercingly blue, so luminous, eyes that a man could die for.

'Porridge, Eden?' Tor had cooked a lot.

'I haven't eaten that since I was a lad ... a boy, I mean.'

Eating at breakfast was something he'd given up years back. Black coffee and fruit juice were more high class; the days of toast with marge and mugs of tea in Streatham were gone. He took a little porridge, struggling to swallow the lumps and leathery skin. The milk in the jug was sour. Tor wore a sacking apron that nearly touched the floor, her expression was stern. None of them wore shoes. Bo's hair was still tangled with grass and burrs. He had a letter.

'Your postman must come early,' Eden said, forcing another spoonful down. The letter was from Ula. Bo read it in a loud, self-conscious voice. '"Ask Mamma to find a hospital in Ireland. It's awful here ... Please ask."'

'Poor little girl. You must be worried about her. Where is your mother, actually? Is she better?'

Tor swilled cold water over her porridge bowl. Bonnie still combed her hair over her face.

'Tor, where are your parents? Are they here at all?'

'It isn't that ...'

'What did you say? Look at me, Bonnie. Where is Bradwell? Where is your mother?'

She threw down her comb and went out, her bare feet making no sound on the stairs. She had such beautiful long legs, such delicate skin behind the knees, he had to follow her. He'd upset her, he hadn't meant it, he half stumbled over a loose board. Missing planks, rot and fungus, what a setting for such a girl. The door of their room was open; there she was, on the bed.

'Don't run away, Bonnie. I want to help. What is it? Please?'

She was by the window, her head in her hands, rocking herself. She needed comforting; he would be bold, he would sit down by her. This mattress was even thinner than his, he felt her fine hair and her ear by his cheek. Her neck drooped so touchingly, he would let her cry, patting her gently. All three of them were much too thin. He could smell cheap shampoo in this room as well as mould.

'It's Mamma, you see. We're worried. Well, not worried exactly, just concerned. Did you guess?'

'I did wonder. She's not here, is she?'

'She's not in her room, she's not at home.'

'And Brad? What about your father?'

'He's gone too. He often does. He goes drinking and upsets Mamma.'

He told her to try not to worry about them. He was here and he would help.

4

He wasn't completely surprised, he had half guessed. No one was dead, it was simply a domestic upset. It was his chance to get down to practicalities, curb his urge to gaze at Bonnie's pale breasts. He must concentrate on all three; Bo's scratches looked nasty, he might need medical care. They all needed properly feeding; they didn't seem properly clothed. Bonnie's hair was warm, like greased feathers near his cheek. He looked into her eyes. Do not fear. I am here to help.

'A drinking father isn't so terrible. Try not to worry so much.'

Her real father had been dead a long time. Very likely she'd expected Brad to be a demi-god, to compensate for what she'd lost. Family circles were rarely perfect. Certainly this one was not. Brad hadn't been a heavy drinker in the army days. Very likely he was still adjusting to civvy street and a ready-made family. He must have been shocked at the deterioration of the Grange and the daunting repairs he faced. He might be missing the army responsibilities. No troops to command now, just a wife and kids stuck in a dull, quiet place. The wife complained, Eden imagined. He'd find out in due course.

All his previous ideas had proved false. The family were depressed, the house a disgrace. He'd come in the nick of time.

Tor and Bo had followed him upstairs. Bo watched him with his goat-like stare that reminded Eden of Brad.

'I'll find your father,' he told them. 'Don't worry anymore.'

'We aren't worried, just a bit concerned. Mamma ...'

'Do you know where she went?'

'She gets so miserable. She doesn't always leave ...'

'Once she went to a hotel,' Bo said sharply.

'And left you alone?'

'We're not neglected. Don't imagine we are.'

Tor was proud, to pity them was insulting. She came to the bed and sat on Bonnie's other side. Bo followed, he looked flushed. Eden told them it would all blow over. Privately he was outraged. He would start a search party right away, the drunken head of the family must be restored. Bo could come too if he liked, and his sisters.

The girls decided to stay at home in case their mother returned. Bo would go with Eden to the town.

The sole of Bo's sandal flapped in the dirt as the two set off along the drive. He still had burrs in his hair. It was gloomy now under the chestnut trees, the leaves hung slack in the heavy heat. The girls had taken the cow to the barn for milking. There was a smell of dung and flying ants swarmed in the air. Bo made little rushes at them, lashing them with a blade of grass. Except for the bubble pipe, he seemed to have no playthings. They might find some comics in the town, or a water-pistol.

'If you see a duck around, let me know,' Bo said. He had two once, but one had gone, eaten perhaps by a fox. Ducks survived better than hens.

'Who lived here before, Bo?'

'No one. We were in England. Dadda was an officer in the war.'

'I know that. I was there. He offered me a job.'

'I'm here to help him. I'm my Da's right-hand man. We can manage.'

'Wouldn't you like me to stay?'

'We can manage, I said.'

His brogue fluctuated. Did he speak like that to gain confidence? Eden cut him a switch, stripping the leaves back, leaving two at the end as a weapon against the ants. A wasp loomed near. Take care, Eden told him, insect bites at this time of year could turn septic. Bo was scratched and scarred enough. Could he have been assaulted or was he accident prone? Nothing would surprise Eden now. Meanwhile, Brad must be found.

There were the white gates again, one propped against the bank, the other half falling from one hinge. There was the gardener's lodge even seedier looking now, in the dull morning light. Drops of rain started falling as they went onto the road. In the distance the donkey brayed again.

Bo said the storm would start in half an hour, he was used to forecasting the weather. He loved Ireland, one day he'd run the Grange. Eden tried to picture it in fifteen years' time with Bo, a strapping young man, and herds of cattle, while Bonnie and her sister skimmed cream and churned butter pats. The picture was unlikely, he didn't want a milkmaid for a wife. He himself knew little about animal husbandry or even the behaviour of cows, bulls and calves. He didn't like to ask Bo. It seemed their neighbours had a bull when they needed one, their cow hadn't calved for a long time. To Eden, the cow seemed dangerously thin.

'I wouldn't mind finding my drake. I saw a stuffed duckling once, all fluffy and yellow. My sisters hate that cow.'

'You are fond of your sisters, aren't you?'

'They have their uses. They need me for their silly games.'

'But you like living here?'

'I do, of course, I'm Irish. Those creatures have no Irish blood. Not like me and Dadda.'

'And your mother? How does she feel?'

'She doesn't belong. No one understands.'

'Understands what?'

The boy said that he didn't worry about his father. He would be in Fagin's Bar.

The rain became heavier, falling straight from the sky on them. The hawthorn in the hedges was pungent. Eden had no jacket with him, the rain felt almost warm. What a good thing he'd spared himself the expense of new clothes, all he'd need for the time being were Wellingtons, cords and some sandals for relaxing in, like the ones these kids wore. If, indeed, he'd find time to relax. A magpie hopped before them. Bo said that the old rhyme about one magpie meaning sorrow wasn't true. The magpie was the sorry one, because of having no mate.

Eden asked about his school. When would he start?

'It's not arranged. I want to go to the Christian Brothers. They teach woodwork and farm management.'

Eden hadn't thought of Bradwell as being Roman Catholic. Did he go to Mass?

Bo answered indignantly. He and his Da were proper Irishmen, not like his mother and those girls. The Brothers had a special bus for the children. He'd be picked up at the end of the drive. His mammy wanted him to go to an English boarding school. He *must* go to a Catholic school, because he might be a priest one day. He wrote verses, that was his hobby, he didn't miss England at all. His mammy didn't like it here; his sisters, poor old creatures, didn't know what they *did* want. As he spoke, the boy lashed his switch at the rain.

A collie dog met them at the town's main street, which was wide, with low grey houses each side, a few shops and some pubs. At the far end was a garage with two petrol pumps and a pub called Fagin Bros. The sign over the door was painted boldly in gold lettering. The church was half a mile further on, there was a sawmill too, Bo said. Eden wondered why it should be called a town; it was a hamlet, depressingly empty and quiet. The rain beat on the pavements, spattering the canvas sunblinds covering front doors. The double doors of the Co-op stores were shut. A notice said 'Back at half three'. The windows on either side were stacked with boxes of soap flakes and scouring powder. A blue enamel washing bowl said 'Washday made Bright'. In spite of the rain you could smell the petrol dripping from the petrol pump opposite Fagin Bros. The collie hung its tongue as if to catch the rain. Fagin's was closed too.

Eden looked over the top of the brass rail that held the red curtains across the window. There was Brad with his back to him, half lying along the bar. He saw the barman coming from the back with a drink in his hand, he had a cruel look on his face. Brad took the whisky, gulped it and reached for his beer. Alternating beer with spirits was a quick way to oblivion, Eden hadn't expected it of Brad. He was wearing the same clothes he'd worn when they'd met in London. Now they looked as if he'd slept in them. His brogues were stained, a slug or snail seemed to have left tracks across his shoulders; buttons were gone, his hands unwashed.

'I'll go first, Eden. Stay.'

Bo pushed the door, his sandal flapped on the step. He touched Brad with his wet chestnut switch.

'I'm here now, Dadda. Come on home.'

Brad turned. He looked at his son with unfocused eyes.

'Has she ... did ... she?'

'She didn't come back yet. Come on, Da.'

Brad went on staring. His mouth was slack, the pupils of his eyes were small. He had the distant look of a homeless person, beyond sorrow.

The collie rested under a table, the marble top made it cool and dark.

'A big storm is coming, Dadda. Eden arrived. See?'

'Eden? You? Here? You're early. How are you? You're a day early.'

'I came yesterday. We arranged for yesterday, Brad. Remember?'

'No matter. You're here. You're welcome. Have a drink.'

5

'There's a storm brewing up. We should go back now.'

'Back? What storm? Have a drink. There's no storm.'

'Another time, Brad. With pleasure. Let's go now.'

As Eden spoke, sheet lightning lit the street. 'Washday made Bright' shone in glory, the brass rail in the window shone like gold. Thunder drowned Bo's voice as he pulled his father's sleeve. Another flash lit the brass letter-flap of the Co-op and the petrol pumps. There were no other people in sight. Bo had said that his father often met the bank manager on the days that he came back drunk. Eden couldn't see a bank or a post office, perhaps they were further on, near the church. Rain washed the petrol drips from the garage forecourt.

'There's no storm. Forget the storm. Have a drink.'

'Come home now, Dadda.'

Straight-falling, hard rain had turned the street into a sheet of water almost level with Fagin's step.

'Come, Dadda.'

Outside in the rain Brad was docile, his hand was light and damp on Eden's wrist. They walked slowly, Bo was a step behind in case his father swayed. Brad kept his eyes half closed. Their clothes soon felt like tight skins that stuck to them. Except for the barman with the hostile eyes, no one saw them arrive or leave. Perhaps more eyes watched from behind curtains and blinds. Perhaps someone peeped from behind the basin claiming to make washday bright. Where was the garage owner, the Co-op assistant? Were there no teachers or priests in this town? The collie watched them leave from the step, the fur on its head and shoulders clotted with wet, then returned to the table. They didn't look back.

The hedges were flattened, beaten down with wet. The road stretched ahead, black and long. The rain thickened to hail-stones, small and light, stinging their skins as they got larger. Eden led Brad by the hand. The only dry parts of him were the soles of his feet. Bo's bare toes gleamed through his sandal straps, his loose flap of sole had gone. Brad tripped. His face, washed of grease and sweat, looked as innocent as Bo's. He placed his feet delicately, straddling them, not noticing the storm; walking without falling took his attention. At last the Grange gates were in sight.

'Steady, Da. Nearly home.'

Bradwell pulled free from Eden and leaned over the broken gate. Drink exhausted you as well as robbing your wits. His hair fell forward like quills as he leaned over the gate. He belched. A stream of saliva followed by vomit poured from his mouth. A clap of thunder broke over their heads. Bo stood by his father, tight-faced. The flowers in the grass under the gate were covered with vomit.

'Come, Dadda. Nearly home.'

Vomit dripped from Brad's chin, glittering. Carroty shreds shone in the pale buff, soaking the roots of the buttercups. His

feet slipped, he grasped at Bo, ignoring Eden's hand. He muttered.

'Brad-well, you are a disaster. You've let the family down. Disaster. Dis-grace.'

Eden took his shoulders.

'Come on. Don't give way. Don't give way now. Let's shelter
here in the lodge.'

They steered him through the gap in the wall and over the
pile of masonry and tin cans in front of the door. It wasn't
locked. The one room inside was dry, bare and clean. It opened
into a lean-to shed where a tap dripped into a bucket. In the
corner a ladder led to a loft. The windows on each side of the
door were without glass, the overhanging eaves kept the room
dry. In the hearth were the charred remains of a log fire. Bo
kicked at a cinder. Ash flew.

'Someone must have been here,' Eden said. It didn't feel disused. It was a good shelter. Had anyone lived here recently?

'It's not used. It's never used. It hasn't been lived in for years.'

Brad didn't speak. He went to the mantelpiece, gripping it
with dirty fingers. The air began to stink of drink.

'Look, Dadda, it's getting light. The rain is stopping. Look.
Light.'

Bo leaned through a window with his hand out. It was dark
still but the thunder had ceased.

'A disaster,' Brad muttered again.

The rain drummed on the tin roof of the outhouse.

'Come, Dadda. Let's go.'

Brad lifted his head from the mantelpiece.

'Come here, you little brat. I want you.'

'Brad, he's only anxious to get back to his sisters. They'll be
worrying.'

'Stay out of it, you. It's not your business. Come here, Bo. Who has been here? Has *she*? ... Answer me, you brat.'

'Of course not. No one has. The rain is stopping. It's gone.'

'Don't, Bradwell. Let the boy alone.'

'What's it to you? I know your game, Eden. I have no ill-usions, no ill-usions at all.'

'What do you mean, Brad?'

'What? I will tell you, I will elu-cidate. You are trying to make yourself indis ... indis ... indispensable. I know your game.'

'You are wrong, sir. I'm doing no such thing.'

'No? "No such thing"? I know your sort. You'll be setting your cap at my daughter next. Oh yes ... Oh yes.'

'Don't be ridiculous, Brad. I only just arrived. You invited me, remember? You offered me the job.'

'Job? What job? There's no job here, can't you see? A disaster.'

'Don't, Dadda, don't be upset again.'

'Bo. My son. My son.'

Brad's mood changed to self-pity again. Hadn't he always done his best? Where had he gone wrong? He deserved better than this. Where was she? Why? Why?

'I'm here, Dadda. Don't be sad.'

'Son. Son.'

The two stood by the fireplace. Eden was excluded. He'd been condemned, the outsider with designs. Not needed. Not wanted here.

He left them. Let them follow or not as they pleased. He had done what he'd set out for, he had brought the runaway back. He must rejoin the daughters waiting behind without proper food or light.

A faint streak of yellow showed over the chestnut trees. The dust and flies were gone, now each leaf dripped. A bird cheeped. He wondered where the magpie was. Bonnie was his main concern, her well-being was all that mattered. He reached the bushes, the grass looked as if it had turned liquid. Rain washed down the steps over the upturned pram. He looked up and saw the girls leaning against their window pane. Rain blurred their faces. How long had they been waiting, heads close, arms entwined? He shouted up.

'We're back. Safe and sound. Bo and your dad are coming behind.'

They didn't wave or answer, staring and waiting. Behind him, Brad and Bo followed, making their slow way.

'Easy now, Da,' he heard Bo say. 'Take your time, Dadda, that's the way.'

Brad went to the lavatory leading from the hall. They heard the seat crash down before he sat down with a great sigh.

Bo waited outside, his face strained and tight still. He tried to smile. His dadda was all right. He was grand.

In the kitchen the remains of breakfast were still on the table. Eden filled the kettle. Bo said his father liked his tea strong.

'Should we check that he's all right? He's a long time there.'

Snores sounded from behind the lavatory door. His father got tired, Bo said. He'd a lot of worry. People didn't understand.

'I want to understand, Bo. I can't if no one explains.'

'It's not his fault. It isn't. It isn't.'

The girls were still in their bedrooms. Eden and Bo drank some tea. The Irish were a nation of tea drinkers, Eden remembered. What a lackadaisical family this was.

The lock was clicking, the door was opening. Brad came out.

'Bo? Where are you? C'm'ere, I want you. I'm going up.'

Eden came behind them. Getting him up the second flight

was worst. The stairs twisted half way up, at the turn Brad missed a step, falling forward on his face. He lay filling the stairway, muttering in a surprised way. He'd let them down. A disaster, he admitted it. Where was she, anyway?

Bo pulled at his hands, Eden pushed and supported him, they reached the attic. Bradwell made for the bed.

To Eden's surprise, the room was inviting; no sign of poverty anywhere. He had expected full ashtrays, dirty glasses, stains and torn sheets. The attic was peaceful and bright. Under the skylight was a brass bed heaped with cushions and silk-fringed shawls. There was a white fur rug as well as Persian carpets. The white walls had jade and rose quartz beads hanging from ornate brass hooks, echoing the greens and pinks of the rugs. A cane hamper spilled satin and silken clothing, there were shoes, scarves, flowery hats. The effect was artistic rather than slovenly. There was disorder but nothing cheap or soiled. He wondered if the mother had left halfway through packing her things. He saw a purse under the bed. Bo kicked it out of sight. The scent of rose perfume was sweet and heady. Brad pitched onto the bed and slept.

Eden felt the tension go out of Bo. Peace at last. His dad was safely back. Brad was the boy's responsibility, his sisters could worry about their mother; the Irish members of the family stuck close.

He lifted his father's feet, one by one; unlacing the shoes, he covered him with a shawl. His father must be left quiet and comfortable. He wrung out a flannel at the washstand, he tenderly wiped Brad's face. He put the china basin beside him in case of emergency. He must have a hot-water bottle. Later, he must have strong tea. Their two faces were more alike than ever, rat-sharp noses, wide-spaced eyes, a lost yet innocent air.

'Does he usually sleep for long, Bo?'

The boy said he would be unlikely to waken before morning. They could go down now, they could all relax.

Bonnie was doing her hair again in the kitchen, her face hidden. Tor was wiping the table in a worried way, her hand moving in circles. He longed to reassure them, to comfort and protect them. Bonnie's hand with her comb was shaking. She kept her eyes hidden behind her hair.

'He's asleep. He's quite all right now, no harm done.'

'It isn't him. It's Mamma.'

'What happened, Bonnie?'

The postman had brought a message from Fagin's farm, just before the storm broke. Their mother was there, she was coming home later.

Eden felt enraged. She had left three nervous kids with a drunken father while she went visiting. Didn't she have any sense of responsibility? Selfish bitch, thinking only of herself. No doubt she was afraid of Brad in that condition, no doubt she found life here a trial. She should have checked before she came to live here, the Irish were different. Irishmen drank to get drunk, drunkenness was accepted lightly. She should have checked up on the state of the Grange. No doubt she missed the parties and admiration she'd been used to, very likely she was a snob as well. If she was lonely, she'd brought it on herself. Her attic revealed a lot about her; her own room was attractive and comfortable, no matter about anywhere else. He remembered the way Bo had kicked the purse away. It wouldn't surprise him if the kid wasn't light-fingered. A lot was wrong with this family. A good thing he'd come when he had. At least they knew where the mother was, the bitch, the selfish snob. She'd be back when it suited her, doubtless.

'Poor Dadda must have a hot-water bottle,' Bo said.

'Poor Dadda nothing. He's drunk, and you know it. He's filthy and disgusting. And stop calling him Dadda. It's silly, it's stage-Irish. Can't you say "Captain" like we do? Can't you be natural?'

'He's my blood father, I'm not like you two. You're mongrels, you have no father. I have my Da ... I love him and he loves me, I'll call him what I like. He's my friend.'

'Friend? Oh, very friendly I must say, coming home in that state, time after time.'

Bickering seemed to give the kids relief, they seemed to enjoy it. The immediate crisis was over, they could relax; scrapping eased tension. What they needed now was a proper meal. He would go now and buy groceries. Perhaps Bonnie would come with him.

But all three preferred to stay. The girls wanted to be here when their mother turned up; it was understandable. Bo had his father on his mind. Eden suggested lighting the range. They could have hot water then. He had never laid a turf fire before; the feel of the sods pleased him, dry and rough, the colour of cork. You laid them on end, round a wad of newspaper. When alight, they smelled like burning leaves, collapsing into orange-coloured ash.

He left the three of them warming themselves and throwing fresh turf into the grate. Though it was hot still, it was damp. The firelight cheered. As he left they started humming their bubble song very softly. Bonnie droned on one note. They were an odd lot, no doubt of that, but he was committed to them.

Another downpour looked imminent, after the lull in the storm. He was beginning to feel part of the place; the dripping trees, the drive, the sodden fields were familiar now. There was the thin cow, lashing its tail. The message on the Co-op door was still there, 'Back at half three'. The town was still empty, the barman in Fagin's still there. At the back of his bar was a small parlour stocked with groceries. Cornflakes, tea, eggs were on a shelf. There were tins of meat and peas. There were stools here where friends of the barman could drink in private. He was surly with Eden, wrapping the purchases without speaking, knotting them with string. Behind were dusty liqueur bottles as well as spirits. A bottle of crème de menthe looked years old. Did Brad buy drink to take home, or did he do all his serious drinking here?

'Very quiet, aren't we?' He planned to be here a long time, he might as well be friendly.

The man was silent, the collie dog slept. Where was the famous Irish bonhomie that he'd heard about? Except for that attic bedroom, everywhere had an air of heaviness and doom. Even Aunt's house in Streatham had some life compared to this place. How shocked she'd be to see it here. 'Be content with your lot. Ambition killed the rat.' He couldn't agree with that. Life had soured his aunt, it wouldn't sour him. Her grey night-time plait of hair, her teeth in the tumbler, her mustard paintwork, were things to be forgotten. He would change everything that he could change. Poor little Bonnie must be rescued. She needed clothes, a proper diet, someone to care.

He had left her holding a towel to the fire for her bath later. Her toes had looked so pretty and pink. They were still sitting there when he got back.

'We'll have a good fry-up, shall we? I got sausages. How about some chips?'

Before they ate they stacked the turf baskets high with turf from the turf shed. They pulled chairs round the fire, they talked with their mouths full, spearing chips and pieces of sausage onto their knives, eating hungrily. They drank a lot of strong tea. Bo hummed and rocked, leaning against each sister in turn. They had combed his hair.

6

Eden checked that Brad was all right before he went to bed. He'd heard of people choking on their own vomit while they slept. He remembered the noisy sleep of the men in the barracks, the snores, groans and cries of the very drunk. 'Be content with your lot?' Most certainly not. His motto was 'Forget your past'.

Brad, having snored earlier in the lavatory, lay quiet and still. Eden tidied the blankets, refilled the hot-water bottle. Bo was asleep before the fire. Efficiency without fuss was called for, no disapproval. Bonnie's peace of mind mattered most.

'I suggest we all go to bed early. Your mother won't be back tonight, because of the storm.'

It was hotter than ever, in spite of the hail and rain earlier.

He woke with a jerk. Someone was screaming in an unearthly manner. A little wearily he wondered if one of them was being knifed. They didn't go in for half-measures in this family. He felt worn out.

Bonnie and Tor were on the landing.

331

'It's another nightmare. He has them sometimes. All right, pet, we're coming, we're here.'

Just a dream, not a soul in torment. He sighed. He tucked his shirt in and followed them to Bo's room where he lay on his back, his eyes staring. He continued the screams, short and sharp. He was so hot his sheets and pillow were soaking, his hair was plastered flat.

'You're sure it's not a fit?' Eden asked.

'Of course not. He has nightmares. He's highly strung, aren't you, my pet?' Bonnie sat on his pillow. Together they soothed and patted him until the screams stopped.

Eden felt he was intruding, he'd felt the same that first time on the lawn. They were complete, they needed no one; grouped on the pillow, an almost holy three, intent on themselves. He looked round Bo's little room, almost a cubby hole, with a set of shelves where the window should be . . .. He'd made a shrine for his prayers, there was a statue of St Patrick and some shamrock. A crucifix dangled from his rosary, his child's missal was on a shelf apart. He lay quiet now between his sisters, tuning his head to their hands that stroked. They hummed.

'All right then, Bo?' Eden felt uncomfortable.

Bo gazed at him. 'We're a lovable little family, aren't we, Eden? Do you find us curious? Do you think I'm spoiled?'

'Oh, I don't know about that.'

Bo took Tor's hand, kissing it smackingly. What a pity Bonnie was tone-deaf, poor creature; she'd never make an opera singer. Ah, me.

'Would you like a hot drink?'

Eden had heard that sufferers from nightmares should be treated gently. Cocoa?

It was one thirty. The storm wasn't over yet, rolls of thunder sounded far off. Bonnie followed him downstairs. He longed to be alone with her, to tell of his admiration. To tell her to be more modest, not to sprawl at the table like that, to do up her nightdress. Some people might get the wrong idea, might take advantage. How innocent was she? All three of them blushed easily, they had that type of skin. Tor was very likely undernourished, all three were in need of love. He wanted to button and bath them, clothe them respectably, keep them smiling and fed. He made a further resolve not to let his desire interfere with his protective feelings. They all needed him, not just Bonnie. Beautiful as she was, lust had no place.

He poured milk into a cup while she mixed cocoa and sugar. 'It's all because of Captain,' she said. 'Mamma isn't to blame.' 'I'm not blaming anyone. I don't like to see you upset.' 'I'm not upset. I'm just concerned.'

She stretched out her long legs. She had a tiny scar high on her thigh. Tor called from the landing in a loud whisper, because Captain must not wake before he'd got sober.

'What are you doing, Bonnie? Hurry.'

'She's helping make cocoa,' Eden answered. Brad wouldn't waken for hours, no need to whisper. He wanted to know about Bo's nightmares. Bonnie said they all had them sometimes, but only Bo screamed. Telling a dream when you woke was the best way to recover. Bo could never remember his. Tor's dreams were of being chased.

'And yours, Bonnie?'

Sometimes they were lovely. Gardens full of tea-roses and love-in-the-mist, small animals, butterflies that made music with their wings, bright sunlight and people dancing. Then it stopped, it went dark. It hurt. He couldn't bear to think of her in pain, she was born for sunshine and flowers. She said the dreams were worse since they'd got here, they weren't used to life in Ireland. They didn't know what lay ahead.

'I wasn't happy when I was young,' he said.

He told her about lighting Aunt's fires, about shopping for her, about trying to please, like a servant. How he'd left and never gone back. She stared at the cocoa and sugar mixture. She said that their mamma should never have married again. She had warned her; it was too late.

'I don't remember Brad drinking in the army days. Life was different. Perhaps he misses his old responsibilities.'

'Responsibilities? We are his responsibility. He's made fools of us, especially Mamma. He pretended he was rich.'

'This could be a fine property; it's small, it's been neglected, it could be restored. Do you miss your real father?'

'He died ages ago, I told you. I knew Captain would let us down. He's made Mamma miserable.'

'What are your own plans, Bonnie?'

'No more studying, thanks very much. I'll never get used to it here. Bo is happy, we are not. He loves Ireland. Mamma has changed.'

'In what way?'

'She's secretive. She cries, too. I won't marry for ages.'

'You may change. Just you wait.'

The way she blushed was sweet, Eden longed to reach for her. He asked what she liked doing.

'I wish I was a dancer, or a singer like Mamma was. But that's impossible.'

'I could teach you to dance. You mean ballroom? Stand up, Bonnie. See? We're perfectly matched.'

Now his arms were round her, sanctioned by ballroom etiquette, nothing furtive, nothing to suggest lust. He felt her thin hand, felt her backbone through her nightdress, felt her breath on his cheek. She was stiff from nervousness and ignorance but her eyes had closed. Her feet started following his. With lips just parted she looked like an angel on the brink of realizing a dream. He knew beyond doubt then that she was made for him, that he must treat her with tender care, he must adore her, must never cause sadness or pain. He increased the pressure of his arm and hand very slightly.

'I don't want to tire you, Bonnie dear. Let's go on talking for a while.'

Her breath was quick, her cheeks a sweet pink. Would he really teach her? She would love that, she said. Her mother had been on the stage, performing might be in the blood. She longed to learn to dance.

'Tell me about yourself.' He longed to know every detail, nothing was unimportant.

She said that when Bo was a baby, she and her sisters looked after him; they had taken it in turns to wheel his pram. They'd had a real garden in Yorkshire, full of flowers. They used to fill the pram with blossoms. She loved roses best, like her Mamma. Tor preferred spring flowers. He pictured them hanging their curls over the baby, the scent of primroses and violets sweet in the air. He pictured them kissing him, singing to him, playing with his toes, rocking him. He longed to kiss her himself. He would teach her to waltz, he would show her the joy of the dance. She'd had troubles early, with her first brother dying, her father dying. He'd like her to rely on him now.

'It will be wonderful, Bonnie. You're a natural mover. I think very likely we're made for each other.'

'What about Tor? Will you teach her too?'

'I will if you wish. Of course. If you like.'

'Bonnie? Bonn-ee.'

'I'll bring the cocoa. Bring the sugar in case he needs more, Bonnie … my dear.'

He wanted to call her his love, his angel girl, his beloved; he mustn't be impetuous.

He paused by the attic stairs to listen to Brad. He thought he heard a snore, then quiet. The sounds of sleeping people were the same, however humble or exalted their class. What mattered was their speech. He had taken particular care to speak slowly to Bonnie. He listened when the sisters spoke. Bo's fluctuating brogue was comic, his 'bedad's and 'ah, me's endearing. He himself must be word-perfect for their world. He ran over his exercise: 'Brown frowned on his way down town. He must save to pay Jane's way.' He remembered the custard cream biscuits bought earlier. Bo might like one.

His sisters watched Bo as he licked the cream fillings with his thin tongue. They piled more sugar into his cup. No wonder they had rather dingy teeth. Bonnie was still childish in many ways, Eden would see that she was happier. He had a lot to offer.

No one felt like sleeping yet, having been woken so forcibly by Bo.

'Eden, what games do you know? What word games?'

He'd never been competitive, hated all ball games. Team spirit meant nothing to him, his interest was in furthering himself. He disliked the idea of word games, they might show up his ignorance. He didn't want to risk revealing the truth about his education. Couldn't they just talk for a while?

'Let's play "Favourites". It's too late to use our brains,' Tor said quickly. Favourite animals, flowers, tunes, books, the list was endless, requiring no skill. You lost a life if you couldn't answer quickly. You must give reasons for your choice. Animals first.

'I choose my duck.'

'A duck is a bird, not a beast.'

Bo said it was the animal kingdom. Ducks found their own food. You could eat them when they got old.

'You've lost a life for being slow. I'll choose the elephant. They make good mothers and are kind.'

'I choose ... a horse. Horses are loyal. Eden, you next.'

'Homo sapiens,' he said nervously.

'Who in particular?'

'Bonnie.'

'*Bonnie?* Sister Bonnie? Bonnie, me darlin', Eden is sweet on you. Imagine that. Eden loves Bonnie, begorra, Eden loves Bonnie, bedad.'

Bo clutched himself, wrapping his arms tightly, rocking with mirth. His sister Bonnie, ah me.

'Stop being so rude and silly, Bo.'

Tears of shame stood in Bonnie's eyes. She leaned forward to strike him. Tor pulled her back. Bo was just joking, take no notice. Bo's mood changed, he turned to Tor, pushing his face into her hand, inviting her to stroke his hair. Darling Tor, she was his best friend. She fondled him, the highly strung little brother.

The front door banged. The mother was back.

'Mamma? You're here. Oh, Mamma. At last.'

'Sweet children. All crouched upstairs? What has been happening?'

'Captain came back. He's upstairs. He's asleep.'

She blinked slowly, she didn't seem afraid or upset. She looked faintly amused. The children were on Bo's bed, he was curled in Tor's arms. Bonnie was aloof and red.

The woman was not as Eden had imagined, not shrinking or

put-upon; in the poor light she was like an older Bonnie, with coarser skin and hair. She kept her eyes wide open and taut. Her cheeks were smooth as dolls' cheeks, her mouth was lined, her hands and neck showed her age.

'Eden came, Mamma.'

She turned to him. What must he think? Had her children been looking after him? The household was somewhat *distrait* just at present; he'd come at an awkward time.

'Mamma, where were you? Are you all right?'

'Why ever not? Don't stare at me, I'm not a ghost. Please, please.' She put her hands to her face.

'We're not staring, we're just looking. We were worried,' Tor said.

'Poor sweets. All is well. Why such agitation? You got my message, I trust. I *should* have let you know sooner ... But ...'

'But, Mammy, you left us a long time, didn't you? We were alone. Luckily for us Eden came.'

Bo eyed his mother shrewdly. He pushed towards Tor's hand. He sighed as she wiped the cocoa stains from his mouth.

7

She was as cool as if she'd been on a holiday.

'Tell me all, my sweets. What has been happening?'

She leaned forward, her knees crossed, a high-heeled shoe dangling from one toe, another shoe under the bed. The girls were still on Bo's pillow, watching her. Were they wondering how soon she'd leave again? The plaster eyes of St Patrick watched the group from the shelf. There was no sound from Brad, upstairs.

'Bo, sweetie, did you see my purse anywhere?'

'No, Mammy.'

Eden remembered seeing him kick the purse under the bed in the attic. Did the boy steal cash to keep his father from drinking?

'Bonnie, cheer up, can't you? Why so subdued?'

'We missed you. Bo had another dream.'

'He did? Tell me, darling, what was it?'

'I don't remember. I never remember.'

Bo kept his face turned towards Tor. The mother stretched out her hand to Eden. Her skin felt dry as holly leaves.

'I *have* been remiss, haven't I? Can you forgive me?'

'That's quite all right, Mrs ...'

'Mrs? Why so formal? Call me Babs. We are Brad and Babs, short for Barbara. My most intimate friends used to call me Bab.'

She had a secret look, as if she was thinking of the days when she'd entertained the troops. Did she still pine for the men in khaki; did she miss their stares, their admiration and whistles, the desire in their eyes? She had traded adulation for the land of shamrock, and a drunk. Her looks were fading, her children thin and sad-eyed. Her house was an overgrown shanty. Yet there was magic here, there was Bonnie. Babs saw him stare, she twitched her lips to suggest a kiss, very likely a habit from her past.

He decided that her nature was base, that her heart was as false as her pink cheeks. She was too old to be called Babs. 'Bab'? What kind of name was that? Brad had made an unwise choice. What did her daughters really think of her? They were loyal, especially Bonnie. Bo didn't pretend.

He wriggled under his sheet, screwing his face like a monkey.

'Little Babsy-wabsy. Get me a drink. I need sweet things after my dream.'

'I'll go. You stay here ... Babs.'

No one had asked what she'd been doing or where she'd been. The Fagins lived two miles away. Now was his chance to prove his worth. He would learn Babs' needs as well as the kids'. He was getting rather sick of heating milk, of running back and forth, of shopping; he was sick of tending drunks, but he would do anything necessary, he wouldn't return to England without a fight, or unless he was fired. For Bonnie he would demean himself. One day she'd be his dancing partner. One day she'd live in the home he'd provided, with a beautiful garden of flowers.

He clanged the pan onto the stove again, he hurled more turf on the fire. That Babs woman ought to be up with her husband, checking that he was alright. He did grant that she had difficulties, but she should manage better, she'd had experience. She only seemed to think of herself.

Was she the type to drink cocoa? She was the gin-and-french class. He could see her sipping from cut glasses, nibbling cherries or olives on sticks, smiling that smile, teetering on those heels. He glanced round the kitchen; he'd wait on her like a slave, ingratiate himself. The fire, the smell of hot milk, the cloth on the table (torn but clean) were his doing. He heard those heels descending, she was coming, smiling that mouth again.

'You're supposed to be the guest, Eden. Let *me*.'

'I want to help. If I can. Anything ... Babs.'

She looked pleased, he had called her Babs. She sat at the table, she peered at her dainty watch. What a criminal hour to be warming milk. She did appreciate his support.

'It's a pleasure. Would you like something to eat?'

There were no biscuits left and very little bread. Waiter, nursemaid, lackey, cook and bottle-washer, no matter, he would comply. If he had a lemon he'd make her Russian tea. He remembered Aunt's tray, the sight of her grey mouth, her warnings. He had proved her wrong, nothing was impossible with the right determination. How well Babs spoke, just like her daughters. Self-improvement took time and effort, he was on his way up. Goodbye loneliness. He didn't care about a stately lifestyle. He had never hunted, fished or shot at animals, never even owned a bicycle, much less an estate car. What he craved was this family's acceptance. He poured weak tea for Babs, who seemed to be giving him the come-on. It was her daughter he wanted, not her. She should be named Mrs Falseheart, with those red-tipped holly leaf hands.

'Don't rush upstairs to the infants yet, Eden. Sit down. We must talk.'

'All right, Babs. I want to be frank myself. It's about Brad. How long has he ... ?'

'Has he what? I beg your pardon?'

'His drinking. He's upstairs, legless. I know about it. Has it been going on for long?'

'Yes, I see. I quite understand.'

Her mouth went slack, she looked at her nails. Her neck was like Bonnie's when it drooped. She was frightened inside like the others, her sophistication was an act.

'I'm not trying to interfere, Babs. How serious is it? I should know about him. He offered me a job.'

She looked up, pushing her lips fetchingly. She couldn't discuss it now, she was exhausted. The infants had obviously taken to him. She wanted him to stay.

'I was offered a position by letter. I didn't expect this. I haven't spoken to Brad about the job.'

'We are counting on you. Brad has been ... He's had worries. It's a change from army life.'

'But the drinking ...'

'He never did before. He needs help with the farm.'

'Farm? I must say I got a surprise.' A thin cow and a duck was hardly a farm.

'Surprise? Imagine how I felt. I had no idea. The state of the place. Brad misled me. Stay.'

'I will do all I can, Babs. There is certainly room for improvement.'

'Improvement? It's plague-ridden. I felt doomed as soon as we arrived.'

'Don't say that, Babs. Don't give up before you start.'

She was strong-willed, she had determination. She could get what she wanted for herself, her attic room proved that.

'There is nothing for us here. The boredom is criminal.'

'Bo seems happy. Does Brad know how you feel?'

'He knows what I'm used to, knows what I need. Any woman would be peeved.'

'I can see you're used to nice things. Your room upstairs . . . very tasteful.'

He could see that Brad hadn't turned out the magical solution to her widowhood. She had ended up in a rundown ruin in a rural area, without much means of support. They were as out of place here as an orchid in a cowpat. He asked her bluntly how often Brad got drunk.

'We never know. Not knowing is so peeving, you can't plan or rely on anything. Don't desert us.'

'I was offered a salaried position.'

'I am sure you will be paid. Brad isn't . . . we aren't destitute, you know.'

She was proud, like her children. What she said very likely wasn't true. Eden might find himself working for nothing. To help Bonnie get away he must earn money. He watched Babs, raise her cup, putting it down before drinking, making her expression appealing again.

'Babs, don't you realize how worried they were? It's lucky I come . . . I came when I did.'

'It's all very well for outsiders to find fault. You don't realize. I have tried my best. Sweet Christ, I have tried.'

'I expect Brad feels upset, he must know he's let you down, neglected all of you.'

'I am upset. I'm let down, I'm neglected.'

'I suppose people in different countries have different ways.'

He knew that sounded priggish, he must defend Brad if he could; he was supposed to be his boss, his provider. Why didn't he get up and come downstairs now, behave in a proper way, assume his proper place? Both he and Babs were at fault, both weak and headstrong.

Babs went on sitting there, shallow, a flirt, trembling and ogling him with those blue eyes, expecting sympathy and support. She must have dealt with heavy drinkers before now.

'You're right of course, Eden; this country is different. They're mad, they love their own voices, they love drinking and fighting. It's the disillusionment of my life.'

'I've hardly spoken to anyone since I got here, hardly seen anyone except this family.'

It was mission week, she said. Everything stopped. The people were in the chapel from morning till night.

'You mean Catholics? Priests?'

The Catholic church had a numbing effect, she said; the people became mesmerized by clergy and nuns. The town was taken over.

'Even Brad? Bo said nothing about any mission.'

'Booze means more to Brad than anything. Bo is a fanatical child, he'll outgrow prayers, I suppose. I sincerely hope so.'

'Is Fagin's Brad's usual haunt?'

'Fagin's? Why do you ask? What did Brad say?'

'He didn't say nothing . . . anything. Er . . . Bo was screaming something shocking while you were out. Loud screaming.'

'He's had a lot of nightmares recently. It's this benighted place.' She rubbed her thumb nail. Poor little Boris was Brad's wonder boy, his golden child, light of his life. Of course, the girls' real father was dead.

'Bonnie said. It must have been a hard time for you.'

His aunt had managed alone. Hardship was as hard as you let it be. Not that he thought anything good about Aunt.

'You probably never met a family like this one, did you? Tell me, Eden, what do you think of us?'

He felt like saying that he thought them a self-dramatizing lot of lunatics, except for Bonnie, of course. He said it was too soon to make judgements. Ask again in six months' time.

'Then you'll stay. I knew you would.'

She gave him her bewitching look again, then pushed out her mouth like a kiss. In old age she'd have a tick if she wasn't careful, her type of looks didn't last. Self-interest made you insensitive. She was probably stupid too. How dare she put her children at risk.

'I'll do whatever I can.'

'Oh, you are wonderful. I worry about the girls. The anxiety ... Bonnie ...'

From outside the kitchen came a crash. Screams sounded from the landing. Eden leapt to his feet. They were at it again. Fresh melodrama. This lot should be on the stage. Couldn't they endure peace for five minutes?

Tor was shouting, 'Don't touch her, leave her. Let my sister alone.' Babs gave a little moan. She spilled her tea, catching her heel in the blue table-cloth, smashing her cup to the ground. Sweet Christ, she was doomed.

Feet on the stairway, bodies falling, a chair falling, a crash, another scream. Eden was there. If anyone laid a finger on Bonnie ... Brad was in his shirtsleeves, grappling with her, falling, losing her, grabbing her.

'Little bitch, I'll teach you to meddle with my things. Stay out of my room.'

Eden felt that his eyes and ears were bursting. He wanted to kill Brad with his bare hands.

'Let her go, or you won't live to remember. Let go of her, I said.'

He shoved Brad against the banisters. He put his arms round Bonnie. Darling, dear one, he was there.

He felt teeth biting his knuckles. Bo was screaming at him now. Don't dare threaten his father, don't touch him. Dadda couldn't help himself. There, Dadda, there.

'It's me. It's Bo. I'm here.'

Brad leaned back against the stair rail. He slipped down, he sat on the bottom step. His eyes were without guile or malice again before he closed them. Whatever had angered him was forgotten. Babs, still in the kitchen, stood twisting her hands. It was criminal, it was all too much to bear.

'I'll get him upstairs again, don't worry.'

Eden dragged him by the armpits.

'He can't help himself, he won't remember,' Bo said.

Babs stayed where she was. Tor had her arms round Bonnie who was in tears.

Brad's hand caught in the banisters, Eden dragged him free. Let his wrist break, he deserved it. Eden wished he had choked on his vomit. Still, it was another chance to prove his ability. He would provide food and drink, create heat, calm nightmares, shop and clean, reassure the anxious, escort drunkards to their beds.

A whisky bottle under Brad's pillow was a clue to the outburst. Apparently the two girls had gone up, Brad had woken to find Bonnie taking the whisky. Was she in danger? He must get her away as soon as possible, settle her, make her happy, teach her dancing. His angel dance-partner-to-be.

He tucked Brad firmly into bed again. He took the whisky and went down. Babs was in Bo's room with her daughters, let her attend to them. The kitchen was quiet. It was after three in the morning, he wasn't doing any more for anyone. He finished the whisky. The fire was out. Let it stay out, he wasn't getting on his knees again.

He straightened the cloth, picked up the broken china. His hand still felt sore from Bo's teeth. He sucked his knuckle. On the floor was a splash of blood. He bent down; it wasn't blood, but one of Babs' thumbnails, false and shining. He threw it onto the ashes in the fireplace where it glowed like a scarlet flower.

8

'Eden, wake up. It's late.'

'Whassat? Sorry, Aunt. I must have slep' it out. I'll get your tea.'

'Who is "Aunt"? What are you talking about? This is Tor.'

'Oh ... Sorry, Tor. Of course. I forgot where I was for a minute.'

The present came back to him. This was Ireland. He had slept late after drinking Brad's whisky, he wasn't with Aunt in Streatham, he would never go back there again. He was living with gentry, on his way to belonging with them. He was at the Grange. He blinked at Tor, feeling dazed. For all he knew, Aunt might be dead now, and her warnings with her. Had his grammar let him down again?

'Is it raining? What's that din, Tor?'

She looked spectral in the light of his bedroom. The rain had got worse, they were being flooded out. The roof was leaking, rain was seeping under the window sills and over the doorsteps; they were in danger of being washed away. Listen to it, that noise was rain. The lights didn't work, the turf in the shed was wet through.

'I never knew Irish weather could be like this.'

Torrents streamed down the window pane, rattling on the skylight outside, dripping onto the landing. No wonder the place smelled like graves. He shivered, still half awake. He mustn't be morbid, there was work to do, there was Bonnie to look after.

'Has anyone been up to Brad again?'

'Mamma stayed with us in Bo's room. It's better if he's left alone.'

Before Eden went down he paused to listen for Brad's breathing. He felt responsible. Babs should have been to him. He would check again, make sure.

Brad was lying in the same position as when he'd left him, his nose tilting towards his pillow, his hands slack on the sheet. His breathing was laboured now, sounding harsh and painful. Eden leaned over him. His lips were blue. Rain was dripping onto the bedclothes through the attic skylight. Brad didn't move as Eden pulled the bed out of the way.

'Wake up, Brad. Sober up, can't you? You're soaked. The family need you. You can't lie here forever.'

He rubbed his hands, he shook him. Brad was inert.

In the kitchen Babs was holding bread to the fire; she moved awkwardly, she held her fork awkwardly as if unused to kitchen chores. There was no more turf in the baskets. Bo was scrabbling for any bits he could find, throwing them into the grate to make a brief flare. His piece of toast lay in the hearth, blackened. He whined to Tor for jam.

'Give me some in the spoon, you creature. I want some. Now.'

'I don't think Brad is well. Have you seen him, Babs?'

'Seen him? I've been trying to cope with all this on my own. What with Bo's whines and Bonnie's sulks, I've had enough. He's doubtless drunk still.'

Babs' face was white, she wore no lipstick, her thumbnail gleamed as pale as the bread she was holding.

'I lit the fire for you, Mammy. I want some jam now please.'

'I'm worried about his breathing, Babs. The roof has leaked onto him. The bed is soaked. I felt I should look at him, I'm glad I did. I hope you don't object.'

'Object? Why should I? Do what you like. I'm on my knees.' Babs waved the fork, dropping the last piece of bread.

Bonnie turned from the window.

'Sulking? I'm not sulking. I hate you. I hate everything. I'm sick of you all.'

'I'm afraid that Brad may have the flu, Babs.'

'Flu? Good. He deserves it after last night. You've seen how he drinks. His chest is weak.'

'Poor Dadda, he couldn't help it. He isn't well, you know that, Mammy.'

'Mamma, shouldn't you explain to Eden about Captain having been in the hospital?'

'Shut your mouth, Tor. Don't talk about it.'

Bo clawed at Tor with his nails, trying to bite her.

'What happened, Tor? If Brad has been ill I should ought to know about it.'

'Don't ask questions. Mind your business. Give me some jam, you cur.'

'There's no more jam, pet, we finished it yesterday. We should tell Eden, he ought to know.'

'Tell me what, Tor? Explain it, please.'

He tried not to speak fast in the heat of the moment. In a quiet voice Tor explained that Brad had been in the local hospital this summer because of his alcoholism.

'I did ought to get the doctor then. Now.'

'You're not to. I won't let you. Cur.' Bo was screeching.

Babs put her head in her hands. Did the child have to make that noise?

'Let me go for the doctor, Babs. Bo can come with me, may he?'

'Do what you like. Get your raincoat, Bo.' He could go anywhere he liked for peace.

Bonnie looked at her mother. His raincoat? What raincoat? None of them had any clothes worth the name. Babs was supposed to have bought them clothes when they got to Ireland. They had little more than what they stood up in. *Clothes?* Really, Mamma, think again.

'Enough, Bonnie. My head.'

Eden went for his demob, raincoat and stout ex-officer's shoes. He'd be quicker going alone, in any case. This place was bedlam. Babs was a disaster, with her selfishness and false red nails. The doctor would be out very likely, lurking in some pub or church. Mission week? Disaster week was more like it. Week of doom, week of drinking, week of floods.

He fingered the cheque book in his pocket. The prospect of increasing his bank balance looked increasingly remote. How shocked his aunt would be over this lot. But he didn't regret coming to Ireland, far from it. Land of dreams, land of romance, Bonnie's land. He would practise his elocution exercise as he walked in the rain again. 'Brown frowned.'

A car was moving through the storm, jerkingly, starting and stalling. An old Morris Minor came into view, drawing up under his window. Black-trousered legs appeared and a vast umbrella. He heard the door bell ring.

'Eden? Could you come down, please?'

What did Babs want? It couldn't be the doctor.

The parish priest was in the hall. He had pushed past Babs, was shaking his umbrella. He had large ears and teeth, he wore galoshes over his shoes.

'Is Bradwell about? Tell him I'm come if you please, Marm.'

'I'm afraid not. You can't see him. He can't see you.'

Her voice wavered. Dislike and fear showed in her eyes.

'Is that right for a fact, Marm? May I ask the reason why?'

'Can I help, Babs?'

'This is Eden, Father. He's Bradwell's new manager. Bradwell is unwell. Eden comes from London.'

'London? So? And how are you now, sir? If Bradwell is poorly he'll want to see me. I'll just take a run upstairs.'

'Father, I have just said, he isn't well. He's asleep.'

'His usual complaint, I take it. I was afraid of that when he wasn't at Mass. He's not been near the chapel since the mission started. He'll be wanting to see me now, Marm.'

Babs looked to Eden for support. This man must not be allowed upstairs. Bottles, soaking furniture, frippery and frills in her room.

'Er ... perhaps you could call later, Father, when he's better? He's not up to visitors yet.'

'Out of my way, sir. Are you plotting to keep a man of the cloth from his flock? Stand clear, let me pass.'

'No, Father. As Brad's wife I refuse to allow it. There is no need.'

'Marm, if your husband has had a slip I need to know about it. There is indeed the need.'

'Slip? Dadda is quite well thank you, Father.'

Bo was in the hall, his blackened toast crust in his hand. He must speak to the Father urgently.

'Wait now, boy. After I've been upstairs.'

'I want to come. Dadda will need me.'

Babs grabbed his arm. 'Stand still. Hold your tongue, don't interfere.'

Eden wanted to tell Babs that Bo felt excluded. He wanted to be with his father, he felt apprehensive. Babs was concerned with being in charge. She ran from her intolerable life when she felt like it, yet she needed to rule, needed power. The Father was a threat to her control; the church's word was law, no one could stop him going up. The attic door closed, they could hear nothing. Was the priest murmuring prayers for the sick, administering the final rites? Touching Brad with oil and water, blessing, absolving in Latin, making the sign of the Cross? Suffering and excitement seemed necessary to this family, if Brad died they'd be lost. Eden smothered another yawn of weariness, he mustn't flag. Diligence, attentiveness, watch your speech. Each new crisis is another chance to prove your worth.

The attic door opened again, they heard the squelch of the Father's galoshes on the stairs; his ears, teeth and bald head came into view.

'No question about it, Marm. I'm experienced in the way of sickness. It's the hospital for Bradwell, right away.'

'I beg your pardon. Allow me to decide what is ... It's my husband, remember.'

'And my parishioner, Marm. I am his parish priest. Remember that if you will.'

'I won't allow you ...'

'Allow me to judge what is best. Was it not me that christened him? 'Twas a mercy I came when I did.' The Father closed his teeth with a snap, scowling at Babs.

'Do you expect me to go on my knees to you? You waltz in without invitation, you start laying down the law.'

'Stop, stop, Mammy. Don't argue with the Father. I must talk to him.'

'Wait now, boy, shortly. You're to start with the Brothers next term. I have it arranged for you. Your Dadda must come with me now.'

Eden spoke slowly and clearly. Might it not be best if Brad went now with the Father in his car? He had seen Brad himself, he did seem very ill. As he spoke he moved out of range of Bo in case he had another tantrum, he wasn't risking those teeth again. There'd been enough combat and violence for the moment. A little ordinary courtesy wouldn't come amiss. He might be expected to make tea for the priest. But Bo was quiet, he'd got his wish, he was to start at the school of his choice, thanks to the priest.

'Pleurisy, Marm; you had thought of that? Bronchitis? Quinsy?'

'Yes, yes. I quite understand. His chest is weak. We know.'

'I'll take him with me now.'

Babs was silent. Perhaps that would be best, easier all round.

'I'm glad, Marm, that you can see reason.'

The priest looked at her with distaste. Protestant woman that she was, without thought for anyone or anything but her own pleasure. Dilatory, neglectful, wrong-headed and, if gossip had it right, loose in her ways. She was apt to visit Fagin's farm a shade too often. That Mick one at the bar encouraged Bradwell in drink. It was high time the Fagin brothers found wives of their own. Nothing like a wife to keep a man straight.

This Protestant one was in another class, from what he'd heard tell. Not that he encouraged scandal, but a priest had a duty to know. The likes of this one and her daughters were a blot on the parish. English, heathen, with time on their hands. The young lad, now, was different; a soul waiting to be snatched from danger. He was unruly, lacking manners, with a nasty temper, but the Christian Brothers would set him right. Marrying outside the church had been Bradwell's ruin, on top of going to England to fight; such action brought no good result.

Tor called her brother. 'Come on, pet, help me now.'

There was work to do if Captain was leaving with the Father. Someone must prepare hot-water bottles for his journey, he must be kept warm. He must have a thermos of tea for the trip. While Bonnie sulked behind her hair, she and Bo would help.

Babs was on her dignity. Naturally she would travel with her husband, she would sit in front by the priest while Brad stretched out in the back. Later she would return with his clothes in a suitcase. The rule of the hospital was that all lockers must be kept empty until the patient's discharge. Without his clothes Brad would be safely contained. Eden thought it unlikely that she'd visit him.

Tor and Bo put bottles, rugs and cushions in the back of the car. Eden and the Father lifted and dragged Brad downstairs. His face looked dreadful, his breath rasped. As Tor wound a scarf round him he moaned.

'Hush, Captain, you're going to hospital.'

'Disaster. Where is ... she?'

Bo did up his shoes. Not to worry, he'd look after things at home until Dadda was back.

'Out of the way, children.'

Babs wore a lavender woollen coat with a nipped waist. The turned-up collar framed her face, she looked queenly.

'Oh, my gloves. Bonnie, be a lamb.'

Bonnie handed them through the window. Babs smiled. Such a thoughtful daughter.

'Weather for ducks.' The Father sighed, adding, 'God bless all here.'

Babs smoothed her lavender kid gloves over her fingers. Father's ears shone like signals in the gloom of the car. He settled his galoshes comfortably. He turned the starter. Brad didn't move. No one waved or said goodbye. They were gone.

Eden slumped against the hall door. Just him and the kids again, time for a breathing space, he hoped. Time to do something about the leaks.

'Come on, then. I'll show you how to keep the rain out.'

First they must put pots and pans under the roof leaks on the landing. Tor and Bo routed under the stairs. They found rags under a basket of empty bottles and newspaper. Eden showed them how to wrap rags round wads of paper, to push into the cracks round the windows. There was no fire, no electricity, but the tension was easier. Soon the sound of raindrops falling into the various containers upstairs made an odd, syncopated beat.

'What shall I do, Eden?'

'Stay by me. Hold this. We'll stay upstairs until your mother gets back. Bo's room is the best.'

Bo lay round his duck on his bed, protecting it. Tor lay next to him. They were curled like spoons.

'Bonnie? Don't look so sad.'

'You mustn't judge Mamma, Eden. I know her best. She changed when we came here.'

'She told me she found it difficult. It's you I want to help.'

Bonnie of the beautiful eyes must trust him.

By the time Babs got back, Bo was over-tired, over-excited and obnoxious. His sisters were trying to calm him when she appeared.

'Must you sing like that, Bonnie? The noise. What is that bird doing here?'

'Mammy, is Dadda all right?'

'Don't bother me. I'm going up.'

'Someone was in the lodge, Mammy. Someone has been there.'

'You nasty little boy, hold your tongue. Let me get some sleep.'

Eden wondered how someone like that could produce someone like Bonnie. Could anyone soften her? She was inhuman.

It was the last time they saw her alive.

9

As long as I can remember I have felt older than Bonnie, older even than Mamma. I have heard of people having old souls; you are born like that. I may have lived other lives before this one. I feel older and wiser inside. I don't remember feeling young, not like Bo or Ula. I was always aware of adult strain.

Ula missed that summer at the Grange. Mamma had planned to settle us in Ireland, then return to Ula to see what could be done to bring her over. But Mamma died instead.

Until we left England, Bonnie and I were close; we didn't need anyone else. We had experienced death early, our real father first, then our first brother as an infant, then our head-mistress at boarding school. Ula had killed her best friend by accident when she was seven. (The friend had fallen under Ula's penknife.) You might think that Ula would be scarred for life, but she grew up a cheerful soul. Our parents going away was worse than anything; you mind them leaving when you're very young, it's worse than death, in a way. I used to know Bonnie's thoughts before Ireland. Then she changed.

Bo loved the Grange. He was a braggart; it would all come to him one day, he was Captain's one blood child, he'd be the owner. He was always a show-off and a pampered brat. Bonnie and I hated the Grange.

She had warned Mamma about marrying Captain. We didn't take to him, my sisters and I disliked most men. Men were better ignored, they rarely understood children. Their wars, their news on the wireless, their money problems, weren't our affair. If they didn't try to understand us, why need we understand them? Mamma had flattered Bonnie into approving of her wedding by making her a bridesmaid. Ula and I had watched from the front pew as Mamma and Captain made their promises and Bonnie stood behind. I wanted Bonnie to trip, to disgrace the ceremony, but it went off without a mistake. The three of them looked gilded with joy. Ula and I wore high-waisted frocks and felt out of place. Bonnie's swishing chiffon and little bolero with flowers was a paler blue than Mamma's. They wore ringlets and high-heeled shoes, unreal as fashion plates. Mamma read a lot of magazines but hated books. Clothes and make up were her passion, as well as popular war-time songs. Her favourite song was 'You'd Be So Nice to Come Home To'. I pitied her when Captain so often did not come home.

Bonnie had turned to us during the service, smiling back in triumph. Mamma confided in her, she knew her secrets. Ula and I were too young to discuss lipstick, bosoms and having babies. Mamma had chosen her.

I remember Captain at the reception, holding his glass tightly in his hand. His eyes were fixed on Mamma adoringly, the drink in his hand mattered, too. Mamma was affected as usual; wriggling her shoulders, blinking behind her eye veil with the flowers sewn on it. She puffed smoke through a long cigarette holder, she smiled too hard, her eyes were hard behind that flowery veil.

'Where is that handsome husband of mine? Bonnie, did you steal him away? She's my eldest, you know, isn't she pretty?'

The guests smiled and toasted the gilded couple and the bridesmaid, yellow bubbles sparkled in the glasses. Bonnie clung to Captain as if she were the bride, loving the limelight. At that moment she believed that he was our passport to family happiness. She was the prettiest, Mamma's favourite, Captain would love her best. A ringlet curled round a flower on her bolero, she was pink-cheeked, with the world in her hand.

For Captain, Mamma had given up entertaining the forces, for him she'd become the mother of Bo. He was born in Yorkshire; our joy, our delight, from birth Bo realised his power. We competed to hold him, to wash and feed him, our lives revolved round his baby smiles. Captain was posted abroad, we lived in a bungalow. Mamma looked after us in a half-hearted way. She tried to make soup from rabbit bones, complaining that cooking roughened her hands. She taught us to file our nails horizontally, drawing the file downwards to strengthen the growth. We had to write polite letters to Captain in Tunisia, to use pumice stone on the soles of our feet. Her own bedroom was always beautiful, but the home in Yorkshire never felt really clean. We used to love the garden; an old man came to tend the flowers. Playing in that garden became my happiest memory. We used to make immensely long daisy chains for Bo. Mamma used to order expensive clothes from London for us. If you had money clothes rationing didn't hinder you. She should have stocked up for Ireland. Instead, we left everything. We had left Yorkshire with romantic hopes and expectations.

In some ways Bonnie was like Mamma. I think she expected to run round Ireland in a peasant blouse and green flannel, a colleen in a story, with black hair streaming in the wind.

We had expected luxury in Ireland. What we found gave us a shock. Captain had lied about his stately home; it wasn't a mansion, there were no servants, no lovely grounds. The food was poor, there were no landed gentry near, no neighbours of any kind except the Fagin brothers two miles away. I don't know what Captain had done before the war, perhaps he just lurked in Fagin's Bar.

Bonnie minded a lot about it, she'd so looked forward to new Irish clothes. She moped in her mirror, combing her hair; she cut her toenails and scrutinized her bust. I have always loved reading, but there were no books here. I wrote in my diary. Peace-time brought no improvement to our lives.

As well as having the old soul, I was the smallest and thinnest. I missed Ula, who had been ill for over a year; I worried about her. Being different from other families seemed a serious worry. Captain had turned out a serious disappointment. It's difficult to feel proud of a drunk.

Bonnie didn't know what she did want. She hated studying, she refused to do it. I wanted to be a nurse. I hadn't told Mamma or Captain about it, they were too busy with their own affairs. They rowed, they wouldn't speak to each other, they shut themselves in their room. And all the time we waited. When would he get drunk again? Our hair, our clothes, the state of our teeth, didn't matter to Mamma now. We felt we were a source of shame. We used to listen to them shouting in the attic, sometimes we hid in the barn with the thin cow for company. At other times they smiled into each other's eyes like they had at their wedding; they went up, they shut the attic door and we

heard nothing. In a way those silent times were worst. It comforted me to think of being a nurse.

When Captain left and didn't come back for days, it was a
relief at first. What you dreaded had happened, the waiting was
over. Then he came back and it started again. Worst of all was
if Mamma went too. I suppose she went to make him feel guilty.
He drove her to it, was he satisfied? When she came back she
stayed in her attic, crying and sleeping. She didn't cook now, not
even rabbit bone soup. Sometimes she let Bonnie up there for
limbering exercises and talk about make up. Mamma worried
about her neck, her bust and thighs. We tried not to let Bo see
we were worried, he liked babyish games and being spoiled.

He defended Captain, his own blood father from whom one
day he'd inherit the Grange. He said that Captain drank
because of money worries, his debts were awful. Mamma was
extravagant. There was something going on between her and
Mick Fagin. Captain was jealous as well as troubled.

Since we got here, Bo started stealing. He didn't spend the
money he took, he hid it or threw it away. I found seven-and-
six once, in the barn by the duck's nest, another time there was
a pile of pennies by the gate. He bit and spat if you questioned
him, he could be vicious as well as a brat. When his front tooth
was loose he bit Bonnie, leaving the tooth stuck in her thigh.
He was terrified of being sent to school in England where he
wouldn't know what was happening. However awful, not knowing was worse than knowing. You knew where you were if you
knew the truth. I suppose that was why he was so religious, sucking up to the priest, saying his prayers in a loud voice in order
to be sent to the Christian Brothers. It must be terrible to have
to love your own father and your religion exaggeratedly in order
not to be sent away. He ran round kissing Captain and rattling

his rosary. His brogue was another pretence. He was always happy when Bonnie and I sang to him, though Bonnie had a hideous voice. I was glad that Ula didn't know about our problems; she'd been quite ill for a long time. She'd probably have to wear a leg iron when she came out of hospital. Bo said he looked forward to pushing her round in the dolls' pram. Poor old cripple, he'd teach her some prayers.

Mamma had always hated religion, I suppose she was afraid of it, the church had so much power. She said that guilt and remorse gave you frown-lines, the past was dead, why fret about life to come? You made your own heaven or hell in the present. People should be free to make up their own minds. She didn't approve of the Brothers' school; they ruled by fear, they instilled lies. Bo should avoid all such holy nonsense and go to a proper English school. Mamma was small-minded, she neglected us, she was selfish, but we needed her. I longed to be able to admire her, she was all we had.

Eden, having known Captain in the army, might be a good influence on him, might even stop him drinking. When I first saw him, his appearance was a surprise. Captain had a ferret-face with blue stubble on it when he needed to shave. When sober he was dapper and neat. You couldn't imagine Eden looking slipshod. It was a hot day when he arrived, but he looked cool. His moustache was the soft kind, not bristling, growing from fine, soft skin. His straight hair was fine too. He looked too frail for manual work, but he seemed determined and sensible. We needed someone to curb Captain's wild schemes when he got drunk. He ranted about breeding Guernsey cattle for export, or training greyhounds for racing. With whisky, his imagination soared. Eden looked down to earth, he might induce Mamma to forget Mick Fagin and attend to her duties.

He was by the laurel bushes when I first saw him, a man with a cheap suitcase and ordinary mac, listening and watching. He wasn't tall, he looked reliable, that was the main thing. Bonnie pretended not to see. She liked showing her legs and her figure off. Pretty Bonnie always had style.

Mamma didn't like her using make up, she used a lead pencil round her eyes, blinking them the way Mamma did. Bonnie got the best presents; seed pearls, watches, a little ring when she was bridesmaid, like Mamma's ring, with opals and rubies, shaped like a flower. Mamma loved jewelry, her make up was expensive, like her clothes, mostly French. She wanted Bonnie as a confidante, yet she wanted to keep her a child. Coming to Ireland changed Mamma, she seemed rather pathetic, a figure of tragedy, often she was sad.

I have kept a diary since I could first write. Memories get confused, you can trust the written word. People fail or betray you, the diary is a constant friend. I suppose keeping one helped my old soul to develop. The one I had at that boarding school is so crammed the pages look black. The writing reflects joy or unhappiness, I have never missed a day. We used to long for letters from Mamma when she was away. Entertaining troops took all her attention, until Captain entered her life.

I wanted to join her and Bonnie in the attic room, all trailing with Mamma's lovely things, but they didn't need anyone else. When Captain came home drunk, Bonnie was excluded. She joined Bo and me and we listened to them downstairs. Mamma was contemptuous of his greyhound and Guernsey cow schemes, they were the ravings of a madman. He accused her of lack of confidence, she and her children kept him poor. She was extravagant, a millstone, useless. She didn't plead or wail, she retaliated. Look what I gave up. For what? You've dragged me down. Then the front door would slam again and he'd go back to the town. Sometimes Mamma would leave then. We didn't ask her to stay, we didn't ask her where she went.

Bo became addicted to sugar in Ireland. I've seen him steal sweets from the Co-op. Once he stole a bottle of gin, I found it under some hay in the barn. Pretty Bonnie got more selfish, but she was fond of Bo, she was loyal.

Marrying a person for protection is a poor reason. Mamma should have waited until she'd seen his home. I expect he would have been a drunkard in any case, but Mamma tried to make him feel small. The Grange was rotting; it must have been nice once. Bo loved it with all his Irish soul.

Mamma must have realized her mistake when she saw those broken white gates, the state of the lodge and the drive. No sign of affluence or even comfort. Captain didn't own a bicycle, let alone a car. How could we shop for our clothes? The one bus to the city left at dawn each day. She didn't speak. We passed the lodge and the laurel bushes, we saw the Grange. Mamma went up to the attic and closed the door. Captain arrived later, having lingered in Fagin's Bar. Once when Mamma left us, the bar closed too. We wondered about that.

I remembered the way Captain had gripped his glass at the reception, the first time he came home drunk. He had that same soft look, he moved slowly, he looked at Bonnie in a special way, his accent was more pronounced, he spoke with deliberation.

'Before any-thing is said on the subject of lateness, I apologize. I was delayed. It will not happen ... again.'

'You're drunk.'

'Wait, now. Ah, wait. Hold your horses. I was delayed. Business. The subject is ... closed.'

'Is that all you have to say? I have plenty to say, I assure you.'

'Now, Babsie, don't take that att-itude. I've been making a deal. Guernsey herd. It can't fail, I tell you. Give me a couple of years . . . 's'going to change. You'll see.'

'Change? How? Absurd dreams of greyhounds and cows? Your mind is addled with whisky and self-importance. I suggest you go upstairs before you fall.'

'I will, Babsie me darling, if you will come with me. Come on up now for a wee lie down.'

He needed a shave, his shirt was grimy, he half fell as he tried to stand. Where was Mamma's dashing officer? He was frightening us. Worse, he was frightened himself.

'Filthy peasant. Look at you. How dare you? Haven't you humiliated me sufficiently?'

'Peasant, am I? You didn't think so once. I was good enough to take on your brats. Peasant, is it? Humil-iated? On your dignity? I see.'

'There is little dignity about life here, I can assure you.'

'Then why stay? You were keen enough in the first place.'

'Look at it. A pigsty. Damp and debris. A disgrace.'

The shouting went on. Captain threw a plate on the floor. Bonnie was crying.

I had been right. Mamma had made a mistake. The bank manager wouldn't cash cheques, the Co-op refused credit, we could only shop at Fagin's Bar. By the time Eden came, we needed shoes as well as clothes. We had one comb between us, we had to wash with kitchen soap. Mamma had stopped wriggling and simpering for Captain long ago, now she watched him with unloving eyes. My periods stopped. Bo stole. Bonnie wasn't my friend.

When I saw Eden watching us on the lawn, I guessed that he'd be our lifeline. He stared at Bonnie, who had her blouse open. She looked brazen, the sun glinted on her tangled hair. His friendly eyes and soft moustache even seemed familiar. He flicked back a lock of hair with his fingers. I may have seen him in a regimental photograph. Soldiers had never interested me. We had been urged to knit for them, Mamma had sung for them, they fought a war that adults loved. They pretended to hate it, war excited them. They prayed for peace, when it came they complained that the old days had gone. Peace for our family was a nightmare. Captain and Mamma quarrelled, we had nothing to do. Now here was Eden from London, watching us; an Englishman with a soft moustache and silky hair.

'Look, Bonnie, someone is here.'

Eden's grammar went wrong sometimes, I don't think Bonnie or Bo noticed. What Bonnie cared about was being noticed and admired. She was the least resourceful. I had my diaries and my nursing plans. Bo dreamed of being a Catholic landowner, restoring the Grange which would be his. Also he might be a priest. He liked writing rather bad rhymes.

He said he'd give hunt balls to which his sisters could come. Bonnie sniffed; priests didn't give balls. Bo said he'd do what he liked. He'd have a peacock lawn and a gazebo where he'd write verses and Bonnie was just envious.

She had dreamed once herself of ancestral halls with polished floors. She told me about it in Yorkshire while she practised dancing, with a cushion for a partner. In the dream, an orchestra of violins softly played, while outside a moon waited to shine on kissing couples. At school we had learned a kind of jitterbugging from some evacuees who were there. Bonnie wanted to waltz with a handsome suitor, so far she'd not had one. There was no one that Mamma would have considered suitable here, no one of standing. I suppose she wanted us to marry well.

It was when Captain tried to attack Bonnie that I knew Mamma wanted her out of the way. Bonnie might grow to be a threat. Poor Bonnie, who Mamma loved best.

'Look, Bonnie, someone is here.'

Someone to trust, someone anxious to please, someone to take over. I trusted my instinct, my old soul was a good judge.

Eden had helped us through the difficult time. Without him we might have all been drowned. He took over the mopping up, he kept the rain at bay. The Father took Captain and Mamma away, Eden showed us how to roll paper and rag together to stuff into crannies, to put pans under the leaks, to sweep the wet from the steps. Some of the rags were old knickers, the newspapers smelled of cats. We must keep dry, he said. What food did we like best? Bonnie said in a strained voice that she wasn't hungry, she was still upset from the row in the hall.

'Worried about your figure, sister darlin'? I fancy a little sand-wich myself, with honey.' Bo was partial to jelly too.

It would be evening before Mamma returned, the hospital was some miles away. Bo strutted about, with his parents away he was boss again. Bow down, slaves, to your lord and master; don't forget who would inherit the Grange. Bonnie watched him with clear eyes. I wished she would talk. People shouldn't bottle up their feelings after upsets. Bo was usually impossible, he showed off, he was arrogant, he stole, bit, screamed like a pampered upstart. It was better than silence.

That night we played games again. I guessed that Eden couldn't spell, had left school when very young. He liked work-ing with his hands, had never been a swot. Bo said he would become an Irish scholar, a local saint even, and a poet. We would draw ghosts and monsters on old envelopes. He would start first with a banshee.

'Look, Eden. You do one.'

Bonnie began to relax as she watched. She would do a goblin. Banshees were bad luck.

'No, no. It's squealing. Look, Eden.'

Eden looked at Bonnie, he felt her hand. Was she warm enough? He put a blanket round her shoulders. He lit a candle in a saucer on the floor. She was a candlelit beauty, a colleen with brilliant eyes. When it was too dark to draw, Bo said he'd make shadows for us. He'd make a banshee, look, Eden, a shrieking banshee. Ay-eee.

'You'll frighten the duck, Bo. Don't.'

He started turning cartwheels.

'Calm down, Bo. Don't get excited.'

'I bought some lemonade early. I'll get it.'

A fizzy drink in a stone bottle. Bo was charmed. A bottle of champagne bubbly. Sham pain? Anyone like some real pain? He staggered, he rolled his eyes, he was drunk. Look, everyone, drunk as a lord, getting drunker. He sang in a falsetto wail.

'I'm forever blowing bubbles, and I am a drunk old man. Me and my duck never had much luck, my daughters are sad, my wife is mad . . . '

'Stop at once, Bo. How can you?'

He couldn't stop, he was carried away, an entertainer, a poet, a mimic, look everyone, he was like his dadda. I could see his sad eyes in the light of the candle, despairing, almost crying. Wasn't he funny? Wasn't he clever; he couldn't stop. 'My daughters are mad, my wife is sad.'

And then Mamma was back again. Stop, Bo, she mustn't hear.

'Out of your minds? Must you make that noise? That bird . . . '

'Mammy, is Dadda all right?'

'Don't bother me, I'm going up.'

'Someone was in the lodge, Mammy. Someone was there.'

'Nasty little boy. Hold your tongue. That noise. I'm going up.'

Had she brought Captain's clothes back? How long would peace last this time?

Shreds of skin had curled from her lower lip. Her mauve eyelids had aged. Had the Father spoken to her about Mick Fagin? If he had, we would never know. She was dead in the morning. The attic skylight blew in and killed her; she was hit on the head, she choked with rain water, having taken pills.

Bonnie and I were not the same after that. My old soul left childhood behind for good. We decided not to say 'Mamma' again. She would be 'she' or 'Babs', but not Mamma. It would be better if we avoided mentioning her until we felt more settled. We would probably miss her one day, but you don't miss what you never had.

10

'Don't let Bo in. Don't let him see.'

I had gone first to the attic to see if she wanted tea.

Only yesterday I'd come up here with Bonnie behind me, and Captain had gone berserk. Now he was banished to the hospital and our mother lay still as a stone.

Last night after she left us, the candle burned into a pool of grease, we felt shivery. Eden said that by morning life would look brighter, we were all over-tired, come along, early bed. The candle smoke smelled bitter. Eden said he'd be up early to try to get a fire going with wet turf mould. We'd been missing sleep lately. Bonnie and I were glad to be in bed.

She was still sleeping when I got up next morning, pale and beautiful. It was just before we fell asleep that we'd made our decision not to say 'Mamma' again. She wasn't the type of mother we needed. Better to look on her as a kind of neighbour, or better still an elderly aunt. We wouldn't write the name 'Mamma', we wouldn't think it.

The rain had stopped in the morning. I felt pleased that Eden was here.

'Bonnie. Bon-nee. Come quickly. Don't let Bo come. Don't let him see.'

She was lying in a mess of plaster and pieces of glass; there were tiles from the roof over the bed. Her eyes were still open, her mouth looked terrible; a shrivelled, miserable hole. The dried blood over one eyebrow looked like mud, the rose-coloured shawl round her shoulders was soaked. The eyes were the worst, they looked accusing. By her head was something wet and furry. Some animal must have come through the roof, a rat or a squirrel had been knocked senseless, but I couldn't worry about that now. Bonnie must help me take the debris off her. A brick must have cut her head. She had no protection from the weather, though the storm was over.

'Get Eden. Don't tell Bo.'

We were experiencing another death, I must stay clearheaded and practical. I had the old soul. Bonnie was shaking again. We must get a doctor or an ambulance. If she were dead, she'd need an undertaker. We'd have to pay a huge amount for flowers. She had loved roses. Did proper roses grow in Ireland or only wild ones? Where was the funeral parlour? They were all Catholic; Babs would hate that, she wouldn't like the Father praying about her. I remembered my dead baby brother lying stiff and cold as Babs was now.

Bonnie was watching with a sick-looking face.

'Stop looking like that. Don't tell Bo. Get Eden.'

But he'd seen. He came behind Eden, he saw the room, he saw the bed, he screamed. He flung himself on her, he rolled her. Wake up. Stop that. Open up your eyes.

'Now listen, Mamma, time to be up and about. Open those eyes and stop playing. Joke over, you hear me? This is Bo, it's orders.'

'She can't. Stop it, Bo. She can't hear. Leave her.'

'Take your hands off me, don't touch me. She *can* hear. She's playing a joke.'

'She can't, Bo. She's . . .'

'She can. She can.'

He put his face to the face on the bed, he rocked her back and forth.

'Listen. Hear that? She's breathing.'

From inside Babs came squelching sounds. He heaved and rolled harder. She was full of liquid inside.

'I told you. I told you. She's alive.'

Her pill bottle was by her, pills were everywhere. She looked so dead. I hoped she hadn't felt the bricks falling or heard the plaster and glass.

Bo turned on Eden. 'It's your fault. Everything is your fault. You keep telling us what to do, you keep explaining. We were all right till you came.'

'Eden is trying to help.'

'We don't want his help. And you can shut up, you fat cow.'

He lunged at me, I didn't blame him. Scratching and biting helped him.

He cried then, falling on top of Babs.

'Don't, Bo. There, there. Don't.'

'Sacred heart of . . . what is this? Has Mammy had some kind of an animal in her bed? Look at that.'

I thought only old people wore hair pieces. She'd had one all along and we'd not guessed, the same glinty shade as her real hair, like a squirrel or a rat or even a little fur crown.

We placed it over her temples, patting it lightly; we arranged a curl over the gash on her brow. She could harm us no more, we must be respectful. Her chin was wet, her eyes stared. As we settled her I knew that she'd not disliked us; we'd just bored her, we weren't exciting. Some people shouldn't have children too young. I wished we'd not discovered the hairpiece or the teeth under the bed. Mamma ... Babs, I could have loved you if I'd not been afraid of you. You did us more harm than Captain because we had you so long.

I have never cried much, I hate the feeling of tears. I felt the hot sticky feeling of them. I looked at Bonnie, her eyes were like syphons. We cried together for something we'd never had and never would have, we cried for the feelings that we'd never felt.

Babs, our lovely mother, had died alone, without kindness, without hair, teeth or dignity. Downstairs, Bo was shouting at Eden. All Eden's fault, all his sisters' fault, fat cows, bloody curs. I blew my nose.

'Bonnie, we'll have to close her eyes now. You have to do that when they're dead.'

'I'm not touching her. You must be barmy. I'm not doing it. You can.'

My fingers were wet, Babs' face was wet. I couldn't do it, such cold skin, soft yet hard. Her eyelashes might come loose, her eyes might roll out. Mascara had washed into her eye sockets, like particles of grit. I remembered the wedding and her eyes behind the flowery eye veil.

'I think you have to put pennies on them to keep them shut. Get some money.'

'You know we haven't any. Leave it, Tor.'

'What about the window? Irish people open it when people die. To help the soul fly to heaven.'

'There's no glass in the skylight, you must be barmy. She didn't believe in heaven, she's not a peasant. Let's go down now to Bo.'

It didn't seem right to leave her. We looked at the skylight, the air was fresh, the sky was blue. We were orphans.

A blackbird started to sing (they had nested earlier, in the laurels) sounding sweet and clear. Babs would have liked that. Bird song was nicer than harps or angels. Bo was still shrieking down below.

'Drink your lemon, Dadda. It will do you good.'
'Tell me that she didn't suffer. Tell me again what she said.'
'Nothing, I told you. I don't know what Father said to her. She went up to the attic, she left us alone.' Captain lay in a corner bed in the hospital, begging to be reassured. He wanted to believe that Babs hadn't been unhappy. He wanted to know what she'd been thinking and feeling the last time she'd climbed those attic stairs. He clutched at Bo with shaky hands. She'd not suffered, had she?
'There, there, Dadda. I shouldn't think she did. You know what the coroner said. The oul' roof fell on her while she was sleeping. She'd taken pills, of course.'

11

'Drink your lemon, Dadda. It will do you good.'

'Tell me that she didn't suffer. Tell me again what she said.'

'Nothing, I told you. I don't know what Father said to her. She went up to the attic, she left us alone.' Captain lay in a corner bed in the hospital, begging to be reassured. He wanted to believe that Babs hadn't been unhappy. He wanted to know what she'd been thinking and feeling the last time she'd climbed those attic stairs. He clutched at Bo with shaky hands. She'd not suffered, had she?

'There, there, Dadda. I shouldn't think she did. You know what the coroner said. The oul' roof fell on her while she was sleeping. She'd taken pills, of course.'

We were at the hospital after the funeral. The days following the death passed in a daze. Brad had been on the danger list himself when he'd heard the news. His temperature rose, he'd abandoned himself to grief and remorse. Had it been his fault? Had he not spent so much time in Fagin's Bar, would she be with us still? Had Mick encouraged him, to suit his own sinful gain?

I suppose he loved Babs as much as he was capable of loving, and their attic had been his heaven on earth.

The nursing sisters exhorted him with grave faces. Less of the self-pity, Man dear, hadn't he his family to love him? Hadn't he a reason for hope? Hadn't his family wanted him, Man dear?

When we arrived he was drinking lemon squash. He was tearful. He'd wanted to follow her to the grave. He'd had double pneumonia the sisters said, we shouldn't stay too long. Just tell about the funeral and leave. I tried to pity him. This was the officer who had swept Babs off her feet, our military stepfather who had gazed adoringly while champagne corks popped and flew. He cried now, he begged for information; uneasy about Mick Fagin, not asking outright, you could feel it was on his mind. Unspoken anxiety nagged at him, he begged Bo to allay his fears.

Who had taken the service? Tell him she'd not suffered. Who had been there? She'd had a happy life, he'd done his best for her, no one could gainsay it. Who had sent flowers?'

'Drink your lemon, it will do you good.'

They made him drink constantly; cups of Bovril, weak tea, milk with egg in it. Weak drinks for a sorrowing man.

Bo was offhand about the service. His mammy had been a heretic, had died outside the blessing of the true church. We had had to travel to a Protestant graveyard, some miles off, she'd not deserved more. He'd behaved with exaggerated piety, intoning prayers in Latin, fervently kissing his beads. There had been few mourners and few flowers. Bo had his inner sorrow like Bonnie and I, but couldn't show it. After the service was over, the town taxi took us to the hospital. I was glad Captain had a corner bed.

The nursing sisters wore clashing beads hanging from their waistbands as they hastened between the beds. The old man next to the Captain scratched and peered between the sheets. 'There y'are. Got you. There now.' His bony fingers pounced and cracked imaginary insects. He looked at us with a grin.

Captain continued sniffing and questioning. His tears might atone for our own dry eyes, might atone for the parish who hadn't cared. That stuck-up woman from England who attended no service, who showed no neighbourliness, was unmourned (except, so it was whispered, for that one at Fagin's Bar). She had got her just deserts. She would be slandered until the next scandal touched the town; she would be forgotten.

Captain wore an ugly hospital gown that opened at the back. The sisters had given him a shave. They had left a small patch by his ear because of a pimple. I hadn't seen him with pimples before. He had lost weight. Bo clicked his tongue. Drink your lemon, Dadda, don't be making that noise, you'll get a coughing fit. There now. Mammy was very likely in some better place, a paradise for heretics. The skylight fell on her, she'd be with her own kind now. There now, not to cry.

'Surely you heard something, some kind of sound?'

'The roof fell, we heard nothing. Accidental death, the coroner said.'

'Were there many flowers for her?'

'A few flowers, white and rosy ones. Fagin's sent a wreath. I brought a flower from it. See, Dadda. Pink. Smell.'

'Fagin's?'

'Smell.' Rose-smelling, her favourite scent.

'The Grange is a ruin. We're not sleeping there now. We moved.'

Captain picked at the flower. He was unconcerned where we had moved, he was consumed with his own unease. More tears oozed from his lids. His was an unfortunate lot, ruined financially, near death, the light of his life gone. Pink roses, her favourite flower.

I told him that the Grange could be repaired, that it would cost a lot. Eden would help. Moving out had been his idea.

'Debris and disgrace. She said so. I am a ruined man.'

'Yes, well, we've lost our mother, remember. It's been a bad time. Eden has helped.'

'Where is Eden?'

'We came alone. He's coming to see you tomorrow. He wants to talk.'

'Talk? I'm widowed. Ruined. Why does he want to talk?'

Bonnie looked at me. His brain must be affected. Would we have to bear that too? She leaned over the bed with a sweet expression, she put her hand on his.

'Listen, Captain dear, Tor and I have been thinking. From now on we're going to call you Bradwell. It's not as if we're properly related, and you're not a Captain any more, it sounds barmy. Tor and I are grown up. We'll say Bradwell from now on.'

Pretty Bonnie smiled. She looked like Babs. Brad had chased her, had tried to harm her, he had made Babs miserable. He must stay in the hospital until we brought his clothes. New names couldn't make new starts, couldn't bring respect. He was sickening. Was Bonnie losing her tender heart?

He had Bo's love. Bo had got his own way about school. He could write his rhymes, be near his dadda, there would be no more rows. He took the corner of Brad's sheet and wiped his face kindly. There, there, Dadda, not to cry. Say a round of the beads for dear Mammy. Smell the flower and pray for her soul.

A nun with a handkerchief the size of a towel came clicking between the beds. What way was this to be carrying on in front of the ward? Shame. Many a sick man here would give a year of his life for a lovely son and daughters to visit and console him. Give thanks to God and his Blessed Mother. Wasn't he alive himself and with a future to live? The sisters would be remembering his family in chapel. Had his wife been a Catholic, he could have had a requiem said. Give thanks, dry those tears.

'Ah, you're very good, Sister,' Brad said in a whining tone.

'You've been quite ill, Brad,' I told him. He must concentrate on getting strong. Eden would repair the Grange roof.

'You don't hold anything against me do you, Tor? Nor you, Bonnie?'

The sister was ringing a bell in the doorway. Time for goodbyes now. She moved towards the man with the scratching fingers. Whiffs of Listerine came from her gown. He plucked my skirt, he whispered that my father had spoken of breeding Guernseys, that he could help there.

Bo climbed onto the bed for a last embrace, the frilled pillow made a frame for their heads. He rubbed against his father's cheek. There, there, no need to fret now. Mammy was in a sort of heaven, a heavenly place for lost souls. She probably had felt nothing when the roof fell. No more tears, drink the lemon.

'Boris, my pal,' Brad moaned.

'When do they bring your tea?' Bo was brisk. He was peckish. He'd relish a little biscuit or a cake with raisins. Don't be crying, when was tea?

I don't remember kissing Bradwell before. He smelled like the nuns' habits as well as wet hankies. At the last moment I pulled back, my kiss turned into a sort of a cough. Bonnie shook his hand, keeping her smile sweet. You never knew with nuns, they might keep him here for years.

Our feet tapped the floor as we left his bed. There were no other visitors. I pushed the swing door. From the other side came the chant of plain song. I looked back; the nun was picking the rose petal from his sheet, straightening his covers, patting his hand. Her lips moved. Give thanks ... blessings, dry those tears ... Now what about a smile?

The taxi smelled of chrysanthemums and also of shoe polish. We had done our duty to Brad the sick widower, taken flowers. He could lie and imagine her grave with Fagin's wreath on it. Perhaps Bonnie and I might get closer with our parents out of the way, but there was still Eden. She changed when he was near, looking at him, listening when he spoke, keeping her eyes wide.

The taxi drew up at the Grange gates where he was waiting for us. He'd insisted that we should visit Brad on our own. Tomorrow he would go and discuss plans for the future, as well as the restoration of the Grange.

In a short time he'd worked wonders on the lodge. The windows had glass in them now. While we'd been at the hospital he'd been cutting back the wild rose bush that had spread itself round the door. He wore old dungarees. Branches and suckers lay on the ground, the rain-dampened thorns hadn't yet grown dark and sharp. He'd cleared all the broken glass and rubbish from behind the broken wall. Old tins and rags lay in a heap. He planned to make a small garden, with a path to the door. There was room for a lawn and flower-beds and perhaps a sundial. The rose, properly pruned, might produce proper blooms. But I liked the single ones with dropping petals and pollen that dusted your hands. Eden would make a warm and weatherproof residence for us until the Grange was restored. Bonnie and I had been keen to move to the lodge. We needed a new start after the past weeks in the Grange.

Bo and Eden slept downstairs on mattresses. Bo was in charge of the fire. Eden had given him a lesson in lighting it with sticks. They found some coal behind the lodge. Bonnie and I slept in the loft overhead. There was just room for our mattresses.

The wettest August in memory was over, the sun had shone for Babs' death and each day since. An Indian summer was forecast. Next spring our garden would bloom. Bonnie helped Eden with the clearance and digging, she'd never worked like that before. She planned carnations and asparagus fern. Her favourite was love-in-the-mist.

Soon it felt as if we'd lived in the lodge for ages. It was safe, I didn't want to leave.

Most of Babs' things in the attic were unusable. We went through her jewellery box, making three piles of her trinkets. Bonnie wanted the rings. I divided the brooches and bracelets between me and Ula, but in the end I kept only the watch. I don't like jewellery, but a watch was useful. It was too dainty for a nurse to use. In a drawer, under her necklaces, we found some papers. It seemed Babs had a little money in savings bonds. Bonnie told Eden, who told us to say nothing about it for the time being. A nest-egg never came amiss, we'd learn that one day. It wasn't a lot, we would need money to restore the Grange. I had hoped to find something that showed that Babs had worried about me. She had never said she loved me, or had hopes, or was proud; she never said much at all. She loved Bonnie, pretty Bonnie of the forget-me-not eyes. Once when I'd had a cold she'd give me a juicy pear, smiling at me. She had cut and peeled it, putting the pieces in my hand. The juice trickling down my sore throat was lovely, the gritty softness of pears would remind me of her, now. Her attic clothes smelled of flood water as well as roses. In the hamper was a picture of our real blood father, looking like Ula. I stared, I couldn't remember him. Why couldn't he be here now instead of Bradwell? The savings bonds might be useful one day but we needed money now. Eden had the good idea of selling the cow.

It had stayed in the barn during the worst weather. We'd always loathed it, time now for it to go. We'd never taken to milking, it was almost dry anyway. It took delight in fouling our shoes or kicking the bucket over. Eden arranged for the Fagin brothers to have it. It was taken off early one morning, we never saw it again.

We had money to settle the Co-op. We wouldn't have to shop at Fagin's any more. We could buy Wellingtons and rain-coats, clothes for the winter. Bonnie bought lipsticks and eye make up. We threw all Babs' stuff away. The cow would have a better life at the Fagins'; they would put the bull to it and make it calve again. They were used to milking and had a real farm. We were left with Bo's duck.

Bo and I went for walks together, Bonnie didn't want to come now Eden was here. Bo was much happier, though he missed Brad. His scabs and scratches healed, he was calmer, his night-mares stopped, he didn't scratch or bite. I showed him how to pull grass stalks gently, leaving the outer sheath behind to keep the part you sucked clean. He hummed as he sucked, his Wellingtons rubbed the backs of his knees leaving red patches. He swiped at dandelions and stirred cow-pats with twigs. He went alone to visit Bradwell, Bonnie and I didn't go again. The hedges bordering the fields smelled hot and a little rotten that summer. Bo still wrote rhymes on scraps of paper. He might turn the Grange into a seminary one day. His plans became wilder as the weeks went by.

'Yes, well, I want to be a nurse myself. I'm not like Bonnie.'

'Eden is a good chap,' Bo said in a wise voice. He said that what Bonnie needed was to become someone's wife. Or maybe the life of an actress would suit her, as long as no one asked her to sing.

'She's much too young for marriage. Don't be silly, Bo.'

'Don't you be so sure, you may get a surprise.'

'What surprise? What do you mean?' Hadn't we already had enough shocks and surprises this summer?

'I mean Eden.'

'What about him? It's not serious. Bonnie is just flattered that he likes her. That's all. She doesn't love him.'

'Oh, doesn't she? She does, the silly cow.'

'You're wrong. You're quite wrong. You're silly.'

I hated him for thinking it about my Bonnie. If she married him she might get a baby. She'd ask me to be bridesmaid and walk behind her, all tricked up in frills and flowers. I wasn't going to be an aunt to anyone, I wasn't that sort. She shouldn't dream of marrying anyone until she was at least thirty. She shouldn't dream of Eden at all.

I remembered the way he watched her, the way he looked at her each time he spoke. He waited on her, he was making a garden of flowers for her. He was even showing her how to cook.

Cooking on an open fire was an art he'd learned at a boys' club. You needed a thick pan with a tight lid. The first cake that Bonnie made was runny in the middle. Eden had laughed tenderly. Bo ate the cake with a spoon. Pancakes were easier, Eden would show her those next time. She'd be the finest cook in the land.

Eden planned to restore the Grange to former glory. He had a book, *Student Guide to Plumbing and Home Maintenance*. It had a section on electrical repairs. He intended to start evening classes with the Christian Brothers, who taught woodwork. Bo wanted to carve religious objects for his altar. There was no time for anyone to become seriously romantic in this family. If Bonnie had any sense she'd learn homecraft to qualify her for earning her living. She might manage a caff, for instance, or become a matron of a school.

I wondered about Ula, I should be with her. She was probably in pain, she was sure to be lonely and worrying about what was going on. In the old days, particularly at boarding school, Bonnie had mothered her. She only seemed to care about Eden now, smiling at him, listening, baking those uneatable cakes. Babs would be shocked at all this. Eden spoke badly, he wasn't well educated, his flattery had stolen Bonnie's wits. Wait, Bonnie, don't be rash; we are different from Eden and people like him. He's kind but he'll never change.

Bo chose another grass stalk, pulling it slowly. We heard it squeak. He said in a mincing tone that he hoped Bonnie knew about sexual intercourse, poor old creature.

'Don't be so rude and crude, Bo. You're always showing off.'

Sex was something we didn't mention. We had found out about it in a dreadful way, on the night our headmistress died at school. Two girls brought soldiers into an empty dormitory. I and my sisters had heard. We crept in and saw a sort of orgy, two under a blanket on the floor, two on a bed. One of the girls was an evacuee from London, the other was our own head girl. We watched without speaking, I felt like fainting. We never mentioned it again. Now here was my little brother talking casually about Bonnie and sex. He smiled in a superior way. I was too prim and priggish, he said. I ought to move with the times.

Bonnie had on her secret expression when we got in again. She'd been experimenting with another cake. You had to line the pot thickly with paper before the mixture went in. The fire must be hot, you had to pile red coals over the lid. When we walked in, we were met by a lovely smell. She had used raisins, nuts, cinnamon and orange peel. It was a perfect cake.

'Isn't Eden clever? He showed me. We used four eggs.'

Eden smiled for joy. She was wonderful to teach, and so amenable.

'You like Eden showing you things, don't you, Bonnie darlin'?' Bo leaned over to whisper something. Bonnie tittered. I felt left out. This cake-making was a bad sign. If she wasn't careful she'd be an old woman with ten children and expect me to be god-mother. Neither of us could knit properly, we hated it. I wanted my own life, I wanted to be a nurse in a hospital. Besides, what about Ula and Bo?

I liked the attic with Bonnie, with just room to walk round our mattresses and the smell of pears and dust in the corners. We hung our clothes from nails in the rafters. It was like a tree house. I slept well, until the night I heard Bonnie go down. Her feet scuffed the ladder rungs. I didn't hear the back door open; she wasn't going to the lavatory. Was she sleep-walking? I knew she was going to Eden, to learn more of his secrets. She would whisper, perhaps they would kiss.

It was the middle of the night. She had a clean nightdress on. She'd been using some of Babs' scent. What had Babs done with Mick Fagin? Had they met at this lodge? I couldn't hear. I crawled off my mattress to the top of the ladder. I craned my head down. Bonnie and Eden were on the floor by the fire. I saw their shadows. They were sitting crossways, her legs were each side of his, in the shape of a squatting bear. Supposing Bo woke and saw? Bonnie was shameless, she had gone down on purpose, she couldn't get enough of Eden. You are disgusting, Bonnie, you are rude. Eden has stolen your wits. I leaned further. What *was* she doing now?

Then it happened. The animal sound, the pants, the whispers, I heard the same words that I'd heard before. It was the same as that night at school, the same words said by the same voice. 'Stuck up bitch, I'll teach you, like I done Red.' Eden had been one of those soldiers hiding under the blanket in the dormitory. He was saying the same to Bonnie as he'd said to our head girl. He was doing the same thing to Bonnie, my pretty sister. 'Stuck up bitch. I'll teach you.' He was the soldier boyfriend of that evacuee from Clerkenwell, the girl called Red, who smelled sickly. The girl with the sniggering laugh. She had brought soldiers to the dormitory to practise intimacy.

A bitch is a female dog. Not my Bonnie, she is noble and fine, she is mine. 'I'll teach you like I done Red.'

I crouched at the top of the ladder till my body ached. Was this what Babs had done? I didn't want to hear, I had to hear. I would never feel the same again. Too much was happening too fast. Bonnie was ... 'Stuck up bitch.'

Eden was just an upstart, he was making use of her. He was unforgivable, he was base, he should be locked up.

Come back, Bonnie.

12

I must have slept, because I didn't hear her come back. Then I had this dream about finding money. I was in a field in the rain and finding money everywhere. First there was a shilling in a patch of shamrock, then a florin further on. A half-crown glittered under a bramble bush, a ten-shilling note was stuck on a thorn. I stretched my hand out, I called to Bonnie that it was all right, we had money. I felt the thorn prick as I woke. The happy feeling didn't leave me, in spite of the shock earlier. Bonnie was there, breathing deeply, everything was all right. Perhaps finding money was a good omen, Ireland might be lucky for us after all. I liked the lodge, I didn't want to go back to England; I had the feeling of belonging here, though I had seen nothing of Ireland except this place, and met few of the people. If only Bonnie hadn't spoiled things, I wanted to shout at her, hit her. I saw. I heard. I know.

Eden was frying sausages on a spirit lamp bought from the Co-op. Bo was trying to light the fire. The lodge fireplace was bigger than the Grange one. He blew the sparks busily, the room was smokey. Bo didn't bother to steal money now. Eden looked calm and cheerful, my own face was the shamed red one. I wanted to hit him with his frying pan. I saw. I heard. I know. You only care about pleasing Bonnie, you're plotting to capture her, you don't think about Bo or me. Your sausages smell disgusting, you are disgusting, give them to Bonnie, she won't say no. She's upstairs asleep with her mouth open, her hair is straggly round her cheeks that are soft as a rose. Did you kiss her mouth, her hair and her cheeks, Eden? Where else did you kiss?

'Here she is. Did you sleep well, Bonnie?'

'Sausages? I'm starved. What shall we do today, Eden?'

'I thought we'd carry on with the garden.'

'Lots of love-in-the-mist,' she said wistfully.

'What about love-lies-bleeding?' I said.

Bo thought that a garden without flowers was best, with room to play. A garden of bubbles, that's what he'd like. Many sizes, many colours, freely floating, filling the air.

I left them talking about the garden. I went up again to enter my diary. I would never forget that squatting bear. I saw. I heard. I know.

'I can't think why you bother with that diary still. You should have outgrown it by now.' Bonnie made a grab at it, she started reading it.

'Saw what? Heard what? Know what?'

My throat felt like dry bread. 'Don't do it, Bonnie. He's not the person you think he is. He's ... he's ...'

'Yes? Who is he? What?'

'He's that soldier. That night at school. Under the blanket. That Christmas. He's the boyfriend of that girl called Red. His name is Ed, he isn't Eden ...'

'As a matter of fact, for your information, I do know. I know everything. He *used* to be called Ed. He *used* to be Red's boyfriend, that's all over. He's Eden now. In any case how do *you* know?'

'I heard. I couldn't help hearing. I heard what he said. The same as that night, that Christmas when we saw.'

'You mean you eavesdropped? You snooped and sneaked. I might have known.'

'I had to, Bonnie. Don't say that. I had to know.'

'You needn't worry. Eden and I have no secrets. We tell everything.'

'How could you? With *him*. He's that soldier.'

The girls had jostled to look at Eden's photograph, only then he had been Ed. Red, the evacuee from Clerkenwell, was only thirteen. She had a vulgar laugh, she smelled of dirt and vanilla essence and was loved by the soldier called Ed. His face, clean-shaven and gap-toothed, had grinned from the frame. He wore a tank beret over stubbly hair. He had written ITALY in the corner, a secret love-code. Ed had taught Red how to dance. Now he made eyes at Bonnie, having changed to Eden. It was disgusting. I saw. I heard. I know.

She told me I was barmy to make such a fuss. Eden was her lifeline, he meant the world to her, as she did to him. He couldn't get enough of her, he'd said so. And just think how kind he was.

'Yes. I see why, now. He's using you. You're a convenience. Can't you see?'

Bonnie's voice changed when she spoke of him. It all sounded so greedy, as if she were a plate of food. He was making use of her.

'We're using each other. You don't understand, Tor, you're too young.'

I understood all right, I saw the truth. She was just thinking of herself.

'I must, Tor. No one else will. I'm not like you. I'm not interested in training. I've got to get away. I just want Eden.'

'And Ula? What about her?'

She said that Brad was Ula's guardian. Perhaps when she and
Eden had settled they would send for her. She didn't sound concerned.

'You mean you'll leave the Grange?'

When we were little we used to play with imaginary children.
Bonnie's were called 'Marigold' and 'Delphine'. My baby was
black. She beat her two with coat-hangers and locked them
under the stairs. She had the same coat-hanger-beating look in
her eyes.

'You don't expect me to stay here? What is to keep me?'

'I'm beginning to like it. I want to be a nurse, but I'll want to
come back. I don't know why.'

'Eden is going to teach me dancing. Proper dancing. We'll
have a flat and a garden full of flowers.'

'When?'

She closed her eyes, swaying romantically. I asked too many
questions. Eden would arrange everything. He'd won medals at
ballroom. As a professional, she'd partner him.

I imagined her dancing in his arms, round their home and
into their garden of flowers. They would travel to far-off lands
and win contests.

'He isn't like us, Bonnie. Do be careful. Babs wouldn't have
approved at all.'

'*Babs?* What has she to do with it? I don't suppose she'd care.'

'She wouldn't like it. Do you ever miss her?'

I thought of the times I had stood on the landing listening to
her and Babs talking about clothes, doing exercises, in a private
world. Bonnie, the bridesmaid, the one who got watches and

pearl rings, the first to hear about Bo, the first to hold him when he was born.

'I can't think of the past. I have Eden.'

'Don't change too much.' She still had a family. Would she forget us?

'I know what I'm doing. Eden is wonderful. He's going to buy me a silk dress for dancing. I'll have sandals with gold straps.'

'You won't go having a baby, will you? It could happen.'

'Oh, could it? And how do you know, snooper?'

'I couldn't help hearing. He's using you. You're just a stepping stone. Don't forget, he comes from the slums.'

'At least I'm not a snob, Tor. You're worse than Babs. You're jealous, aren't you?'

'No, I'm not. Of course I'm not. But he's a pretender, he isn't real. The way he speaks isn't real. Haven't you noticed?'

'What's wrong with change? What's wrong with trying to improve? He hated his old life. He wants me.'

'Don't you mind about Red? Don't you care? It's horrible.'

'It's not. It's over, past. Dead. He's mine now. He's changed and I've changed. I'm dying to learn to dance.'

It sickened me to think of her in Red's trashy wake. Red of the thin red lips and coarse talk, Red of the bitten nails and tin rings. She'd had experience with boys. She had an influence on the school. The girls had watched and copied her. She had taught us to frizz our hair. Because of her, nail polish had spilled over our school blouses. Because of her, we knew the Lambeth Walk. Life in her Clerkenwell sounded jolly and noisy, never lonely.

You couldn't compare Bonnie with Red. My Bonnie was sublime as well as noble. She hummed and swayed round her mattress, with a pillow clutched to her chest. She knew about real kissing now. Pretty Bonnie, stay as you were.

Bo's head appeared at the top of our ladder. A party? He'd join us with the duck. And then we were dancing in a ring round the mattresses; we waved our arms, we joined in Bonnie's song. Bo imitated her terrible voice. Happiness was hard to catch, it dissolved in your hands so easily, floating, alighting, bubble-frail.

'Don't look so serious, Tor.'

'Don't do anything rash will you, Bonnie?'

'What are you talking about? Who is rash?' A rasher of bacon was what Bo would relish. He didn't like sausages so well. Who was rash?

'Shut up, the two of you. And take the duck off my bed.'

I knew she would go creeping down again tonight, smelling of roses, to learn more of the secrets of life. Their limbs would entwine, they'd hug and whisper. Once you started, you had to go on until you'd learned all you could learn. You didn't think about the consequences, only your own need.

I thought I could hinder her by staying up late. I would sit by the fire and spoil their privacy. I would keep an eye on her, as Babs should have done. Though the lodge was only two rooms and we had no privacy, I felt secure now. Eden mustn't spoil it. Bonnie must be chaperoned. Baking cakes and dreaming of dancing was one thing, running off with an impostor, another.

'Go to bed, Tor. Stop yawning.'

'Poor old soul, little Tor is worn out.' Bo picked up one of Babs' magazines with pictures of models with long legs and thrusting bosoms. Their eyes were like Bonnie's, watching and waiting.

'Go on, Tor. You're dead beat.'

The lodge lavatory was a small shed at the back with a broken door. You had to hold the string tied to the latch, but even that was better than the Grange. The board with a hole in it over a drain wasn't comfortable. Small animals rustled in the undergrowth outside. I would stay out there as long as possible, put a stop to Bonnie's behaviour. A spider caught the light from my torch, motionless, watching and waiting. Insects had never frightened us, we used to play with them, cradling them in hankies and matchboxes, christening them, racing them, fondling them. Woodlice were best. Don't do it, Bonnie. He isn't right.

Something large was snuffling and scratching outside the door, a badger or a fox perhaps. A little boney-legged hedgehog was scuttling through the weeds. Its black-tipped spines looked so charming, the fur framed its eyes like a flattened moustache. I would have liked to have caught it, I would like it as a pet, to put insects in the way of its routing snout, to give it a happy home.

'Stop fussing over it, Tor. They're vermin. They're flea-ridden. Go to bed.'

I made the old meat-safe into a nest for it. I got a cushion, I put out a saucer of milk.

The dish was licked clean in the morning, the cushion in the meat-safe looked dented, but I never saw it again. Eden said that hedgehogs were the gardener's friend, ridding the flowers of slugs and snails. Would it sniff round the roots of his love-in-the-mist? Would its fleas bite Bonnie's limbs? Searching and wondering about it kept my mind off her. What I dreaded most was that she'd have a child.

13

The Indian summer continued, the hot dry days passing slowly and lazily. Brad was still in the hospital under the care of the sisters, I still loved the lodge. It was like living in a dolls' house. We were two couples, Eden and Bonnie, Bo and I. There were no irksome chores, Eden cooked lovely food. We sunbathed in front of the lodge, we walked in the fields, sucking grasses and singing songs.

Each morning we ate our porridge outside in the morning dew. A donkey brayed far off. It wasn't the Ireland of fiction or expectation. It was the quiet that I loved, the little wild flowers, the fuchsia in the hedges outside the gate, the straight road that stretched to the town. Bo was fatter and more gentle.

The day that the letter came, he and I were watching Bonnie picking roses. I sat on the wall. Bo was licking his bowl. The duck was by Bonnie's feet. Once they were picked, the petals fell quickly, pollen fell on her bare toes. Bo was to start at the Brothers' school in a fortnight. My own future wasn't settled, but I'd written for information about nursing. The sun was hot on my head.

Bonnie knew she looked beautiful, stretching up to the roses. Her shirt colour was the same colour as the sky and the flowers. Eden was at the back clearing the growth round the lavatory; he'd make a path before the winter, so that we'd keep dry. Restoring the Grange was a long-term project, he'd make the lodge comfortable first. I looked forward to the winter. The less I worried about Bonnie the better; she was adult, she must look after herself. I had written to Ula about Babs dying. England seemed another world; poor little Ula, she hadn't answered yet. The postman was late. I watched the duck picking round Bonnie's feet. I will think of Ula and ducks and hedgehogs. The postman may have a letter from her. Bonnie was sick this morning. Her period is five days late.

Eden was a man of worth and integrity, the way he worked proved that, but not the man for my sister. Why didn't he speak of his past, was he running from something? He and Bonnie meet each night, I can't stop her. I will think about becoming a nurse.

I love buttercups and dandelions, yellow for sunshine; ducklings, yellow for egg yolk and champagne. Yellow for vomit, sick faces, bile, yellow for despair. I wondered if Eden had found any stolen money. Bo had stopped stealing and Brad was safe.

How long will he stay sober when he comes home again? There isn't room here, could he stay at the Grange? I love this peace, this green and sunshine, the serenity of this life. I want time to stand still, for nothing to happen to Bonnie, for things to stay as they are.

I tried to see Ula's and my own future. I could specialize in orthopaedic nursing and look after her, we could live here in peace and prosperity. She and I would survive. Bo would thrive with the Brothers, he was intelligent, he loved his father. If only I could wave a wand and make Bonnie a virgin again.

'There's the postman. Look, there's his bike, I see him.'

Against the pink sky, far down the road, he was pedalling slowly, his sack limply hanging on his back. He reached the gates, he dismounted, pausing, staring. The lodge had changed. Smoke came from the chimney, the windows had glass, the front was cleared, there were flowerbeds, there was a table with plates on it. Bonnie, lovely in pink, posed with flowers in her hands.

'Hullo,' she said in a throaty voice.

He stared with brown pop-eyes. Had it been him who had gossiped about Babs and Mick Fagin? Don't think about that, Babs is dead. I wanted to warn the postman not to idolize her. Bonnie was not what she seemed, she was vain and wild, loose in her ways. Eden had stared like that when he saw her blowing bubbles, look what happened. Turn your eyes away.

She would arrange herself fetchingly on her deathbed for the undertaker, a natural seducer of men. Why should she feel the need to conquer if she was Eden's girl? Just you wait, Bonnie, until you find yourself crooning lullabies with your awful voice. You'll be tired, you'll be tied, the cost of motherhood is high.

'Hullo,' she said, going to the gate. 'We've changed our residence. Isn't it sweet? We live here now.'

The letter wasn't from Ula. It was addressed to Eden.

He came from the back, he rested his rake against the wall. He took the letter, not speaking, not opening it. He put it in his jacket, hanging over the wall. Love made people secretive, he and Bonnie had their sealed world. Why should he hide the letter from her? He could be a murderer or a bigamist. Why didn't he ask her to marry him instead of filling her head with dreams of dancing and gardens? He should be planning wedding bells, diamond rings and champagne.

We weren't an ordinary family, we never would be. We were too sensitive, took life too much to heart. We might not succeed in what we tried, but we must try. Bo would soon be an ordinary school boy at a local school, I had my nursing plan. All Bonnie seemed to do was stare at her stomach with a fixed look, or smile into Eden's eyes.

If there was a child there, it would blight her. She wasn't suited to becoming a teenage mamma. She should be eating oranges and fish oil instead of stuffing silly cakes and posing with roses. Squatting like a bear with Eden each night might amuse her, it didn't amuse me at all. Bonnie, don't have a child, have a period.

She'd always been like clockwork, never suffered from cramps or headaches like me, never bled for more than four days, could time her first drop of blood almost to the minute. Spots, greasy hair or nasty feet never bothered Bonnie. But now she'd lost her common sense. She would need special clothes if she were pregnant. She would swell and her milk would drip. She needed cash and a wedding at once, this week. What was Eden doing about it?

The letter could be about plans for their future, it might have money in it. Perhaps I misjudged him, he might be planning a home in England where he could establish a wife. If Bonnie was about to give birth, she ought to do it in style. Be proud, pretty Bonnie, and don't expect me to deliver it or sing to it. I don't like motherhood. If it's a girl don't call it some dainty name like Marigold, just teach it to be tough. Love it. Meanwhile what about calcium and vitamins? Stop staring at your stomach, stop eating cake and kissing Eden. My old soul is getting tired.

'Good news, Eden, I hope? Nice little letter?' Bo could be as sweet as Bonnie when he liked.

Eden twitched his fingers. His moustache looked stiff as wire in the morning light. If the letter was about money or jobs he'd open it. It was cruel not to tell Bonnie, she looked unhappy. He should be holding her hand, showing her his letter. She fiddled with her flowers, with the hand that should be wearing a ring. She put the flowers down and went up to the loft.

'Well, aren't you going to read it, Eden?'

He scowled, he took his rake and went to the back again.

'Bo, I'm sure Eden is up to something. He doesn't want anyone to see his letter. I think we should find out. We must read it.'

'Ah me, Tor. No.'

'Ah me, yes. It's our duty. We must read it for Bonnie's sake.'

'He'd kill us.'

'I'm going to look. Go on, your fingers are quick.'

Cunning was in Bo's blood. He slit the envelope silently. I filled the kettle from the outhouse tap. We might need steam for re-sealing. There was Eden by the lavatory, digging, with his back to the lodge. The undergrowth was cleared, the hedgehog would be unprotected. Had he thrown the meat-safe away?

'Tor. Come here. Listen to this.

Dear Ed. Long time no see no hear. I heard you was in Ireland I'm still fancy free. Mum has our little boy, he wants his Dad now. Don't forget our arrangement long time no see or hear love Red.

'Who is it? Who is Red?'

'Hush. Keep your voice down. Don't let Bonnie hear. Red is . . . It's awful.'

'Who is she? Who?'

'It's Eden's old girl-friend. He used to be called Ed.'

'Did he tell you? Who is she?'

'We knew her once. Not Eden. She was evacuated to our school, ages ago. Before you were born. Don't let Bonnie hear.'

'You never told me, you never said. What does it mean, "our little boy"? This Red and Eden must have some secret child.' Ah me. Ah tangled love.

'It's a . . . disaster. Eden isn't right for Bonnie. I said he wasn't. It's a disgrace.'

'Poor, dear little Bonnie.'

'Keep your voice down. It's the worst thing that has ever happened.' My Bonnie. Did Red want Eden back?

She might even be married to him. Pretty Bonnie, where are you now? You ran twice to the lavatory this morning, I heard you. Being sick is a sign of a child. It's no good hoping it won't happen, I think it has.

'Quickly. Put it back. He's coming.'

Reseal the envelope, put it in his jacket. Eden is banging the back door. Now he's running the tap over his hands. Will he notice the paper is torn?

Bo and I stood in the doorway, not looking at him. We heard the envelope crackle, heard it being crushed in his hand.

'Everything all right, Eden?' Bo's voice was full of concern.

Eden cleared his throat. He flicked his hair back.

'Listen, kids. I got to . . . I have to leave. To London, actually. Right away, 's'matter of fact.'

'Oh dear. Why, Eden?'

'Something come up ... came up. A bit of business. Where is Bonnie?'

'Here I am. Up here.'

Her sandals appeared at the top of the ladder, her tanned legs and her shorts. She looked ill. She had heard Bo reading the letter. I was afraid she'd be sick again. She kept swallowing, Eden's pink shirt accentuated her pale colour, a petal had caught in her hair. Now, Bonnie, the time has come to assert yourself. Be proud, demand your rights. Insist on reading that letter, ask what it means. Eden hasn't told you everything, he'd hiding something. Be tough.

'Must you go, Eden? I don't think Bonnie is well. Don't go.'

'You never said, Bonnie. Not well, dear? What's up? I won't be gone long. It's ... business. Will you be all right?'

She nodded.

Another time she must come with him, he said. She'd be better resting at present. If she felt poorly the crossing might not agree with her. Rest. Take it easy. All right?

The way her hands dangled and her eyes begged made me angry. Stop being humble, Bonnie, take a stand. Fall in a fit, threaten him, slap him. But she said nothing.

'Must you go, Eden? Is it absolutely necessary?'

He looked irritated as he answered me. Unfortunately, yes.

Was he already longing for Red's scrawny arms waiting to grab him? Would they lurk in Clerkenwell doorways? Would he sniff her vanilla and dirt? She must have power over him, her letter was a magnet. Pretty Bonnie came second, Red wanted him, Red came first. He had taught her to tango, dipping and darting round cheap dance halls. Who will teach Bonnie the hesitation waltz?

He left the next day for the night boat to Liverpool. Bonnie even helped him to pack. We leaned over the lower half of the door watching him leave us, his raincoat over his arm. He was thinner now and browner than when he'd first come. Loving Bonnie had improved his looks. If she'd had more experience he might have ignored that letter. Bonnie had given him too much too quickly. She'd had no practice, having had few men in our lives.

Bo waved him off importantly. 'Have no fear, Eden. I'll mind the ladies while you're gone.'

We watched until he was a tiny figure down the road. We were three on our own again.

'Bonnie, darlin', you'll be the blushing bride yet. Don't despair, you'll walk down the aisle on my arm.'

'Shut your mouth, Bo, don't tease her. Can't you see how Bonnie feels?'

Bo said he knew a lot more than we thought. Who could make fires burn? Who brought the coal in? We'd miss him if he wasn't around. It would be as well if he slept up in the loft tonight, in case we got afraid in the night.

'I'm not having you near me, you little Irish rat, or your duck either.' Bonnie spoke with venom, but her face looked better. Nothing stopped Bo, he was irrepressible. He started inventing a rhyme. He walked round the table chanting. 'I'm forever blowing bubbles, sister Bonnie lost her man, stole her heart away, leaving her to . . .'

'Oy oy. Anyone at home?'

Silhouetted against the evening sky was a young woman with frizzed hair. She had thin lips, a spotty neck. Her small eyes peered through her fringe.

'Red.' I would know her anywhere.

'Tor and Bonnie. I sort of guessed. Where's Ed?'

'Why are you here, Red?'

Bonnie's face was flushed, she jumped up, agitated.

'I'd had an idea we'd meet one day. Long time no see, Bonnie.'

'Why are you here? Eden left today. He's not here, he went to London.'

'He got my letter, then? He done well for hisself I must say, living in a Grange. Is this it?'

Bo unbolted the door for her, bowed over her hand. In the absence of his father, he was her host. A thousand welcomes to Ireland and to the Grange.

'You their brother? Bit small for a Grange.'

Bo explained. He was Boris. We'd had a flood. His father was ill, so was Ula. He was in charge. Red must look on the lodge as her home.

'Bo, what are you saying?'

'I mean it, Tor. Red is welcome. She has come a long way.'

'I'll stop for tonight. Pity I missed Ed. What happened to your mum?'

For a moment I saw the lodge through Red's eyes; small, bare, poor. But I had been happy here, especially outside, in spite of Bonnie. I didn't want Red to sneer. In spite of the trouble, death and worrying about Bonnie, it was a happy summer.

She stared at Bo's duck. She wasn't keen on birds, feathered things got on her nerves. She'd come on the off-chance, looking for Eden. The pub in the town told her the way.

14

The way she spoke was unforgettable; her stare, her nasal whine, were the same. She seemed even thinner, without bust, stomach or calves, thinner than any of us. Her bitten nails matched her velvet dress and the satchel hanging from her arm. She walked with a little lurch, almost like a dance, because of a broken high-heel. She had no coat or luggage. What had Eden seen in her? I looked at my Bonnie of the beautiful eyes and figure. Red said she was out of cigarettes.

She said if she had the choice she'd stop on at the Grange, no matter how flooded. This lodge wasn't much. And fancy letting that duck on the table. Ducks lived in filth, they got on her nerves. She wasn't keen on animals at all, excepting for her dog. Bo said he loved the duck.

'That all the animals you got, then? Thought you was supposed to have a farm?'

'Did Eden write? How did you know?'

''Course he did. Where's all the animals? Ain't you even got a dog?'

Bo explained about the Grange. Empty for years, then

404

flooded and spoiled. About the cow that was gone. How we were short of funds, temporarily, of course.

Red nodded. Right, she'd caught on. What went wrong? Where was our parents?

'My father is in hospital. Double pneumonia with complications. I am the only son.'

'He drinks,' I told her.

'Right. Shame.'

'He's rather a bad case.'

I didn't care if I upset Bo. I liked telling her. It was like a revenge. Brad didn't deserve loyalty.

'My dad's a boozer. Doesn't do to make too much of it.' If not that, it would be something else, men being what they were. Her dad used to blacken her mum's eyes, bust her nose once, when he was wild. He'd calmed down since he got older.

'Did she mind?'

'Takes a lot to upset my family. I never forgot you, specially Bonnie.'

'And I remember you, Red.'

She said that the school was a right load of toffee noses. Did we ever hear from that head girl?

I didn't answer. I couldn't bear to think of that night of the orgy. ('I'll teach you, like I done Red.')

She was contemptuous about our clothes. We looked bloody poverty stricken, our sandals had seen better days. Bonnie flushed again, we liked the way we dressed. We liked sun and a simple life.

'Simple is right. You don't seem so good, Bonnie. You poorly or something?'

'Of course I'm not.'

I remembered how sick she'd been this morning. Morning sickness could last all day. I knew she was pregnant.

Red sat down, she took her broken shoe off, flexing and rubbing her toes. She had a chain anklet. She said it was a shame about Ula being so poorly. What about our mum?

'She's dead. Didn't you know? Didn't Eden write about it?'

'Go on. Never. Dead?'

'We never settled. Our mother (we call her Babs) ... never settled. She hated Brad drinking.'

'You mean she done herself in?'

'Of course she didn't. The roof fell on her.'

'Oh, right. That's really a shame. You don't seem too upset. If it was my mum, I'd die too.'

'It was upsetting. Very upsetting. Eden was a tremendous help.'

''Course I never had no posh family. Governesses and that, but we got our feelings. I think the world of my mum.'

'Eden is rebuilding the Grange. It will take time.'

'Is he now?'

Bonnie told her that we did miss Babs in our own way. Her death was horrible.

Bo wanted to hear about Red's mother. Never mind now about our mammy, talk about Clerkenwell.

'Mum is all right. I think the world of her. She's got my little boy.'

'Aha.' Bo leaned forward eagerly.

Red's world was another planet, enthralling as a film or play. I remembered the stories she'd told us at school. She'd missed her mum then, the market on a Saturday, jellied eels and chips. I loved the sound of their parlour, the shiny coal scuttle, the fur rug before the fire, the dog called Bones. Her parents drank beer, sometimes her dad became wild. Red and her mum had no secrets, thick as thieves they were. She didn't want to change,

she loved Clerkenwell, she didn't want to leave. She'd never forgotten that school of ours.

Bo leaned, his elbows on his knees. He did admire her.

'I like your hair. Is Red your real name?'

'Ethelreda. Red to my mates. I always wear red, you might
have observed. Me and Ed were a team, won the Saturday spots
regular; my best partner, was Ed. You mean you let that duck on
the bed?'

'Duck relishes a little comfort.'

'Who sleeps up there?'

'Tor and Bonnie. I sleep down here with Eden. I mean Ed.'

Red sniffed. She said Ireland was a right dead-alive hole.

'Stay, Red. You'll like it. I'm starting with the Christian
Brothers. My sisters aren't Catholic, though.'

'You watch them, kiddo. Those Brothers will sour your
brains.'

She said she didn't encourage religion in anyone, she never fancied prayers. You had to make things happen, not sit waiting and
praying. Dead quiet, this place was. How did we pass our time?

'I like reading. I'll probably be a nurse soon and look after
Ula. Bo likes religion and writing rhymes. He had his own altar
at the Grange.'

'What about Bonn here?'

'She makes cakes don't you, Bonnie? She likes arranging flowers. She wants a garden.'

Our pastimes sounded boring and limited. I added that I liked
animals too, I might even be a vet as well as a nurse. We'd not
had experience of animals, though Bonnie once had some mice
that were killed during the war.

'What do you do for laughs? Have you seen the latest Fred
and Ginge picture?'

We never went to films. Red knew the ups and downs of all the stars, all their romances. She could chain-smoke, drink beer, dance the rumba. She was an experienced poker player as well as knowing about boyfriends and what they did. She knew the words of all the popular songs. She yawned. She'd be bored stiff if she had to stop. Some of her back teeth were decayed, her tongue was thin, pointed, a yellowish shade. What in others might be unattractive was acceptable in Red. She had style.

Bonnie spoke. Did Red remember teaching the school to do the Lambeth Walk? Those long ago winter nights were safe to remember. Bonnie's present and future were uneasy.

'That's not all I taught you. You were an ignorant lot till us evacuees came. How old was your mum when she passed on?'

'Not old. She couldn't bear this place.'

'It was the skylight. The flood blew it onto her head,' Bo said.

'It was Brad's drinking,' I said.

'Can't say I blame her hating here. A shocking shock though. She must have slept heavy. Luckily you're four of a family, you got each other still.'

'True, Red. Very true.' Bo sighed. Ah me.

Red herself only wanted one child, being an only herself. How was Ed in himself?

'He's restoring and rebuilding the Grange, I told you. Ireland's his home now, he's employed by Brad,' I said firmly.

'Oh, right. We'll have to see about that. I'll have to look at this Grange. I wouldn't mind living somewhere posh for a while. A holiday, like.'

'No one can live there. It's uninhabitable.'

'What's up with old Bonn? You look a right miserable misery.'

'It's no wonder. Bonnie is having a child.' The words popped out before I could stop them.

'Shut up, Tor. It's not true. It's nothing to do with you. Shut up.'

Bonnie was frantic. Bo danced about with delight, his rat's face bright with smiles. His little Bonnie with a child in her? Fertilized like a flower? Was Ed the bumble bee? He'd be an uncle. He crossed his arms, flapping his hands. Sister Bonnie with a child. Ah glory me.

'Can't say I'm surprised. Ed's kid, of course? He don't change. Why didn't you say?'

'Why should I? It's no one's business. It is Eden's actually, if you must know. Yes.'

I felt sadder for Bonnie than I could bear. Bo picked up two knives. Bonnie must knit for the babby, he clicked the knives, knit-knit-knit. He'd make up a poem for the birth.

'Silly bitch.'

'So you see, Red, she'll have to marry Eden. She can't have a child on her own.'

'She can't, can't she? Why can't she?'

'It's different for us. She isn't like you, Red.'

'It's different, is it? I'll tell you what's different. Ed is mine. We got our arrangement, we made it years back. He belongs to me. He's mine.'

'What arrangement?'

'Arrangement to settle when the time came. To settle somewhere when the time was right. The "when" is now. My little boy needs a dad. Right?'

'You mean you'll marry?'

'Might do. The point is our arrangement. I need him, so does my boy.'

'But what about Bonnie?'

'She'll have to manage, won't she?'

'But Eden and she ... they ...'

'Ed would never settle permanent, old Bonn's not his type, not deep down. You're none of you like us.'

'She needs him.'

'I need him more.'

Bo asked why now, especially. Her boy had been all right without Ed until now. Red said she wanted to take up dancing again, she wouldn't mind turning pro. Which meant practice, right? For which she needed Ed. Red and Ed, back in harness, old time partners in the dance.

'Red ... Ethelreda, can you show me the rumba? I'd relish a little display.'

'Later, kiddo. Wish someone had a fag.'

'There's some of Bonnie's cake.'

'Sod cake, I need a smoke.'

'Watch me, Red. Is this right?' Bo pranced round the table waving his hands.

'Astaire had nothing on you, kid. The thing is, Bonn, you only think you want Ed. You're scared. Right? He'd soon get on your nerves.'

Bonnie's words ran together, her cheeks went a hectic red. Red didn't realize that Eden *wanted* to change, he *wanted* to forget his past. He wanted a different world. He looked different, he spoke differently. She wouldn't know him now.

'Yeah? He always had high ideas. Inside he's weak. He always needs someone to copy. He needs to lean, he doesn't take the lead. It's not accents or manners that counts. Besides, I need him for my partner. Ed and Red.'

'But he loves Bonnie.'

'Love? I know Ed. I'm sure he does.'

'Tor is right. He adores me. We're made for each other. He said.'

'He can adore anyone he likes far as I'm concerned. Only, he's mine.'

'But the baby, don't forget that, Red.'

'She can have it or don't have it, it's up to her. Trouble is, you none of you got no fight.'

'It's different for you, Red. You're not blue-blooded.'

'Blue-blooded? You mean snobs. You're used to the easy life. You flop when things get rough. You're leaners too. Ed's weak but he's mine. I know him. Right?'

'What do you expect Bonnie to do? She'll ruin her life.'

'Want my advice? Get rid of it. Forget it happened.'

'It's dangerous, Red. It's illegal. How?'

Tears came into Bonnie's eyes. Eden wouldn't allow it. Not their child.

'Ed? Wouldn't he? Have you asked him?'

'But how?'

Bo paused in his rumba practice, busily thinking up a rhyme for the occasion.

'Changing partners in the dance, Red and Bonnie share romance.'

Bonnie looked at him with hatred, tears still on her cheeks.

'You and your silly rhymes. I'm sick of you, do you hear?'

'Leave the kid alone. What you need now is cash.'

'We haven't any.' Eden was cashing Babs' bonds for us, the money hadn't arrived.

'I can see that. Poverty stricken.'

Red would get Ed to send some. Quicker the better. The operation was best. Get rid of it. Start fresh.

'Isn't there another way? Where would Bonnie go?'

London was the quickest and best. There were other ways, Red said, but not so certain. You could drink gin in the bath tub, you could jump off tables or swallow quinine. You could shove a knitting needle up you. A special doctor was best. For which you needed cash. Leave it to her, she'd get Ed to send some back, quick as possible.

'I've been feeling so sick, Red.'

'Yeah? Right. Stop feeling sorry for yourself.' Red poked round the lodge. Could she see up in the loft? Fancy sleeping on the floor. She liked the smell of pears. Bo and I stayed downstairs. We got out the cake. We didn't speak. He beat the two knives on the table and tried his rumba step.

Red said the lodge could be all right if it was furnished. She and Bonnie had stayed up the ladder a long time. We heard Red's snickering laugh. They smelled of Babs' scent when they came down. Red wore a pair of Bonnie's shoes. She wondered if our mum's ghost was about in the Grange. She and Bonnie would go there after tea. And what about this altar of Bo's?

After we'd eaten the cake, Bo and I watched them walk along the drive together. We couldn't hear what they said. Bonnie had her spongebag and two towels over her arm. Red fancied a bath.

15

Rain soaked his hair, ran down his forehead, splashing from his ears and chin. His trouser hems were soaked. The sting of the rain on his roughened hands took his mind off his grief. He stood straight-backed and dripping, watching the funeral.

The mourners and their umbrellas were grouped round the grave. Mud was trickling into the newly piled earth. It looked shadowy, like the ending of a film. It mustn't end, not yet. A mourner sneezed, a bus swished past outside the wall. Rain from the church guttering overflowed. He had helped staunch the wet before, he could do nothing now. If it could be a film, he could watch it again, could watch her standing on the lawn, thin and lovely, reaching to the bubbles in the sun. A family in Ireland, in a garden, inviting him to stay. Now it was over, he was outside again.

He should be the chief mourner, he'd been the chief love of the deceased, had known her intimately. They were made for each other. But no glances of comfort came his way, no friendly handshakes or pats. He was disgraced. Rain and damp weather would always remind him of Ireland, but this was England now, and Bonnie was dead. Rain seemed to wash the colour out, even the grass looked the colour of graves.

There was Tor, standing where he should be, her face in her hanky. Someone held an umbrella from behind. That must be Ula at her side, white and ill-looking in a leg-iron. No sign of Bo or Brad. Bo must be heart-broken. Was he in Ireland with his father? Was he tending the fire in the lodge? Tor and Ula, look at me, I want to be part of you. Don't keep me out, I am bereaved.

The moment was coming, the coffin was being lowered, his lovely one was on her way. He wanted to shout out. Stop! No! Don't do it. He was guilty, but they were too. They were in it together. Stop. Don't. He was apart, stick-necked in the rain, while they wept together. The wet ropes slid through the coffin bearers' hands. Their knuckles glistened, the ropes slackened, she was out of sight without a goodbye. Don't go, Bonnie, my dear one. I need you, you are my reason for living, all I desire. My heart and soul, I trusted and loved you. Don't go, Bonnie, be my guide. Your thighs, your breasts, your hair under my fingers are part of me. I can't bear it. I'm part of you. I see you reaching for bubbles, I hear your voice singing. Girl on the lawn, don't go. I'm here.

He must speak to Tor, must explain to her. He'd only wanted to help. The money from the bonds was nothing, he'd wanted money quickly, had gone back on the buses for Bonnie's sake. He'd saved, he'd scraped, couldn't get money fast enough, had taken too much, often, from his day's takings. Because of her he'd thrown caution to the winds. His sentence was harsh, but he'd asked for it. He'd done it for Bonnie's sake. Now, tethered like an animal, he couldn't help no one, not even himself. He stepped forward, was pulled back sharply, he felt the grip of the cuff on his wrist. He couldn't walk to the graveside of his dear one. A common prisoner detained at His Majesty's pleasure, he couldn't even wipe his tears. He needed a handkerchief, his face was wet, his right hand wasn't free. He felt like choking, his hanky was in the wrong pocket, he was trapped. Tor and Ula, look at me, can't you see?

'Here you are, Mack.' The man at his side handed him his own hanky, freshly ironed, still in its square. Ed took it, breathing the smell of it, starched linen, product of loving care. He mopped and blew, nodding his thanks to the jailer who smiled at him.

He could afford a smile, he had a home somewhere, Pentonville most likely supplied comfortable quarters for wives and families. This screw had a wife to love and tend him. Bonnie, dear, I intended to find a real home for you, I wanted to sort something out. I'm your love, your intended bridegroom, you did believe that, didn't you?

No flowers from him, no carnations or love-in-the-mist. The coffin had white flowers as it went down. The priest prayed inaudibly. Bonnie disliked prayers and priests, no one had consulted him about the service. He must go back now to his prison cell.

He saw Tor put away her hanky, turn to her sister in the leg-iron, putting her arms round her, kissing her. Tor, speak, don't leave without a word. You trusted me once, you relied on me. I made the lodge fit to live in for those happy summer days. I am still reliable, still mean to help you. I am loyal, I will stay true, I'll never change. I ran risks for Bonnie's sake, I stole for her and got nicked. I'll be out again, I'll come back to you, I will rebuild the Grange. Don't go, Tor. Look at me.

She looked, and her face changed; she looked disgusted. Keep away, you're not wanted, know your place. A prisoner in hand-cuffs has no place here, you're not like us, go away. Get back to where you belong, leave us to our grieving, leave us alone.

The younger sister limped forward to throw a flower. White flowers look grey in the rain. Farewell, elder sister, rest in peace, goodbye, don't forget us. Here is your flower, wet and grey, adieu.

Tor, look at me again, wait for me. Young sister, don't leave me on my own. I can't bear life without you, can't bear to lose you. Speak to me, say something, Tor.

'Come on, Mack, better be going.'

Mack. Mate. Jack. Chum. Life inside forced you to accept any name. You became one of the herd whatever your name was, just another of society's rejects. He was a petty larcenist with a record of grievous bodily harm. For Bonnie's sake he'd become a convicted thief, was getting his payment. Carelessness, over-ambition, over-confidence had been his real crimes. Aunt's advice wasn't true, he didn't believe her. Ambition hadn't killed the rat; he wasn't dead, Bonnie was. Bonnie, his loving sweet-heart, his dear one, was gone from him. The whole world, outside and inside, was a huge trap waiting to get you. Murderers rapists and burglars were his comrades now.

'Mack. Time to be getting back to the Villa now. Do you hear?'

You need patience and long sufferance for prison work. Ed was causing the staff extra work. There were too many villains inside, without providing escorts to funerals. They had all pitied Ed for losing his girl. He must be cuffed though, no matter what happened, couldn't risk him doing a runner with his record of GBH.

'Mack!'

Ed felt the tug on his wrist again.

'I must speak. Just a minute. Wait, Tor.'

'Doesn't look as if the party wants to speak to you, Mack.'

Tor was walking away now, with Ula limping behind her. He must, it was his last chance, he must drag the screw after him.

'Tor. Wait. Please.'

She spoke to him.

'*You.*'

He wanted to scream at her, he was heartsick, she must believe him. He had stolen the cash for Bonnie's sake. When he came out he would help her and her family. They were involved forever, it was meant to be. She mustn't imagine he wasn't good enough, he was changing and improving, he intended to change a lot more. They must stick together, shared memories still bound them. Bonds like that couldn't be broken. He would come back, he would help; they were conjoined.

'Come on, Mack. Back now.'

'For Pete's sake, get my name right; it's not Mack, it's Ed, short for Eden. Get it right for once, can't you?'

'Sorry, Mack. I mean, Ed.'

He stood still, his head was lowered now, the rain was blinding him, but he wasn't beaten, he'd fight till he died. They belonged to him, he belonged to them, it wasn't over.

He heard the footsteps in the wet behind him, slicking over the grass, he felt the hand touching him, he smelled that perfume again, familiar as cake, sickly-sweet, cloying, foul. ('Be content with your lot. Ambition killed the rat.')

'Ed. I couldn't get here any sooner. I'm here now. Right? Poor old Bonn, silly bitch. Fancy doing that to herself with a knitting needle. Nasty. Dangerous. I warned her not to, silly cow.'

'You shouldn't of come. Why did you? You shouldn't of ...'

'Stop away from Bonn's funeral? Not me. Not after all we

been through. A right miserable misery you are. You didn't have to half kill that copper what was bringing you in. Why didn't you go quietly? If you had, you wouldn't be inside now.'

'I was trying to help Bonnie. I did it for Bonnie. I loved Bonnie.'

'Yeah. 'Course. I know that. Shame. I'm here ready and waiting when you're out again, same as always. Red and Ed, back in harness, ready for our arrangement. Long time no hear, no see.'

GOOD BEHAVIOUR

Molly Keane

Introduced by Marian Keyes

Behind its rich veneer, the estate of Temple Alice is a crumbling fortress, from which the aristocratic St Charles family keeps reality at bay. Aroon, the unlovely daughter of the house, silently longs for love and approval, which she certainly doesn't receive from her elegant, icy mother. Her handsome father is fond of her but above all he thrills to the chase – ladies and servants are equally fair game. Sinking into a decaying grace, the family's adherence to the unyielding codes of 'good behaviour' is both their salvation and downfall. For their reserved façades conceal dark secrets and hushed cruelties.

'A remarkable novel, beautifully written, brilliant . . . every page a pleasure to read'
P. D. James

Virago Modern Classics
978-1-84408-324-4

HARRIET SAID

Beryl Bainbridge

Introduced by Linda Grant

A girl returns from boarding school to her Merseyside hometown and waits to be reunited with her childhood friend, Harriet, chief architect of all their past mischief. She roams along the shoreline and the woods still pitted with wartime trenches, and encounters 'the Tsar' – almost old, unhappily married, both dangerously fascinating and repulsive.

Pretty, malevolent Harriet finally arrives, and over the course of the long holidays draws her friend into a scheme to beguile then humiliate the Tsar, with disastrous, shocking consequences. A gripping portrayal of adolescent transgression, Beryl Bainbridge's classic first novel remains as subversive today as when it was written.

'An extremely original and disconcerting story'
Daily Telegraph

Virago Modern Classics
978-1-84408-860-7